Dabresha Goes to France; An Urban Girl's Adventure Outside of Her Comfort Zone

© 2016

Anastascia Duchesse

To Maudie, May God Bless you in all your life adventures! Xoxo Anastascia Duchesse

Chateau Foveo Publishing
info@cfbooks.net
Pasadena, CA

Chateau Foveo Publishing
Copyright ©2016 by Anastascia Duchesse
ALL RIGHTS RESERVED

Anastascia Duchesse
Dabresha Goes to France; An Urban Girl's Adventure Outside of her Comfort Zone

ISBN: 978-0-9974064-2-9

Cover concept and photographs by Anastascia Duchesse
Cover design by Lyan Kwan (www.lyandesign.space)
Editing by Joshua T. Adams (EditorJoshTada@Gmail.com)
Book manufacturing by McNaughton & Gunn
Printed in the United States of America on FSC paper

This book is dedicated to Nohemi Gonzalez and to every other courageous dreamer who was fearless in stepping outside of their comfort zone.

Que Dieu Vous Benisse

God Bless

Reposez en Paix Nohemi
(10/19/1992 — 11/13/2015)

♦ ~ *Contents* ~ ♦

PART ONE : THE COMFORT ZONE

PART TWO : THE WORLD

DABRESHA GOES TO FRANCE

PART ONE : THE COMFORT ZONE

"The world is a book and those who do not travel
read only one page.." -Aurelius Augustine

DABRESHA GOES TO FRANCE

Chapitre 1 : The Laydees

Bonjour, Je m'appelle Dabresha! Et c'est mon histoire.

(Hey y'all, I'm Dabresha! And this is my story.)

"Da BREEEZY be EEEAZY!"

I whipped my head around even though there was no need to. I already knew who was calling me at full volume from the other end of the school hallway. Only my loud hot mess of a best friend would be bold enough to yell something like that without caring who or what was around to hear her. We stopped walking so she could run and catch up to us, then I threw my chin up with a smile to say,

"WHAT IT DO BOO?"

My girl Laydee was a trip! Always loud and saying (in most cases, screaming) exactly what was on her mind whenever and wherever she thought suitable. I admired her confidence though and wondered if she had been born with her obnoxious ways or had acquired them sometime after birth. She was constantly changing her hair color; today her hair had dark red highlights and tomorrow could be anyone's guess as to what she'd do with it. She had more tattoos and piercings than any other girl I knew, and more than enough sass to complement her style. It was all good though because her 'idgaf' attitude made her fun to be around, and hanging with her was like watching a reality show where every new episode involved Laydee trying to out-do herself and take it up a notch. I can't remember her being so brash when I first met her back in high school, but I guess I changed a little since high school too, don't we all?

"Dang Laydee, could you be any louder? I don't think the roaches in the basement heard you," I teased. "My science teacher sure weren't happy when you walked up in my class yesterday; he almost booted me and told me to join you outside. You didn't have to shout from the doorway to ask to borrow my lighter!"

"Yeah, yeah, well I needed to melt my eyeliner and it was urgent," Laydee replied. She fished my dark blue lighter out of her front jeans pocket and dropped it inside my purse as our mutual friend, Antoinette, appeared from around the corner, dressed in her usual boring attire. Wait, let me rephrase that—I'll call her wardrobe 'eccentrically plain'. Not a day has passed on earth where Antoinette wasn't wearing something African influenced or simply too old for her; it was like her and her mom came from a family of caravan traders who shared the same closet and covered up from head to toe. I've never been through Nette's closet before, but I've grown under the assumption that it opens up to a desert land of old jeans, wool turtlenecks, dull colored long skirts, and head scarves of every geometrical pattern hanging on cactus branches. I imagine her closet being like the real-life version of a cartoon character's closet, full of the same exact outfits from front to end.

I can't forget to mention the pulls, you know those long oversized flowy tops with no sleeves that older ladies wear in the winter? Yes, I think Antoinette has stock in those things, and I think she missed the memo about African print going out of style in the 90's. She's like a young high yellow version of Erykah Badu, and so proud of the darker half of her culture. Today, she's wearing a black turtleneck, dingy jeans, some pointy cowgirl-ish boots, and a turquoise headwrap to match her oversized feather earrings.

"Whatever y'all, I got official business to discuss so listen and follow me to the spot," Laydee said haughtily.

The three of us stared at Laydee with anticipation as we filed around her while walking down the hall and leaned toward her to get a better listen. Our other friend, Tamina, was our third. Tamina never talks much so I forget she's around sometimes, but that's my dawg. Tamina and I nearabout grew up together; well we went to the same elementary school and all and I've always looked out for her like a sister. Right before middle school, she moved to California where apparently all the girls weigh a hundred pounds, even the black girls!

She says she never felt like she belonged there. She also said it never rains there, and I wish the weather was like that in Texas because the rain and humidity here makes it hard for me to maintain my hair-do. I don't know about you, but getting my hair done costs time and money, and those are two things I never have enough of. The smallest amount of moisture can ruin a fresh press and curl, it drives me nuts! Anyways, Tamina moved back to Texas last year and started attending the same junior college as me, so we naturally started hanging out again like she never left. Miles and minutes didn't detach us, so I know we'll always be friends.

Laydee led us to post up by the arts building where we usually found each other between classes. It was an area with some concrete tables and benches that all the cool kids seemed to gather frequently (and by cool, I mean the black students). I humored myself wondering if we should post a sign there that said 'blacks only,' or if one may have been there when the school first opened in the sixties. No one would probably notice the sign amid all the graffiti and street art on the tables and benches anyway.

Once Laydee was certain that she had everyone's full

attention, she continued with her announcement.

"So there's 'sposed to be a mess of St. Patrick's parties this weekend and we need to decide which ones we're gonna make an appearance at, ya heard me?"

I rolled my eyes at Laydee, who had succeeded once again at fetching all of our attention for a stupid reason. Like always, we thought she had something important to say, but that's Laydee, a-k-a Laydee-T-The-Queen-of-Hype. She can make the smallest piece of information seem like the biggest news story in the world—she'd be a perfect 'hype man' for an up and coming rapper!

"Girl, we're not thinking about parties right now, we fixin' to finish all these damn tests!" I said with a groan.

"That's right," Antoinette chimed in, "these midterms ain't no joke!"

All the tests I took in high school definitely could not have prepared me for what I've come to discover in the form of college exams: long demented official-looking sheets of paper that every student suffers through at least twice a semester. Now, after four semesters at Saddle Ranch Junior College, I knew I needed to step my game up. I should have been ready to transfer to a 'real school' by now (i.e. a university), but I was nowhere near that point.

My dad says community colleges are a trap (well Maurice is my stepdad kinda sorta, but he's *like* a dad so whatever). He says the sooner you get through with them and transfer out to a university, the better. This is one of the few times I can admit Maurice might be right. I knew too many people who had went to the same college for years and never finished nor transferred out. My friend Rodrick for example, he's almost thirty and started going to SRJC when he was my age! He may already be in his thirties to tell you the truth, but he always avoids talking about his age when the question is thrown at him. He has a smooth shaven face and is always cracking jokes. When anyone tries to ask him about his age, he just sidetracks the question with "don't worry 'bout mine and I won't worry 'bout yours," or, "I'm old enough to kick it."

I didn't want to be one of those full grown students like him or a few others I knew at the school. I can't imagine still taking classes here ten years from now—heck to the no! I can barely stand taking classes now, and even if Rodrick might have some sort of situation delaying him from finishing, he alone has inspired me to not become a 'super student'. That and the fact that Maurice says I have to leave the house if I don't finish classes here and transfer this year.

Laydee was on the same track as me, delayed for whatever reason and goofing off whenever possible. Antoinette, who was a year younger than both of us, had actually surpassed us in class credits and was preparing to transfer to Grambling University, one of the top historically black universities in the South. *Oooh* I know she's going to have fun at that school! But me, I couldn't personally move that far for school or really anything for that matter. Not that I wouldn't want to, it's just a little too far for me. It probably takes half a day to drive there and I am not a fan of road trips or traveling; the only times I've left Texas was when I visited my aunt in Louisiana. I love Beauconte, my quaint southern town where everything is familiar. Here, I know I'm never too far away from help if anything serious goes down.

"Whatever Miss Louisiana, thinkin' you all that 'cause you leaving us already!" Laydee smirked at Antoinette, who rolled her eyes at her before proceeding to twist her neck to wave to one of her classmates she saw walking into a bookstore a short distance away.

"Don't hate, it's not my fault y'all been slackin' since you got here," Antoinette said defensively. "I'm a Christian on a mission, I ain't got time to waste!'"

She pointed her index finger towards Laydee and I, and she had every right to. We had both been treating our classes kind of casually, but I was ready to stop that and had been ready for a while to be honest. I recently asked my supervisor at the restaurant I work at if he could limit my schedule to weekends and day shifts so I wouldn't be up too late at night and too tired for my morning classes. Maurice was also nagging me about the fees for the school; financial aid had helped us with some expenses, but didn't cover all of the costs involved for the school. More time in college meant more money out of his pocket, so I knew he'd be far from happy to hear I was falling behind and livid if I ever stopped going to classes altogether since he already 'invested' so much money in my first few semesters and said he'd kick me out the house if I didn't get it together.

Tamina was spared from Antoinette's accusatory finger since she was also on the right route with her school credits; she already got accepted for transfer to a school in Georgia and was waiting on letters from another school in Tennessee and two schools in Texas. No matter where she ended up, it meant that there'd be a fifty percent chance she'd leave Texas again, our crew would be reduced to half, and things would never be the same.

We fit well together, the girls and I: crazy Laydee, timid Tamina, and nerdish Antoinette. I'm the chameleon because I'm the link that jelled us all together, and depending on the day, time, or situation, you might see me partying with Laydee, studying with Antoinette, or vibing out to soft jazz at a 'zen' café with Tamina. We nicknamed ourselves 'The DLC' (the daddyless crew) because none of us have our real Dads around, and although we're so dissimilar in other aspects, somehow we just match, and it pained me to think that we might all be living in different cities by the time the year was over.

"Don't trip Antoinette, I'm about to get on your level, trust! I'm going to the advisor right now to see what I can do to straighten out my classes," I said matter-of-factly. Laydee clutched my forearm.

"You're gonna leave me too? All y'all just gon' up and leave and forget about me?" she joked with a fake cry. The tiny dice on her labret lip piercing was more visible whenever she made her pouting face. We shared a laugh at Laydee even though deep down, I felt the same way she did.

"I'm not tryna camp here any longer than I have to and you know that Laydee! Quit playin' and come with me, maybe you can speak with one of the other advisor people," I suggested.

Laydee shrugged her shoulders and threw her nose up at the invitation before saying,

"Like y'all said, we need to focus on our midterms, so I gotta get to the library and study for my history test."

Antoinette, Tamina, and I gave each other a look.

"Study, huh?" Antoinette said before she shook her head and we all laughed. Laydee was not only the queen of hype, but the queen of losing her focus for some boy. She looked at us with an innocently puzzled expression on her face.

"What's so damn funny?" she snapped.

"Nothing. Just try to remember to study the book more than Dominican Chris, okay girl?" Antoinette teased.

"Whateva lightbright! For y'alls information, it's a group study session so there's going to be a *group* of us there. Stop thankin' what you thankin'," Laydee snapped.

"No one's thinking anything, we just know Laydee Sharlaine Taylor too well!" I chuckled, causing even Tamina to laugh.

Her name still cracks me up, and yes, her real name is Laydee. I, like most people, presumed it was some sort of nickname at first, but nope, that's the God-given name on her birth certificate and I made her show me to prove it! Her parents must have predicted that she would live up to be just as outrageous as her name, however I don't really know what my parents were thinking when they named me. I've only met one other Dabresha in my entire life and her name was spelled funny. She was from South America or South Africa or something—somewhere far away! I don't know what Dabresha means or how they came up with it, and I still haven't completely gotten used to it and all its uniqueness to tell you the truth.

Mostly everyone calls me Bre because it's short, sweet, and to the point; easy to pronounce, easy to spell, and it doesn't confuse people. It saved the questions and puzzled looks that usually accompanied 'ghetto names' whenever I had to introduce myself to 'non-ethnic' folks. If there was one thing on this earth I couldn't stand, it was hearing someone mispronounce my name, or watching someone's eyes squint when they tried to repeat it after they heard me pronounce it. Name mistakes like 'Bredisha' and 'Durisha' caused my ears to pound like hearing jackhammers on concrete—I had heard every possible erred existence of my name since I could remember!

"Psssh, anyways, I'll link up with y'all after. I'm already late so I'll holla," she called out as she started heading towards the library.

"Late for your date!" Antoinette called out as she stuck her tongue out at Laydee.

Laydee offensively raised the palm of her hand in our direction then twisted her wrist around so there was just one finger left up in the air (I'll let you guess which one). She scurried off to her date, or 'study session' or whatever it was. The boy in question was one of those pretty boys who dressed with a style that was a cross between preppy and geek. He was a boy we knew for a fact she'd been crushing on for a while, so we knew she was elated when she found out that they would be in the same history class that semester.

Of all the little spats Laydee and I have, one thing I could be sure we'd *never* fight over is boys. The type of boys Laydee seemed to crush on were never my type and vice versa. She liked those skinny light-skinned boys with the light eyes, and to this day I have yet to be even slightly attracted to any of the fellas she's picked up—they just ain't my type! Well I'm not sure exactly what my type is; I mean I can't define it precisely and with certainty, I just know it's not light skin, not patterned-dress-pants-wearing Dominican Chris, and not the same type as Laydee's. I do have a specific type right now—my scrumptious chocolatey Florida boy Darrien! We call each other 'D-squared', or I should say I call us that to tease Darrien because he hates 'couple names'. He is all of that, all mine, and far off Laydee's radar.

Tamina had to take off too, so she left our little group and headed to her obligation, whatever it was. That girl was far from outspoken, and whatever dictionary antonym exists for the word outspoken should be replaced with the word 'Tamina'. She never talks much about what she does when she's not with us and we never press her too much because we all know she doesn't like to talk. She's the complete opposite of Laydee and the only one in our crew who doesn't drink or smoke, and Laydee doesn't conceal the fact that she isn't too fond of Tamina. Laydee thinks Tamina is hiding something, like she's a fugitive who popped up in our little Texas town on the run from California. Antoinette and I never pay Laydee any mind when she talks mess about Tamina, though there were a few times I had to set Laydee straight and tell her to lay off of her. Let's just say that Tamina and Laydee were the two gals in our little group that you'd never see hanging out on their own; you might find Tamina chilling with Antoinette on campus or fixing up my hair at my house, but it's pretty much guaranteed you'd never see Tamina with Laydee unless Antoinette or I was around.

Antoinette and I strutted down the crowded walkway toward the administration building, which was noisy and cluttered with dozens of other students. Midterm week was the deadline for withdrawing from classes, so I reckoned that's why it was busier than normal. Thankfully, I had already withdrawn from my hardest class, an early morning French class I was forced to register for as a general language requirement, and didn't have to deal with the ruckus. It sucks having to endure general classes before you can take classes related to what you're actually interested in, but I guess I can't complain too much since every college student has no choice but to suffer the same misfortune. So, after showing up late countless times and missing a few quizzes and homeworks, I was nearly failing! I decided it'd be best to try the class again another semester, a semester when I'd hopefully have my car fixed up and wouldn't have to rely on dilly-dallying public buses to get me to school all the time.

Starting classes before 9:00 in the morning should be illegal; I'd ban them if I could! 7:40 am French class was torture for me because I usually didn't get home from work until after midnight and had to wake up early enough to catch a bus an hour ahead of time. Foreign language classes aren't the easiest to take that early in the morning either. I don't think my brain was built for more than one language, or maybe it just wasn't built for French. I swear half the things that teacher lady said went in one ear then sidestepped right out the other. I did alright in Spanish back in high school, but all the Spanish classes (and ASL classes, my second choice) were full when I tried to sign up for them at SRJC. I thought it might be an interesting deal learning how to pronounce all the funny looking words on my beauty products, but that class was first-degree torment. The grammar was impossible to figure out, and though the pronunciation sounded exotic and whatnot, it was really difficult to repeat. It just didn't make any sense!

Antoinette walked with me to the admin building so she could finish submitting more transfer papers. I was honestly a little jealous of her finishing her transfer before me but I congratulated her anyway—she worked her nerdy little behind off for it, not to mention she had been taking classes every summer and winter to get ahead. I wondered how she could stay so motivated and focused, I really wish I could! That energetic DNA just ain't in my body the same way it's in Antoinette's though, and 'the smarts' just don't come easy to me.

Antoinette's studying psychology and wants to be a social worker when she finishes school. She was one of the first people I became friends with back when I started taking classes here; we were in the same dull astronomy class with the dullest teacher I've ever had, Mr. McClain. He was even more confusing than that uppity French teacher, Madame Riviere. Mr. McClain talked in monotone and always looked at the back wall when he gave his lectures, never at all the people in front of him. It was like we were invisible and he only stopped to take notice of us if one of us dared to raise our hand and interrupt his wall-staring contest.

Antoinette is a math tutor, so she helped explain some of the concepts that I struggled to understand in that class. I thought I would enjoy learning about stars and constellations and all that, but I was fooled by my academic advisor when she recommended it. I swear half of the class is math formulas and might as well be calculus! Okay maybe I'm exaggerating, but there was a little too much math in that class, so I despised it. Then again, maybe if this school stopped hiring dull, confusing teachers, I could enjoy what I'm learning and be more motivated in my classes!

During one of our first study sessions, Antoinette invited me to a Black Student Body event she was hosting and we've been friends ever since. She's the vice president of SisterCircle, one of the 'cultural clubs' they have on our campus. I went to a few meetings to support her, but I'm not interested in going every week like she does. It seems like all they do is complain about black men, politics (which I could care less about), and controversial rap lyrics, then discuss current events that 'set us back'. I'd go more often if they'd talk about more interesting things, or even open the meetings for boys to attend (hey now!). After homework and real work, I don't have time for campus clubs anyway—I got bills to pay! My cell phone, my rent (yes, I have to pay Maurice a little something every month), my car repairs, my parking tickets, it all adds up. I'm still trying to save up for a better car too, so I'm torn on which obligations I should take care of first.

Right now, the '93 Buick Regal Maurice gave me is sitting on the street collecting dust, rust, and cobwebs. One of the neighborhood kids drew a picture of a ball sack on the back window and another wrote 'ashes to ashes' on the front hood (probably little Sierra or Mikey from down the street!). Someone else in the neighborhood casually knocked off my side mirror without bothering to leave a note, and both of the back tires look deflated. It's far from functional, and I'm debating on whether I should keep saving up to invest in a new clutch, alternator, ignition, car battery, *and* side window, or whichever completely craps out first.

I won't forget to mention the cracked windshield and the car's need of serious detailing—it's a black hole of expensive repairs. Being car-less makes me feel like a wingless pigeon forced to hobble around on my claws and stoop in the back of city buses to get around, but I've already spent too much money on that dumb car and just can't afford a new one. My job, my school, and my house certainly aren't walking distance to each other; they're pretty much on three different outskirts of Beauconte! I get rides every now and then from my friends and my boo, but it ain't easy linking up with them with all our schedules being so different.

I waved Antoinette off as we headed to our respective destinations in the admin building; hers at the end of the first floor's main hallway and mine up the elevator on the fourth floor east wing. I entered the reception area of the advising center to find at least a dozen other students waiting in the lobby's outdated maroon-colored chairs. I wrote my name on the clipboard outside Mrs. Vanderkamp's office and avoided filling in the column by my name where I was supposed to write the time I came in. I knew I was behind schedule because the name above mine signed in at 11:17 and my appointment was supposed to start at 11:00. I flipped open my cell phone to verify; 11:23. I decided to write 11:15 in the blank and took a seat anyway, hoping she wouldn't notice my minor delay in the midst of all the sloppy signatures and chitter chatter of other students.

Mrs. Vanderkamp appeared from her office a few minutes later and I hurried to greet her.

"Hi Mrs. Vanderkamp," I blurted with forced enthusiasm just as her lips were parting to summon the next person on the list. She gave me an uninviting stare.

"Miss Davis, your appointment was at eleven. I'm sorry but you're going to have to wait until I see the other students now."

I pleaded with her to let me go ahead of the others, hugely stretching the truth to say that I had to stay late in class to discuss an important assignment with a professor, then by explaining that I had to get to work soon after.

"Well fortunate for you, it appears my next appointment

has decided to also come late or cancel perhaps, so I can fit you in for a few minutes now if you'd like, but just a few," she said sternly.

I sighed when Mrs. Vanderkamp motioned me to come in to her royal headquarters. I was irritated with myself for showing up late, but just as irritated with her attitude. My little delay couldn't have possibly been that big of a deal; I didn't even know how it happened! But 'lateness' seems to happen to me a lot. I swear I was keeping track of time right before I left the chillout spot by the arts building. Oh well, all I could do was try not to let it happen again.

"Hello *once more* Miss Davis, how can I assist you today?"

I handed Mrs. Vanderkamp my school transcript records and promptly told her about my goals for the next semester (or two, or three). I hoped not more than two. I really dreaded the thought of having to go to SRJC any longer, so the goal was simple: get out of junior college and get to a university ASAP! I'd be cool with escaping the overcrowded and run-down SRJC grounds to go to a university, then graduate and get a good job where I could make bank and pay off all the loans I'd be taking out. There were only a few required classes that I hadn't completed, and I hoped I could finish them the next semester.

"You would have been eligible for transfer after one more semester, but there's a problem," Mrs. Vanderkamp asserted. I stared at her wide-eyed and inquisitive, waiting for a response.

"Your language requirement," she said bluntly as she shuffled through my wrinkled transcripts and glanced at her computer screen.

"What about 'em?" I asked meekly.

"You're required to take two semesters of the same language subject. I see that you already took Beginner's French 101 and barely passed with a C-. You need to take the second section of that class, French 102, and it's only offered in the spring. You won't be able to take it until next spring even if all your other classes are done, therefore your transfer process can't begin until that time. Also, you really need to bring up your G.P.A. because your current grade point average will make a transfer application less likely to get approved. Furthermore, it will disqualify you from financial aid and make you ineligible to attend here if it isn't brought up by the end of this term, so I would look into re-taking the 101 course as well. The French 102 is the class you dropped earlier this semester, right?"

I gave Mrs. Vanderkamp a blank stare even though I completely understood what she was saying. Playing dumb helped me get away with things sometimes, or at least get some leeway out of potential lectures or punishments. If there was one thing on earth I couldn't stand, it was adults nagging me about *me* or speaking down to me about my choices. I'm grown! Therefore I don't need no other adults on my back telling me what they *think* I need to hear. I've pretty much been taking care of myself since I was a teenager and know all I could possibly know about the real world and how messed up it is. Now all I need to do is prove I know a little something something by getting through college.

I defended my reasons for dropping the French class by explaining my work and car situation to Mrs. Vanderkamp as plainly as possible. Had I *known* that the class was that important to my transfer process, I might have pushed through it and tried to bring my grade up!

I wish I could have known then that the few minutes I'd spend sitting in her office that day would completely throw off my afternoon and ultimately start the sequence of events that would eventually imbalance my semester, my year, and my life.

Chapitre 2: Oooh I Can't Stand Mrs. Vanderkamp!

"Why ain't you tell me that when I came a few weeks back to drop the class?!" I demanded. I was full-blown upset, and Mrs. Vanderkamp's stringy blond hair and heavy country accent were starting to irk me.

"Ineligible to attend means kicked out, right? If I get kicked out of school, I'm done. My dad ain't havin' it!"

I could feel my frustration heightening the longer I sat in her office; my muscles started aching and my head started throbbing. I stifled a yawn as I briskly folded my arms, slouched back in my seat, and thrust my legs straight out in front of me so that only the heels of my sneakers were touching the ground. This is how it all starts, I thought to myself. This is how someone becomes a super student. They are forced to wait unreasonable time lengths for 'required' classes and eventually give up!

"It's not my job to keep repeating things you've already been instructed to do and should have also researched on your own. I'm here to *advise* you on your progress, and it's common knowledge that students can't keep attending classes if they're not performing," she replied. She pursed her thin, dry, lips together and leaned forward toward her computer. I imagined myself leaning over her desk and slapping her across the face. I'm a nice gal and all but don't set me off! Right now, Mrs. Vanderkamp was doing a damn good job of that. I shook my head in disbelief as Maurice's baritone-voice replayed in my head: "*If you don't transfer by end of the year, you're gonna have to go Bre-Bre. School is not a toy you play with, and the only way I can be sure you're not foolin' around is if you finish in decent time.*"

I didn't absolutely love still living at my folks' place, but I was comfortable there and I knew I wasn't financially ready to get my own apartment yet. I would need a second job to afford even the most basic space in an ugly part of town! Then again, the thought of my own place didn't seem *that* terrible. I wasn't sure how much longer I could put up with my little sister (and 'roommate') borrowing my things without asking, waking me up before my alarm went off, and living like a complete slob!

I could've *killed* her last week when I found out she borrowed my brand new Houston Rockets jersey dress without asking. She tried to hide it in the back of my side of the closet with a huge slit down the side! When I asked her about it, she said it must've been designed that way before I bought it, but I know exactly what it looked like when I first tried it on. Plus, it smells like *her* body spray and has deodorant stains on the side, so I know it was worn by SOMEBODY and it sure as heck wasn't Maurice. If I got my own place, I could do whatever I wanted whenever I wanted and keep everything clean without having to worry about somebody else messing it up. I wouldn't have to worry about my accessories and clothes disappearing from my side of the closet or reappearing damaged, so paying rent at my own place would hypothetically pay for my peace of mind.

Now's not the time for me to make any kind of major moves though because if I get kicked out of school, it'll all hit the fan anyway. I still have a heap of other things to take care of with my checkbook and my bank account keeps struggling to maintain a triple digit balance for more than a few days. I think I could get by a few more years before I'm officially considered too old to still be living with my parents. I'm barely twenty now, just barely! So it doesn't look so bad. I stopped my worrying long enough to tune back into the pompous broad in front of me.

"I can't take the class in the summer? It'll be easier for me with my work schedule to do just the one class..." I interjected.

Mrs. Vanderkamp proceeded to explain that the particular class I needed was not offered at our school in the summer, and that my only option would be to take the class at a community college in a neighboring town. Oh how I wished I could have registered on time and got the Spanish classes I wanted in the first place! I'm never procrastinating on anything at this school again. This college system is straight up wack if you ask me; it's too much work, too much money, and too much time. My high school economics teacher told me it took her twenty years to pay off her student loans—two decades! The same amount of time I've been alive?! Sounds like fraud if you ask me. Psssh. Anyways, Mrs. Vankderkamp ended her speech by telling me the class I needed was also being offered through a unique study abroad program.

"You would have to go to France to take that class," she said with a blatant smirk. My eyebrows flexed inward and I scoffed. Why was she smirking, and why would she suggest something crazy like that? Probably just to spite me! Shoot. Well, I'm going to have to start looking for an apartment and another job! It's not going be easy either without my car running right. I knew Maurice would harass me to see my grades like he did at the end of every semester and I wouldn't be able to stall him out too long. An apartment search would be added to my already tall list of things I gotta do, after fixing my car and paying for my traffic tickets. Oh, and asking my boss for a fat raise! A big enough raise to get me all the money I need before summer vacation. My looming headache throbbed stronger as I started to gather my things to leave Mrs. V's royal quarters. I gave Mrs. Vanderkamp a sideways look.

"I don't got money to go to France for a class, I barely *have* money to take classes here," I snapped. I snatched up my giant red leather Louis V purse and abruptly stood up as I was sure the honored privilege of the noble Mrs. Vanderkamp's 'few minutes' was up. She sighed and bit her bright red lip as I stood up to leave.

"I can check and see if there's another solution, but otherwise I have no other suggestions. I'll research alternative options and you can stop back by tomorrow? My only open time slot is 8:15 and I'll need you to bring your current progress report. Will you be able to make it?"

"I don't have class tomorrow and I work early afternoon. Do you have anything open the day after?" I asked.

"I'm all booked up until spring break Miss Davis, so it's your choice, but I need to know now so that I don't give the time slot to anyone else."

A few explicative words bounced around my head. An early morning appointment on campus on the one day I don't take classes? Just. my. dang. luck. I nodded my head and forced a fake smile—I couldn't wait to wake up early and come back to this lady's office on my 'school day off'... I was absolutely thrilled! "Alright I'll show up," I sighed, rolling my eyes toward the ceiling. I clenched my fist and bit the inside of my cheek as I left Mrs. V's office (two things I often did to help me hold my anger back and this time it wasn't working). Maurice sure wouldn't be happy to hear about this! I dreaded the inevitable conversation and my thoughts played around with different ways that I could present the news to him, strategically and casually, so he wouldn't get all uptight.

My legs felt like two-ton weights as I dragged my feet to the elevator. I didn't have energy to take the stairs, so I pushed the arrow down button several times and waited for it to come to my level. I stared at the crack between the metal doors, thinking *open already!* Could this elevator take any longer? Why was there only one elevator for this entire building anyway? I paced back and forth for what seemed like eternity until I heard the pleasant 'ding' and the doors finally creaked open. The ding sound oddly lightened my mood even if it were just for a moment.

I situated myself in the back of the elevator and looked down at the torn carpet escaping the metal lining in its corner. Just as the doors started to close, a tan hand with a velvet red scrunchie around its wrist came piercing through and stopped the doors from closing. A girl I recognized from a class I took last year got on and smiled at me, but I looked away after acknowledging her with a short nod. I didn't know the broad so it wasn't necessary to say hi to her, plus my Uncle Otey told me several times when I was little that I should never get too friendly with anyone that wasn't black. I think her name was Mary or Maria or something Mexican like that, and I only remember her because she was one of the few Spanish folks in that class and basically one of the few on campus. She used to sit two rows in front of me and was always typing in her phone and twirling her long wavy hair with her pencil whenever the teacher turned to write something on the board. Yeah I remembered her, and today she was still dressed like a tomboy with way too much make-up on—she was quite the catch!

I crossed my arms and leaned against the back wall of the elevator while the ball of my foot bounced anxiously. The elevator stopped at the next floor down and I prayed the ride to the ground floor wasn't going to be an extra-long trip with new people getting on at every floor. I did not have the patience, especially after lady Vanderkamp done ticked me off. I groaned and looked at the wall as the doors opened at a lazy speed. A heavyset older woman wearing a gray and black dress suit got on the elevator and a strong smell of fruit and cinnamon radiated from her jacket.

"Good morning young ladies," the woman said in a singsongy voice as the clunky elevators doors slowly screeched to a close. I glimpsed up as the woman joined us. I recognized her from the school's newsletter but didn't know her name; I just knew that she was one of the administrators who organized the cultural events on campus. Great! Just what I needed: a talkative teacher-type to lengthen this ride (why am I not off this elevator yet!?). I should have just taken the stairs; I heard climbing stairs makes your thighs thicker and your butt bigger and I could use a little help in those areas.

A soft, warm hand gripped my shoulder and I glanced up at the lady and gave her a sharp look. The stout older lady had placed each of her hands on both mine and the other girl's shoulder and was smiling at us very sweetly. I stepped back and gave her a blank stare before slowly rolling my shoulder out of her grasp. I always got uncomfortable when strangers touched me, no matter who they were or what the reason was. The woman began to talk quickly.

"I don't know what either of you are planning for your summer, but I want to let you both know that the SDAO still has several scholarships available for the study abroad programs this June. Have either of you heard about them?"

Mary-Maria and I both shook our heads and gave each other a quick glance before reverting our attention back to Ms. What's-her-face. She removed two sheets of paper from a thick stack of medium-sized yellow flyers tucked under her arm and handed one to each of us.

"Take these flyers young ladies. Studying abroad is a wonderful way to enhance your college experience and learn about other cultures first-hand. The deadline for these awards has been extended until Spring Break and very few students have applied. I strongly encourage you to look over them and turn them in before the new deadline."

I hesitantly grabbed the flyer even though I wanted to tell her no and be gone from school already, but I followed Mary-Maria's lead and accepted the paper, placing it in a side pocket of my purse where I usually placed 'ready to dump' trash items like my empty bottles of miniature liquor shots.

"We need our black and Mexican babies to travel," she said with a smile as the elevator slowed its speed. Mary-Maria and I glanced at each other before turning our necks back to the older lady.

"The applications are at my office on the second floor, so please stop by anytime if you have questions about the programs. This summer there are two programs in Europe, and I hope you both *strongly* consider filling out an application."

She pulled out two business cards from her jacket pocket and handed one to each of us. I didn't want her handing me anything else and considered giving the paper and the card back to her so she could give it to someone who actually gave a damn.

"Thank you," I heard Mary-Maria mumble as I flipped over the business card. 'Ms. Myrna S. Cole: Student Diversity Affairs Organization Director' it read in bold cursive letters.

"Oh yeah, uh thanks," I added quietly as Myrna Cole walked off the elevator with brisk speed. She was unusually nimble for her size, but her swiftness didn't make the elevator operate any faster. A short, quiet laugh escaped my chest once the doors started closing and Myrna Cole was out of sight. I glanced over at Mary-Maria after briefly eyeing the front page of the flyer. There was a photo of the Eiffel Tower next to a picture of a tall skinny clock with a pointy roof.

"Anyway," I told Mary-Maria to break the awkward silence. "So... this scholarship pays for people to study in a different country?" I asked casually after realizing my little laugh had caused the uncomfortable silence.

I looked down at the flyer and then back at Mary-Maria, who seemed intent on reading it. I didn't know why she was concentrating on the flyer so much—I know this chick wasn't about to take any part of that lady's half-minute promotion serious or really consider the random invitation to take off to another side of the world.

"I think so," she replied with the thickest Spanish accent I had ever heard. She shrugged her shoulders and tilted her head. I side-eyed her with curiosity before I readjusted my stance to face the front of the elevator. She continued to concentrate her gaze on the flyer as I slowly folded Ms. Cole's business card in half and tossed it into my purse's side pocket next to her flyer. I looked over her shoulder to see what part of the flyer could possibly be so mesmerizing to her; there were bold blue subtitles illuminating from the corners of the flyer with the headings: 'Discover. Make Global Awareness. Earn Credit. Explore.' Mary-Maria nodded her head as if she was in agreement, then kept her eyes fixed on the flyer as the elevator finally opened its doors on the ground floor.

"You gonna apply?" I asked her in awe as I followed behind her off the elevator and walked with her down the hall. The amusing situation helped distract me from the little gust of emotions I had just succumbed to inside Mrs. V's office. She flipped the flyer over to the back page and nodded her head again.

"Yeah I guess, I mean, why not? It's not due 'til Spring Break, it's free to turn in... it looks cool to me. If I don't win, oh well, but I might as well take a chance."

She continued to read the flyer and I stared at her with wide eyes. She was talking about going to Europe so casually, like it was a weekend trip to New Orleans or something.

"I've always wanted to go to another country. Both my parents are from other countries," she continued, "and it looks like they'll pay for everything but the plane ticket."

She flipped the flyer back over and didn't take her eyes off it long enough to notice the crazy look I was giving her.

"I don't have summer plans besides the usual niece and nephew babysitting. I just broke up with my boyfriend and I'm not working right now so I'll ask my papa about it. Two of the England classes are classes I need," she concluded.

I stared at her with disbelief. Was this chick really ready and willing to disappear to the other side of the globe on a minute's notice, and on top of that for school? This Mexican chick was surely entertaining.

"You ain't scared 'bout nothin'?" I asked her in a high-pitched voice as she started to saunter towards the main area of campus, "and don't you need a passport?"

"No, not scared. My best friend's sister did something like this... I mean they wouldn't send us anywhere dangerous right?" she asked, flipping the flyer back over again. "The girl I know that did this, she went to school in Barcelona with other kids from her school and some tour guides. She talks about how fun it was *all* the time, and I mean, she did come back alive in one piece."

We shared a laugh as I tried to remember where exactly Barcelona was. I didn't think it was in Mexico, so I figured it was somewhere in South America. Or maybe it was in Europe? I would have liked her to clarify, but I didn't want to look stupid by asking, so I tossed the question aside.

"I dunno... it seem like too much to do in a short time, and it look like the program starts two months after spring week."

"Well that's two months to get ready," she interrupted. "I don't know about you but I could use a break from Texas."

Of all the random comical moments that had surfaced in my life, this one definitely had to be near the top. It was like the start of a bad joke: an old lady walks onto an elevator and invites two country girls to Europe. The crazy Mexican girl takes the lady serious, the broke black girl stays realistic.

"I guess," I replied, shrugging my shoulders. "You're Mary, right? You were in one of my classes last year?"

"It's Miryam, Miryam Oseguera. I had a English class with you," she said, nodding her head. "You borrowed my notes a few times you were running late. You're... Debbie?"

"Dabresha," I quickly corrected her as I cringed (Debbie was the worst of my name mistakes!). "But I go by Bre."

Our small talk ended when we started to split off on different walking paths. "Well good luck!" I called to her half-heartedly. "You too!" she called back.

That broad must be on drugs. My mind tried rewinding to the conversation that had just occurred moments earlier with Mrs. Vanderkamp, but the thought of Myrna Cole appearing out of nowhere and promoting some farfetched trip with some probable scheme behind it made me laugh out loud again. People like Ms. Cole are too optimistic for their own good, or it's their job to pretend to be. The few times I've seen her on campus she was always smiling for no reason, and this last encounter practically took the cake. She must be rich and probably doesn't have any bills to worry about.

And what was up with that random statement about black and Mexican babies? I ain't her baby so I don't know why she called me one in her little speech. She probably says the same thing to everybody so she can get commission or something to advertise those scholarships. Regardless, the invite was funny to think about and it definitely lightened the fuzzy mood I was in. I mean, really though, why would I even consider going to France for classes? I don't speak French and could never speak French. I passed the first French class by a whisker and can hardly remember anything after 'bonjour' and 'merci'. I got too much going on in Texas and I could never pile enough money for a plane ticket that probably costs something like five thousand dollars. I've never flown before and don't plan on getting on a plane anytime soon, especially after them terrorists hijacked those planes in New York a few years ago. No sir, I'm staying in Texas right where I need to be. What's out there anyway that I can't find in the biggest state in the biggest country of the world?

As I walked away from the admin building, I flipped open my cell phone to check the time. I had just missed a text message from Darrien asking me where I was at. I decided to call him up instead of writing him back for two reasons: I had just gotten a full set of long acrylic nails, so text messaging was a lengthy ordeal. Secondly, though I had enough time to take the bus to work, I wanted to see Darrien, so I created the excuse of needing a ride. It seemed like I hadn't seen him in forever even though it had only been a few days. My girls tease me and tell me I'm sprung when it comes to that boy, but I'm not. Ain't nothing wrong with having love for your boo, right?

We've been going steady for about four months now. We met in science class and started talking more and more outside of school as time passed. He's a little quiet sometimes, but I think that mysterious part of his personality is sexy, even though my girls disagree. They tell me it ain't good to not be able to sense what's on your man's mind, but I don't see nothing wrong with it. He trusts me and I trust him for the most part, so that's all that really matters. He's a few years older than me, and though we don't got a huge amount in common, we get each other. Plus, he's the best friend of Laydee's live-in cousin, so she keeps me posted on the little extra details of his whereabouts.

I sat down by the rail of the top step that led down to the school's cafeteria courtyard. Darrien didn't answer my call and I wondered what he might be up to. He had a gig making announcements for the campus radio station a few times a week, so it was normal for him to turn his phone off while he was recording in the station's studio. He was a part-time student and because I knew the schedule of the few classes he took during the week, I knew he couldn't be in class. I re-dialed his number just in case he didn't hear his phone, but it went to voicemail again. I texted him back and told him I was leaving campus to go to work, hoping he'd get the hint that a ride would be nice. I flipped through all his text messages from the past week and, while waiting for him to reply, I pondered on whether or not I should ask Tamina or Antoinette for a ride. Tamina used her grandma's car to get to school on occasion, and Antoinette had her mom's van every so often, but neither one of them had their very own cars.

Laydee didn't have a car, but she didn't have a job either, so being car-less didn't really bother her like it bothered me. In fact, Laydee didn't even have her driver's license! She said she didn't need one since she could rely on 'fly boys with fly cars' to get her around. Laydee cracked me up sometimes, especially when she seemed dead serious saying silly stuff like that and was really okay with using boys for favors! But I liked my independence, and being independent had its perks too! (Plus, Laydee hates to mention she failed her driver's test when she accidentally hit an armadillo and swerved off the road).

I stood up from where I was posted at the top of the stairs and started walking off campus towards the bus stop, abandoning the idea of asking anyone for a ride. I shouldn't ask for rides anyway unless I *really* need one, and though I wished I could get home to get ready for work faster, I had more than enough time to get there and wouldn't have to be concerned about my boss jumping down my back for being late again. I had a few hours to kill and the weather was favorable for the first time in a long time; it was warm but not too humid and this was rare in Texas. Plus, I needed to walk off some of the day's frustrations and come up with ideas of how to approach Maurice about my 'unsatisfactory' college progress.

I leaned against the fence behind the bus stop and reflected on the heavy cloud that hung over me. My stepdad's rules might as well be engraved on the backside of the Ten Commandment tablets, and he was not the type to bend them for anyone. If I thought about it long enough, maybe, just maybe, I could find a way to get him to 'bend' (though I could never expect him to break them for me).

Could I succeed in breaking the news to him softly and explaining it to him innocently? Maybe if I told him every single detail, like how it was hard getting to and from school and how I was tired from working late to pay *his* rent, maybe he would understand! But that excuse didn't work in the past and I knew better than to try it again. Maurice was set in his ways and his laws were concrete. He was a straight-forward, no b.s. man, and every time I seemed to mess up around the house, he would remind me that I was an adult and could easily be kicked out if I didn't obey the rules which were: take the trash out every other day, come home by midnight or let him know whose house I'd be at, and don't make trouble (i.e. don't get arrested, don't bring home no babies, and don't get lifted). He also said I'd better make sure to introduce him to any young fellas that took interest in me, so I forewarned Darrien that an introduction between them would need to take place soon.

His most important rule for me was to finish school, and I don't know why it was so important for him. I mean, he didn't even finish school if I remember correct! So I didn't know why he was putting so much pressure on me to be a 'pioneer' for the family. I didn't know if I could ever live up to his standard nor why I was chosen to break the so-called pattern. I wish Maurice was more like Tamina's mom; she told Tamina that school was a waste of money and that government assistance could pay her enough to get by. In one aspect Maurice seemed unfair; I couldn't think of anyone else in our family who had gotten through college before and I hoped my little sister would be given the same ultimatum when she finished high school in June. If she didn't start college, maybe she'd be forced to move out and I could finally have my own room *if* I weren't to get kicked out first.

I smiled at the thought of my own room, then it faded when I realized I could be homeless in a matter of months. I knew Maurice would never literally throw me out on the streets, but then again I wasn't sure what he was capable of. He was a rigid man, and even though he always seemed to be busy working or passed out sleeping, he did have the upper hand in a lot of my decisions. Dang. Maybe I should surprise him and move out so I could have 100% control of my life. This whole 'responsibility' and 'example setting' thing was never my idea. It's more annoying than when one of my CD's starts skipping on my favorite track.

Chapitre 3: Kinfolk

When Darrien surprised me and swooped me up from the bus stop that day, he could tell that something was bothering me. He pulled up to the curb in front of the bus stop and motioned for me to get in his car. Before I could even open my mouth to let him know what was going on, he said,

"Just chill shawty." I was pleased he had showed up to find me even if he hadn't responded to my text messages. I wanted to tell him all my frustrations with Mrs. V, but I doubted he wanted to hear them. He's calm that way and never seems to get worked up over anything, and he doesn't like 'drama' talk even if it's just school-related. I don't think I've ever seen him once show frustration or lose his temper, so we balance out since I've been known to lose my temper quite a few times.

He smacked the side of my thigh as I sat down in the passenger seat of his car. His three simple words made me feel better as we drove across town to my house. Darrien dropped me off on the corner like he usually did when he knew Maurice was home; we could see his burgundy work truck poking out from the driveway from down the street, so whenever that happened, Darrien let me out at the stop sign and turn to drive down a different street.

"You sure you don't want to stop in and say hi to my kinfolk?" I asked him as I carefully opened his passenger door so it wouldn't scrape the curb.

"Got business to handle right now," he casually replied as he adjusted his rear view mirror with his fingertips.

Maurice told me that any fellas that dropped me off or picked me up ought to come in the house and introduce themselves, but Darrien insisted he wasn't ready to do that, or didn't have the time, when I've asked him before. I'm sure my dad intimidated him a little, Maurice intimidates everyone! But Maurice is a good dude—after all, he was doing an okay job taking care of us, TWO GIRLS, on his own.

As I got closer to the front porch, I could smell the scent of a delicious down south dinner in progress. My sister Delilah could cook anything under the sun and make it savory! I had a little talent in the kitchen too, but Delilah's food was always on point. She usually got home before Maurice and I, so she had ample time to experiment with recipes in the kitchen. Maurice worked long hours in construction and never had energy to cook, and since he couldn't even make rice without burning it, Delilah always made sure there was a hot meal ready for him when he finally got home.

Mmmmm, what was that smell? I tried to guess what was cooking before I thrust my knee into our busted front door—it wouldn't open unless we lifted the knob and lunged at it simultaneously. The screen was also hanging on by a thread, the frame was splitting, and the deadbolt was rusted beyond measure. It was a pitiful sight, but our door helped keep salespeople from pestering us too much. I'd like to think that's why we haven't fixed it yet, but Maurice keeps insisting that he just hasn't gotten around to it even though it's been over a year.

I jerked the door closed as I stepped in and made a quick right down the narrow hallway in the opposite direction of the kitchen. I dropped my bags in the bedroom that Delilah and I shared; I eyed my phone charger on her bed and snatched it out of the socket at the foot of her bed and placed it back on my dresser. This was the umpteenth time Delilah had poached my charger and not put it back where she found it. She keeps saying she's gonna find hers or buy her own, but she's been saying that forever and

I'm tired of her using mine without putting it back!

Nevertheless, what smelled like jerk chicken, mashed potatoes, and greens soothed my temporary frustration. Even when Delilah worked my last nerves, her cooking always found a way to earn my forgiveness. It could have been chicken fried steak and baked potatoes, and I was ready to dig in either way! I couldn't quite pinpoint the exact combination of food she was preparing, so I asked her as I entered the kitchen.

"What you grillin' up ova there D?" I called out as I poured a glass of water from the fridge.

"Nothin' for you!" she teased, making me chuckle as I gulped down my water. A cold drink was exactly what I needed after a long day at school, and water tasted so good after I went too long without it. I wanted to drink some sweet tea or cola, but could hear all the old folks in my ear telling me to stay properly hydrated in the Texas heat.

"Just messin'.. chicken and 'taters. It's almost done."

I heard the pan sizzle as she tossed the potatoes in the frying pan on the stovetop and I poured myself a second glass of water.

"You finish ya homework?" I asked her over my glass of water. She replied with a simple "duh!" before she added to her defense with,

"I ain't tryin' to hear him nag me about school *all* the dang time, so I finished before I started cooking just like he want me to."

Maurice told me to nag Delilah about her homework since he was rarely around to do it because three months earlier, her schoolteachers called and told him she was in danger of failing her senior year of high school. She hadn't been doing her homework and was ditching classes, even though we thought she was at school. Up until this year, Delilah was doing better in high school than I ever did, so we were surprised to find out that she had been low-key fooling around the whole year. Maurice told her she had better finish her classes right or move out, so she got her act together and started pulling her grades back up. That was Maurice's other rule: get good grades or get out! He said I could only stay at our house if I stayed in school, and that's the only reason why I registered at SRJC in the first place. I didn't want to, but I knew I wasn't ready to move out the summer after high school.

Preventing my eviction wasn't the only reason I signed up for classes at SRJC; I knew Laydee was going to go there and she told me a lot of cute boys would be going there too. SRJC ain't a fancy, brand new Ivy League school or nothing, but it's the closest college to my house. Part of me wanted to move out and use my hostess paychecks to pay rent at an apartment somewhere and have freedom; freedom to come and go as I pleased, freedom to play my music as loud as I wanted, and freedom to do *whatever* I wanted! I could only wish it'd be that simple though, and the hostess salary surely wasn't enough to pay my own rent and pay all my own bills, even when I combined them with the little extra money I got from the financial aid office at school. Maurice was fair enough though, and that's part of the reason I stayed living at his house (that and the fact that I liked having extra money to shop with). As long as I told him where I was going, who I was with, and when I'd be back, he was cool, and as long as I didn't make too much noise coming home, my sister was cool too.

When he wasn't around, I would play my music as loud as I wanted to anyway, especially if Delilah wasn't there or if we could agree on which CDs or radio stations to vibe to. There were rare fantastic moments when I had the house completely to myself, and when these miracles happened, I savored them. But the fact of the matter was this: I was twenty years old and I wasn't trying to spend any more of my young adulthood than I already had at the house I basically grew up in.

A lot of my friends had already moved out of their folks' houses and they were doing alright. Antoinette had started living in a dorm, and I knew a few others who were renting apartments on the south side of town where rent was cheaper and crime was more frequent. Dorms didn't seem like a terrible idea, but I wasn't sure if I'd want one if I'd still have a bunch of rules to follow. Antoinette said that alcohol wasn't allowed at the dorms and that they got random inspections by school staffers. I also think she said only athletes could live at our schools' dorms, but I didn't see the point of moving to a place that had almost as many rules as living with parents anyway.

If I were to move out, I could finally spend some real time with Darrien, somewhere away from campus where we could just chill and not have to worry about nothing or no one around us. Darrien has an apartment twenty minutes away, but he shares it with two of his friends and a cousin. His place was always a busy mess with people constantly stopping by, so I hated staying over there for more than a short spell. There was only so much discomfort I could take when I visited his place and had to look at dirty clothes and sneakers scattered across the floor, dishes piled up in the sink and on the living room tables, low-rider and nudie magazines on the kitchen counters, and topped-off ashtrays on every flat surface. It should be against the law for too many boys to live in a place by themselves; with no female around helping to run the place, it was no wonder why it always looked a disaster! But Darrien was comfortable there and didn't see no problem with his place. What else can I say? Boys will be boys.

"Suppa's ready!" I heard Delilah shout. I ran to the dining room to set the table before Maurice appeared out of his cave. I switched on the living room TV before I sat down; a newscaster was talking about a stabbing that happened at a house party the weekend before and police still hadn't ID'd the body yet because the boy's face was impaled beyond recognition. All they knew was that the boy was between fourteen and seventeen years old and was wearing red Nikes.

"It has now been nine days since this incident happened on the 2200 hundred block intersection of Cedar and Howard Street. If anyone has any information regarding this disturbing incident, please speak up and call the Sheriff's Department immediately. All reported information will remain anonymous. Parents, please be mindful of where your children are. Again, this is a teenage boy, about five feet ten inches, wearing a gray sweatsuit and red tennis shoes..."

"Faulty shame whoever did that boy like that," Delilah mumbled under the clanking sound of her scooping the potatoes into a ceramic bowl with a metal spoon. "They got detectives askin' kids at school about it but no one knows nothing supposedly."

I nodded my head in agreement as Maurice appeared. He walked straight to the living room as Delilah and I eagerly waited for him to join us at the table, plucking the remote control off of the couch as he started flipping through channels.

"I don't want to hear any more of this bull," he grumbled as he changed the channel. "Ain't nothin' but foolery on the news."

"Here goes grumpy bear again," Delilah whispered as I stifled a laugh. Delilah and I always made fun of Maurice and called him a big black bear because he was always tired and cranky even though he constantly seemed to be napping. On a normal day, he was closed up in his gloomy cave of a room with towels over the windows to keep the sunlight out, and he would only come out of hibernation to eat or use the bathroom. To drive the point home, his frequent yawns resembled the growl of a giant bear that just came out of his habitat. I guess construction is no easy job, and I'd never want to do it if it makes people that tired!

Aside from construction, he also worked graveyard shifts as a security guard a few times a week at the same hotel property I worked at. Thankfully our schedules were so different that I rarely had to worry about seeing him while working at Zoe's Roasthouse; the diner was tucked away deep inside the hotel and he only kept watch outside and in the parking lots. When I do get a glimpse of him patrolling the grounds on my late shifts, he pretends like he doesn't see me, but I know he's watching. He's actually the one that told me about my job when he saw the sign posted that they were hiring. I already had a cashier job at a grocery store in the center of town, but decided to apply anyway since the hotel restaurant paid a little higher and working at a four-star steakhouse inside a three-star hotel felt more sophisticated than running a register at a discount grocery store.

Delilah still works at that same grocery store I used to work at; she pretty much took my spot because I quit a few weeks after she started working there. The hotel restaurant hours were plenty and I was busy enough with school, plus, working at the same place as her made me realize that there is such a thing as 'too much Delilah'; I already had the privilege of dealing with her constant bratiness at home and didn't need to deal with even more of it on the clock. Working with her for three weeks was two-and-a-half weeks too many, and it wasn't easy trying to cover for her on the days she was late or broke something or short-changed her cash register. I couldn't stand my co-workers asking me about my sister's mistakes or whereabouts since I had nothing to do with how she worked.

So, even with each person in my family working their tail off, we still always seem to be low on cash. Hopefully this college stuff pays off like they say it will and I get a real nice job when I finish. That is the point of going to college anyway right, to get a good job after and make lots of dough? My leg shook as I sat down, restlessly waiting on Maurice to choose a channel, and thought about updating him on my semester setback. I wasn't in the mood to argue nor provoke The Bear during dinner, especially a dinner that looked this delicious, so I decided to hold off on the conversation for the meantime.

Maurice the Black Bear released an inoffensive growl as he plopped down in his usual seat at the good end of the old, square, chestnut table that had been a fixture of our dining room since I could remember. The table had a broken leg with a flat block of wood wedged in between the table and the floor, and just like the front door, Maurice had been promising to fix it for a while. We were still waiting for him to come through on that three year old promise and the other dozen promises he made to fix up things around this old house, so it was guaranteed we'd be waiting for a while.

I think Maurice preferred sitting in that particular seat since my Mom used to sit across from it. The seat was always empty, but keeping it there made us feel like she was still here eating with us, and I could only imagine her teasing Maurice to fix the table.

"*Reece*, when you gon' fix up this damn table? My food is sliding off my plate!" she'd say in a playful voice, and he'd always reply "I'll get to it woman." I think Maurice liked hearing Mom nag him; couples are funny that way sometimes and actually like having something small to spat about. Maurice Franklin was a man of a few words, almost to the point of silence after my mom passed, but we could usually tell when something was on his mind even when he didn't talk.

When he played loud jazz records, hummed along to

Motown tunes, or came out of his cave to read the newspaper in front of the living room TV, it meant everything was fine. When he constantly rubbed his neck during dinner or avoided eye contact, it meant something was bothering him at work. On nights where he didn't come out to eat with us at all, like the day Delilah's school called to tell him she was failing, it meant he was upset about something. However because of his crazy work schedule, we rarely could tell if he was genuinely upset or simply just too tired. I once found an empty bottle of gin in his room too, so I'm sure the other reason why he didn't come outside on those days he was feeling bothered was because he preferred to be alone with his bottle.

My sister and I think he purposely avoids telling us his work schedule so we didn't plan on bringing people over the house. Though his schedule is inconsistent, Delilah and I have a good sense of when he's set to work the night shifts because he usually gets to sleep right away after his construction job. Now the times he had to work graveyard on Saturday nights, those were the best nights, and luckily I hadn't been caught yet bringing my gals or Darrien over, *especially* Darrien. Delilah promised she wouldn't snitch as long as I didn't say anything about her sneaking away to her friends' houses or inviting her own friends over on those nights. Between all the disagreements and sisterly clashes, our secret outings and covert chill sessions were one of the few things Lilah and I could agree to stay hush-hush about in front of Maurice. I'm sure Maurice suspected we had people over against his wishes on occasion, but since he could never prove it nor find evidence, we both stayed in the clear.

"Your Aunt Trecee called the house for you Lilah, said she tried to get ahold of your cell and you didn't answer," Maurice stated as he stuffed his mouth with a fork full of moist, simmering potatoes that were so tender they almost slid off the fork. Maurice loved him some potatoes! He always stocked them up in our pantry because they were inexpensive and could be made a million different ways. I loved taters too, but not *that* much, and of all the foods my sister cooked, I'd have to put her Tex-Mex at the top of the list. You ain't had real Tex-Mex until you've tried Delilah's sopes and enchiladas, and do not disturb me while I'm eating them! Tex-Mex was pricier than the other fixins she cooked since it required so many different ingredients, so though we didn't get to indulge in them as much as I would have liked, I loved the moments we were able to afford those more elaborate meals.

I wouldn't pile my plate up too high today though; I had started a diet the week before and was eating less in anticipation of my Spring Break plans, so smaller portions and occasional exercise had become a part of my already busy agenda. I was planning to get a new swimsuit and wanted to slim out, so I only placed a small scoop of potatoes on my plate once Maurice finished refilling his plate. We both looked at Delilah and awaited a response.

"Oh yeah, I know. I was busy when she called but I'll call her back," Delilah replied with a slightly defensive tone and a look of mild irritation on her face.

This is one of the reasons why Delilah and I didn't get along so much; she had all the time in the world to run her mouth when her friends called, but acted like it was inconvenient to spare a few minutes to talk to my Mom's only living sister and my favorite aunt. She knew it was upsetting to Maurice, but she ignored my Aunt Trecee's calls more often than not.

"Maybe if you stopped talking to *Jay* so much you could find some time to talk to Auntie," I said casually. Her mouth dropped open as she squinted her eyes and shook her head at me, kicking my shin under the table just light enough so that I wouldn't react.

"Shut up! You swear!" she scoffed as she rolled her eyes and raised her fist at me when Maurice wasn't looking. I laughed and helped myself to the chicken. It was cooked to perfection and damn near looked like something off of a Smithony's Barbecue commercial. My mouth watered as I dug in for my first bite.

"Who's Jay?" Maurice demanded in all seriousness. He barely looked in Delilah's direction; his attention was on the TV screen peeking in from the living room broadcasting the basketball game he found during his anti-news tirade. He looked her dead in her eye and she averted her gaze down at her food, pretending not to notice his stare. Delilah avoided responding until Maurice pressed again.

"Well, who is he Lilah? Is that your booboo? That's what y'all call 'em nowadays right? Your booboo," Maurice joked with a poker face expression. The corners of his mouth strained not to smile as I cracked up at his pronunciation.

"It's boo Dad, and no, he's just a friend from school. Bre's making stuff up 'cause that's what nosy people do good with!" Delilah snapped. She stuck her tongue out and sneered at me. I smiled and continued to dig into my meal, trying to pinpoint the combination of seasonings Delilah used to make the chicken so I could attempt her recipe next time I cooked. I definitely tasted some black pepper and parsley but I couldn't figure out the rest, and if I tried to ask her she wouldn't tell me either. She says all her recipes are top secret and anyone who asked would have to pay for them—she doesn't even let me stand next to her in the kitchen when she's cooking! It's all good though and I won't step on her toes as long as she continues to cook up food this good.

Delilah casually helped herself to a scoop of vegetables as she attempted to get back at me for calling her out on her little boyfriend.

"So how's Darrien?" she asked me as innocently as could

be. I flinched at Delilah and squinted my left eye as Maurice jumped in to defend me.

"Your sister is old enough to go steady with somebody. *You* still need to wait until you finish high school like I done said before. You don't need no more distractions."

A huge smile overtook my face before I helped myself to another bite of my food. I was gratified with Maurice's response, and the food tasted so much better with him on my defensive line.

"I would like to know more about Darren though," Maurice continued. He shot a look in my direction and raised his bushy, black eyebrows at me before bringing his attention back to the basketball game playing on the television.

"Darr-i-en is just a friend from school," I teased, mocking Delilah's high-pitched response and correcting Maurice's erred pronunciation of his name. That was one humoristic quality that Darrien and I shared; people often mispronounced our names even though neither of our names seemed too difficult in my opinion, especially his. I understood people slaughtering my name on occasion, but there was no excuse for his. Mine wasn't *that* hard either though: DA-BRE-SHA. Why did so many people growing up have a problem getting it right? I used to dread the first week of every school year when I was little because I hated correcting my teachers when they did attendance. Thankfully, my college teachers didn't take attendance the same way so I didn't have to deal with those same annoyances.

"Ooooh, we forgot to say grace!" Delilah gasped. We all stopped eating, put down our utensils, bowed our heads, and repeated our usual brief, dull, blessing. We had become accustomed to saying a tiny ten-word grace before we ate dinner, but Delilah and I never said it when Maurice wasn't at the table; we pretty much only said grace to respect his wishes since he insisted it was an imperative thing to do before eating.

The three of us quickly reclaimed our utensils after blessing our food and went right back to filling up our bellies with Delilah's delicious cooking. I had to give my sis silent props; her meals were always on point! But I rarely told her because I didn't want her head to get bigger or for her to think that I needed her cooking. If I did, she'd probably act like even more of a brat and cook less often to spite me after a spat. It's crazy how you can't tell folks what you honestly want to say sometimes because they might start acting funny on you.

We finished our meal in our typical quiet manner, occasionally laughing at something that came up on the TV commercials. I enjoyed the days when all three of us sat down to eat dinner together, even if it meant Delilah kicking my shin or Maurice concentrating more on the basketball game than on anything else. Men and sports are two unusual things, and I could really care less about the latter. I never watch sports and never had an interest in playing them. I took some dance classes when I was little, but I don't think dance can be considered a real sport. It requires a lot of practice and it make you sweat, but it ain't like basketball or running races.

I *loved* to dance back then, those were the days! There were few moments you *wouldn't* see me dancing around the house, happily practicing a routine that I learned from one of my after school teachers. Tamina used to come over sometimes and practice with me; she was in a dance group that we started way back then, and we use to perform in talent shows and local gigs. We won a few trophies back in the day if I remember right, but those days were definitely long ago and are now just a distant, foggy memory amongst the blur of the rest of my childhood memories. Now when I hear old folks tell me that time goes by too fast, I believe them much more than I did before.

I hurried to scrape the vegetables tidbits from my plate

into the kitchen sink when I remembered that Darrien had told me to call him after supper. I rushed to get to my room before Delilah came in so I could have at least a little bit of privacy on the phone with him. I'd hang up or go outside if Delilah showed up, depending on how the conversation was going (sometimes Darrien liked to talk about smashin' if you know what I mean). I still needed to do dishes before I started on my homework; Dad's rule was that whoever didn't cook had to do dishes, and though I hated that chore, I didn't mind doing them if it meant Delilah would cook.

Washing dishes meant risking harm to my manicure, and I hate messing up my nails. It took me a while to do dishes after my fresh weekly manicure, so I got in the habit of using latex gloves to protect my nails whenever I had to. It might sound funny to you, but manicures and full sets are not cheap these days and they are essential for my happiness! Darrien told me he loves a pretty girl with pretty nails, so that being said, I do what I have to do to make my nails stay lovely as long as possible and to limit my visits to the salon cashier. I liked feeling pampered while getting my nails done, but the stylists get on my last nerve sometimes. I couldn't stand them talking around me in Japanese or whatever language it was, and always telling me to 'relax my hands' when I'm there. What the heck does a relaxed hand look like anyway? I swear I almost cussed one of them out last time after she told me that b.s. three times and smacked the back of my hand with the nail filer.

I pulled my cell phone out my pants pocket as I headed down the hallway to my room, dove stomach-first onto my bed, then held down the speed dial button that linked to Darrien's number, #1 of course! The phone rang a few times before connecting me to his voicemail; he didn't mention he was working that night, so I didn't know why he wasn't answering. He must've been busy with something important, and whenever he couldn't answer his phone for whatever reason, we started texting even though it took much more of my time to type words on my phone with my acrylics on. Texting was cheaper though since the family phone plan had unlimited texts (but limited daytime minutes), so I wasn't too badgered about it.

'*I called, no answer. what u up to?*' I started to type, then slowly erased the message letter by letter and simply replaced it with '*i called...*'

I didn't want to seem all nosy and such asking where he was at. I especially didn't want to be one of those bugaboo females always checking in on her man, so my short version of the message would hopefully elicit the same results. He would probably reply with where he was at or explain why he couldn't answer, so any reply would be good enough for me.

I waited a few minutes for a response, which sometimes felt like holding my breath when I was waiting to hear back from that boy. I got up and put my phone on the top of my blackwood dresser where I usually left it to connect it to my charger. I decided to take a shower while I had the room to myself, so I quickly lathered and rinsed, threw on some sweats and a tank top, then started to brush my teeth with the bathroom door wide open so I was in earshot of hearing my phone ring if it sounded off.

I strolled over to my dresser with my toothbrush hanging out of the side of my mouth and flipped open my phone to check if it rang while I was showering. There were no new calls or texts, so I was at least relieved I didn't miss anything and plopped the phone back on the top of the dresser. I moseyed back towards the bathroom in the corner of the room Delilah and I shared. Our bathroom was very covert: it had a narrow doorway and could easily be mistaken for a storage closet (and was about the size of one). Our room was technically the master bedroom of the house because a few years ago, Maurice graciously offered to trade his room for our old one to give us a little more space. I loved having a bathroom in my room even if I had to share it; it made getting ready to go out so much easier, and getting ready to do pretty much anything easier since I only had to take a few steps to check the mirrors instead of running down the hall.

Even better, the sliding closet doors had giant mirrors on them so if Delilah was hogging the bathroom mirror, I could still check my appearance inside my room. It was lovely! Even lovelier before the second mirrored door fell off to where it was currently resting at the bottom of the closet under our massive collection of shoes. I was secretly happy that my sister's feet were two sizes smaller than mine so I never had to worry about her borrowing any of my kicks or heels without asking. I know she borrows my stuff already, it's just hard for me to prove it when I don't notice anything missing right away. She's lucky I'm too busy to take inventory of all my clothes and accessories because I'm sure I'd catch her borrowing my stuff more often than not.

" ♪ *GET BACK, you don't want problems with meeee,*
CLACK CLACK, I take my paper seriouslyyyy,
GET BACK, GET BACK, CLACK CLACK! ♫ "

I ran to pick up my phone; the ringtone playing the chorus to one of my favorite rap songs signaled I had a new text message. Finally! Took him long enough! I flipped open the phone and scrolled to the envelope icon that was blinking impatiently on the front screen. New message from... Aunt Trecee. Merde (a cuss word and one of the few words I remembered from French class!). I laughed to myself thinking about how old folks like Aunt Trecee try to use the internet and send text messages like us young folks. Aunt Trecee didn't even know how to text until I taught her a year after she bought her phone, and it was times like these I wish I never had.

I casually opened the message to see what she wanted. *'Hey niecy, just want to say hi. Call and let me know if u still plannin to visit on spring week. love you!'* I sighed as I slammed my phone shut. I forgot to tell Aunt Trecee that I made plans to go to Florida with the girls for Spring Break, and as of the week before, the plans had become official. Spring Break was looking to be the livest one yet! Laydee had family in Daytona who had graciously agreed to lodge Antoinette, Tamina, and I for six whole days, and I was especially looking forward to it since I had never been on a real beach before (the shores of Lake Beauconte don't count). Spring Break was less than two weeks away, and within two weeks I could finally chillax.

I already gave Zeke, my stiff-necked boss, the heads up that I planned to visit family for spring break, so that he'd be okay with my mini-vacation request. I wouldn't exactly tell him that those plans had been altered to me visiting Laydee's family in Florida and partying on the beach with a fake ID for the week—it wasn't necessary for him to know anyways! I wouldn't be telling a bold-faced lie, just leaving out a few details right? It wasn't like there was a shortage of people working there anyway, so it shouldn't be a problem, hopefully. I'd make sure to confirm with him next time I worked, then start looking for outfits and the perfect swimsuit at the mall.

Maurice said it was okay for me to go as long as I checked in with him when we got there and gave him all the information of where we were staying. I'm glad he never pressed me too much on everything I did; he trusted me to stay out of trouble and I loved him for that! I also hoped he would keep all my previous responsible decisions in mind when I told him about my tiny school setback situation later on. I decided to hold off on that conversation until after Spring Break so he wouldn't punish me and forbid me to go to Florida with the girls. Yup, definitely a better idea to delay that little talk until after the trip, even though I might get in more trouble for waiting to tell him... Oh well, I'd figure that deal out later.

Right now, it was time to focus on my biology homework assignment. As usual, I had waited until the last minute to do it, but I felt I got things done better under pressure. My last minute assignments seemed to get higher grades than my carefully planned out assignments (well at least that's what I told myself). The biology assignment would be due the day after tomorrow, but tomorrow I was working a full shift and had to meet with Mrs. Vanderkamp again early in the morning. I could always skip that meeting if timing became an issue since it wasn't mandatory or anything, it wasn't like a court date! But it was semi-important so I knew I'd have to force myself to get there on time and pretend like I cared about my classes.

I couldn't stand people who took offense to the smallest things, and I personally couldn't stand Mrs. Vanderkamp. She reminded me of those cougar ladies that tried too hard to dress 'hip' even though she had to be well into her forties. Her dyed blond hair and low-cut blouses were too much for someone her age, and her redneck accent made my skin crawl. Unfortunately, she was the academic advisor for all students with last names 'A' through 'H', so I didn't have a choice but to put up with her until I could bolt my way out of that school.

My biology homework for the night was confusing like it typically was. We were learning about rainforests and ecosystems and about how much danger our planet was in from destroying them. Teachers had been warning us about our planet being in 'danger' since elementary school, but it still looks like the same planet if you ask me. I think they exaggerate things to make us want to recycle and save the planet and all that crap, kind of like how they exaggerate the importance of college. I low-key think college is just another way for the government to get our money, but I wouldn't say that out loud. I knew people with college degrees who were working regular jobs and driving regular cars, and dropouts who were making bank! But I'll air out my grievances about that another time.

My homework assignment emphasized the fact that there would be no more rainforests by the end of the century if humans continued to cut them down. I didn't see the importance of the lesson since people didn't live in rainforests anyway, so I quickly scribbled down some answers to the reflection questions at the end of the chapter. The teacher in this class rarely marked homework questions wrong; she just gave us credit for trying to do it, so I never spent too much time on her assignments. I wrote out the vocabulary words on a separate paper like my teacher requested so I could turn them in when they were due. I couldn't care less about what I actually learned in that class; I didn't get why I had to take it anyway since it had nothing to do with what I was going to major in, but I guess all colleges have the same base classes and every student has no choice but to suffer through them and get them over with.

I wasn't exactly sure what I was going to choose as a major, but I knew it had nothing to do with ecosystems. Sometimes I felt like I was learning the same bull from my classes in high school, which means some could consider college to be a half-waste of time, but I guess others would consider it an advantage since we had already learned a lot of what the professors talked about and were able to get through some classes a little easier. That's one of the few benefits of this school nonsense, I suppose.

* * *

" ♪ *GET BACK, you don't want problems with meeee,*
CLACK CLACK, I take my paper seriouslyyyy,
GET BACK, GET BACK, CLACK CLACK! ♫ "

"That best not be Aunt Trecee again," I said to myself. Sometimes she accidentally sent messages twice without realizing it, and this is why people over the age of forty should not have cell phones! Maurice had a phone but rarely used it (he barely even knows how to use email!). He never texts and pretty much only keeps his phone around for emergencies. Occasionally, he'll reply to one of our messages if we ask him a specific question—he knows the routine! Aunt Trecee really needs to join him in limiting her cell phone and internet use.

I flipped open my phone and clicked again on the blinking envelope icon. New message from... Antoinette. Dang. I mean it's cool to hear from her and all, but it's not Darrien.

'Hey lady, can I borrow your green Coogi top this weekend, the silky one with the silver straps?'

I popped my gums and quickly typed back *'sho'*. I didn't mind letting Nette borrow my clothes; she could use a little extra style! She only broke free from her typical boring attire if she stepped out with us on the weekends. Though she didn't stray too far from her jeans and sweaters, she at least let her hair down instead of covering it under a wrap. She also put on lip gloss and wore blouses that showed just a little bit of flesh. My clothes were loose on Antoinette, but I think she preferred her clothes that way. It's like she's afraid to wear anything too tight or even the least bit risqué. The only skirts she wears are the ones that go down to her ankles, and she's the only young person I know that wears those kind of skirts. She never wears halter tops or tank tops even though she could easily rock one—she has a cute little figure! In the end, her style was her choice and I wasn't going to knock her for her fashion sense (or lack thereof).

I meandered back to the bed I had converted into a study space and tried to focus on the biology assignment again. My eyes continually shifted to my phone as I tried to focus on the homework; I couldn't stop glancing at my phone even though it wasn't sounding off. Darrien drove me crazy when he didn't answer my calls or respond to my messages as quickly as he should, but I knew he'd get back to me when he could. Before I knew it, the clock showed (and my body felt) that it was late. Time had flown by in the midst of my assignment and I still hadn't heard back from my Darrien. *Where is my boo?* Maybe he never got my message?

I thought about re-sending it, but decided not to; if he hadn't gotten it, he should have at least seen my missed call. I sheltered a yawn and convinced myself to stay keen on finishing the bio assignment, but then I remembered there was still a pile of dirty dishes waiting for me in the kitchen sink. I scurried to the kitchen and quickly scrubbed the three sets of plates, silverware, and pans that were still crusted with flakes of leftovers, and carefully loaded them into the already crowded dish rack. I wondered where Delilah might have been; the TV was on and I saw her books out on the living room table, but she was nowhere in sight (she was probably down the street with one of her loud friends!). I was pretty sure The Bear was hibernating in his cave and unaware that Delilah might have just snuck away from the house without permission. I never ratted her out though, not unless she *really* ticked me off. If she got caught then she got caught, but I wasn't going to worry as long as she came home.

I plopped back down on my bed and attempted to finish the tail-end of my biology assignment, but my eyes were so heavy and I was battling to keep interest in the subject material. I began to drift off into sleep in an upright position with pencil in hand, leaning against the wall that hugged my bed. I snapped back awake a short time later when my phone's text ringtone went off again. Much to my dismay, my last text message of the night came from a club promoter, and because so many promoters had my number, I couldn't even guess which one it was.

'Come see superstar Texas rapper Kingston Midas perform his hit single "Short Dress Shorty" this Friday at Club Monaco. Ladies on the guestlist free before midnight. Gents, dress to impress or digress!'

I groaned and gathered my homework into a pile, deciding it'd be best to finish the rest of the assignment sometime the next day. I'd find the time somewhere, maybe on my lunch break since there were only about a dozen questions left to fill out. I pushed my book and papers onto a neat stack on the floor and snuggled under the zebra print comforter that Aunt Trecee gave me for Christmas a couple years back. I *loved* that blanket; it was so comfy, thick and cute! I couldn't ever imagine replacing it for another blanket, and Delilah knew better than to ever try and borrow it.

I ignored my desire to change into pajamas and dozed off with the light on. Since Delilah would be coming to bed any moment after me, it was easier for me to get to sleep with the lights on so the lights wouldn't make me snap wide awake whenever she came in. My eyes had gotten used to sleeping with the lights on, so it was all good as long as I was under my blanket. I hoped to have a nice dream, something to make up for the bad dream I had the night before. I tried to think good thoughts as I slowly lost consciousness, and before I realized it, I had reached my REM state (thanks psychology class!).

Chapitre 4: Baby Girl

" ♪ Get up, get up, get doooown!
Then drop it to the muh-fuht ground!
Get up, get up, get doooown!
Then drop it to the muh-fuht ground! ♫ "

I staggered like a wino towards my dresser and snatched my cell phone off its charger as my wake-up call sounded off. My phone was my alarm clock, my calculator, my calendar, my social link, and so much more; I still couldn't believe that one little device could do so many things! I rubbed my eyes and groaned at having to start another day, pressing the snooze button as I stumbled back to my bed and placed my phone on the pillow by my neck. Ten more minutes was all I needed to feel right and refreshed, so I snuggled back under my zebra blanket and zoned out for a second time. I could hear the slight commotion of Delilah moving around in the kitchen, but the clank and clatter of pots and pans was barely noticeable as I savored my precious minutes of additional slumber.

The alarm went off again as promised, but I pressed the snooze button once more. I was certain I would have enough time to get dressed, eat a quick bite, and get to the bus stop even if I slept a little longer. I didn't sweat about it because twenty minutes was all I really needed to get going in the morning, though I usually gave myself twice as much time since my hair and makeup took me a good spell. All ladies need that little bit of extra time to look fresh! But I was just going to the counselor's office and not to any actual classes, so I figured I wouldn't need as much time perfecting my look anyway.

"Shiii-yooot," I screamed as I glanced at my cell phone. I missed my third wake-up call and accidentally turned my alarm off. I now had less than an hour to get up, get dressed, *and* be inside the administration building. My thoughts wrestled each other as I hurtled out of bed, avoiding using some choice profane words that I would have most definitely preferred to use in such a case. I was trying to break my bad cursing habit after accidentally letting one slip in front of Maurice and a few of my friends' parents. They all scorned me for my verbal errors, but I didn't give two craps what they thought. They act like they never cussed before themselves! I couldn't remember when or where I started swearing so much, but I knew hanging around Laydee wasn't helping since Laydee rarely completed a conversation without dropping a few F, N, and B words.

Shoot. Now the near impossible task of getting to campus in less than an hour was going to be a certified challenge. I threw on a pair of casual jeans with a sweatshirt and abandoned the idea of make-up. I packed my school purse in a fury, viciously bumping into anything and everything that was in my path as I tried to flee my room. If I ran that threatening quarter mile length between my house and the bus stop on the main road, I could make it just in time for the next bus *if* I was lucky. Luck never seemed to be on my side though, so I feared today wouldn't be any different and I'd miss the bus and be forced to wait half an hour for the next one.

I zoomed out the front door, almost forgetting to lock it, and debated on whether I should try to call someone for a ride or make a break for the bus stop. As I flew off the patio stairs and brought my walking pace to a light jog, I started thinking over the schedules of anyone who might be able to give me a ride. Was today Wednesday or Thursday? What time was it? I think Tamina was already on campus and Antoinette should have already been in class. I ravaged through my purse and tried to feel around for my phone with my right hand while poorly stabilizing the purse with my left; neither task was easy to accomplish while sprinting down a bumpy beat-up sidewalk. At that moment, I didn't care if anyone in my neighborhood may have seen me looking like Aunt Jemima while running down the street and scrounging through my purse with a du-rag hugging my head. I could fix my appearance on the bus, but getting to the bus stop on time was my only concern.

"You gotta be kiddin me mayne!" I moaned between gasps for breaths. I realized I had forgotten my phone on my pillow, so the chances of getting a ride from ANYONE vanished in the thin, morning air. There was a payphone right near the bus stop I could use, but I didn't know any of my friends' numbers by heart except for Darrien's. My pace quickened as I rounded the corner. I didn't see a bus driving away in the distance and the benches at the bus stop were full of other people, so I silently thanked God that all my running hadn't been a complete waste of time (Amen!).

I doubled over and grabbed my knees to catch my breath as I positioned myself beside the half-dome shaped fence that surrounded the blue bus stop benches. I shook my head furiously as I threw my purse on top of my feet. How could I oversleep like that?! I didn't even drink or go out last night! Exactly a minute later, the giant dingy blue bus appeared when it rounded a corner in the distance. It slowed down to a loud squeaky halt in front of the bus stop, lightly brushing its giant rubber wheel against the curb. I tried to use my last bit of energy to climb the sticky stairs and greet the bus driver, but only a loud exhale came out of my mouth.

I jammed my bus fare into the entrance meter before tip-toeing past all the other riders and taking a stance holding onto a high rail near the back exit. All the seats were full, and I hoped there were no dirty old perverts around looking at my booty, which was eye-level to everyone that had a seat in the section I was standing in. The main thing I couldn't stand about riding the bus was that it seemed to be the assembly point for suspect looking people; pervs, molesters, kidnappers, and rubbernecking old men seemed to accumulate there all the dang time, never allowing me to be at ease while getting around town. I connected my earphones to my CD player and started playing music to take my focus off the fact that my legs were dog-tired and I was dying to sit down.

When the bus halted to let off an elderly couple a few stops down the road, I made a dash to claim their seats. I whisked my purse on the adjacent seat, vowing to move it only if someone eyed me or asked. I started furiously digging through my purse to search for the papers that Mrs. Vanderkamp requested me to bring. *Shoot shoot shoot!* I had forgotten the papers in the stack of homework by the foot of my bed, however my irritated look was replaced by a gleaming smile when I discovered that my phone was in the depths of my purse all along and I wouldn't have to spend the entire morning without it.

Any amount of time without my phone seemed endless, and I dreaded the days I messed up and forgot to take it with me. I flipped it open to make sure I hadn't missed any messages or calls. Nope. No messages of any sort, and specifically none from Darrien. Had he not gotten my message the night before? I hoped my phone hadn't malfunctioned like it had done in the past and tripped up sending my messages. I tried not to stress about it since I knew Darrien would eventually get in touch if we hadn't communicated in a couple days. I leaned my head against the bus window and allowed my eyelids to lower quite a ways down.

"Bresha? That you bay-bee girl?"

I flipped my phone closed and threw it back in my purse as I tried to identify the gently strained voice that intruded through the earphone I had just jammed into my ear. I forced a smile as I looked up at Ms. Pat, one of the elderly ladies I knew from the community church. I had at least twenty minutes remaining on my bus ride and dreaded the fact that Ms. Pat had approached me and insisted on sitting down in the seat next to me. I was in no mood to chat with church folks, but I chucked my purse onto my lap to make room for her, then removed the earphone and slightly turned down my music.

"How ya doin Ms. Pat?" I asked with all banality, secretly wishing the bus could speed up so I could get off faster.

"I'm fine baby! Tried to wave you when you got on but didn't think ya sayne me."

"Oh, sorry ma'am," I innocently replied. I thought I *may* have seen Ms. Pat out the corner of my eye when I first got on, but I avoided making eye contact with her and any other possible 'familiars' since I looked a mess. I forced my back against the hard plastic bus seat and adjusted my posture to a slight slouch. I knew this ride was going to be long now.

"We ain't seen you 'round church in a while, hopin' you gon' stop back by soon. The folk miss ya and ya family, hopin' y'all getting around B'connie okay."

There it was; the church promotion. It seemed like Ms. Pat and a few other people in the neighborhood were always trying to promote going to church. Sometimes I wondered if they were all undercover church employees with quotas for expanding the congregation. They were almost as persistent as the nightclub promoters who handed out flyers anywhere and everywhere young folks gathered and blasted endless text messages to everyone's phones.

"Yea, we good Ms. Pat, thanks for askin'," I told her, "and

we'll be back by the church soon," I fibbed, knowing that the word 'soon' was perfectly vague. I couldn't remember the last time our family went to church together, with the exceptions of the appearances we made every year for Christmas and Easter. Maurice was always too tired for church after his night shifts and I usually worked on Sundays at the restaurant. Ever since my Mom passed away, our family had begun making fewer and fewer appearances. Even when my Mom was around, we still didn't go all that often. It didn't bother me much since I knew church was just one more thing to add on my already busy schedule. Unlike my other obligations, church was optional, and I couldn't be fired or be failed for not showing up.

"Oh you missed a beaut'ful service few weeks back, fer Black Hist'ry Month, the child's choir did a African dance and the taynaygers put togetter a lil' play, it were so great. Wish you coulda sayne it! I remember when you was doin' dem lil' dances with dem kids by the church, you's so good Dabresha, so good" she babbled.

"Yea, I *was* good, but I don't do that stuff no more. I be workin' a lot and going to school and all so I don't got time for none else, 'specially with my car actin' up.."

Ms. Pat interrupted me before I finished my thought.

"Yes, Sista Hayes was tellin me 'bout you going to the lil' college down on Lincoln Ave with her daughter. You go baby, you get your schoolin' done now. We all so prouda ya baby, so proud…"

Ms. Pat's hair bun tumbled to the side of her head as she nodded enthusiastically. The failing bobby pins began to show as I wondered what anyone could possibly be proud about in *my* life. My grades at school weren't anything to brag about and my mediocre job had just written me up for tardiness for the second time last week. Above all, I was broke, and probably would be until I finished school and got a better job. Who could possibly be proud of a car-less, penniless, C-average student? I started fixing my hair as Ms. Pat continued to jabber and her own hair continued to unravel.

I fidgeted in my chair, anxious to escape the grasp of Ms. Pat's conversation. It was the second time that week I had been referred to as a baby and it bothered me even though I knew Ms. Pat meant no harm by it. I breathed a sigh of relief when Ms. Pat's wrinkled, veiny hand used all its might to squeeze the rail beside her knee and she slowly got up from her seat. I noticed Ms. Pat's loud floral shirt had come untucked from the back of her long, brown corduroy skirt. I didn't bother to let her know; it made me uncomfortable when I had to correct people, especially elders, and I secretly wanted to give her some hairstyling tips in addition to tips to help her coordinate her clothes better. I would never put a pink and red blouse with a long brown skirt, nor end the outfit with flat white loafers, yet Ms. Pat was wearing exactly that, proudly.

"Well I'm about to go make groceries baby, hope to see ya round church pretty soon," Ms. Pat called out as she waddled to the exit door and gestured me goodbye. "Have a blessed day now."

"You too ma'am." I quickly threw my purse back on the seat and replaced my right earphone so I could jam to my music again. Listening to crunk music in the mornings got me pumped up for the rest of the day and made me want to dance! Or shove somebody! The energy in Southern rap is undeniable and it's rare that I go even half a day without vibing to it. The music helps the days and the minutes go faster, especially when I'm on the bus, and that's why I made sure every alert in my phone was a ringtone of one of my favorite rap songs when it sounded off.

It would only be a few more minutes until the bus got to

my stop and I knew I'd have to damn near run to the administration building to get to that appointment on time if that was still even possible. As the bus started to slow to a stop, I pushed my way toward the exit door and flew down the stairs the moment the doors popped opened. I pretended not to notice the unpleasant stares of some of the other people around me who were already standing at the exit and should have technically gotten off first. I cut around the corner and rushed through the school's front parking lot, being careful to make sure my purse didn't hit nobody's car and making sure I didn't step into the path of any drivers that may have been in just as much of a hurry as I was. I had almost reached the browning lawn that housed the 'Welcome to Saddle Ranch Junior College' sign when I heard a familiar voice say, "Ayyye!".

I twisted my neck around and threw a huge smile on my face as Darrien's candy-colored Chevy pulled up to the curb next to the sidewalk I was standing on. His roommate Keith was in the passenger seat and they were dressed fresh, just like I loved him to look. My face lit up as I ran over to him and he rolled down his tinted window. The pleasant tinge of cherry Cigarillo smoke flowed out of his car as I gripped the window sill and leaned in to give him a kiss on the cheek.

"I ain't hear back from you yesterday," I said softly, then I stepped back and scrunched my eyebrows at him. "And why you up this early?" I asked him with an inquisitive expression on my face. I placed my left hand on my hip and tilted my head to the side as he forced a plastic red cup into my hand.

"Try this," he said, directing the cup towards my mouth. I took a huge sip and made a sour face. Whatever bitter concoction was in his cup was way too strong for anyone's morning; it felt like tiny burnt pieces of glass had materialized in my neck as it flowed down my throat like lava. He let out a chuckle and I pouted at him, though I adored the way he always laughed with a singular elongated grunt. That boy loved getting faded!

"Chasin' paper so I can keep the Chevy nice and keep taking you out nice places," he replied smoothly. His attention stayed focused on his front windshield as if he was looking for somebody. His roommate barely took notice to me as I peered into the car. I wondered why Darrien was up so early since he usually didn't start classes or work until the afternoon, and I hoped he wasn't up to no good again.

Darrien was with Keith when he got arrested last month, and I had to empty my bank account to bail him out. Darrien said the charges weren't serious and he'd only have to pay some fines, but he never told me exactly what transpired. All he said was that he got pulled over while he was leaving his homeboy's house and that the cops tripped off of finding a little bit of weed in his car. Supposedly the weed was Keith's, but Darrien had to go in because of a bench warrant he forgot about. Darrien always seemed to get irritated when I asked him too many questions about that incident or pretty much anything, so I tried to avoid nagging him to keep him levelheaded.

He told me he was shy about our relationship since it was his first 'real' one and he didn't like showing affection in public. I understood where he was coming from since I also was also an amateur in the dating game; I hadn't really dated anyone since high school, (and that 'relationship' ended when he cheated with my ex-best friend), so I get why Darrien was hesitant and I didn't pressure him into displaying our relationship more publicly. I just wanted to make him happy and be there for him if and when he decided to open up, so I didn't get offended when he barely spoke to me in front of other people like in the parking lot that morning. He was with one of his 'boyz' and I knew that boys especially hated showing love in front of their friends. It was an unwritten rule that all boys followed so they wouldn't appear whipped, or God forbid, weak. It bugged me that I still felt like I hadn't really gotten to know him all that well even though we had been dating for a while. I guess relationships are funny that way though and you can still feel like something's missing even when you have a man.

I handed the red cup back to Darrien after I took another sip and shook my head as the last of the lava dissolved in my chest.

"We gotta get to the spot simp," Keith said under his breath. Darrien tilted his head at me, and without saying a word, gave me a look that said 'you know the deal!' I took a step back from the car and watched him roll his window back up, then waved him off, fully aware that I had just lost a few minutes on my journey and was fixing to be even later to my appointment.

I continued to think about Darrien and his 'secretiveness' as I darted to the pathway that led to the admin building. Once in a blue moon, Darrien dropped small hints about why he acted so guarded and how his past life in Miami influenced his low-key persona, but the hints were never sufficient enough to know the full story (it seems like every black person got a story!). I just knew that his past wasn't all that dandy, much like mine, and that we surely related to each other on that level. He was fun to spend time with and easy to talk to, but I knew there was something more underneath his undeniable swagger and stylish clothes. That's what I liked about him most: the way he dressed. My momma used to say that you could tell a lot about a man by the way he presented himself, and Darrien *always* looked fly—even in his pajamas!

As I dashed across campus, I spotted Antoinette standing by the library in the distance talking to one of her Black Student Association friends.

"Hey girl!" Antoinette called out, motioning me to come over. I quickly made the detour as a bead of sweat escaped from the edges of my questionable hairstyle.

"I can't chat now Nette, got an appointment, but tell your mom to stop talking 'bout me at church!" I joked.

"Aww you saw Miss Pat? You know she always asking about folks!" Antoinette chuckled, "and my parents want to know when you gonna go to church with us again by the way, they said they can pick you up if your dad can't give you a ride."

"Okay coo," I replied with strained enthusiasm. "I'll see when I can go but I gotta talk to ya 'bout it later. I *really* gotta bounce."

"All right girl, bye!" Antoinette called out, resuming the likely boring conversation I supposed was taking place between her and her club friend. I often wondered where Antoinette got her motivation from. Not only did she get good grades, but she was involved with a lot of events on campus. Most important, she was a good friend who always found time to chill after her school work and school gigs were done. She was always talking to people about campus events and study groups; she was a nerd in that aspect but still cool to kick it with. Maybe I could do better in school if I borrowed a little bit of her motivation, but I know I'm not as smart as her. People like Antoinette are born with special intelligence and special gifts, and those are two things I just don't possess.

Antoinette must have inherited her stamina from her mom 'Sister Hayes', the person responsible for influencing her bohemian desert fashion. Sister Hayes was a hairdresser who ran her own salon and usually wore long African garbs even if the bottom of her pulls sometimes dragged on the floors. Sister Hayes was also an active member of Beauconte Baptist Church, hence her frequent conversations with Ms. Pat. I don't know how

Antoinette found time to go to church every Sunday since she was busier than I was with classes, campus events, part-time work, and swim practices, but I guess she made sure to find time since it was the only day she could see her brothers and sisters during the week and she admittedly missed them (all five of them!).

The Hayes family was large and solid, and at times I wished I could be a Hayes and have two loving parents and a host of nice brothers and sisters around. I disposed of those thoughts every time they came up though and brushed them off as foolish. I had Maurice, my sister, and Aunt Trecee, and my friends were there for those necessary 'female' conversations. To me, it's pointless wishing for more when I had just enough to get by. I was never the wishing type anyway, and I felt like nothing good could ever happen to me even if I tried to wish or pray for it. I don't consider myself pessimistic, just more realistic in my thinking. I found it silly when people hoped and dreamed for things that would never happen, so if I didn't wish or pray for anything, then I could never get disappointed.

Chapitre 5: Not a Good Fit

I impatiently paced back and forth in front of the elevator of the administration building, rapidly pushing the button several times with the hope that the elevators would drop faster. I was short of breath from rushing to the building after my brief chat with Antoinette, and I think Darrien's drink had made me a little dizzy. I closed my eyes and tried to slow my breathing as the elevator slowly made its way to the first floor. The elevators at this school were soooo slow, and they seemed to go slower when I needed to be somewhere faster. As soon as the doors popped open, I hopped in and pressed the button for my floor. The elevator jolted as it started to ascend, so I leaned against the wall to keep my balance.

I let out a short chuckle when I thought about the last time I was on the elevator and Ms. Cole appeared out of nowhere with that stack of yellow flyers like a club promoter. I dug through my purse and glanced at my cell phone to check the time, then rubbed my eyebrow with the back of my hand to wipe the sleep out of my eyes. I tried to think of a good excuse to tell Mrs. Vanderkamp if she pressed me about the delay; I could only think to say that the bus was late, but I just hoped the question wouldn't come up since I was only ten minutes behind.

I speed-walked down the corridor and made a sharp left, nearly bumping into Mrs. Vanderkamp, who was standing in the hallway quite a ways away from her office talking to her co-worker Mr. Johnson. I wasn't a fan of Mrs. Vanderkamp, but I did have to give her props on her shoe game. She was poised in shiny blue stilettos that were hugging the stubs of her fresh-shaved legs. The shoes matched her shiny v-neck blouse which, unsurprisingly, revealed too much of her chest.

I approached her on her left side and wondered if it would be rude to tap her on the arm or better to stand in her line of vision and wait for her to wrap up her conversation.

"Another cancellation, another wasted time slot. You know how it goes..." I heard Mrs. Vanderkamp say as I got closer and opted for the silent, hands-off interruption. Mrs. Vanderkamp and Mr. Johnson both craned their necks simultaneously to peer down at me. I forced a grin on my face and apologized for interrupting, then subsequently for my tardiness.

"Oh don't fret Miss Davis, I'll still be happy to help you. We have to chat quickly though because my next appointment starts in about 10 minutes," Mrs. Vanderkamp replied in the kindest manner I had surely ever seen.

"Hopefully," Mr. Johnson laughed as he winked at Mrs. Vanderkamp, who giggled before smiling back at him. I had never seen Mrs. Vanderkamp in such a good mood, but didn't mind it as long as she wasn't upset about my delay. She placed her arm around my shoulder, turned me toward the direction of her office, and motioned for me to follow her. She walked ahead of me as we got closer and held the door open for me to enter. As I sat down, Mrs. Vanderkamp flipped over a yellow plastic sign that hung on her door from its current message of: 'Be Right Back,' to its opposite side that read: 'Cell phones are not needed for academic counseling. Thank you in advance for turning them off.'

Mrs. V rounded her huge, L-shaped mahogany desk and sat in her plush gray chair to face me. I plopped down on the hard plastic guest seat and placed my purse on my lap, hesitating to explain to her that I had forgotten the requested paperwork and hoping she wouldn't ask about them. Mrs. Vanderkamp glanced in the square compact mirror that was attached to her computer and fixed her make-up and hair. From my view in the guest chair, the back of the mirror looked like some sort of information placard, so several times a day when students thought Mrs. Vanderkamp was looking at time schedules or school calendars, she was probably verifying that none of her blond hairs, eyebrows, or fake eyelashes were out of place.

"It's good you made it but I'll have to be quick, and hopefully one of the options I found you will help," Mrs. Vanderkamp started. She shuffled through a pile of folders that were scattered across the corner of her desk, carefully ensuring that her shiny nails and perfectly lotioned hands wouldn't get damaged between the papers.

Mrs. Vanderkamp presented me with a few possible options to help me amend my class situation, none of which were to my liking. There were two nearby colleges offering the language classes I needed during the summer, and a third college even further away offering the class in the fall. All three establishments would take at least two hours to get to on the bus, so I knew getting to any of the schools would be a hassle without my car. I was planning to work full-time in the summer and save up money to fix it, and possibly start looking around for an apartment. When I tried to explain this to Mrs. Vanderkamp, all she said in response was,

"Well Miss Davis, it's about time you decide if your priority is work or school."

I poked my lip out and my muscles tightened as I sat in front of Mrs. V. I was no longer at ease and felt myself getting angry, though I wasn't sure at who. Angry at Mrs. Vanderkamp? Angry at myself? Angry at my car for causing me so much dang trouble? I wasn't sure, but I knew I was angry and when I got angry it wasn't a pretty sight. People like Mrs. Vanderkamp could never understand how hard it is to do work and school at the same time, especially without a car in this day and age. I doubt she *ever* had to worry about bills or getting kicked out her house by her parents and she's probably been well-off her whole life.

I dryly thanked Mrs. Vanderkamp and carelessly flung the papers she handed me in my bag. I turned to slide the chair backwards and started to get up, but I wobbled a little bit and had to grab the armrest to balance. Those little sips of whatever was in Darrien's cup had done a number on me at eight in the morning! I hoped Mrs. V hadn't noticed something was 'off' about me (or noticed a funny smell on my breath).

" ♪ *GET BACK, you don't want problems with meeee,*
CLACK CLACK, I take my paper seriouslyyyy,
GET BACK, GET BACK, CLACK CLACK! ♫ "

Ms. Vanderkamp shook her head as I quickly switched my phone to silent and prepared to leave her office, even though her 'phones off' rule didn't matter now. I meant to turn it off before the meeting started but I forgot! I never understood why teachers trip off of phones ringing when it really isn't that big of a deal. Most of my teachers spaz out when our phones go off during class, and even though Mrs. Vanderkamp was just an office worker, she reacted the same way.

"Sorry 'bout that, but I got one last question," I said in a shaky voice while looking over my shoulder with my back slightly turned to Mrs. V.

"You *have* one last question? Yes, what is it?" Mrs. Vanderkamp replied. I could tell she was a little put off by my attitude but I didn't care to say the least. She glanced back at her mirror and used her index finger to smooth out some of the concealer that was clumping under her eyes.

"I found out that summer study program in France is offering two classes I need, and there's scholarships for 'em…" I started.

"Yes, that's correct. There are two study abroad programs

this summer and one of them's in Paris. Scholarships are available for both programs as there weren't a sufficient amount of applications turned in this year, like previous years, but these programs cost money Miss Davis, even with scholarship help." Mrs. Vanderkamp began to shuffle through some other papers on her desk.

"Yes, I know. But... I can apply right? And if I can't get a scholarship, I can take out another loan right? That's what the flyer said, I have it somewhere," I replied. I rummaged through my purse and attempted to find the wrinkled up yellow pamphlet I carelessly tossed inside of it the day before.

"I know what the flyers say and I know all about the programs Miss Davis, however you have to understand that these programs aren't just for anyone. They're for *motivated* students willing to commit their time, serious effort, and expenses to the program. You can't just withdraw these overseas classes whenever you feel like, and if you miss those classes, huh..." she scoffed and raised the palm of her hand towards me. "You miss those classes?? You might as well come on home before they send you home. I'm sorry but that program's just not a good fit for you."

Mrs. Vanderkamp began to write something on a post-it note and was unaware of the ice cold glare I gave her. How could a middle-aged white lady possibly know what would be a good fit for me? She may have been older and already had her college degree, but what did she know about me personally that qualified her to give me any type of guidance? I knew I could be a better student, but I didn't like anyone else calling me out on my imperfections. Mrs. V casually stuck the post-it on the right side of her computer screen, and I could see the ink through the paper read 'call Manny for hair appointment'. She began to rearrange the folders on her desk again.

"I know the programs aren't easy and I know I'm not a

straight A student, but just to be clear, those are the classes I need for my language requirement, right?" I responded with a defensive tone.

"That's correct Miss Davis, but realize that a program like this will only bring you more student debt. You've told me that you didn't want to borrow more loans, and the amount you need for this type of program would put you above the maximum loan amount for your next semester."

"But those classes will get me on track right?" I interrupted, tilting my head at Mrs. V and placing my hand on my hip.

"Miss Davis, I'm not going to argue or waste time discussing this with you when I know it's not worth your time. It's just not a good idea for someone taking classes at your pace and frankly not for someone in *your* financial position."

I edged toward the door and thanked Mrs. Vanderkamp a second time with a half-smile while I started to make a hasty exit. My head was hanging low; I felt defeated and just couldn't figure out why Ms. Cole made the program seem attainable, yet Mrs. Vanderkamp made it seem nearly impossible. I reflected on it as I dragged my feet back down the hall toward the elevator. It descended and stopped to let someone on at that same floor Ms. Cole had exited on the day before. Just as the doors started to close again, I stuck my arm in between them so they would pop right back open. I got off the elevator and decided right then and there that I was going to pick up the study abroad application at Mrs. Cole's office despite anything Mrs. Vanderkamp may have just said.

I knew I'd probably never turn it in, but it felt sensational to take some sort of action that defied Mrs. Vanderkamp's orders. I could at least use the application as a prop to show Maurice that I *tried* to fix the class situation, but was only given absurd solutions. I cautiously wandered into the office, which had an 'SDAO' placard next to its entrance, and approached the receptionist sitting at the front desk. I scanned the little office for Ms. Cole, who was nowhere in sight, and hoped I had come to the right place.

"Can I help you?" the receptionist asked in an oddly polite manner, glancing up from her PC with a smile. There was an odd-looking mosaic lizard figurine sitting on top of her monitor and it had big, bulging eyes. The receptionist, whose nameplate read Harmonie, didn't look that much older than me, yet she spoke and was dressed professionally like the other adult staff members roaming around behind her.

"Yes, umm, I... I came for a scholarship application? For the France summer study.. thing?" I searched the room for some proof that I was in the right office. I hated looking dumb in front of other people so I hoped to correct my mistake in advance before it was too late to recover.

"Oh yes, you're in the right place," Harmonie replied with a smile. She adjusted her glasses as she walked over to a far counter and grabbed a thick packet of stapled papers out of a huge stack. My eyes widened as I prepared to jump ship and abandon the idea of the application since it looked to be thousands of pages long.

"The first few pages have more information about the programs. I'll give you two applications just in case. Good luck!" she replied as she eagerly handed me the packets. "We extended the deadline until the Tuesday during Spring Break, so feel free to contact our office if you have any questions before then."

I slowly clutched the packets and thanked the young receptionist, quickly making my way back down the hall towards the elevator. I remembered my phone had sounded moments earlier at Mrs. Vanderkamp's office, so I flipped it open to see who was hitting me up. A big grin crossed my face when I realized it was Darrien. He had sent a text message that simply read, *'u need a ride today?'*. Without fail, hearing from Darrien put a smile on my face. My pensive expression transformed into one of bliss.

I texted him back right away, letting him know that I'd love for him to drop me off at home before I headed to my midday shift at the hotel restaurant. *I'll take you so we can chill together,'* he replied a few seconds later. I giggled as I walked back towards the parking lot, happy and nearly forgetting everything else that had just happened that morning. My frustrations with Mrs. Vanderkamp and my unplanned visit to Ms. Cole's office vanished when I stopped by the ladies room to check my hair and apply a little make-up before Darrien came to swoop me up.

He appeared a little later than the time he said he'd come in the same area of the parking lot that I'd just seen him earlier, but my excitement overshadowed his delay. He reached over from the driver's seat and pushed the door open for me. I gracefully eased in the passenger seat, poorly trying to conceal a smile, and greeted him with the kiss I never got to give him earlier that morning.

Chapitre 6: The Boo

"What's that in ya hand?" Darrien asked, briefly glancing down at the application packets. I slammed his car door shut and adjusted the passenger seat so I could sit back a little more comfortably.

"Nothing, just school papers," I replied as he rolled up all the tinted windows in his car. He gradually turned up his car stereo as loud as it could go. The bass from the speakers shook the gravel on the ground as his car skirted out of the parking lot a little faster than I'd have liked him to be going. I *loved* riding in his car and sitting next to him, surrounded by the music and forgetting about everything else. All that mattered was the bass in the speakers and the moment, and no conversation was needed. I glanced over at him every so often while he drove, adoring the way his head nodded to the beat of the songs and how he gestured and mouthed some of the lyrics. These were the moments I felt safest, with him in his car, and with no interruptions besides his occasional phone calls that prompted him to turn the music down for a brief moment.

Oh I wish I could cruise around all day with him! Drive across town in his stylish whip and find new places together—but I knew the ride would have to come to an end just like it always did. Even before he installed the sound system, butterfly doors, two-tone interior, and custom twenty-two inch wheels, I loved riding around with him because I was *with* him and loved the moments we had together.

Darrien's Chevy made a smooth stop outside my house. We got out the car and started walking up the path to the front porch.

"D, stop!" I said between giggles as I pushed his arm away from my stomach. I had told Darrien countless times to not touch me outside my house! We had too many nosy neighbors around, particularly the Sheffields across the street; they were that typical, old, snoopy couple who rarely left home and liked to gossip about everything they'd seen throughout the day. I always had to keep a lookout out for them whenever Darrien (or really anyone) came over since I knew they could possibly report who they saw, or think they saw, to The Bear.

"I can't help it Bre. You lookin' better and better every time I see you and I don't know how much longer I can wait."

Darrien got behind me and wrapped his arms around my shoulders. I flirtatiously pushed him away a second time.

"D, I'm serious! You tryna get me caught up or what?" I whined.

"Ain't nobody around shawty, wind down," he said with a smile. He leaned against the wall next to the front door, accidentally ringing the doorbell while I hurried to unlock it. I wanted to get us both inside quickly just in case the Sheffields were doing their usual surveillance. I let him in first, playfully pushing him as I scanned the block, then slammed the door closed. No Sheffields in sight. The only person I saw in the neighborhood was lil' Mikey from down the street riding around on his bike without any shoes on.

"Sit down, watch TV or somethin' while I get dressed," I ordered Darrien, and he obediently plopped down in Maurice's favorite recliner. I walked down the hallway, peeked into Maurice's room, and let out a sigh. I was certain he was at work since his truck wasn't in the driveway, but I had to make sure so I could relax better. I always feared he would make an appearance at the very moment Darrien and I decided to give into temptation, but no, he was nowhere in sight and shouldn't be for a while. As I entered my room, I heard Darrien switching through TV channels and could hear when he stopped on a channel playing rap videos. That boy loved rap music just as much as I did, and definitely let it be known by blasting it in his car everywhere he drove.

I began to arrange my side of the room since it was a bit messy from my rushed exit a few hours earlier. Nonetheless, my little mess didn't compare to the catastrophe known as Delilah's Side of the Room, so after I made my bed, organized my shoes, and folded up my clothes and pajamas, there was a distinct invisible line of whose side of the room belonged to which person. I organized my books and papers into a neat stack on my dresser and fished my work uniform out of the closet. I made sure the black pants and white long-sleeve collared shirt with pearly buttons were both clean and ironed straight before I put the pants on and threw on a tank top. I kept the shirt covered in a plastic dry-cleaning bag because it tended to get wrinkled and dingy if I wore it too long before my shift. I had just pulled my tank top over my head and down to my belly button when I felt a large hand slide down my left shoulder. I jumped and turned around to Darrien pushing his face against mine. He grabbed my bare waist and started to guide me towards my bed.

"Didn't I tell you... to wait... in the living room?" I mumbled between his kisses. They felt *so* good but I knew they had to stop. I diverted his grasp, took a step back, and pushed him onto my bed.

"Yeah, I been waiting... a long time," he replied with his adorable laugh. He started to slide his hand under my tank top and he kissed me again.

"Boy don't start now. You know I got work," I said nervously, rolling my eyes with a smile. Darrien was always pressuring me to get intimate with him, but we never seemed to be on the same page, ready at the right time or at the right place, and now was *definitely* not the right time nor place. I could hear my heart pounding as I lifted my work blouse from the space on the bed beside him and started walking towards the doorway. He crept up behind me and plucked my shirt out of my hand, forcing me to turn around and give into another one of his irresistible kisses. He shut the door before I could escape and pushed me against it, kissing my neck and shoulders as he started to lift up my tank top.

"You ain't got work for another hour right?" he whispered. I giggled as his hands moved across my stomach and I hoped he couldn't feel all the fat around it. I had been trying to lose fifteen pounds before summer, but rarely had energy for exercise and sit-ups after long days at school and long shifts at work.

"Darrien, I'ma hurt you for coming in my room like this!" I pouted. He ignored my playful threat and continued to give me more of his delightful kisses. He turned me around and started to guide me towards my bed again. I loosened his grip on my waist and pushed him onto the bed a second time, then rushed to rescue my work shirt from the floor.

"I still need to get ready for work boo, you understand right?" I gave him a kiss on the cheek. I could sense Darrien was excited and a little peeved when he blandly replied "I guess, just hurry up."

He got up from my bed and slowly let himself out of the room. I heard his phone ringing in the living room and silently thanked God for the perfect timing of the call to help interrupt Darrien's upteempth attempt to swoon me—the boy is impatient!

I finished combing my hair, dabbing on my make-up, and started to pack my purse. I crammed the science homework I didn't finish the night before inside my bag since my break at work was going to be my only chance of getting it done before class tomorrow. I looked around the room to ensure that there was no evidence of Darrien's presence there, then headed to the living room. I was surprised to find Darrien leaning against the front door, looking down at the phone in his hand.

"You want sum'in to eat?" I asked him as I threw my purse and work uniform on the couch.

"Naw I'm good. Actually gotta run a last minute errand, so I gotta take you *right now* if you want the ride to work still." Darrien had a look of disappointment chiseled on his face when he opened the front door to head back to his car. I hoped he wasn't mad at me. I hoped I hadn't let him down.

I hurried to get my things together and rushed outside (for the second time that day) to his car. He already had the engine started and he barely acknowledged me when I got in. I rode with him silently as the music blasted through his car's speakers all the way to work; I didn't mind showing up to my job a little early, but I did mind that Darrien seemed to be in one of his 'moods' during our ride. I gave him a kiss on the cheek anyway before I walked through the side entrance of the hotel. Darrien didn't say a word, he just gave me a small nod.

I couldn't stand when Darrien copped attitudes like that; it was like he had multiple personalities or something. He was a walking puzzle I couldn't put together, because depending on the day, the time, or the hour, he could be in one state of mind or another. His more playful side had a sense of humor and was easy to communicate with. Then there was 'D. Dare,' his low-profile and slightly impatient side. D. Dare is what his friends and roommates called him, and D. Dare is usually the personality he put on when we were around his friends. I wasn't too fond of D. Dare, but I always knew that Darrien would reappear eventually. I was in love with Darrien's playful side and did my best to tolerate D. Dare on those other occasions he emerged.

I jammed my headphones into my ears as I walked down the hotel's hallway and through the entrance doors of Zoe's Roasthouse. I tried to walk through the foyer full of people waiting to be seated in the entrance lobby, but a bony hand firmly grabbed my forearm before I could even take two steps toward the break room.

"Can we have a table? We've been standing here for infinity." A tall, wide-eyed brunette lady with bangs stared at me with a peevish expression on her face, awaiting a response. I gently removed my forearm out of her grip and removed my earphone from my ear as two other ladies stood up and joined her from their seats on the lobby benches. They all looked annoyed and not a single one of them displayed a hint of a smile.

"Hi, someone will be right with you," I replied with a strained smile. I elevated my other arm so the brunette and her cohorts could see the hanger carrying my work shirt and perhaps take the hint that I wasn't ready to work yet. The Brunette-With-Bangs folded her arms and glared at me, or rather I should say she glared *through* me. I tried not to appear irritated by the lady's unnecessary seize of my arm or stank-faced look, and jammed my earphone back into my ear. She placed her hand on her hip, stretched her neck as high as it could go, then grabbed my shoulder as I attempted to walk past her towards the employee break room.

"You work here, don't you?" she asked with a look of disgust.

"I'm not clocked in yet," I strenuously added. It took all my might to not respond to the lady in the manner I would have preferred to (which would have included a stank face of my own and a few choice curse words).

"So you don't know how to seat people when you're off the clock?" she asked in a condescending tone. I took a step back and held my breath while I scanned the restaurant floor for my boss or one of my co-workers. If there was one thing I couldn't stand about my job the most, it was having to bite my tongue and restrain myself from snapping on people as rude as her. I don't know who the lady thought she was, but I knew that if we were *anywhere* but my job, she would never get away with talking to me the way she was right then!

I bit my tongue as Zeke's customer service mantra played like a military cadence in my head.

'When They Fret, Show Your Regret.

Don't Analyze, Smile & Apologize!'

He had repeated those foolish phrases so many times that they might as well have been ingrained on the soles of my work shoes. *Smile Dabresha, just apologize and smile!* I tried to convince myself to follow the mantra in that moment, I really tried! But I just couldn't bring myself to deal with the Brunette-With-Bangs in any other way than to back away from her. I was afraid of losing my temper and letting this lady potentially be the one to get me fired! I exhaled when I saw Zeke appear in my peripheral vision and thanked God for his timing.

"Are you the manager?" I heard the Brunette ask Zeke as I turned around to briskly walk away from both of them. I rolled my eyes once I was out of sight of the other customers since I already knew what was about to happen: Brunette-With-Bangs was preparing to complain about having to wait for 'infinity' to be seated, which was probably less than five minutes in real time, and would tell Zeke that I gave her 'attitude' during her endless seating delay. Zeke would likely offer that broad a discount on her bill while 'smiling and apologizing' the entire time, even though she was far from deserving of even half a pardon.

I couldn't *stand* her type, and by her type I mean snooty, entitled, and likely bigoted customers that regularly dined at Zoe's.

Because of her and the hundreds of people like her whom I was forced to interact with on the job, I knew one thing was certain about my future: whatever work lay ahead for me would not involve dealing with stuck-up folks who thought they could talk to me any kind of way.

I tried to brush off the episode as I burst into the break room and sat down at the cleanest table. I had forty minutes to finish my science homework and change into the rest of my uniform, and was planning to use those forty minutes right. Just as I propped my book open and started skimming over my class notes, the break room door swung open, and Zeke waltzed in and approached the table I was sitting at.

"Hey Bresha! I know it's early but I need you to start sooner than your schedule today. Rita called sick and we're slammed right now," he said with squinted eyes.

I looked up at the clock on the break room wall and back down at my homework. I hadn't even started working on the assignment and was in no mood to start smiling in people's faces quite yet thanks to Darrien and Brunette-With-Bangs.

"Don't mean to bust in here and bother your school work, but we need an extra man, I mean person. It'll pay out overtime on your check too since you probably won't get a lunch break," he concluded.

I placed my pen in the crevice of my text book and closed it. When Zeke asked something, it was usually a non-reciprocal demand, so it meant I didn't really have much of a choice to decline his invitation to start working early. I knew I needed to finish my science assignment, but money motivated me just a tad bit more. I was looking forward to dropping dollars in Florida for spring break and not worrying about the prices of the abundance of drinks and souvenirs I was going to buy. I also really needed to stay on Zeke's good side while my vacation request was still pending.

"I'll step out in a minute," I answered, raising my index finger. Zeke nodded and straightened his shirt collar before he swiftly hurried out the break room. I put my homework assignment back in my notebook and reminded myself that I'd need to finish it before bed or on the bus the next morning, then walked towards the break room lockers. I pulled a miniature banana schnapps shot bottle out of the side pocket of my purse and downed it as fast as I could. I always kept a shot bottle or two handy just in case I needed a quick 'pick me up' during the day. I checked my hair and lip gloss in the employee restroom mirror while I buttoned up my blouse. I turned my phone to vibrate, threw it inside my purse, and squeezed the bag into my assigned employee locker.

"Here goes," I grumbled as I walked out to the hostess stand and greeted the next customers in line... with a smile!

Chapitre 7: Shoes and Purses

I got home late that night dying to get to right to sleep, but as luck would have it, my slumber had to be delayed. Delilah was wide awake with all the lights on in the front part of the house. I gave her a sideways look when I entered through the front door and tried to quietly jerk it closed behind me.

"What you up for?" I demanded. I threw my purse on the floor next to the sofa and sunk into the couch. I was so tired from the day's events that I was willing to fall asleep on the couch right then without even attempting to hobble to my bedroom. My clothes smelled of condiments and without even looking in the mirror, I knew my hair was probably a mess too.

"I've been doin' homework and cleanin', but *you* of all people shouldn't be questioning me on anything until you explain *this!*" Delilah held up a small, elastic-looking object that I couldn't identify from across the room. She walked up closer to me with a huge smirk on her face then threw it on my lap. I flinched and jumped up off the couch when I realized what it was.

"Ewww! Where'd you get that? Don't be throwing rubbers at me!"

Delilah let out a loud laugh, then covered her mouth and looked back towards the hallway. We both quieted down to listen for The Bear; Maurice was hibernating and would get angry if we woke him up, but he was a heavy sleeper so we weren't too paranoid about that happening. That man could probably sleep through fires, tornadoes, and hurricanes! He also snores as loud as a bear, so we could usually hear if he woke up for whatever reason while we were in the living room.

"First off, mind ya business. Second off, that ain't mine!

Laydee flicked a bunch of those at us as a joke when I had the girls over last week and I thought I picked 'em all up. She had a huge supply from the clinic... one must of fell somewhere behind my dresser."

"Mmm-hmmm, riiigghht." Delilah gave me an accusatory stare. I lifted up the back of my hand and shooed her away as I plopped back down on the couch.

"I am too tired to be dealin' wich you right now, and you nasty for even touching it if you think it's used anyway."

Delilah grinned and jumped to sit on the sofa next to me, then threw her bony legs across my lap.

"Aww big sis is grumpy wumpy! It's okay, I won't tell nobody. We all get caught up sometimes." She hugged her arms around my neck and started dramatically rocking me back and forth while squeezing my shoulders tight.

"Moo ya legs Lilah, and go ask Laydee yourself. She was foolin' around slingshottin' those at me, Nette, and Mina, tellin' us we needed to get 'some' in our lives. I ain't gotta explain none to you anyway, who you think you is?" I tried to push her away from me, but her playful grip was tight around my shoulders.

"Okay, I'll believe you and your angel friends for *now* even though I know Laydee ain't the only one tootin' in your little crew! And trust me, everybody knows Laydee is true to the first half of her name. Y'all full of it!"

"Girl go somewhere, go to bed better yet! I am too tired for your blamin' games right now."

I rolled my shoulders to loosen Delilah's grasp from around my neck, then scooted away from her to the other side of the couch.

"Speakin' of your angel friends, I saw Antoinette and her little sis' Jayna on the bus earlier, they gon' stop by next week. I thought we didn't resemble much but those girls don't look none alike!"

"Antoinette's adopted." I said bluntly. "That's her foster family."

"Oh," Delilah replied, "My bad."

"Like always," I snapped.

"Dang alright, I'll stop bothering your grumpy behind about Darrien's condom. I need to ask you some else anyway."

I rolled my eyes at Delilah. She was hoping to corner me into admitting to something, but the truth was, she was completely wrong. Darrien and I had ran a few bases but definitely hadn't reached home plate yet. I wanted to and my body definitely wanted to every time he started talking to me and touching me a certain way, but we just hadn't gone all the way there in our relationship yet.

"Whatchu want?" I asked her. Whenever Delilah got in my face, it was usually because she needed money or a ride, and since my car was out of commission, I doubted it was the latter.

"Can I hold twenty bucks so I can get my hair done?" she asked. Bingo, I nailed it!

"Gal, you never paid me back from last time I let you 'hold' money. Plus you just got your hair did last week!" I grabbed the back of my neck and groaned. I was losing minutes of precious beauty sleep because of Delilah.

"Psshht I know I know, I'ma get you back everything I owe next check. I got deep condition last week but now I'ma get braids and Jayna's gonna hook me up for a real good price! I just need a little bit more ends than I have on me."

"I ain't got it," I said bluntly. "Good night!"
I slowly lifted myself up from the couch and started towards our kitchen to grab a glass of water.

"Come on Bre, I'll get it back to you, I swear!"

I ignored her as I opened the fridge and started to pour

myself a glass of water. I sure wasn't in the mood for Delilah's begging and wasn't going to sit there and force myself to listen to her.

"Fine, be that way! You and urrbody else act like you ain't got a spare twenty but y'all be forever at the mall buyin' up shoes and purses and fake nails. How you got money for that and nothin' else?"

I gave Delilah a deranged look. Sure, me and my crew were known to take quite a few trips to the mall, but we usually only bought things off the sale rack. Sure, my collection of shoes and purses had grown substantially to the point where I no longer had space for them on my side of the closet, but having fresh fits and clothes was a necessity. Shopping made me feel better when I was in a funky mood, and wearing the freshest gear helped me feel, well—fresh! I loved getting compliments for my outfits and I couldn't help but want to keep myself looking as fly as possible all the time.

I loved having lots of accessory options to choose from when I put my outfits together, so keeping a mass of jewelry, belts, and shoes almost guaranteed that no one would ever see me in the same exact outfit twice. My mom used to be like that too, always accessorized and dressed spiffy whether she was at work or at the corner market. I kept some of my mom's jewelry after she passed, but we had to sell a lot of it to help pay for the funeral.

I also kept her favorite bottle of perfume; it was a half empty pear-shaped turquoise bottle that she says came from France, and the scent had some sort of hibiscus in it. The bottle is empty now, but I keep it because I can still smell small traces of it and I want to fully replace it one day if I can find a place in America that sells it. You'd never think my family was broke by the looks of us, that's for sure—even Maurice has style when he's not in one of his work uniforms.

"What I do with *my* money is *my* business so stay your nosy behind out of it. How about you stop showin' up late for work and start makin' your own dough? Your job called the house twice last week lookin' for you."

Delilah smacked her lips and stormed off down the hallway ahead of me, stomping her skinny legs and making sure to slam our bedroom door. I couldn't stand my sister and her drama queen antics; she always pouted when she didn't get her way and acted hostile toward me for days whenever we disagreed on something.

That night, I didn't care how mad she got. I was tired, still contemplating whether or not to finish my science homework, and still put off from the way Darrien acted earlier that day. I knew Darrien would get over it though; he was my boo, and there's no such thing as a perfect relationship. I just wish he'd communicate more.

I sent him a text before I went to my room that said *'thinkin' bout you..'* with a smiley face emoticon. I didn't expect him to respond since it was late, but hoped he still wasn't feeling agitated about earlier. To my surprise, he wrote back pretty quickly.

'All good shawty, just lemme know when you ready to show me the juicy figure to match them juicy lips of yours ok ;)'

I smiled as I turned my phone to silent and went in my room to get ready for bed. Delilah was buried under her blankets and didn't say one word to me as she pretended to be asleep (I could see the light from her cell phone illuminating through the blankets). I felt my heart beating a little louder as I thought about Darrien. That boy sure knew how to work me up! As I threw on my pajamas and crawled under my blankets, I pondered on what Darrien might think about the application I picked up earlier that day for the study abroad scholarship. I wondered if I should tell him about the application before actually wasting time filling it out. Would he even be okay with me leaving town for a little while to take some classes? If he wasn't cool with it, then I'd just toss the applications in the trash. It seemed silly to do the application in reality, but even sillier to not even try. I messaged Darrien to casually let him know about it. *'I'm thinkin' bout taking classes in Europe this summer. Wanna visit me while I'm there?'*

'if that's what it takes,' he replied.

'I'm bein' for real though, it sounds legit. I'ma do an application and keep you posted. Good night boo!' I replied. He didn't respond back but I imagined he was thinking that I was either crazy or that I was joking. He'd know the truth soon enough, and he didn't seem fazed by the information so I'd feel better about filling out the application with his consent.

Whether it was Florida, France, or home plate with Darrien, all the possibilities of the near future seemed fab. I'd be making big moves sometime soon and couldn't wait to see how things could go that spring. Even if nothing transpired at all, it still felt nice to think about what could happen in the months that followed (hopefully good things and not bad). I curled up in my zebra comforter and fell asleep that night with a smile on my face, ready to tackle whatever lay ahead.

Chapitre 8: Bre Bre and Laydee T

The sirens wouldn't stop wailing that day. They got louder and louder as I neared closer to Maurice's house; I was walking home from middle school with a huge grin on my face, pleased that I had gotten a perfect score on my vocabulary test. My grin slowly vanished as my footsteps slowed down and my heartbeat started racing. Several of my neighbors were standing outside and they were all gawking at Maurice's house.

"Niece! My niece!" Aunt Trecee was screaming. She ran up to me on the sidewalk before I even had a chance to approach the front lawn. She was holding Delilah's hand and Delilah was trailing behind her looking around, scared and confused. Aunt Trecee fiercely embraced me, pulling Delilah next to me and forcing the three of us to hug. Drying tears were streaked down Delilah's face and Aunt Trecee began to cry.

"Where's mom?" I kept asking over and over again, my voice muffled as my face smashed into Aunt Trecee's velvety blouse. She kept hugging me, rocking me back and forth, but wouldn't answer my question. I thrust myself out of my aunt's grasp and looked up at the scene: two police cars, a coroner's truck, an ambulance, and Maurice standing on the front porch talking to two police officers. Maurice looked sullen and kept rubbing his forehead. My mom's boyfriend of a year whom had moved us out of our apartment and into his house just a few months before looked the most defeated I had ever seen him look.

"She's been sick for a while," I heard him saying to the officers. "She stopped drinkin' last month to try and help it but she's been coughin' up three weeks now and didn't want to see a doctor. She wouldn't let me take her and her insurance wasn't good. She didn't want hospital bills." I broke away from Aunt Trecee and ran up to confront Maurice. "Where's my momma?" I kept yelling at him, "Where's Momma?"

Maurice shook his head with a look of disappointment chiseled on his face, as if he was aching to respond.

"She gone," he said. It was the most serious I'd ever seen him look. His eyes were sinking far back into his sockets as if they were trying to crawl inside and not see anymore.

I started backing away from him in disbelief. What did he mean 'she's gone'? I looked around and realized everyone standing on the sidewalks were now staring at me; the paramedics, the cops, and the neighbors all had contorted sympathetic expressions on their faces.

"Whatchu mean she's gone?! Where's my momma?! Let me see her!" I started sprinting up the pathway that led to our house, but the police officers and one of the paramedics grabbed me and blocked me from passing.

"Get out my WAY! I *live* here! I wanna see MY MOM!" I was crying to them. Pleading. The hefty emergency workers blocked all of my attempts to bypass them until I was winded and could no longer try. They were twice my size, but I still tried to push them away before I took a step back.

"Niece, stop!" Aunt Trecee cried. I tried one last time to charge past the uniformed men, but failed and collapsed on the sidewalk and started gasping asthmatically. Aunt Trecee tried to peel me off the ground but I refused to get up. When one of the police officers tried to help me up, I started swinging, hitting, and punching everything in arm's reach. It took a group of them to get me to finally sit still.

"Let off and let me see her! I don't belee you, SHE'S NOT DEAD!!!"

I got up and started running down the street, mortified, devastated, and short of breath. I only got a few yards away before I fell down again. How could the same mom that saw me off to school that morning not be alive anymore? She was acting strange that week, and she hugged me longer than usual when she said goodbye that morning and told me to do good in school. She probably knew her illness was overpowering her, but she still sent me off to that damned school. I would have rather stayed home with her, maybe force her to see a doctor, but my momma hated hospitals and didn't want to die in one. She said she didn't like the way the doctors talked down to her or made her worry about things. She knew something was wrong and she didn't tell me. *Why didn't she tell me?*

She called Aunt Trecee the night before and asked her to come stay with us for a while. Aunt Trecee packed her bags immediately, got on the road first thing in the morning to make the drive from Louisiana after she called our other aunts and uncles and told them something was wrong with momma. Aunt Trecee came twenty minutes too late, found her sitting on the living room sofa holding Maurice's hand. The ambulance was already there and had been for a while, trying to wake her up. The police showed up soon after.

"She got two daughters in grade school, the father's not around," Aunt Trecee told the police, so they tried to find us and pull us out of school. They found Delilah and brought her home, but I had let out of class by the time they got to my school and this was before I ever had a cell phone or a pager. They couldn't find me walking home because I took the long route that day and was goofing off with some of my school friends.

"Can we still live here without our momma? I don't wanna live back where we used to live," I heard Delilah asking Maurice, one of the last things I remember hearing that day. Everything else is still kind of foggy.

Only two of my mom's five siblings came to the funeral, including Aunt Trecee. Uncle Otey was in jail that year for trying to pull off that stupid robbery with my biological dad, whom was out of jail by then but still didn't show up to the funeral. The rest of my aunts and uncles said they didn't have the money to get to Beauconte from wherever they were. I haven't seen most of my mom's sibling since before her passing, and don't care to see them again.

I despised that dream, yet it would come back to me all the time, grim memories replaying in my sleep reminding me of the worst day of my life. I didn't go to school for almost a month afterwards and didn't talk to none of my friends about it. I didn't want to talk to anyone and even now I try to avoid the subject of my mom's death. The tears had drowned my eyes and distorted my vision the rest of that day, that week, that whole month that my already shaken up world finally came tumbling down. I don't remember anything that took place the rest of the evening. All that has happened since that day and up to now is still kind of foggy, full of sirens and commotion. To this day I hate the sound of sirens, but living in Beauconte, I still have to hear them every single day.

* * *

I awoke early Sunday morning thanks to the invasive sound of my text message ringtone screaming out from under my blankets. Through blurry vision and cold sweats, I focused my eyes on the phone screen just enough to read a text message from Laydee.

'Let's link up and talk... stepdad's trippin again. meet me at Westriv.'

Laydee is one of the few people that can get me out of bed

at eight in the morning on a weekend for no real reason, and that morning, I was all for getting out of bed and away from my bad dream. Whenever Laydee 'needed to talk,' it usually meant she was fighting with someone in her family and needed to escape her house (or had just been kicked out for the hundredth time). I replied to her message and told her I'd be there in an hour, then got up to get dressed. I put on my comfortably cute pink and black velour jumpsuit and threw on my favorite pair of black double-hoop earrings. I wanted to look presentable just in case we ran into folks at West River Plaza, which often happened in a town our size and especially on the weekend.

This was set to be another Bre Bre and Laydee T shopping spree (those are the names we used when the two of us hung out alone looking for mischief). Laydee is my BFF after all, no matter what! We bicker every once in a while, but at the end of the day, that's my main and we have each other's backs.

Don't get me wrong, Antoinette's kind of my BFF too, and Tamina also in a different way, but Laydee and I have more in common and have known each other longer. We both love fly fashions, parties that pop off, and parties full of boys wearing fly fashions—crunk is a lifestyle! We used to get into a lot of trouble together back in our high school days; ditching classes, fooling with the bus drivers, driving our teachers up the wall, fighting the shit-talking girls, distracting the cuties by any means necessary, and sneaking out to parties at night—you name it, we've probably done it!

One time, we both got arrested for shoplifting when we were teenagers, and that's kind of the incident that brought us closer together and certified us true 'partners-in-crime'. We thought we were so *slick* putting on designer bathing suits under our clothes in the Macy's dressing rooms and popping off the tags. We were both sure we'd get away with leaving the department store with more than five hundred dollars' worth of merchandise, but boy were we wrong. I guess the department store folks knew what we were up to the entire time, so it was a cinch for them to stop us when we tried to leave the store. The mall security guards were already waiting for us outside and everything! We found out one of the girls working there was hiding in the dressing room and listening to us ripping the tags off. She also caught on to us trying to talk in code hoping no one would catch on to what we were up to.

That ride in the back of the police car was the longest ride I'd ever taken, and those handcuffs left purple bruises on my wrists for weeks. Maurice had a look on his face like he could kill me when he picked me up from the police station that day and he grounded me for the rest of that year.

We don't steal anymore—well at least I don't! It's just too many nerves for a little bit of merchandise and I never *ever* want to go to adult jail, so I try to behave by society's standards (with the exception of using a fake I.D. to get into clubs and an occasional restaurant eat-and-run).

Laydee and I have been tight ever since that day, but even with our history, Laydee never tells me exactly what's going on with her when she 'needs to talk'. I have to dig stuff out of her and chip away at her conversation like it's frozen in ice and I'm holding a tiny pick. I have to talk to her for hours just to get a small piece of information, but when we meet up and start shopping together, we usually forget about everything else and just focus on finding good deals on stylish clothes.

Laydee's kind of funny that way, but I think we all kind of are. When I'm feeling really down about something, I usually keep to myself and listen to my crunk music. Tamina doesn't answer her phone or try to find us at school when she's upset about something, and Antoinette just acts like everything's okay all the time and she's pretty damn good at it. We can all sense when something's bothering someone in our circle, but avoid talking about the problems too much. I guess as long as we're there for each other, that's all that really matters, and the problems eventually fade away, or at least they seem to.

I found Laydee at the plaza sitting by herself at the food court gulping a huge fountain drink out of a tall cup with a big red straw. Her leg was shaking vigorously and she had a nervous look on her face. Something was bothering her and it definitely wasn't the cleanliness of the unmopped floors she was staring at. Her hair was messy and her makeup was too; her eyes looked glossy as if she'd been crying or didn't get any sleep (or as if she had just lit up a fat blunt!). *'Daaamn girl, what happened?'* I *wanted* to say, but instead, I just sat next to her and started talking about how gross the breakfast sandwich I picked up from the mini-mart on the way there was.

"What took you so phuggen long?" she interrupted me with. "Girl I almost had to scrap and had no back-up!"

"Scrap? Who you fightin' with?" I asked her with wide eyes.

"Remember Shareena from high school? The broad with the gapped teeth that I gave that black eye to when she was talkin' mess about my weave? She call herself tryna start some by the bus station, had two of her dusty stripper friends from the Phoenix Club with her. I ain't even seen her since high school and that broad still startin' mess. She *lucky* I ain't in the mood today!"

"Girl next time send me a text and tell it so I can be ready. She still around?" I asked as I stood up and started to unhook the back of my hoop earring. If I had to fight, I needed to be on deck, de-accessorized with my hair pulled back. I coolly scoped out the plaza before I plopped back down in the plastic chair next to Laydee. My guard was up in case Shareena or any of her stripperettes wanted to step to us. I have never lost a fight and did not intend to lose my first one to Shareena's crew at West River Mall!

"That bee-yach know better! I'll make one call and get all my sisters and cousins here and it's over."

I wasn't in the mood to fight neither, but if it had to be done I'd handle business. I wanted to ask Laydee what was *really* bothering her, but she wouldn't tell me straight away even if I tried. So, we chatted about anything and everything except for whatever provoked her to leave her house so early that morning. I told her about how Delilah was working my last nerves and how she had found the 'rubber souvenir' Laydee left at my house. Laydee laughed and I could tell her mood was lightening as we talked, and I could feel her invisible guard slowly melting away onto the food court tile.

"My bad folk! Didn't mean to set you up like that," she chimed in.

"Your bad fo sho! Thankfully Lilah found it and not Maurice. I know he be sneakin' into our room sometimes, I've caught him! Said he was just tryna check the plumbing in the bathroom... it weren't even broken!"

We got up and started walking around the strip mall and dipping into the different boutiques. The mall had just opened so there weren't too many other people in the stores. It was perfect shopping time! I loved shopping when there weren't other folks bumping into me or eyeballing me for whatever reason. Laydee and I had an effect on 'non-ethnic' people that would usually cause them to stare at us for whatever reason. Sometimes there were stares of fascination that would usually end with a compliment about our hair or make-up. Other times there were hater stares or stares of disgust; people just didn't like our presence, or simply put, just didn't understand 'us', and they sure had no shame in letting it show on their faces. Sometimes I'd stare right back at them and smirk until they got embarassed and looked away. It's crazy how you can feel out of place even when you're in your hometown and in your own country.

For that reason, I preferred strolling through the mall when it wasn't crowded. It was like the mall was all mine and I had first dibs on everything before people started ransacking through all the merchandise. That morning, I scored on two pairs of earrings, some berry lip gloss, some mango color pointed-toe pumps, and a cute sparkly tank top that said 'beautifully black'. Laydee didn't buy anything, but she lingered at the mall's tattoo parlor to look at the art books and think about what she might get next. She was deciding between something small on her ankle or some sort of landscape on her back... that girl is so brave! Needles freak me out to the max, so getting a tattoo is highly unlikely to happen for me.

One time I tried to get an angel piece for my mom on my arm. I went with Laydee during one of her regular visits and paid the artist and everything! But I just couldn't bring myself to actually let the needle touch my skin and I jumped out the chair before it did. Even now, the sight of needles make me nauseous. Thankfully the tattoo man was nice and let me have all my money back.

As we thumbed through the art books, I told Laydee my thoughts on taking the classes in Paris, and clarified to her that I meant Paris, France and not Paris, Texas.

"Is you phuggen sur-ee-us?" she responded, lending me an irrational look.

I chuckled and explained how I'd already discussed the possibility of the trip with Mrs. Vanderkamp, Ms. Cole, and Darrien, and brought up how my Mom used to talk about Paris a lot. I told Laydee all the details I could remember from the brochures and the websites I peeked at regarding the trip, then told her I would only need to come up with money for a plane ticket if I won the scholarship Ms. Cole told me about.

"Girl, you need to keep your big, black behind in Texas," she responded. I laughed and looked at her with my head cocked to the side.

"Why for?" I asked her with a smirk.

"They got all kinds of foolishness and foreign diseases out in that part of the world. And how'd we know if somethin' happened to you? What if you need back-up in a fight?"

I sighed as Laydee continued to ramble.

"Do you even know French?!" she concluded.

"I'd be learning while I'm there and there'd be other people looking out for me. I ain't worried about fights or diseases girl, it can't be *all* that bad. I heard guns ain't even legal in France so I doubt their streets are anything compared to ours. I've seen one too many people get stretched out in our neighborhood and we've been here our whole lives, wouldn't you want to at least try and get away from your house and all the drama?"

"If you wanna put it that way," Laydee said, rolling her eyes. Her phone started ringing, so she stepped outside the tattoo shop to answer it. I checked my own phone while Laydee started blabbing to make sure I hadn't missed any calls or texts. I called Darrien and invited him to meet us at the mall, but he told me he couldn't come because he had to work. Once Laydee was done blabbing on her phone, we continued to dawdle around the mall until about noontime when she told me she had to get ready to babysit her nephew. I needed to get ready for work that afternoon, so we went our separate ways and that was it! But I had to borrow some change from Laydee when I realized I lost track of my spending and didn't have enough money for the bus fare home.

Laydee T and Bre Bre concluded yet another successful day of shop-nanigans. We flirted with a couple of cute boys, innocently of course, talked about parties with a few familiars, and shared a cinnamon soft pretzel before we took off (those things are delicious!). I hoped Laydee felt better after our little outing—I sure did! Shopping always slowed my mind and brought a smile to my face; it was the natural cure for the blues (just like my momma used to say).

More importantly, whatever was bothering Laydee didn't seem to be bothering her anymore. Mission accomplished: My BFF felt better, I forgot all about my bad dream, at least for now, and I was going home with a bag full of new stuff. What more could a small town Texan girl ask for?

Chapitre 9: Texas Style

We're about to get *crunk* this weekend, hey hey hey! I'm about to tell you how it goes down in Texas, but I'm only going to say it once so pay attention. If you've never been to the South and have no intention of going, no offense, but something is wrong in your head! I'll break down a little history to you about the best part of the U.S. of A, just in case you've been living under a rock and have no idea how bomb it is.

The South consists of about a dozen states depending on who you ask, with Texas being the biggest, baddest, and best! Louisiana, Tennessee, Mississippi, the Carolinas, the Virginias, Alabama, Georgia, Arkansas, Kentucky, and Florida are somewhere in the mix—sometimes people throw Oklahoma and Maryland into the parade even though a lot of us Southerners think of them more as distant neighbors.

Some of the best hip hop and jazz music was born in the South, and it's also home to the Mardi Gras festival. The South operates some of the greatest soul food establishments the world has ever seen, and here in Texas, the TexMex cuisine is on point. Lastly, we got fancy ways of styling our teeth, our cars, and our hair that the rest of the world will never be ready for.

The best thing about the South are the parties! Spontaneous gatherings are a huge part of our culture; cookouts and functions materialize on the spot in a host of casual locations and all are welcome. I'm not just talking about college shindigs either; I'm talking about functions that involve the whole neighborhood and take no notice to anyone's age or the time of day. Sometimes they kicked off in parks, or in parking lots, and every once in a while on someone's front lawn. Anywhere large groups of people could gather and loud music could blast out of decked out cars was a potential location, and if a barbeque grill was available, the size of the function could grow exponentially. People would show up by the masses to partake, and their only requirement was that they came prepared to have a good time and good conversation. Drama was taboo, but drinks and a little dancing was A-OK.

Last weekend was a perfect example of why I love the South. There was a gathering at Baylor Park and there were at least sixty folks there chilling and chatting. The barbecue grill was flared up high and people were passing beers and wine coolers around like footballs. My whole crew made an appearance and had a genuine good time. We spent a good amount of time talking to some young folks from Arizona who were 'passing through' on a road trip. Everyone there could tell they weren't Southern by the way they dressed and the way they looked slightly out of place, so we took turns picking on them, all in good fun of course.

"Does everyone in the desert wear bucket hats?" I heard an old man ask the Arizonans.

"Ain't the South gorgeous?" another guest inquired of them.

The South is a *gorgeous* place indeed, probably the most gorgeous place in the world! I haven't seen much else of America, but I'm pretty sure it doesn't get better than this. Southerners are full of style and full of soul. We have a unique way of dressing and speaking that non-Southerners often don't understand. People say we wear a lot of bright colors, that we talk funny, and eat too much fried food, but we're just doing 'us'. When Westerners or other foreigners like the Arizonans come visit the South, we can usually spot them in a crowd. They're the ones with the odd clothes, frazzled hair (since they don't know how to handle the humidity), and 'funny talk'.

We *love* our Southern culture and many of our families have been here for generations. My family has roots all over the South, and both my natural parents are true Southerners. They met at a friend's party and were in the South their whole lives as far as I know. They had me some time later, and though they were never officially married, they lived together long enough to be considered spouses under Texas Common Law. Their union never mattered anyway since Maurice eventually stepped in and took over the job my real dad was supposed to do. Maurice, too, is one-hundred percent southern, born and raised as an only child in Arkansas to a family of corn farmers. Both his parents died when he was about my age, so he ultimately sold their farm and used the money as payment on the house in Beauconte. To sum it up, my heart and heritage are in the South, and I can't ever imagine leaving it.

On the flipside, the South has a dark past shadowed with reminders of a racist history. This part of the country was at the center of the civil rights movement and was at the core of discrimination and injustice less than half a century ago. Sometimes it still seems like there's just as much racist bullcrap happening today as there was back then, but at least now black people can do as we please. We can vote, go to school, and start businesses just like the white folks! Most importantly, we can gather peacefully whenever and wherever we want to without having to worry about getting hosed down.

In my group of friends, Laydee was the ringleader of finding out where the neighborhood gatherings were taking place. Laydee was unquestionably the 'social' one of our group and the one that associated with people from every little clique at our school. Laydee definitely loved to party, even more than me, but her main motivation for staying in the party scene was to mingle with the sorority chicks. She was aiming to get recruited into the most popular sorority group in the South, the Beta Lambda organization, so she made sure to do her best to impress the sorority leaders she saw at the functions.

I thought about joining a sorority when Laydee told me how exciting it could be—she said the step shows, excursions, and parties were just a small part of all the things the sorority could offer. What Laydee failed to tell me was that sororities cost money to join, so once I learned that little piece of info, my interest pretty much diminished. I had enough bills as it was and wasn't about to invest money joining a 'club' that would take up even more of my time. Sorority stuff was more for people like Laydee anyway; sociable people with ultra-self-confidence and lots more time on their hands.

A day after the Baylor Park function, Laydee alerted our crew that there would be a St. Patty's function popping off at the movie theatre parking lot that night and that the gathering would be packed with fly boys with fly cars. She sent all of us one of her typical hyped-up text message invites:

'Wake yoselves fools! We got green cars to grab on and green drinks for the puffing impaired (Tamina), let's roll out in an hour!!'

Tamina, Laydee, and I rallied up at Antoinette's dorm to get ready and dress up in our best green and black outfits. Laydee threw on a white tank top and green jeans with a Celtics hat, I wore a dark green one piece jumpsuit, Antoinette wore my Coogi top and Tamina wore black jeans with a mint green V-neck blouse. My squad looked fresh and the function was everything fun and flirty. When we first showed up, things were kind of quiet so we kept to a corner of the lot, then we started to branch out and mingle with folks when more people started showing up. Laydee went and brown-nosed some of the sorority girls she saw then started dancing with a boy that owned one of the cutest cars there (she always migrates towards the boys with the nicest cars).

Antoinette chilled with some basketball players she knew from our school and stayed talking to them the whole time. Darrien rolled through so I sat in his car and chilled with him for a little bit, then he had to take off shortly after so I just hung out with some other folks I recognized from around the way. All of us chatted and danced with a good number of folks—I even saw Tamina batting her eyelashes at one of the boys there and she rarely talks to anyone when we show up at these things!

We all had a fabulous time, but I think my time there was slightly more amplified than everyone else's. I helped myself to too many of the Irish Bailey drink mixes that were being passed around and apparently, I threw up in a trash can and almost messed up my brand new shoes! Thankfully, the trash can was out of sight from where everyone was posted, so Tamina was the only one to know what happened since she walked with me to find it. Antoinette decided it was time for us to go shortly after that, which was right around the time the function was quieting down. I knocked out in the car on the way home and didn't wake up until Laydee flicked my ear after we had pulled up outside of my house. She tried to push me out of Antoinette's car, but I stayed solid as a rock and wouldn't budge (so I was told).

"Girl, go!" Laydee whined, as she tugged at my shoulder. "Already took us forever to get here with Antoinette's Grandma driving."

I guess I was unresponsive, so Tamina and Antoinette got out the car to help me walk to my front door. I had an arm around each of their shoulders and my high heels felt tighter and stickier than ever as I dragged my feet to the porch.

"The Bear's here, don't be loud," I told them in my drunkenness. They both laughed.

"Girl, you're the only loud one right now. Gimme your keys so we can set you up on ya couch," Antoinette responded.

"Shhhh," I told Antoinette. She playfully rolled her eyes. "You gotta lift the knob left and kick the door when you turn," I said with slurred words.

"Girl hush, I know! I carried you through this door plenty of times," Antoinette replied.

"You go overboard with the drinks sometimes Bre. You gotta know when to tap out," Tamina added.

"Okay officer, yeessss maaaaa'am!" I shouted. They both continued to giggle as they forced my front door open.

"We love ya anyway though, now rest up," Antoinette added. She forced my keys into my purse and placed it on the living room table as I stumbled to my couch. I flung my high heels off across the living room and went right back to sleep. I woke up a few hours later with drool on my cheek and an odd urge to look at all my schoolwork. I guess thinking about schoolwork at three in the morning was the *other* side effect of too much Irish whiskey!

I crept into the bedroom as to not wake up Delilah, then snuck my school bag out of my room and dumped all the papers inside of it on the living room table. I propped up the piece of paper that had my work calendar mapped out on it and arranged the notes from all my classes next to it. Shoot. I was scheduled to work the next three days in a row and only felt *semi*-confident about the material on one of my FOUR midterms. Within one week, I needed to prepare for all of the exams and finish the application for the study abroad scholarship *if* I was even going to do it. The application would be like a 'midterm' in itself and would require just as much time work as all my midterms combined.

As I shuffled through my class notes, I weighed the pros and cons in my mind, wondering if doing the application would really be worth the time. I could always put off the application until the end of the week after midterms were done, but that scenario wouldn't leave me with too much time to finish it before

I had to leave for Florida. Even if I got accepted into that scholarship program, could I *really* pack up a few bags and disappear to the other side of the world? Could I muster up the courage to do something so crazy that none of my friends or family could understand? They'd probably think I was kidding at first, or that it was a foolish plan that fell out the sky and hit me on the head, but if they really knew me, they would know that my desire to go to France was never exactly spur-of-the-moment.

I always dreamed of traveling the world when I was a little girl, but that's all it was, a child's dream. Where I come from, traveling is something reserved for the 'elite' society; people who can easily buy plane tickets or take private jets to faraway destinations in the blink of an eye. It's for people with extravagant jobs that pay for them to do fancy business deals in all corners of the Earth and for the types who don't have to worry about saving up money for hotel rooms. Thus, it's definitely not for people in my neighborhood. I only know of one person in my entire circle of family and friends who went to another part of the world, and it was for military service. I've been brought up to think that going anywhere away from the South was just too difficult, or just not all that important. Yet, there's a part of me that never listened to what other people told me to do.

The only grown person I knew that openly talked about traveling was my mom. When she was around, she loved shopping at foreign markets and cutting out pictures from magazines that showed fashions from all around the world. She used to have a keychain of the Eiffel Tower on her car keys, and I loved playing with them and pretending I could drive. It made me feel like a real grown-up when I held her keys and imagined that I could take off in her car to go anywhere under the sun. I used to ask her about places I'd hear about in school, like the Grand Canyon and that mountain with the faces carved in it. I asked her about the Eiffel Tower keychain all the time because I thought it was made of real gold and really pretty. I think I was five years old when I first asked her what it was.

"It's a tower" she answered, "like a skinny building."

"It's a real building?"

"It sho' is Bresha! It's big and it's made out of glitter."

"Wooow, really? I wanna see!"

"You can see my keys as much as you want baby girl," she laughed lovingly, jingling her keys as she handed them to me.

"No, the big tower! Can we see where the real tower is?"

"The real tower's too far away baby, but maybe one day I'll take you because I really want to see it too."

I was so naive and gullible when I was a kid—I believed almost anything a grown-up told me. When my mom took Delilah, Aunt Trecee and I to Las Vegas two summers later to see the Eiffel Tower, I was so happy, it might as well have been a trip to the moon! I was confused at the same time because I remember my Mom telling me the tower was made out of glitter, and even though that tower in Las Vegas was tall, it wasn't as big and tall as I thought it'd be.

"It's not glittery momma, there's no sparkle," I told her, upset, "and you said it was cross the ocean but we drived here!"

I remember poking my lip out while my mom tried to comfort me.

"They must have took off the sparkle baby. Don't work yourself up naw. This tower here is the big tower's little sister, and the big tower's far across the ocean. The towers are two sisters, just like you and Lilah. The big sister is taller and older, but it looks just like the little sister, and they're both lovely little somethins."

Too often, she would pinch my cheeks every time she told

me I looked like Delilah, and I would scrunch my nose up with a repulsed expression. I didn't think I looked anything like Delilah and *hated* when people asked if we were twins. Thankfully, we filled out a lot differently as we grew so people don't ask us that silly question anymore. I developed curves, whereas Delilah grew two inches taller than me and looks more stick-like. (Lilah used to get made fun of in grade school because she was one of the skinniest girls there!)

At the end of that trip to the fake Eiffel Tower, my mom gave me my own Eiffel Tower keychain and a matching necklace and charm bracelet. My Aunt gave both me and Delilah our own Eiffel Tower jewelry racks to keep our earrings and accessories on. I still use that jewelry rack and keep the necklace and bracelet on it, but the necklace is broken now. I wear the bracelet on special occasions, especially on days I really need some luck. I wore it the day of my driving license test, my high school graduation, and on my first day of college. It's one of the few things I still have that my Mom gave to me. I feel like it gives me strength on the days I need it most, and it must really work since I was wearing the bracelet on the day I met Darrien!

My dreams of traveling are always stunted by a very specific memory I have growing up. It's crazy how a lot of my childhood memories are blurry, but this one is crystal clear. I can still hear the words my friend's mom used to scorn my elementary school dance teacher for supporting our dance troupe's dreams of performing all over the world. There was a time when three of my kid friends and I practiced dancing together and had entered a few competitions in our neighborhood. Jakeisha was our group leader because she had been dancing the longest and knew the most moves, and Tamina, Larae and I made up the rest of the group.

I remember this particular night we won first prize at a talent show for our dance routine to a Michael Jackson song. We had practiced the routine every day for months until we had gotten sick of the song and had sweat the baby hairs of our edges out. My mom had sewed together matching pink and purple headbands and arm bands for us to coordinate with our all white costumes (which were really just white shorts and t-shirts). We were too pumped up to stand still when we won and we couldn't contain ourselves—we were kids! We started jumping up and down backstage and throwing our prize flowers in the air.

I remember so clearly how my dance troupe used to talk about different cities we wanted to see on tour after we became famous for our routines, or after we would get hired as backup dancers for Janet Jackson or Destiny's Child. We each contributed a city to our tour list and created our future tour stops: Larae chose Tokyo, Tamina chose London, Jakeisha picked Rome (because she heard the best 'pitha' in the world was there: Jakeisha had a lisp lol), and I chose Paris since I knew the Eiffel Tower was there and heard from my mom that there were extravagant boutiques in the shopping capital of the world.

I had always been curious about what the Eiffel Tower looked like in real life and if it was as sparkly as momma claimed. Our school teacher Ms. Becker told us we could take our dance routines anywhere we wanted if we worked hard at our routines and kept practicing. *Practice makes perfect*, Ms. Becker would tell us over and over. *Ten times more makes you ten times better. A thousand times more makes you a thousand times better.*

Ms. Becker was quite talkative, and that night, I accidentally walked up behind her having a heated conversation in the backstage area with Ms. Mallard, Tamina's mom. I could see that Ms. Mallard was angry with Ms. Becker, but they couldn't see me because I was hidden behind the big blue velvet stage curtains. They were standing mere inches apart, and I could tell the air was tense between them. I heard Ms. Mallard tell Ms. Becker that

Tamina had been asking her too many questions about traveling since she started participating in the dance group, and every time Ms. Becker tried to interject, Tamina's mom interrupted her. I only caught part of their conversation, and it was the part when Ms. Mallard said,

"You know *damn* well ain't none of these kids ever leaving past the county line, especially not mine and not on my dime."

I could see the two women glaring at each other like they were about to duel. Ms. Becker shook her head and started to walk away, but Ms. Mallard grabbed her arm and gridlocked her retreat.

"My daughter's head don't need to be messed with young Miss Becker, that's all I'm simply trying to say. Don't be giving her no false hope—let me raise my child truthfully."

Right about then, I turned to leave, but the dust from the curtain started irritating my nose and I sneezed. Both of them looked in my direction as I scurried away to sit in the audience like they had instructed us to do earlier, hoping neither Ms. Becker or Ms. Mallard recognized that it was me eavesdropping on them through the dim backstage lighting. I ran into the audience area without looking back and found an empty seat near the front so I could be as close as possible to the stage for the second half of the show, which was designated for the younger performers and that Delilah was selected to perform in. I intended to sit near my parents but I couldn't find them and the audience seats were too crowded for me to be picky. The seat I found was one row in front of Larae's family, and I asked them if they had seen my parents.

"They left quick out the side door, arguing about..." Larae's mom started to say.

"They said you did really good," Larae's dad interrupted, giving his wife a stern look and squeezing her wrist. It was one of those moments where I could tell the grown-ups were withholding information from me, like they often did, because they thought I'd be 'too young' to understand whatever they wanted to say. Even if Halfy said I did well, I wish he could have told me himself. Halfy was the nickname Delilah and I gave our biological father since the only thing we felt he contributed to our upbringing was half his DNA; he was in and out of our lives like a revolving door, up until I was about ten, and we haven't heard from him since.

I knew he couldn't stay during the whole show because he supposedly had to work, but I didn't know why my mom took off when she did. Many years later, I found out that that was the night of Halfy's first arrest. My mom saw him buying drugs from a guy in the parking lot, and he stormed off when she tried to snatch the baggy away from him. He sped off in our family car and didn't care for how fast he was driving, got into a fender bender, questioned by the cops that showed up, and charged for having the drugs (and lots of them).

So while that argument was happening outside unbeknownst to us, Delilah sang pretty damn well! She belted out a classic SWV song with cool precision and I was shocked that her voice actually had range. I cheered so loud for her (this was back when we got along better) and was so happy for her when she ended up winning second place in in the junior competition! She gracefully walked back on stage and accepted her award in front of the audience so her long, beaded, navy blue gown. She had practiced that performance so many times in the mirror that week, right after momma had found that dress for her at a thrift store and sewed it up so it wouldn't drag on the floor. Delilah's eyes were full of light when they locked with mine as she scanned the audience while collecting her prizes. She mouthed the words 'where's momma?' and I shook my head to try to hint to her that she, nor Halfy, was there.

I thought about the argument between Ms. Becker and Ms. Mallard while I sat in the crowd during the rest of the talent show. I didn't fully understand the context of the argument then, but as I grew older, the words started to make more sense.

Chapitre 10: Pressure

Money doesn't run in my family. It never has and probably never will. I've accepted that though and it doesn't bother me much since I know most of my friends are in the same muddle. Whenever I thought back to that night of the talent show and how Ms. Mallard didn't want Ms. Becker filling our heads thinking about things we could never do, I couldn't fault Ms. Mallard for keeping it real. It made sense, but even as a youngin' I didn't think it was necessary for Ms. Mallard to talk to Ms. Becker the way she did. I'm pretty sure Ms. Mallard talks to Tamina in that same condescending manner, and that helps explain why Tamina is so gosh darn timid. In all our years of knowing each other, I rarely saw Tamina step out of her shell and I was never very fond of her mom. Ms. Mallard's not the nicest woman, but aside from that, it was only a matter of time before we grew up and started seeing the reality of our limits for ourselves.

The conversation between Ms. Mallard and Ms. Becker resurfaced in my mind as I chilled with my girls the next day at yet another function. This time it was an afternoon mixer themed around the upcoming spring break. We didn't get all dressed up for the 'Springtime Hop Off' like we did at the St. Patty's party, but we were still looking cute with our school outfits on and made sure to wear lavender, pinkish, and light blue colors that were thematically 'springy'. All throughout the afternoon, Laydee interrogated me about my hesitation to go to Florida for Spring Break. I told the girls I was starting to have second thoughts about joining them after looking over all the assignments I needed to get done. It was so hard to say no, and of course Laydee wouldn't understand the importance of getting my work done.

"Whatchu mean you THINK you ain't goin?!" Laydee

demanded in a tone so brusque and piercing that it probably
startled everyone within earshot. I told Laydee and the girls that I
wanted to finish the application for Paris and was starting to
doubt that I could get it done by the time we were supposed to set
off for Florida the following Friday.

"So you 'bout to change *all* our plans for that France
shit?" Laydee persisted while her eyes bugged out. She gave me
one of the craziest looks I had *ever* seen her make. I guess she
really wanted me to go to Florida, heck I really wanted to go too!
Laydee pleaded with me a thousand ways and tempted me with
every scenario we had already gone over before to try to convince
me to go: the boys, the VIP access to the clubs, the all-day drink
passes and non-stop parties—I knew about all of it because I
planned it with her! Whenever we mentioned Spring Break to
someone at that mixer, Laydee made sure to reiterate that *four* of
us were going to Florida.

Don't get me wrong now—everything about going to
Florida seemed fantastic! But that was until I found out about the
possibility of going to Paris for basically free, and though it wasn't
a sure thing, just the chance of going somewhere new for a short
time sounded even better. I *love* my city and my hometown, but I
also love the idea of a change of scenery in a place I used to dream
about seeing. I liked the idea of not having to come home to
Delilah's loud phone conversations or Maurice's mood swings,
and trying to live on my own for a little bit. I hadn't left Texas
since I visited Aunt Trecee in Louisiana two summers ago, and
haven't really ever left the South. Florida was surely going to be a
good time, but something about going overseas seemed even
more wonderful if not nearly insane! A trip to Europe could be
my escape from all the b.s. in Texas, and I think that's what got
me secretly even more excited about it.

Laydee was persuasive in her methods in getting me to

stick to the original Spring Break plan, so much so that I kept changing my mind that afternoon. The cute little 'springtime' beers that were being passed around did not help me stand up to Laydee's persistence either—at one point I considered abandoning the study abroad application altogether! But by the time the afternoon had ended, my decision had changed from 'probably not', to 'maybe.'

The pressure overwhelmed me, but I managed to shake it off and enjoy myself at the mixer. Everything that could possibly happen was up to me to *make* it happen. I could stay up late studying every night if I needed to, or call out for one of my shifts at work, or just not do the application at all if it came down to it. If I managed my time right, I could probably get everything I needed to do that week done properly and on time. I hoped to find a solution that would make my friends happy while I was taking care of business. I left the mixer a little early to get a head start on my homework, though I didn't stay up long since I was fatigued (and tipsy) by the time I left that gathering.

That whole week, I studied like I had never studied before. I went to the library instead of sitting on my bed with my headphones on; I didn't want Delilah or Maurice bothering me not one bit. I posted up on the second floor of the library every day that week, in a corner where fewer people passed by as to help avoid distractions or interruptions from any possible familiars (though most of the people I hang out with don't go to the library anyway). The whole week of midterms, my thoughts were a hurricane of the periodic table of elements, the Civil Rights movement, the new swimsuits I had been eyeing at the mall, statistics formulas, and the incomplete essay for the study abroad application. Crazy enough, the study abroad application became the least daunting task in comparison to the other midterms, so I felt a bit of relief whenever I switched tasks to fill some of it out.

During one of my trips to the library, I spotted a book on photographs of Paris as I was walking up the creaky, wooden steps to the second floor. I turned to descend the steps, snatched up the book, and started thumbing through it. There were vividly colored landscape portraits of lush gardens and medieval castles, and of course several images of the Eiffel Tower. There was a picture of a long building with a huge glass pyramid in front of it, and another of a long and wide tree-lined street with a giant concrete arch at the end of it. The images inside were absolutely gorgeous and all the pictures were impressive to look at. Wouldn't that be something, a girl like *me* posing in front of these places? I imagined myself standing in front of the glass pyramid throwing up deuces, or posting my Chuck Taylors up on one of the garden benches. I picked the portrait book up off the shelf a few times that week before it eventually got checked out by someone. This book further sparked my interest in completing the application.

I didn't even see Darrien that week, but he said he understood that I was busy and needed some time to myself. Besides, he had plenty to do himself since he made his own Spring Break plans to go to Vegas with his boys. He said it was a business trip, something involving a t-shirt company he was going to start with his roommates, so he didn't invite me for that reason. He and his boys were going to walk the strip promoting their t-shirts, and try to make some sales while they were out there. He promised he wouldn't be wilding out at the clubs or kicking it with other girls, and I promised I'd hurt him in case I heard different!

It was exhausting trying to focus on one single aspect of my suddenly eventful life, but I managed to be as productive as I could every single day until one by one, I knocked my exams out. Even though I wouldn't know my scores on them until the next week, it felt so good to finally finish them and lift the weight off my shoulders. I felt twenty pounds lighter!

All that remained by the time Thursday afternoon came around was the 'fun stuff' to think about: Florida and France! Both were definitely still options even though I hadn't even started packing for Florida and the rental car we picked out was set to take off the next morning. My study abroad application still needed serious work, and I hadn't even made a dent in the most important essay parts of the application. I sat down at the living room computer that was tucked away in the corner behind an old bookshelf. We barely used that computer because it was slow and outdated, but it did work for the simple stuff like typing up documents. I was debating on how to start one of the essay questions when Laydee called. I closed my eyes and grabbed my forehead when I answered, hoping the conversation wouldn't take up too much time.

"Is you done packin'?" she asked. I shook my head as I stared at the blank computer screen.

"Girl, I'm trying! This application is askin' like a million questions," I replied.

"Here you go with that application stuff again. Just do it later and come on, I'm hittin' the mall and gettin' more things for the trip."

I was silent for a moment. I thought about how I could squeeze a trip to the mall in between everything else I had to do that day. As much as I would have liked to break away from what had become that week's routine of intense concentration and studying, I still wasn't done, and the application needed to be finished.

"I can't right now Laydee, I really don't have time for nothing else but this."

I heard Laydee pop her gums and let out a sigh.

"You really gonna make me walk around the mall all by my lonesome self? I'll just find one of my sisters. You're wack.

Bye."

Laydee hung up the phone. I shook my head and smirked as I plopped my chin on my palm and continued to stare at the computer screen. I glanced at the application propped up next to the computer and read over one of the questions: 'What is your primary motivation for pursuing international studies?'

'I JUST WANT OUT!' I started to type on the computer screen, then I slapped the 'backspace' button on the computer keyboard repeatedly to erase my silly answer. I had several reasons for wanting to 'pursue international studies' a.k.a. escape Texas, but wasn't sure how to phrase it in a way that the school would want to hear. I started to type whatever I could think of, and tried not to let my mind wander too much while I formulated my responses.

It would be less than 24 hours before the crew loaded up the car to start the half-day journey to coastal Floridan party paradise. If there was one thing that sounded unappealing about going to Florida, it was definitely the drive, but I knew the leg cramps and motion sickness would be worth it once we set our freshly pedicured feet on that white sand and began our weekend at the Spring Break capital of the South. Being able to chill at one of the world's most beautiful beach cities with my best girlfriends at my side would make the journey worth the hassle. Not probably, but definitely.

As I worked on the Paris scholarship application and time continued to fly by, I started to realize that Florida just wasn't going to be possible if I wanted to finish it right. For me to get the application done correctly *and* on time, I would have to abandon the idea of Florida and my friends altogether. The application needed to be in the campus office four days after the vacay started, and I was not going to risk taking the application with me and trying to finish it on the road to Florida, furthermore worrying about finding a post office that could guarantee that the application would land in the right hands and in the right department at my school on time. Florida wouldn't be much of a vacation if I had worries and concerns swimming around my mind every time I took a dip in the beachwater. I would be *super* upset if I found out that the application arrived a day late and was automatically thrown out.

I sighed as I thumbed through the reflection questions at the center of the application—they were nerve-wracking! I found some of the questions to be very personal, though there were some easier ones about my health history, my family, my finances, and past travels (that was the easiest question to answer, I haven't traveled anywhere!). There was even a question about where I saw myself in the future, and I wasn't sure how to respond. I didn't know what to write—I'm not a writer! But eventually I just let the words flow through my pen and wrote fluidly on notebook paper before looking at my words thrice over and starting another section. I wanted to give myself the best possible chance by turning in the best application possible. I wanted to make sure that missing what could be my only chance to go to Florida with my best friends would be worth it. I couldn't remember ever winning anything worthwhile in my entire life, but this thing, I wanted to win. I needed to go to Paris.

After I wrote out my responses to the first half of the questions, I began typing as carefully as I could on the old computer. I kept typing and correcting until my wrists and knuckles ached and until my back felt like it had a rod going through it from sitting so long. I took a short break to drink a glass of water and text Antoinette to stop by, then went right back to work. I kept my phone on silent and only picked it up once to check on Antoinette's reply.

Antoinette stopped by my house a couple hours later to

take a look at everything I typed before she went back home to finish packing her suitcase. I always asked for Antoinette's help when I had big English essays to do because she was really good with grammar and spelling and always gave me good advice on my writing assignments. I also remember my psychology teacher from last year telling us that it was harder for people to catch their own writing mistakes, so it was probably best to have my essay looked over by another pair of eyes.

"Not bad Bre Bre! This is the best I've seen you write. You're off to a good start," Antoinette said before she gave me a few suggestions on how to structure my essay. As she was leaving, I broke the news to her that I wouldn't be going to Florida.

"I want the essay to have a good finish too, so I can't roll with y'all tomorrow," I told her.

"I kinda figured you might stay behind, but don't worry girl, we gon' rep Texas for you all the way! And when summer comes, we'll plan something even bigger next spring break," she assured me.

I hoped whoever made the decision to award me the chance to study in Paris would understand my story, my past, and my... anguish. In my two decades of existence, I have seen and heard a lot of terrible things! Without even considering my family woes, I was never sure if my past was unique or if it was just as nutty as everyone else's. Was seeing people get shot at, beaten to death, or drugged up supposed to be normal? Do people everywhere get pulled over and arrested simply because of what they look like? Was my childhood supposed to be riddled with funerals and fear?

I hoped the 'decision-making committee' would understand my desire to try this thing I'd never thought I'd be able to try before and get away from the turbulence of central Texas. Maybe that's why I never talked about traveling much with my friends, because I didn't want to seem foolish, but traveling has definitely crossed my mind more than once even if I never spoke about it. It was crazy how the opportunity just appeared right in front of me that day in the elevator two weeks before. I wondered about Miryam and if she had decided to turn in an application. I wondered how many other people were doing their applications at the same time as me, and if I actually stood a chance against all the other kids at the college with better essays, better grades, and better luck.

I was so jittery when I finally printed the first page of the essay that my thumbs wrinkled the corner of the paper, leaving a small imprint on the edges. I decided it'd be better to print the entire packet at the library over the weekend, and also look over the application at least a few more times. Maurice's printer had some temperamental glitches, so things didn't always look like they were supposed to when they printed. I wanted my application to look perfect when I turned it in even if my writing was far from being it.

Shortly after Antoinette left, I sent a text message to Laydee and Tamina, letting them know that I wasn't going to make it to Florida with them.

'That's 2 bad, it won't be the same without u! but good luck on your application and we'll bring u souvenirs,' Tamina messaged back.

'You suck. u really bailin' on us at the last minute like that!? it's whateva...' Laydee wrote, *'btw, just got word that the bruhs are throwing another gatherin' so just make sure u ready to party 2nite!'*

Chapitre 11: The Bruhs

Whenever 'The Bruhs' threw a party, it was guaranteed to jump off. The Bruhs were part of the biggest fraternity on campus, so naturally, the sorority sisters migrated towards them when they organized something, and Laydee usually followed in suit. Somehow someway, Laydee was able to convince the whole crew to make a short appearance there even though the party was quite a ways away from campus in a town called Cinderwood, and we all had plenty to do that night in Beauconte. Cinderwood was, to put it nicely, a *questionable* part of town—it's where my Mom raised Delilah and I when we were kids before we moved to Maurice's neighborhood. Even though Maurice's place is only a few miles away, living there made a world of difference in the sense that I didn't have to look over my shoulder as much when I walked down the street or worry about stray bullets coming through the living room window.

Maurice was firm in letting my mom know that he didn't like us living in *that* side of town. Don't get me wrong, Beauconte is far from being crime-free, but when you turn on the news, the majority of incidents are in Cinderwood. Assaults, robberies, and homicides are regular news over there, if they even show it on the news, and houses get raided so often over there that people nicknamed the place 'Cinder-Hood.' Even with all that considered, my girls and I still rallied up to make an appearance at the Bruh's party out there. We were all quite familiar with the house the party was at and none of us had been personally involved in any incidents out there before. We knew how to handle ourselves and watch our backs in case any fights or shootings started like they did at other parties we went to.

Antoinette and Tamina picked me up once they were sure their packing was done, then we scooped up Laydee on the way there since she lived closer to that part of town. I made sure to carefully save all the application work I had started typing onto a floppy disk and on the computer desktop before safely placing my handwritten notes under my bed. After several long hours sitting at that computer desk, I was looking forward to getting out of the house and loosening up a little before I had to start working on it again. I knew I'd be on track with finishing because I didn't have to work the entire weekend. Zeke already gave me the days off I asked for Spring Break, but I called in and let Zeke know I was free to pick up extra hours afterwards since my Spring Break plans were now cancelled.

My crew showed up at the Cinderwood party looking absolutely fly. The party was jumping and the crunk music was blasting to where we could hear it down the street before we even parked. There was so much excitement in the air, especially from the girls! They talked about Florida with every single person they ran into, though I overheard Laydee mentioning how displeased she was with me for backing out of the trip. I was excited too, but not in the same way as the girls. I was just excited about having the next few days without work or school and being able to chill out for a moment! Days like those were rare, so I was definitely going to take advantage of the free time as soon as my study abroad application was done.

The girls and I decided beforehand that we would all leave the party at a decent hour so they could rest up before they started their drive to Florida and so I could do a little more work on my application. Laydee didn't ridicule me about going to Florida that night; her cousin Misha had agreed to join in on the trip at the last minute and happily took my place in the carpool. I heard Laydee and Tamina talking about the trip with some guy who none of us recognized from school.

"We're leavin' as soon as the sun peek out. She ain't goin' because she thinks she goin' to France or some shit," I heard Laydee tell the dude while pointing at me. I glared in their direction as the guy let out a long laugh and Laydee didn't even try to stop him. I rolled my eyes at Laydee. She didn't need to be telling my business like that, especially to some random guy she just met a moment earlier. Within the first hour of being at that party, she had already told at least a dozen people that she was going to Florida and most of them were now aware that I had 'cowered out' of the awesome vacation. This particular fellow that Laydee was chatting with smirked at me and gave me a sour look before taking a sip of whatever was in the styrofoam cup he was holding.

"Ain't none of y'all b****s going to France," I heard him mutter. Laydee laughed at the guy's comment and changed the subject, nonchalantly, as though his comment wasn't rude at all. I was honestly surprised she didn't have my back—she could've told this dude what the deal was instead of making me look like a complete fool! First off, who did he think he was to say what I could or couldn't do, especially without even knowing me? He didn't know anything about me, my school, or my scholarship application. *Boy* would I love to let him have a piece of my mind, especially if I were to win the trip! But I kept my peace and ignored him instead. I folded my arms, turned away, and went to the kitchen of the house where all the drinks were laid out. I wasn't in the mood to argue or explain myself to a hairy dude wearing wrinkled clothes and dirty shoes. He definitely stood out in the crowd of people who had put a lot more effort into their appearance that night.

The kitchen was surprisingly empty with the exception of two 'lovebirds' making out in an empty space next to the fridge.

The boy had the girl pinned up against the wall and they kept bumping into the fridge, making the boxes of cereal on top of the fridge wobble and shake. They were kissing loudly and groping each other like they had no home training! I turned my nose up at them and concealed them with the door to the fridge as I opened it up. I quickly scanned the fridge racks for a cold drink, and couldn't help but listen in on the likely drunken conversation that the lovebirds were having. They sounded so ridiculous trying to talk between sloppy kisses—it was gross! As I closed the door to the fridge and popped open a can of beer, I did a double-take at the sudden recognition of the voice that was coming from the female counterpart of the shameless couple. I dropped the beer can and my mouth dropped wide open.

"DELILAH?!" I screeched. I couldn't believe what I was seeing! My little sister, one-half the shameless couple, was wearing hoochie shorts, magenta high heels and looked too indecent for words! She had no business being out that late on a school night, especially at a college party in Cinderwood. I hadn't seen her in a couple of days, and according to Maurice, she had been picking up extra shifts at her job was supposed to work late that night. Delilah giggled and playfully pushed the boy she was with away from her and out from the corner of the wall space next to the fridge. I didn't recognize him and had never heard her mentioning having a new boyfriend. Delilah patted her hair before readjusting her black lace midriff blouse and running the back of her hand across her lips. Her lipgloss had naturally gone awry during her scandalous episode.

"What it do sis? I'm just chillin' with my man," she responded matter-of-factly. Her eyes were bloodshot and her speech was extremely slurred. She licked her lips and ran the back of her hand across her mouth again to catch a glob of saliva from running out the corner of her mouth.

"Your man?" I said loudly, "I *know* Maurice don't know you here and I'm sure he'd love to hear about your *man* since he look a little too old to be messin' with you. And is that a college dude? 'Cause it sure ain't Jay." I glanced over at the 'boy' and looked him up and down. Whatever his age was, he looked way too old to be involved with my 17-year-old sister. His eyes were hanging low and he had a huge smirk plastered across his face.

"Well he don't go to your school," Delilah started, "and I'm way past J-Day. That fool's in my rearview." The guy scoffed and staggered away towards the living room where the core of the party was taking place. He was probably irritated that Delilah had stopped pleasing him and that I had interrupted their little moment.

"He's trippin'... anyway... stop naggin' me alright?" Delilah said as she gestured to shoo me away. Her words were strung together like a plastic choo-choo train and her eyelids were hanging just as low as her 'man's'. I had never seen her like that before, so far from her right state of mind, and it was unnerving. I noticed she was holding a drink cup next to her leg and I snatched it out of her hand and smelled it. Delilah started laughing. I. was. fuming. A small crowd started to gather by the kitchen entrance as Delilah sluggishly tried to reach for the cup and reclaim possession of it with her hands. I threw the cup into a sink behind us, and whatever was in it splashed on the walls and on the floor beside it. Delilah rolled her eyes, folded her arms, and started to walk in the same direction her 'man' went. I grabbed her arm when she tried to pass me.

"Are you high!?" I asked her. She laughed again. This time her laugh carried on too long.

"OK. We're goin' home. NOW," I told her punctually and clearly. Everyone from that section of the party was now looking at us. "We'll see what Daddy says about your new 'man' since you wanna pretend to be grown," I emphasized with air quotes.

"So *you* can do whatever you wanna do? You only two years older. And if anyone's pretending on anythang it's *you*, Dabre-sha. Walkin' around with ya broken ass half-ass car and ya half-ass boyfriend and half-ass life," Delilah rambled. She placed her hands on her hips and cocked her neck to the side. I was mortified by her *audacity* to take the argument to the next level with personal blows, especially in front of other people!

Laydee ran into the kitchen to try to calm the noise.

"Don't trip y'all, they sisters, they always fightin'" Laydee told the crowd. She walked straight up to us and shot Delilah a wide-eyed look before she spoke to me.

"What are y'all *doin*?" she said harshly between puckered lips. "You know I'm tryna get in good with the Greeks. Please stop showin' out!"

The sorority sisters Laydee had mingled with earlier were eyeballing all of us, and I could tell they were starting to gossip. I put my hand on Laydee's shoulder and turned her so her back was to the party crowd.

"Laydee, my LITTLE sister is here drunk and who knows what else! She told us she was workin'. She needs to go home *now*," I retorted as quietly as my anger would let me. It shocked me how much I almost sounded like a parent in that moment. Delilah and I didn't have the smoothest relationship, but she was still my little sister and I needed to look out for her.

"Okay, so she lied so she could come out with her friends," Laydee said plainly. "You act like you ain't never done the same!"

I winced at Laydee. Was she *really* defending Delilah right now? I grew irritated and didn't care anymore to lower my voice.

"First off, yes I have snuck out to a few parties, but I wasn't dressed like a trick and I was with *y'all*, not some stray dude. She shouldn't be here," I said defensively. Delilah slipped away from Laydee and I and began to pour herself another drink on a nearby counter.

"Leave da gal alone Bre. Ain't no sense talking to her now anyway cuz she ain't gon' listen. Just deal with her later when she's thinkin' straight," Laydee pleaded. Delilah nodded at both of us in agreement, then she picked up her coat off the kitchen counter and ran outside to try and catch up with her 'man'. Antoinette came in the kitchen and told us it was time to go, saying her family needed their van back earlier than planned, but I knew she was just telling us that so we would stop arguing. Antoinette hated arguments and especially hated when anyone in our circle fought, but this argument was bonafide necessary!

We all gathered our things and quickly walked outside the party towards Antoinette's van. Laydee, of course, plopped herself in the front seat and claimed control of the radio station before anyone else could. I didn't say a word to anyone until Laydee opened her big mouth again.

"I'm just sayin', I don't boss my sisters around 'cuz they're old enough to handle themselves. It ain't that big of a deal, your sister's business is her business so just let her do her."

I sneered at Laydee and held the palm of my hand up toward her face. I wanted to snap back at her soooo bad and remind her that every single one of her sisters were streetwalking, gangbanging messes because nobody looked after them, but I tried my hardest not to knock her with personal blows. Everyone in my crew knew her family was screwed up, even more lopsided than mine, and I wasn't going to remind her right then about what she already knew.

"Is my sister not my business though?" I retorted, "you want me to walk right by her and act like I'm okay with old dudes grabbin' on her at a grown folks party?"

"It ain't like she's marryin' the dude, she was just havin' a good time like we were all *trying* to do before you started goin' off and killin' everybody's buzz. Ain't Darrien like four or five years older than you?"

"Yes but our relationship is le-gal," I emphasized, "and I don't appreciate you taking Delilah's side nor offering your opinion in my family business since *your* family is the last I'd take any kind of advice from."

"Bye Dabresha!" Laydee yelled, she folded her arms and turned up the van's radio as loud as it could go. Tensions stayed high that night as we made our way home and I wanted to slap Laydee. While Laydee and I continued to exchange heated words during the ride home, Antoinette pouted and Tamina just sat there quiet, looking uncomfortable and awkward. I went OFF on Laydee so much that I forgot to confront her about dissing me in front of the Dude-With-the-Dirty-Shoes at the party!

Antoinette naturally tried to play peacemaker and mediate our argument as she usually does, but neither one of us were in the mood to reason with each other. I was convinced that I had every right to intervene when I saw my sister and did not agree with one single point Laydee tried to make.

On our way back to Beauconte, we spotted a Red Bull truck outside a convenience store handing out free drinks. The energy drink companies often parked big trucks displaying their logos around town and hired promoters to hand out t-shirts, drinks, and merchandise. I normally picked up all the free handouts from the promo trucks, but I was too angry to even try to interact with anybody, promoter or not. Laydee being Laydee, however, plastered on a fake smile and rolled down the van window to gleefully ask the promoter for the free samples.

"Can I get three please?" she shouted to the promoter. "These bee-yoches need stimulation!"

Chapitre 12: Spring Break

I wish I could say I let loose and had a grand ole time, but I'm not going to lie, my Spring Break was kind of wack. Thursday night, after I came home fatigued and furious about seeing Delilah at that party, I struggled to work on the application. My whole weekend was dedicated to my repeated review of my application packets. Thankfully, I was able to use the backup application Harmonie gave after the mistakes I made on the first packet were too many for me to accept. I hadn't worked that hard on any project before in my life, so it'd be a bittersweet incredible feeling to hand it in and watch it disappear forever.

I spent a lot of time wandering around the house; there wasn't much to do since my closest friends were in Florida and Darrien was in Vegas. The college scene was dead and the town was eerily quiet. Between working on my application and catching up on some much needed rest, I exercised and tried to make progress on my goal to lose fifteen pounds. I focused on stomach exercises because I was hoping that all the weight would disappear from my waist area, or maybe shift below my waist and fill out my hips and booty so I could be shaped like the girls in the Swishahouse videos (if only!). I caught up on some much needed house cleaning and reorganizing and messed around with some recipes in the kitchen since Delilah was acting stuck up and not cooking for me on the days that Maurice wasn't there for dinner. She had better been feeling grateful that I didn't tell Dad about seeing her at that Cinderwood party. I decided to let it go and focus on my own ish, and possibly use the information as a bribe later on to threaten her with if she ticked me off again.

I thought about catching the bus to visit Aunt Trecee in

Louisiana like I had originally planned, but Zeke had already agreed to put me back on the schedule at work and I didn't want to keep changing my mind with him and give him another reason to write me up. Instead, I called Aunt Trecee and spent a good deal of time on the phone with her and caught her up on everything that had transpired over the past month. It was the most we talked in a long time if not ever, and if it wasn't for her being able to talk so much during spring week, I probably would've died of boredom.

I had the house to myself on Friday afternoon—thank God—and was lounging on the living room sofa when the house phone rang.

"Where's your sister?" Aunt Trecee exclaimed before I even got a chance to say 'hello'. "I saw a picture on her webpage that I don't like and I been tryna call her but she don't call back. I even tried to message her on that Facespace website and she ain't answering."

Aunt Trecee told me about her various attempts to get ahold of Delilah via phone, social media, and email. Aunt Trecee was such a character, always trying to 'keep up' with us young folk and our gadgets and not ashamed to admit it!

"Aunt Trecee, you know you need to stay off the intranet if you ain't sure what you doing," I chuckled. I always found it funny when old folk tried to mess with *our* technology.

"I know gal, but I gotta make use of the computer your uncle left me. I be shoppin' on there and watching videos—there's so much on the intranet! Plus it help pass the time some days when I don't feel like doin' nothing else."

"You so crazy Aunt Trecee," I said lovingly, then I told her I had something important to say.

"I'm listenin'" she answered while stifling a cough.

"Last week, one of the black teachers at my school told

me about studyin' abroad. She said I could take classes in another country and try for a scholarship to go there. I'm going to try and do it. They got a program in France this summer…"

"Are you serious niecy?" my aunt interrupted in a shrieky tone. "I'm so proud-a you. I always knew you had the smarts."

I stopped my aunt before she got ahead of herself. She was always so positive about things before they even happened. Turning in an application wouldn't mean anything. Getting accepted would mean something *if* it were to happen.

"It's nothing like that auntie, it's just a thought. But I wanted to tell you first. I probably won't even get accepted, and I still have to talk to Maurice…"

"They'd be *foolish* not to 'cept you. You'll get there niecy. I can see you there havin' a wonderful time and all. Oh I'm so proud."

"Auntie, calm down. I got big things to think about before I do something like this. My job… my car… I don't even got a suitcase!"

"Dont worry 'bout the small stuff niecy. You'll get there if it's in your heart to do it. I can see you there! Standin' in front of the *real* Eiffel Tower. 'Member how upset you was when we took you to the tower in Nevada? Even then you was so smart you figured out what we was up to."

"It's not that I don't want to go auntie. I really do! But…"

"Dabresha Lynn, stop talkin' 'bout this all calm and whatnot. This is cotton-pickin' big! A girl like *you* travellin' across the world, you're gonna make hist'ry! Whether or not you get 'cepted, I'm already proud of ya baby girl."

I didn't know how to respond to my aunt and didn't understand why she was so proud of me even though I hadn't done anything special. All I did was pick up an application. It was just an application, not a guarantee.

"Thanks auntie," I concluded, feeling her support lifted me up. "I'll tell Lilah to call you *if* I see her, but I don't know where she really be at half the time."

I heard her cover the phone receiver with her hand, and through muffled voices, I could hear Aunt Trecee chatting with somebody. She probably missed the little hint I was giving her about my irritation towards Delilah; my aunt often sat on her side porch when she talked on the phone so she could greet her neighborhood friends passing by (and probably smoke a cigarette though she keeps telling me she quit).

"Okay Miss France," she said. "My niece goin' to France y'all!" she screeched.

"Auntie stop! Who you talkin' to? I ain't even turned in the application yet!" I tried to say sternly.

"Well make sure it get turned in then. Ms. Charles and me and all us will be waitin' for you to tell us 'bout it. Dawnisse would be so proud."

I sighed. Whenever someone mentioned my mom, I would try not to get down on myself but it was so hard. Even though she had passed away six years ago, I could feel my eyes steam up and my body weaken whenever Aunt Trecee talked about her. My mind would get cloudy and the dryness in my throat would get real. I missed my mom so much.

"Thanks auntie. I gotta go start my laundry so I'ma let you and Ms. Charles chit-chat. Love ya," I finished.

Her neighbor, whom I had spent some time with during my past visits with Aunt Trecee, got on the phone. I remember visiting Ms. Charles' house when I was a kid. She was always chattering with Aunt Trecee and they often went to bingo together at their favorite casino in Shreveport.

"Is this true what I'm hearing? Miss Bre traveling? I remember how much you loved playing with that puzzle of the globe when you was little. Don't you worry yourself about being in a strange land now. Psalm 146 say God looks out for the strangers in new places. I can't wait for you to show us pictures Bre!"

I shook my head in disbelief. My aunt had really prematurely told her friend that I was going to France. I tried playing it off as if it were insignificant.

"Hopefully Miss. Charles. I'll let you know if it all work out," I said hesitantly. Why couldn't these old folks understand the difference between possibility and for sure? Nonetheless, I vowed to do my best on my application. Now that Aunt Trecee and her friends were on my back, I had to make sure my application was solid. I got off the phone with them and went right back to work on it.

I had a clearer idea of how to finish my essay by the time I looked over my final draft, so I let the words flow through my pen and onto my computer screen. I concentrated until my head throbbed like I had been blasting base in my ears for days. This was finally it!

When I printed my final draft the next day, I was a mix of nerves and happy. I was elated that the application was actually done, but nervous about what the people reading it would make of it. Antoinette wouldn't be around to look over it either, so it was all on me now. I had spent so much time on it throughout the last few weeks that I was certain it was decent, but who knows how the people making the decisions on all this really think. Would they be able to tell that it was completed sort of last minute and turned in on the extended deadline? Would they be able to tell that I worked so hard on it and fixed it a dozen times or that I had put more effort into this one paper than I had into any paper from any other class in my entire life? I hoped they would be able to see my efforts and have a sense of how hard I tried. I couldn't remember the last time I had tried so hard on anything, so this thing was truly a big feat for me.

I read the application over probably fifty times that weekend before I personally walked it into Ms. Cole's office at school on Monday. I secured it in a manila envelope and made two copies of it just in case anything were to go wrong with the original. I walked up to the reception counter with this uneasy feeling of extreme confidence mixed with hesitance. The two emotions were trapped in bubbles that bounced around my body and knocked into each other in playful juxtaposition. Confidence. Hesitance. Confidence thrusting my legs forward, hesitance pulling me back. When I handed the envelope to Harmonie, both feelings burst in thin air and all that was left was nerves.

Harmonie seemed calm and complacent at her desk inside the SDAO office, and she assured me that my application would be securely placed in line with the other applications. My countless hours of hard worked disappeared into a tiny white cardboard box, never to be seen again. The feeling of accomplishment was immense though and didn't disappear into that cardboard box; I had finished something that I had started for the first time in a long time, and it felt really good to have gotten that far.

"Do you know when we'll know if we won?" I asked Harmonie politely. I didn't want to go stir crazy the next few weeks waiting for them to contact me, *if* they were going to contact me at all.

"They will email you with a decision by mid-April," she assured me. Three weeks seemed like an eternity away, but I guessed it would be worth the wait. I knew patience was a virtue, but unfortunately it wasn't a quality that I possessed much of and impatience was probably my least pleasant attribute. I would have to grit my teeth and bear the wait until I knew the outcome.

* * *

I spent the rest of my spring break contemplating the application, scrutinizing the copy I had of it, and obsessing over how I could have done better on it. I let off a little of my anxiety to Aunt Trecee and, like a good aunt, she listened. She was always there to cheer me up when I needed it most, and always seemed to know exactly what to say if I told her something was bugging me. I'm glad she listened because I didn't tell anyone else about the application, not even Zeke or my other co-workers, because I didn't want to get too ahead of myself. I didn't want to feel stupid when they asked me about it in the future and I would have to tell them I didn't get selected. I worked my extra shifts and made a little extra money. I kept all my thoughts and anticipation to myself, which was easier than I thought it'd be. I waited patiently for my friends to get back to town so I could try and let them know how I was feeling, and I couldn't have been happier when I heard they arrived home safely that weekend.

The girls were too tired to hang out when they got back from Florida Saturday night, so we agreed to catch up over brunch at The Waff Spot, our favorite waffle joint, the following morning. The cool ambiance, the generous prices, and the fluffy banana pancakes kept us coming back there whenever we needed some good eating! The girls wanted to sleep in on Sunday morning, rightfully so after half a day on the road, so while I waited on them to get ready for our noontime brunch date, I decided to watch morning cartoons on the living room TV while I casually looked through my history notes and filed down my fingernails.

Delilah came bursting into the living room with the

vacuum roaring loud as all heck. She had headphones stuffed in her ears and was humming to her music. She zig-zagged the vacuum at least a dozen times back and forth across the living room, which was completely unnecessary in a living room as small as ours and further unnecessary while I was watching TV. After becoming irritated from the vacuum noise and her blocking my view, I grabbed the remote off the living room table and held down the volume button so the TV sound increased as high as it could go.

"I CAN'T HEAR THE TV!" I said loudly over the vacuum's noisy whirring. Delilah pretended not to hear me and kept passing the suction over the same areas she had already vacuumed while humming along to her stupid music. The vacuum was so loud that when the house phone rang a moment later, I almost didn't hear it. I nearly tripped over the vacuum cord when I jumped up and rushed to try to get the call, but whoever was on the other end hung up before I could get to it. I tapped Delilah on the shoulder.

"I missed who called because of your vacuuming and I'm expecting somethin' important. Can you shut it til I'm at least done watchin' TV?" I yelled.

"Oh yeah, you got a message on the answering machine the other day," Delilah said plainly. She steered the vacuum past the TV and began humming to her music again.

"What'd you just say?" I said loudly. I walked back towards the house phone and squinted at the digital screen on the face of answering machine sitting next to it. The answering machine indicated there were no messages, new or old, in its stored memory. I walked back to Delilah and grabbed her arm.

"From who it was? There's nothing on the tape," I shouted, over-enunciating my words and putting extra emphasis on the way I mouthed my words so she could follow what I was saying through her headphones. Delilah took two steps back and shrugged her shoulders, then started to guide the vacuum away from me.

"Whatchu mean you don't know?!" I demanded. "You must've checked it if it ain't there no more," I yelled as loudly as I could over the rumbling of the vacuum. Delilah turned to face me.

"I don't know, something about some trip and some application. Must've of accidentally deleted it," she said with a complacent look on her face. She turned around and started to strut back across the living room with the vacuum leading her way. I walked around her and planted myself directly in front of her vacuuming path, crossing my arms and giving her a hostile stare.

"You don't remember what the message said? And how you 'accidentally' delete it?" I shrieked.

She shrugged her shoulders again and poked out her bottom lip. I saw a hint of a smirk form in the corner of her mouth.

"Ooooh, you stupid witch!" I screamed. I snatched the vacuum cord out of the wall and positioned myself so that I was head-to-head with Delilah, my chin raised and only inches away from hers. I raised the palm of my hand next to her cheek and drew it back like I was about to hit her, then stuck out my index finger. I had to use all my might to stop myself from squaring off with my sister for the first time since we were kids!

"You knew I was waitin' on my school to call, I told you it was important!"

Delilah looked right through me as if I were a piece of glass and didn't say a word. She tilted her head slightly and let her face muscles relax before looking up at the ceiling and releasing a sigh. She backed away from me and bent down to pick up the vacuum cord, then began to walk it back towards the wall socket.

"I said it were an accident," she said casually. She plugged the vacuum back into the wall and let the noise takeover the tension in the air. I shook my head and raised my hand higher in the air.

"You LUCKY I don't wanna mess up my nails!" I shrieked. I stomped down the hallway and slammed our bedroom door closed so hard that one of the family pictures hanging up in the hallway came toppling down from the nail it was hanging on. I lunged to sit on the very edge of my bed and began to rock back and forth, trembling as I imagined all the ways I could hurt Delilah. Both my legs and my head were shaking furiously, and I felt that I could spring up off the bed and clock Delilah in a split second if she were to walk inside the bedroom.

I snatched my phone out of my jeans pocket and furiously began to scroll through my contact list, debating on who I should call to let everything out. Before I could make a decision, my phone rang and I instantly answered it. Aunt Trecee called at the perfect time to stop me from murdering my sister!

"Aunt Trecee, get your niece before I hurt her!" I yelled into the receiver. I could still hear the vacuum running in the distance when I bounced off the bed and began to pace back and forth.

"Child breathe. Tell me slow what's gone on," Aunt Trecee replied.

"She deleted my school's phone message Auntie!" I yelped, trying to use all my might to restrain my curse words. "I been at the end of my tether all week wonderin' on my Europe application and she gonna delete the message knowing damn well it was important. She say she don't remember what was on it, my ass! She did it on purpose! I hate her and can't *wait* to get away from her dumb behind!"

My voice cracked as my outburst turned into a whimper,

and I stopped myself from crying in the middle of the second sob. I was not going to let Delilah get to me like that! Aunt Trecee was silent for a second, then she stifled a cough and began to speak slowly.

"I know you fed up right now niecy, so I'm not gonna hassle you 'bout your cursing. But she's your sister Bre Bre. She's in a funky mood for whatever reason and you can't let her set you off like that. Get out the house, get some air, and don't hurt her okay? I'll try to call her and sort things with her. Dawnisse and I use to spat too, that's what sisters do, but we still loved each other no matter what. Just let it go for now and get back to enjoyin' your spring week. I'll check in on ya later on after things calm down. I love you," Aunt Trecee concluded. She slowly hung up the phone as I sniffled and tried to steady my breathing.

I threw my phone in my purse and quickly walked out of the house. I sent a text message to Tamina, who was supposed to be my ride to brunch, as soon as I stepped foot on the sidewalk. *'Don't need a ride to the Waff Spot, see you in a few,'* I wrote.

'okay, see you there' she replied as I quickened my walking pace.

The three mile trek to the Waff Spot didn't seem as long while I was trying to cool down from the fire-breathing dragon feeling that Delilah had incited in me. The girls were already sitting down waiting for me when I burst through the glass entrance doors and stalked towards their table.

"What's wrong?" Tamina asked as I slid into the seat next to her.

"My sister is all wrong, I almost beat her behind before I walked here," I snapped.

"Walked? Dang she must of really ticked you off," Antoinette chimed in.

"Y'all still fightin'?" Laydee asked as I plucked a menu out of the dining table's syrup rack.

"She's chidin' me on purpose Laydee! Now I gotta wait 'til Tuesday to find out what's goin' on with my trip. They called and she deleted the message and their office is closed 'til then," I responded.

"That's two days, chill out," Laydee said, slightly rolling her eyes.

"Jayna did tell me she's been actin' stuck up at school. Maybe she just needs some space," Antoinette added.

"It's whatever. Y'all just pray I don't hurt that girl before her graduation," I replied. "I'll have her limp across that stage with a black eye and a shoulder cast if she keeps it up!"

I flagged down a waitress and ordered my usual plate: banana pancakes, chicken sausage and grits. Laydee ordered an omelette and hash browns, and Nette and Mina both ordered waffle plates with bacon and eggs.

"I don't mean to bring funk on y'all," I said once the waitress walked away, "so let's hear about Florida! Tell me the good, bad, ugly, and fab," I demanded the girls as we waited for our plates.

"It was so live!" Laydee bursted, slamming her hand on the table. "The beaches were crowded as all hell and fun as all ever. We got VIP to a different club every night, one night we saw David Banner in the VIP booth! And my cousin hooked us up with drink passes to all the beach clubs. We saw J-Kwon and Lil' Flip in concerts too, girl you missed out! Oh and Tamina got a boyfriend," Laydee smirked.

"You go girl!" I added as Tamina shook her head and looked up toward the ceiling.

"We all met some nice fellas out there, but Laydee's puttin' extras on it like she always do," Antoinette laughed.

The girls caught me up on every detail of their week in

partying paradise, and I really started to regret skipping out on the trip after hearing about how much fun they had. I tried to focus on all the exciting stories they told me, but my mind kept wandering to what the answering machine message Delilah deleted could have possibly said. Had the school already rejected my application and tried to let me know? Or did I mess up somewhere and they wanted to tell me it was incomplete? Either way, I could not have been more eager to go back to school on a weekend than I ever was that Sunday.

When Tuesday came, I got to campus an hour early and went straight to the administrative building. I skipped up the flights of stairs and burst into the SDAO office with incredible energy, running straight to Harmonie's desk. Harmonie was caught off guard when I started talking a million words a minute, but she smiled anyway and looked at me with a curious expression on her face.

"Hi, I applied for the study abroad scholarship last week. My name's Dabresha D…"

"Yes, Dabresha Davis, how was your break?" Harmonie interrupted.

"It was good but someone tried to call my house last week and my sister erased the message, please call my cell phone from now on. I don't know what it said and…"

"Oh yes, we called because you missed question twenty-nine on your application, the question about your immunizations to date, but we were able to get the information from the registrar's office and fill it in for you," Harmonie said, giving me a reassuring smile.

"So nothing's been decided yet?" I asked her to clarify.

"Not at this time, but you should be getting a call within the next week with the committee's decision," she replied with a smile.

"Thank you," I said, disappointed. I slowly walked away, discouraged, and with a sudden hatred for the concept of time. That week could not have gone by any slower, and I dragged through it, anxious and worried. I knew the application was heavy on my mind because I kept daydreaming about Paris during my classes, and when I would look at my class notes every evening, I'd notice a lot of spelling mistakes, missing words, and my handwriting looked atrocious. Every twenty-four hours felt like sixty, and every phone call on my cell phone was a moment to hold my breath if I didn't recognize the number.

Three days later, I got a call from Ms. Cole on my cell phone.

"Miss Davis, do you have a moment to talk about your application?" she asked, and then she gave me the news.

Chapitre 13: The News

I CAN'T BELIEVE I GOT ACCEPTED! I can't believe this is really happening to ME! Dabresha Lynn Davis! I'm going to school in Europe for a month and a half?! This can't be real. This can't be happening to me, no ma'am!

The craziest part is that it all started with a random encounter in an elevator. To think that the school chose *me* of all people to do this program, I just can't believe it! My friends probably won't believe me either. I have to tell Maurice! And Delilah—even though she's been dancing on my last nerve lately. I wonder what they'll say and if they'll believe me. Woowww. Six weeks in PARIS! I need to go shopping to prepare! And do more shopping when I get there!

I need to figure out what to do with my hair. What a nice change to only have to worry about that. More importantly, I need to make sure I save up enough money to hold me over for the six weeks that I'll be there. I'll need to ask my boss for some extra shifts at the restaurant at the end of the semester. I'll need to buy the plane ticket first, somehow, then books and supplies when I get there. Oh my Lord. No one'll probably ever believe me. I don't even believe me! They'll think I'm nutty as a fruitcake, but they will have to take me serious once I get on that plane! And come back with stylish new clothes, souvenirs *and* even some school credits!

I'll send them postcards with pictures of the Eiffel tower and the Mona Lisa on the front. I'll use a chat room to talk to them from overseas if I can! Jee-sus. This can't be happening. Is this really happening to *me?* I'm gonna start a countdown. 47 days until Europe. 47 days until I get on a plane for the first time and start a semi-vacation (still gotta do a little school work!). Aunt Trecee will be so happy for me. I'm going to call her as soon as I get home. I'm going to tell her she was right for believing in me. She was right for telling me I could do anything I dreamed of, with or without the smarts.

I'll be the first person in my family to travel this far. I might be the first one to ever leave the South! I guess luck doesn't avoid me all the time after all... maybe luck finally started feeling sorry for me and decided to help me out. Soon, I'll be traveling across the world for close to nothing of my own dime because of my newfound luck. I'll have a break from Delilah, a break from work, and I'll be seeing things I never thought I'd get the chance to see before. I think things are really going to be different now. It'll be a nice change.

And I'm going to get on a plane! If that don't put pepper in the gumbo I don't know what will. I've told my friends fifteen, maybe forty times that I would never get on a plane, but I'm going to have to since there's no other way to Europe. God help me survive that flight! Forty-seven days... and fourteen hours.

* * *

I walked up the pathway to my house that day feeling like I was floating on clouds and wearing one of the biggest smiles I had ever worn. I was too excited and couldn't hold it in! I wanted to call so many people but couldn't decide who to call first, so I listened to some crunk music while I reveled in the news and tried to decide. I scrolled through all the contacts in my cell phone list and pondered on who to tell first. Would Darrien be excited for me? Should I call Antoinette first since she helped me with my application? Or call Aunt Trecee because she believed in me? I just couldn't decide!

I planned to burst into blabber the moment I entered my house and give whoever was there a big hug. If Maurice was home, I would thank him for allowing me to go on the trip. Not all parents are as cool as Maurice—I ran into Miryam at school and she told me her dad wasn't keen on the idea of her going on the trip under any circumstances, scholarship or not! It would suck to win a trip anywhere and then have your parents tell you you're not be allowed to go—shoot I'd hate Maurice if he did that to me! Thankfully I didn't have to worry about that. Hard as he was, he was still supportive.

My smile widened as I got closer to the front door of my house. I turned down my music and took my headphones out of my ears once I mounted the front porch. I could hear loud voices coming from inside the house, but assumed it was the TV or Delilah having another one of her hyped up phone conversations with one of her loud friends. As I started to open the front door, I confirmed Delilah's voice as the one speaking loudly, but she wasn't speaking in her usual, jovial tone. It was an argument, a loud one, and Maurice was on the other end of it. My smile faded as I stepped inside the house to try to speculate the various possibilities of what the argument could be about. Maurice was definitely a man of a few words, so I rarely heard him argue with anyone. Delilah must've be getting reprimanded for doing something *else* stupid, and I secretly hoped she was about to get punished for it. In my eyes, Delilah was just an annoying senseless brat who was overdue for a good whooping.

I completely turned off the music in my headphones and tried to decipher what the argument was about before I closed the front door shut. I could tell Delilah was crying between her exchanges with The Bear, and I could hear his raised voice roaring so angrily that it nearly gave me chills. I could feel the friction in the air as I closed the front door and tried to interpret the first full phrase I could.

"I'm going to ask you one last time and you better make me the truth Delilah. Why else would they be calling for you, huh? Don't bullshit me gal."

I approached the kitchen with careful steps, and took a peek at where the altercation was taking place. Delilah was standing by the hallway entrance and Maurice was facing her from across the kitchen table. Neither Maurice nor Delilah took notice to me when I dropped my bag by the front door and inched past them towards the hallway. I didn't want to become a part of their feud and was hoping to slide past Delilah to take refuge in the bedroom. Maurice's voice was so aggressive that it was difficult to try to slip past them without being drawn in. I felt like ducking a couple of times to avoid the shrapnel of his growls ricocheting off the walls.

"I told you, I DON'T KNOW!" Delilah screamed. I took another step towards the hallway leading to the bedroom. My attempt to bypass the situation was squashed when Maurice called me by name.

"Dabresha, do you know who the doctor called for? Because I know damn well you was working the day they said on the answerin' machine. *Someone* in this here house went to a pregnancy clinic and it sho as hell weren't me. Was it you Bresha?" Maurice demanded. He snapped his finger and his eyes lowered toward the area of my stomach; he glared at it intensely before his eyes came back to my puzzled face. My belly, even with all its stubborn fat on it, showed no sign of surprise under my tight-fitting white tank top, however Delilah's flowy black blouse was concealing, and it looked like she had gained weight in her midsection.

"I ain't been to a clinic since my check-up last year," I replied quickly, lowering my head. I glanced over at Delilah from the corner of my eye and she broke out in tears. My sister sobbed uncontrollably like she was a little girl again—I hadn't heard her cry like that in a decade! I backed away from the kitchen and crept towards the hallway while shaking my head. Every ounce of excitement that I had a moment earlier had vanished with the firm snap of Maurice's finger.

"I'm sorry!" Delilah wailed. She buried her eyes in the palm of her hands. Maurice ignored her as he passed her and started to stomp down the hallway to his bedroom.

"I've already arranged to miss work for your graduation, so you best be there," Maurice snarled from down the hall. He slammed his bedroom door as loud as he could so the whole house shook in the aftermath.

I stared at Delilah in disgust. Delilah sobbed even louder as I darted past her to get to my room. My vision was blurred during my escape—I was full blown frustrated! Delilah had singlehandedly ruined the moment I had been building up all damn day to share my wonderful news. I would have to wait for a more suitable time to tell my family, and I groaned at the thought of how long Delilah's breaking news could linger and take over the whole household vibe. It could be days, maybe even weeks, before the house got back to normal if it ever did. I reflected on the time Delilah got arrested for shoplifting the year before, and how Maurice didn't talk to either one of us for nearly a month. This news could make him hostile for months. Maurice had always told us to be careful with boys and to not get ourselves knocked up. I had followed Maurice's instructions since the day I first started having 'feelings' for boys, but I guess my sister hadn't. Was Delilah really pregnant?

I already thought very little of my bratty little sister, but even I could have never predicted anything like this. Come to find out, Delilah was already six weeks pregnant and had gone to a clinic earlier that week to try and ward off her worst fears. Delilah's anxiety must have caused her to overlook important sections of her clinic paperwork, particularly the sections that asked if it was okay to leave messages at the phone numbers she provided. When the clinic called the house to provide her with her pregnancy and health screen results, the results that she couldn't wait around for that day because she had to get back to school, Maurice intercepted the call and cussed out the phone technician in a moment of weakness. Maurice had come home earlier than usual from work that day because of a power outage; Delilah would normally get home before Maurice and succeed at erasing any messages from her school or her job, but this day she was unsuccessful.

Maurice came home early that day hoping to enjoy some downtime in a quiet, empty house. He planned to take a short nap before his rambunctious step-daughters came home from school, but he too, was unsuccessful at his task because the clinic called twice just as he closed his eyes to try and savor some much needed peace and quiet. His voice was weak when he answered the phone, and he mumbled a hesitant "yes" when the clinic receptionist asked for a 'Miss Davis.' Maurice suspected that his daughters were growing up rapidly day by day, but he could have never expected a pregnancy. He downed a glass of scotch and waited for 'Miss Davis' to come home and explain the basis of the clinic's call. I arrived home ten minutes after Delilah and was able to hear the nucleus of the most shocking arguments to ever take place in that house on Berry street.

No news I could provide would ever compare to the news of my sister's. I dismissed the possibility of sharing or celebrating my great news and chose to go to bed instead, without calling Darrien or responding to any of my unopened text messages from earlier that day. Sleep was the only thing that sounded good to me that moment, so I fell asleep fast and I slept good, making sure to bury my head deep below my pillows so I wouldn't have to hear any more of Delilah's sobs or Maurice's growls if they started arguing again.

Not much was on my mind that afternoon besides the clear shock of my sister's pregnancy. I don't remember a lot of dreams, but that afternoon I clearly remember dreaming about standing in front of the Eiffel Tower. It was unusually small and ugly, and the skies around the tower were dark and ominous looking. The tower had jagged, rusted edges and gothic statues were protruding from its sides. It looked like something from a horror movie.

Delilah's surprise pregnancy had certainly thrown me off that day, but I didn't focus on it too much or let it bother me—afterall, Delilah deserved any mess that came her way. Delilah had been trying to act 'grown' for so long so her situation was her own fault and her own proper punishment. I hoped it would force her to act right and be a more mature sibling, and I hoped it would make her realize that making grown-up decisions came with grown-up consequences.

* * *

I woke up from my nap a few hours later, determined to tell at least one person my good news. The sun was almost set outside and the house was completely dim and silent, so I could tell that Delilah had probably taken off somewhere and that Maurice was probably still cooped up in his cave, preparing for his evening work shift. I patted my hand around my bed and felt around for my cell phone. I dialed Aunt Trecee and was surprised when she answered since she was an early sleeper who usually went to bed right before sunset.

"Hey niecey," Aunt Trecee answered in a high pitched voice, stifling a cough.

"Aunt Trecee, I won it! I'm going to EUROPE!" I cried out. I couldn't contain my excitement even though I had just woken up groggy a moment earlier and my voice was muffled and scratchy. I felt like I had won the lottery! I had never won anything before, and my scholarship was the closest thing to it since the original cost of the trip was almost seven thousand dollars. Putting it in perspective, I had just won all that money!

"That's wonderful niecy! I knew you was gon' get it, I just knew it. My lawd my lawd, my niece going to France!"

"London too! The first couple days of the trip is there and we land there!" I added. I was so giddy as I told my aunt all the details I could think of and probably repeated a few more than once without realizing it. My heart pounded as I told her how the school notified me by phone earlier that day, and how the scholarship would take care of almost every expense associated with the trip. I told her how skeptical I was about getting on a plane, and how excited I was to see the real Eiffel Tower.

"If it makes you any less nervous Bre, I'll tell you now that it won't be your first time on a plane really. Your mom and I took you girls to Virginia for a family reunion before you could remember. You and Lilah was both still in diapers I think."

I laughed at the thought of my sister and I walking around in diapers; I remember seeing a family photo of both of us in diapers and it was one of my favorites. We were two plump chocolate babies with thick curly hair and someone had snapped the perfect photo of us holding onto the coffee table in our old living room gazing at the camera, shirtless and all. I wanted to search around mom's old boxes to try and find the family pictures someday, but had never gotten around to it.

I felt a little more at ease with my Aunt's reaffirmation that

I shouldn't be worried about getting on a plane. I had already heard dozens of times before that driving was more dangerous than riding an airplane, and there must have been some sort of truth to it because car accidents happened all the time and I rarely heard about plane accidents, and if those terrorists hadn't hijacked those planes a few years back, the planes would've probably landed safely where they was supposed to go. Those were crimes, not accidents, and it hasn't happened again since that day.

"I'ma find my old suitcases out the garooje for ya and lend you my camera so you just snap everything you can and show me what it's like over there. I've always wanted to go to Europe, but never got a chance."

"Of course I will," I replied. "I'm gonna buy some disposable cameras too and take pictures of everything I see twice over."

I told my aunt about my intentions to find a temporary part-time job before the summer came. I wanted to save up as much as I could so I could have some extra spending money when the time came for me to take off.

"You know miss Nora down on Brighton Creek by the church? She told me she was lookin' for a babysitter for her grandkids a couple days a week. You remember them two little bowlegged boys?" Aunt Trecee asked.

"Yes," I replied, "Jordy and Jerlin. Can you tell Miss Nora I'm interested?"

I wasn't a very experienced babysitter nor was I very enthusiastic about watching after the kids in question, two hyperactive preschoolers, but I figured any extra money would be good for my summer. I was willing to work every day if it meant I could save up hundreds of dollars to ball out in the shopping capital of the world!

"This trip is gonna be such a wond'ful experience and do

you some good. I know your momma's proud of you Bre Bre," Aunt Trecee concluded through another muffled cough. I nodded.

"I hope she is and I hope she gives me strength on that plane ride!" I joked. My aunt's throat seemed to be clogged up when we shared a laugh.

"You sick again Auntie?" I asked her, concerned.

"No baby, just allergies showin' out again," my aunt replied.

I had already expressed concern about my Aunt Trecee's smoking habit years earlier, and as far as I knew, she had quit and was living a healthier lifestyle a couple hours away out in Louisiana. Her voice sounded like she had started up again, but I didn't want to ask her because she would probably snap at me. Aunt Trecee had tried to quit smoking several times over the past few years, but I suspected she had yet to completely eradicate her addiction. I could hear the smoke in her voice and in her cough, and I despised the smell of cigarettes (though I didn't mind Cigarillo smoke as much).

She changed the subject by asking about Maurice and Delilah, unaware of the events that had taken place that afternoon. I told my Aunt that they had a spat earlier that day, but resisted going into detail. My aunt would eventually find out everything anyway, and I had no desire to talk about Delilah's drama while I was sharing my good news. I wanted to keep the conversation focused on my accomplishment, my excitement, and my summer.

I wished my aunt well as I got up from my bed and retrieved my backpack from the living room. It was hard not to smile as I started to work on my homework assignments. It surprised me that I couldn't stop grinning the whole time I worked on the assignments, and I couldn't ever remember smiling so much while doing homework. I was happy to be in a quiet house and ecstatic about finally having something good to look forward to. Within a matter of months, my worries and cares would vaporize over the Atlantic Ocean and I would be experiencing things in a part of the world that I had only dreamed of before.

Chapitre 14: Fixin' for France

The last few weeks of school evaporated faster than dew on a summer day. I finished all my classes with proper grades: a B in African-American studies, an A in Statistics, a B- in Biology, and a B+ in Geology. It was my highest grade point average yet, but I didn't boast about it to no one. I would be in Europe in a month, and the trip seemed a stitch more important than everything else.

Aunt Trecee let me borrow her suitcases since we didn't have any at our house; she sent them over with the stateline bus shipping service and I picked them up from the bus station when they arrived. Aunt Trecee put all three of the suitcases inside each other, like those little wooden Russian dolls they sell at the swap-meet, but instead of painted wood it was a set of three rectangular beige luggages with maroon floral patterns. They were hideous by my standards, but they would get the job done. She also left me her credit card inside the smallest suitcase's tiniest pocket, along with a digital camera and a note that said: 'a camera and spending money for u, 'bout $200. Try to bring some souvenirs. love you.'

I quickly realized it was going to be a difficult task deciding what to bring with me on a six week long trip. I would need at least five club outfits to wear on my nights out, and at least two pairs of cute heels and walking shoes. I would also need to bring a pair of comfortable flat shoes or slip-ons for walking around the residence. Above all else, accessories, sunglasses, jackets, and daily clothes options were going to be essential, and I wanted to bring a few fitted caps with Texas logos so I could represent where I'm from!

It was tedious trying to decide how many pairs of socks

and undergarments to bring, and I hoped the laundromat would be easy to use out there. I wondered if their washers and dryers even worked the same! I had a lot of decisions to make, and the pamphlet I got in the mail from the AIS-American Intercontinental Studies program repeated the phrase 'pack light' several times throughout its pages. I was going to pack my way, no matter what it said; I needed six weeks of clothing and accessory options to accommodate my various fashion moods!

As soon as the semester ended, I started a routine of throwing things into the suitcases that I thought I might need. I'd leave the open suitcases lined up against the wall by the foot of my bed, and throw things in as the idea came up. It was like a puzzle game where I would rearrange things every other day, and the suitcases still wouldn't close right. I almost broke the zipper on the small suitcase, which was safeguarding my most precious shoes, and when I tried to close the largest suitcase, it looked like it was pregnant and kept falling over whenever I tried to stand it upright. I hoped the suitcases wouldn't need to be pulled around too much and that the wheels and handles would help ease the heavy load. Thank *God* these suitcases had wheels!

I've never had to pack for any trip before, not besides weekend visits to Aunt Trecee's house or a friend's sleepover. I couldn't wait to leave the house for my first real 'grownup' trip. No family would be around telling me what to do and I was too excited for words!

I wondered what the boys would be like out there, what the food would taste like, and what the clubs and the people were like. I wouldn't exactly be checking out the fellas, just curious to see how they dressed and spit game (and I wouldn't give Darrien too much detail of these particular curiosities of course!). I'd just be a quiet observer. I couldn't wait to see Par-ee, the place I had only read about in magazines and seen in so many movies, and the place my mom set my heart upon. I couldn't wait to live my dream. Five. more. weeks.

My friends were just as eager as me to know about what the future of my trip would hold, and when I began to talk to them about the trip, they had a plethora of questions of their own.

"How are the clubs out in Europe? And the college parties?" Laydee asked me one day while we were walking around the mall on a Wednesday afternoon. I told her I wanted to shop for fresh gear to wear in Europe, and she came along with me to 'acquire' a few things for herself.

"Hopefully just as trill as the clubs in Texas," I answered her, "I'll let you know in five weeks, and I'll come back early if they suck," I joked.

That day, it hit me that I'd be trapped on another continent if I ended up despising it, but I hoped that wouldn't be the case. No place in the world could ever be as vile as sharing a place with Delilah, whom, by the way, recently started waking up several times throughout the night to run to the restroom and vomit. I got tired of hearing the patter of her feet across the bedroom floor in the middle of the night, and hearing the noise from the old plumbing pipes running through the house walls every time she flushed the toilet.

* * *

"Are there black people out there?" Darrien asked me one night while we were driving to my house in his car. He had picked me up from work that night and we were sipping on strawberry milkshakes that we had just ordered from the Rocky Diner drive through.

"There has to be," I replied as I took a sip of my milkshake and cringed as I felt the rush of cold liquid give me a brain freeze. "I saw 'em in the pictures in my French book. I'll let you know in five weeks." He didn't ask me too much else about the trip after that day, and I was surprised he didn't have more questions.

"Best behave yourself out there woman," he joked as he slapped the top of my thigh.

"Me, misbehave?" I asked innocently as I finished off my shake. He let out his adorable laugh as he turned up the music to his car stereo and we drove around Beauconte with the bass blasting.

* * *

"What's gon' happen if you need help somewhere and no one understand you? Who you can talk with if you got any problems?" Maurice asked me one day when he walked in my room and interrupted me in the middle of my suitcase-packing-puzzle game. I was sitting on the floor near the foot of my bed rummaging through the suitcases trying to find my favorite jacket.

"I'll be alright Pops, they'll be counselors there, kind of like teachers. They 'sposed to look out for us when we need something."

"Alright Bre, just stay outta trouble. Don't talk to no funnyheads and keep alert like your mom taught you how to do where you used to live. You're gonna be on your own next month, so don't be foolish," he concluded.

"You too Maurice? Why everybody think I'm gonna show out and act a fool over there?" I asked him with a serious expression on my face.

"It ain't that, it's just we don't want to have to get on a plane and come find you if something go wrong. We like being on the ground," Maurice joked.

"I won't act up, please believe, so you won't need to worry and I'ma pack the knuckle rings you gave me just in case," I replied. I stood up and walked toward my dresser, then opened the top drawer and pulled my custom purple brass knuckles out from the back corner of the drawer. I held them up and showed them to him as visual proof of my back-up safety plan. If anything serious were to go down, I'd be ready to fight, and I'd do what I'd have to do to keep my friends and family 'on the ground'.

* * *

The questions and criticisms I got from my friends and family were overwhelming, and I didn't know how to answer a lot of them. They kept asking me things like I was the expert on Europe travel, and criticizing me for not having answers. I had to keep reminding them that it was my first time leaving the South! I didn't know much about anything over there, at least not yet.

The whole month of May was an overwhelming blur. I had so much to think about, but not much time to reflect. The only thing that was clear was the fact that I would be on a plane within the next month, holding my breath and praying that the plane didn't crash. I would be one of hundreds of people sitting still in a giant, white flying cylinder, soaring through the sky at five hundred miles an hour across the Atlantic Ocean. I'd be praying that I'd land safely at the airport with all my luggage and sanity intact. I wondered what Darrien would do without me around, or if he'd miss me as much as I'd miss him. That boy drives me crazier than he'll ever know! In fact I've tried to let him know before, but he wasn't trying to hear it. One month until Paris, and until then, the only way I'd be able to take my mind away from thinking about the trip was by grinding at work. Work would keep me from thinking too much about everything else, and I'd be making money, so I'll just stay thinking about stacking that paper!

Chapitre 15: False Notification

I wasn't having a good day when I went to work on Friday afternoon; it was Memorial Day weekend and the dinner rush had started early, so not only was Zoe's Roasthouse busier than usual, but the lines of people waiting to get seated and get their three-day weekends started at happy hour were consistently long. I struggled to smile through my uneasiness, and acted as if everything was fine. It was hard to focus on seating the crowds of anxious diners with all the thoughts about Europe floating around my head. I was feeling tired about preparing for my trip and was upset that I had to take passport photos that morning and my hair hadn't come out looking the way I would've liked. On top of that, the old man photographer at the passport photo place copped an attitude when I told him I didn't like my picture and he wouldn't let me retake the photo, well at least not for free. He could've told me that my earring was crooked and that my hair was sticking out of place on one side, but nope, he just let me sit there and pose for one of the worst photos I could possibly take!

The anticipation of my trip to Europe overwhelmed me every single day; I still wasn't sure if I'd have enough money to truly enjoy my time there and thinking about getting on a plane instantly made me nauseous. Doubts kept slowly creeping in as the days crept by, but I decided I would take the trip no matter what, and would not allow anything, not even doubts, try to stop me. I had less than a week to earn the rest of the money for my plane ticket, and a few weeks remained before I would actually take off. Part of me still couldn't believe that I had gotten accepted into the program in the first place. Every time I checked my email, I half expected to see a message from the school informing me that I had been accepted by mistake and was not eligible to attend school overseas.

'Dear Ms. Davis, our sincere apologies for the false notification of your scholarship award and program acceptance. We apologize for any inconvenience this may have caused. Better luck next time,' I imagined the message would say. The amount of self-doubt and anxiety flowing through my veins was enough to fill up Lake Beauconte, but the feelings faded away when I cleared my thoughts and repeated this same phrase: *They chose me and I'm going. The only thing I have to worry about is money!*

The proof was in the pamphlets, in bold Courier font, in the form of a series of email messages and inch-thick information packets that had been arriving in my mailbox on floral colored paper over the past weeks. The proof was in the smiles and small talks that Ms. Cole and her office staff had been passing off in the campus hallways before the semester ended—it was like everyone in that office knew about my trip and wanted to congratulate me on winning the scholarship. It felt so nice to be congratulated and to finally be noticed for something. I really was on cloud nine!

Bonjour & Bienvenue à la France Ms. Dabresha Davis. The headline was bold and clear at the top of the official notification letter I got in the mail from the SDAO office. **Hello and Welcome to France** the subtitle clarified. **'Welcome to *France.* Your journey begins on June 23rd. Congratulations on being selected to attend one of the most prestigious universities in Paris.'**

At some moments, I was blissful at the thought of the trip, but feelings of worry continued to shadow my excitement. Could I really survive six weeks across the world without my family, my friends, and above all, without money? I knew Maurice wouldn't be able to help much financially, but I was content knowing that he had not even hesitated in allowing me to go on the trip. I'm sure he appreciated me doing something good with myself, in strong contrast to Delilah who kept missing curfew and was again in danger of not graduating high school. *I'm almost there*, I kept thinking. I'm only $340 away from affording the plane ticket. After that, it's official!

I gazed out the giant glass windows that faced my hostess stand at Zoe's Roasthouse, staring at the parking lot of the small town world I knew and was preparing to leave behind. My palm hugged my cheek while my elbow rested on the chic, wooden booth that welcomed the restaurant guests. I was only halfway through my shift, and the last half of my shifts habitually slowed down to a crawl. Daydreaming about my trip helped pass the time, and thinking about Darrien helped me to smile through my boredom. I was so zoned out during that particular shift at work that I nearly jumped when Zeke tapped me on the shoulder shortly after I seated a ritzy family near a window table.

"Hi," I said startled. Had I accidentally given away a reserved table? Did I forget to ask another set of guests for their drink order? My eyes widened as I surveyed Zeke's expression. I quickly took my elbow off the hostess stand since Zeke had reprimanded me in the past for 'looking bored' at the front counter. I was supposed to stand with good posture and appear interested in my hosting activities at all times. I snapped out of my slouch and half-grinned at Zeke.

"The party in the banquet room wants to see you," he stated, offering a half-grin of his own. I scrunched my eyebrows, confused as all heck. What person dining at this kind of restaurant could possibly want to see me? Certainly, no one I knew personally could afford to eat here.

"Who is it?" I asked Zeke politely, "you sure it's for me?"

"Not too sure. Just go see and I'll manage your post for a bit."

I looked at Zeke with squinted eyes and hesitated to leave the hostess stand. He lightly pushed my shoulder in the direction of the banquet room. "It's okay Bresha, we finally startin' to slow down."

I peeled myself away from the hostess stand and cautiously walked down the dim-lit hallway that led to the entrance of the banquet room, trying to identify the voices echoing out the room before I got to the doorway. Surely there had to be some mistake. I had been told many a time that I had a 'familiar face,' a face that reminded people of relatives or friends, so maybe the banquet group had mistaken me for someone else.

I peered into the room and scanned the small crowd of older faces. There were about a dozen people there talking amongst themselves, all dressed up kind of fancy and business-y. I instantly became flustered and was certain that I had been summoned by accident, but then a familiar voice called my name as I started to back out of the doorway. I smiled a sigh of relief as I turned back around; Ms. Cole motioned for me to come to the other end of the large oval-shaped table she was seated at.

"I remember you saying you worked here, just thought I'd say howdy," Ms. Cole voiced with a warm smile. There were a few envelopes scattered across the table in front of her, between a series of ceramic coffee cups and glasses full of ice water with several droplets of condensation stuck to the sides. Ms. Cole introduced me to the people sitting closest to her; all were staff members of the college, and they all smiled at me and congratulated me on my trip. I found it unusual that all of Ms. Cole's associates seemed so interested in me; they asked me a myriad of questions about all different kinds of things including my schooling, my family, and my life. They asked the usual questions regarding how excited I was, but also asked about my personal goals and my hobbies. I wondered if it was their job to pretend to be interested in the lives of students, or if they were just trying to fluff up some small talk.

To ease my apprehension, I asked a few questions of my own to the people sitting closest to Ms. Cole and asked them if they had any advice to give me. An older man named Clarence gave me some tips on traveling through Europe, and another woman, who introduced herself as Bernadette, assured me that my trip would be well worth the butterflies in my stomach. I asked Ms. Cole if Miryam or any other students from SRJC would be going on the trip.

"Yes there are a few more who've been selected for other programs, but unfortunately, Miss Oseguera won't be attending."

I frowned at the news. I had run into Miryam in the school hallway the same week I won the award and found out that she had also won a scholarship of her own. We had hugged and I was so excited for her, but she said her parents, particularly her dad, weren't completely on board with her decision to go abroad; they told her that she needed to stay home and watch after her younger siblings and that her family duties were more important than any reason to leave Texas. I could tell Miryam was really upset about it and may have even had some mild resentment toward her family over it, but she congratulated me anyway and wished me luck on the journey. Miryam promised to 'press' her parents and try to convince them to change their minds in the weeks before the trip, but Ms. Cole affirmed that the convincing didn't go too well. In that regard, I was even more thankful that Maurice was a more lenient type. He didn't put up much resistance when I told him about my intent to try studying in Europe, and to my surprise, he actually reacted very calmly. He even told me not to worry about paying rent for the entire summer!

My cheeks hurt from smiling so much by the time I told

Ms. Cole and her associates that I had to return to my hostess stand; Zeke had peeked in the room and gave me a look that implied he was ready for me to come back to the front, or that the restaurant was starting to get busy again. I made the effort to smile at Ms. Cole and her associates again when they finally left the restaurant an hour later, though my fatigue and job jadedness had long already kicked in. It felt kind of good seeing someone familiar at work, even if it was only someone only slightly familiar from school. It made me feel special to know that someone who came into the world-class restaurant knew *me*! Surely my co-workers had to be a little envious and a little curious about my connection to the people in suits and ties that requested my presence. I couldn't help but smile.

Rita, the stout, older waitress that had assisted Ms. Cole's banquet party throughout the night, approached me a few minutes after they left.

"The banquet group asked me to give this to you," she said, lending a peculiar glance. I slowly grasped the plain blue envelope Rita was holding while she waited for an explanation.

"Thank You Rita," I said abruptly as I set the envelope down on my hostess stand. I could feel Rita gawking at me from the other side of the foyer, waiting for me to open the envelope or justify why I had received it.

"They work at my school," I interjected. Rita grimaced as she strutted back to the main room of the restaurant and as soon as she was out of sight, I carefully tore the tape off from the corner of the little blue envelope.

I quickly removed a tri-folded blank sheet of paper from the envelope and a smaller gray piece of paper fell from inside of it, whirling down in a funnel shape before it glided across the tile floor. I gasped as I squatted to pick up the piece of gray paper off the floor and slowly stood back up. It was a check, and the title line was addressed to Ms. Dabresha Davis (AIS airfare) in the amount of $734, on behalf of the SDAO staff, and endorsed by Ms. Myrna Cole herself. On the memo line were written two familiar words that I had come to know very well: Bon Voyage!

Chapitre 16: Three Suitcases, Two Passport Photos, One Mission

I darn near sprinted to the bank the next morning with the check that Ms. Cole gave me—I had to make sure it was real! I had never been given a check that big for anything to tell the truth, so I felt antsy carrying it around in my purse. I kept checking to see if it was still nestled inside every few minutes because I was flat out paranoid that someone would steal it or that it'd fall out and a breeze would pick it up and blow it away into a sewer drain. Even though the check funds weren't going to me specifically (hence the words AIS airfare in parentheses after my name), it still felt like the greatest present. I was amazed at how nice Ms. Cole was, and though she hadn't given me her personal money, I knew she had a hand in setting up this favor.

Either way I looked at it, I had truly lucked out running into Ms. Cole that very first day on the elevator. If it wasn't for her, I would have never thought it possible that I, of all people, could travel overseas. If it wasn't for her, the idea of studying abroad and applying for a scholarship would have never even crossed my mind. She was an angel in disguise, concealing her identity behind dress suits and lace fronts. For reasons I could not understand then, she wanted to see me succeed and do well in my studies and ultimately in my life.

I planned to cash the check at the bank, stop by the post office to mail off some final paperwork, then pick up some of the 'recommended items' from the program packet at Wal-Mart. I already had more than enough clothes and shoes to go there with, so I wasn't going to waste money buying things I didn't need. I was just going to purchase things I didn't have that the study program recommended.

Darrien met me at the bank parking lot and let me borrow his car. He left me his keys and I barely had time to give him a hug before he hopped in his roommate's car, which was following right behind him, and took off. Once my bank trip was done, I was going to buy some healthy groceries at the market. I really wanted to lose a few pounds before the trip so I could feel at least a little better about my body while I was overseas. I was already disappointed in myself for not losing fifteen pounds by summer like I planned to, but if I lost even just a few before I went on my trip, I would at least have a start on that goal.

When I walked inside the bank, the lady working there looked at me so crazy when I asked her how much it would cost to exchange currencies and buy stuff with my ATM card overseas. Her name plate read Londa Rae and she was always feisty. I hated having to go to her window whenever I went to the bank, but since it was a small bank with only a few tellers, it was almost guaranteed that I would have to deal with her on any given visit. She's one of those people that doesn't seem to like her job or the customers she has to deal with, yet continues to show up at work month after month with a stuck-up attitude and fake smile. Don't get me wrong, I'm not in love with my line of work either and I doubt anyone I work with truly loves serving stuck-up rich people in any capacity! But I don't let my resentment show *that* much and don't rub my mood off on other people.

Besides, my boss doesn't play. If we look like we're crabby about something, he will tell us straight up. He fired a new hire one time because he always showed up to work looking tired and rarely ever smiled, so a few customers lit up Zeke's voicemail with complaints. I guess that's what customer service is though; you have to show up and smile no matter what because customers will only come back if they liked the way you treated them. Londa Rae's boss probably hadn't gotten that memo about good customer service, so Londa Rae got away with being rude to people as often as she pleased.

"Give me a moment while I find that out," Londa Rae answered with slight irritation in her voice. "We don't get questions about overseas transactions often so hold on."

I rolled my eyes as she walked away from her window to consult with one of her co-workers about my inquiry. She came back to her station a minute later and gave me a look of disbelief.

"What country is you traveling to?" she asked brusquely. She scrunched her nose up at me and squinted one of her eyes.

"I'm going to two countries: England and France," I answered assertively. I smiled afterwards, realizing that I never thought those words would leave my mouth the way they did. I was really preparing to travel, and it was crazy how things happened so quickly and how so much changed in a matter of weeks. If you would've asked me two months ago if I had planned to travel anytime soon, I would have laughed in your face and called you insane.

"Hmm," Londa said softly. She gave me one of those quiet 'hater stares', but I kept on smiling. No one in Texas, not even 'Londa Rae the Queen of Mean', could take my happy away that day. She slid a pamphlet to me through the small half-circle opening of the bullet-proof glass window of her desk.

"Look through this here pamphlet. It has all the prices the bank charges for making purchases in different countries. Europe is page four."

I grabbed the pamphlet and started to thumb through it. It was thick and had all kinds of information on using bank funds overseas. There were *so many* countries listed inside the pamphlet and I wondered how many countries actually existed in the world. I would only be visiting two, and the thought made me curious about how big the world actually was, and how small Texas, even with its massive size, really was in comparison. I had never thought of Texas as small before; Texas was big and everything's big in Texas! But Beauconte was just a tiny part of a small section of Texas, which was just one state in all of America, and America was just one country in all the world. I started to daydream a little, then snapped out of my daze when Londa Rae interrupted me with a banal "is there anything else I can help you with?"

"No thanks," I replied. I made sure not to say ma'am because I'm not wasting my breath for just anybody! I did feel a little guilty for having secret pleasure in telling Londa Rae that I was going to travel though. I would be leaving small-town Beauconte while she'd be stuck working in her dull, unhappy little glass cage. I wanted to scream, 'Look at me! I'm going somewhere and you're not!', but I pushed my ego aside for the time being since My mom always used to tell me that it was better to keep quiet and listen then to talk before thinking. In this case, my mom was probably right. My mouth would get me into trouble if I truly said what was on my mind (and it surely had many times in the past).

I jovially left the bank, doing a little skip and hop once I was out of the building, then let my happy bubble burst when I plopped down in the front seat of Darrien's car and remembered my packing was nowhere near complete. Two large suitcases and a carry-on bag was not enough space for all the clothes, shoes, and accessories I wanted to bring, not to mention the books I needed to pack! But limits were limits and I couldn't afford to pay the airline extra money to bring any more bags with me. The days leading up to the trip were an endless tunnel of stress and confusion.

Maurice offered to help me pack, but I knew he would only hinder me more than help. No one but me could make the best decisions on what to bring, but that didn't mean it was any easier. I couldn't even decide what I should wear on the plane ride! I'd be stuck on that plane for ten hours, so I would need to make sure I had a coat and things to keep me busy in my carry-on bags just in case it was cold or really boring. My mom loved crossword puzzles and word searches in magazines, so I thought about searching the attic for some of her old puzzle books and bringing them along with me. It'd be nice to have some of her momentos with me, and even nicer to have time to try and look for them!

Maurice told me that they usually play movies and give out free food on longer flights, and boy did I hope he was right! Ten hours seemed like an eternity at first, then I thought about the other things I've done that I spent at least ten hours on. I've worked a ten-hour overtime shift more than a couple times in the past when someone called out sick. The drive to Florida would have been more than ten hours if I would've gone on the spring break trip with the girls, so in that regard, ten hours didn't seem so bad after all.

Was anyone else I knew from my school going too? Would I even have time to join in on the parties Laydee specifically planned for me and the crew to celebrate my leaving? I was surprised when she mentioned them, then wondered if it was even necessary for me to attend 'goodbye' parties when I was only going to be gone for six weeks. It's not like I was moving away forever, but then again, *what if* something happened to me while I was gone and I never got to see my friends or family again? It occurred to me that it probably was necessary for me to make some visits to say some proper farewells, the first and most important one of course to Darrien. He seemed a little fazed about me going on the trip at first, even though he initially said he was fine with me doing the application, but he eventually came around. He warned me he might be too busy to see me the days before my flight, but he promised to try his best to make some time to visit before I took off and maybe take me to my favorite seafood joint for a dinner.

After I left the bank, I drove to the AIS-affiliated travel agency to buy my plane ticket. I had to wait in a giant, dark green plush lobby chair for a little bit until of the agents became available, but didn't mind the wait because the chairs were comfortable and I liked looking around the room at all the posters on the walls that had pictures from places around the world.

When my name was finally called to meet with an agent, I was back in my happy bubble and couldn't stop fidgeting while I sat in the chair across from the agent. The process was easier than I thought it'd be and it went by so quick! Larron, the man working at the agency, was really helpful and gave me lots of advice about flying overseas. He could tell I was new to the whole business of travel and had a tiny bit of apprehension about my journey, but he told me that flying these days was completely safe and that I shouldn't be worried about anything. He pretty much repeated what every other older person I came across had told me, and also gave me advice about making the flight seem shorter.

"Whenever I have a long flight, I don't sleep much the day before. That way, I knock out on the plane," he said with a friendly wink behind his thick framed glasses. Larron didn't appear to be too much older than me, so I was surprised to hear that he had taken quite a few long trips and had so much advice to give. He was lighter-skinned and slender so he definitely wasn't my type, but he was nice and his simple advice helped put my worries at ease.

I made a mental note to use his sleeping trick for my own flight because I could really care less about looking out the plane window and seeing the city or the clouds outside—I don't even like heights! All I cared about was landing, so if I slept through my flight then it wouldn't seem so long, especially if I wouldn't be able to remember it.

As I left the agency, I sent Laydee a text message telling her that I was definitely down to step out with the girls the nights before my flight. I would be ready to party and waste my last nights away, not caring about what time I got home, before taking my last nap in my bed in Texas for a while. I'd make sure my bags were fully packed so all I would have to do the next morning is drag my luggage (and myself) into Darrien's car before setting off on the hour-and-a-half long ride to the airport.

Before I returned Darrien's car to him, I picked up groceries on my last errand in town. I carried a list of snacks I wanted to pack for the plane ride and just enough food to last me until the day of my flight. I was standing at one end of the frozen food aisle at the market when I noticed a girl standing at the other end. My ears perked up when I heard her speak, not because I was listening in on her conversation, but because her voice sounded so familiar. I couldn't pinpoint from where, but everything about the way this girl talked was reminiscent of someone I knew. She had a strong southern accent, and I mean *strong*, and spoke with a distinctive lisp.

"And this fool talkin' 'bout, Keish, you know I luh you, then got the nerve to ask me why *I'm* thrippin'," the girl said.

I studied the profile of the tall girl with the mocha complexion, the girl undeniably having the loudest phone conversation in the entire market and whose lisp could clearly be heard from aisles away. She was unrecognizable as she stood behind her shopping cart even though I was certain that the voice struck a familiar nerve. I inched towards the girl, extremely hesitant. I didn't think it was someone from my college, and I didn't want her to think I was rubberneckin' in her conversation either. Maybe it was someone from high school? Or maybe even middle school?

I made my way closer to the girl, pretending to scan some items on the small shelves nearest to her.

"He be workin' my last sthraw, I swear! And he ain't even paid lasth month's child support. I don't even know why I put up with his bullshee-yith. *Fool* is dumber than dirt."

My mouth dropped wide open when I finally realized where I recognized her from, and I walked up to to her with a huge smile on my face.

Chapitre 17: When Did You Win The Lottery?

"Jakeisha girl?? I thought that were you!"

The girl I recognized in the corner market forced her neck around and gave me a blank stare, muttering 'hold up' to whoever was on the other line of her phone call. She covered the receiver with her hand.

"It's me, Dabresha Davis!" I cried. My eyes widened with the huge hope that I hadn't just made a mistake in identifying this girl.

"Oh wooooow," Keisha gasped. "I'll be damned!"

Keisha stepped from behind her shopping cart and threw her arms around me and we hugged liked we hadn't seen each other in a month of Sundays, but in all actuality, we hadn't! The last time I remember seeing her had to be over a decade ago. Keisha was one of the girl's in the dance troupe that Tamina and I used to be in, the one that wanted to go to Italy when our troupe was supposed to go on our world tour!

"Bre-Bre Davis, what the heck you been up to? I ain't stheen you since elementary! Isth you still over there on Cinder sthreet?"

I couldn't stop smiling. I never thought I would run into an old friend at the corner market of all places, and that this old friend would have grown to be so tall and thin.

"Not too far away, over on Berry Street now, workin' and takin' classes at that junior college on Lincoln. Actually just got accepted to a study abroad program in Europe for the summer, I'm leavin' in a few weeks!"

It was hard for my voice not to raise itself when I told her about the trip. I wanted to scream my news to everyone I crossed paths with ever since the day I found out I won, but didn't want to feel like I was bragging to anybody.

"Study broad, what that mean?" Keisha asked curiously.

"It means I take classes at a school overseas, in Paris." I replied, waiting for Keisha's next question to come. I wanted to talk about my trip so badly with someone who would listen and I hoped she would. I knew my girls were tired of hearing me talk about it, but it was hard not to.

"Hmm" Keisha replied blatantly.

"Where you been though? You got up, moved and didn't tell nobody! And you got so tall!" I beamed as I envied Keisha's stature. I remember Keisha always being one of my taller friends, but boy had she grown! She had to be at least 5'10", and the Timberlands she was wearing shot her up to a solid six feet.

"We in Georgia now. I'm justh out visitin' kinfolk next couple days," Keisha replied, glancing at her cell phone. "Oops!" she said with a smirk when she realized she had forgotten about the person on the other end of the phone. Whoever it was had hung up in the midst of our reunion.

Our conversation was interrupted by the sudden appearance of a small boy with nappy hair who looked to be about seven years old. He started tugging on the base of Keisha's shirt.

"Can I have a Starburst please?" the boy asked politely, looking up at Keisha.

"Boy didn't I thell you to wait inside the car wich yo cousin? Go back to the car, NOW!" Keisha screamed. The tone of Keisha's voice alarmed me a little. I didn't think yelling at the little boy was necessary.

"But you said I could have Starburst if I acted good on the train," the little boy pouted.

Keisha gave him a stern look, then started counting down

from five while looking straight past him. The boy ran down the aisle and outside the market in tears. I empathized for the little fellow because he didn't look like he deserved that kind of treatment.

"These lil' goons don't be listhenin' to no.body!" Keisha yelled between gritted teeth, disregarding the sensitive ears of the other people in the market who were peeking in our direction. I laughed nervously as I waited for Keisha to turn back to our conversation.

"You got a little brother now?" I asked surprised. I remember Keisha being the youngest in her family, so I presumed her mom had another child since she moved off.

"Girl that's my son. Sorry I didn't inthroduce you to his bad behind but he don't be followin' directions."

I tried my hardest not to look surprised while I tried to mentally calculate how old Keisha must have been when she had that little boy. She was my same age and I remember us having birthdays a month apart, and that boy had to be at least five or six.

"Congrats," I said quietly to fill the silence. It's not like Keisha was the only person my age I knew with a kid, but something about the situation still astonished me. Keisha must have had him right when she started high school. I couldn't fathom having kids anytime during my high school years or even now! Part of the reason why I gave Darrien a hard time about getting intimate was for the simple fact that every person I knew my age with kids certainly didn't plan on having kids when they did, and I didn't want to end up with an unplanned baby like them.

"Girl you'z a lil' late for congratulations. Da boy starting kindergarten in Augusth and his sisther sthartin' pre-school, but thanks," Keisha responded. I searched my mind for something to continue the conversation with. I could not imagine having TWO kids at my age, let alone one.

"You 'member my sister Lilah, right? She pregnant now, so I'll be an auntie soon. None of my own yet though…" I added, with a slight sense of unexplainable guilt. I suddenly felt bad for Delilah. Bratty or not, she would be taking on one of the biggest challenges a young person could ever have in a matter of months (seven more be exact). She was barely old enough to look after herself, so being a mom would not be easy for her.

"Girl sometimes I wish I had none of my own," Keisha joked, "and what was you sayin' 'bout Yurip? What the heck you goin' all the way out *there* for?"

"I'm taking classes there. My school got programs for students to get school credits there."

Keisha gave me a confused look, then checked her phone again.

"Okay when did you win the lottery? And can you take me with you? Shoot. I could use a break from the baby daddy and the kids," she snickered, letting out a long, high chuckle. She picked up a bag of brown sugar from the shelf next to us and dropped it in her shopping cart.

"Oh it ain't like that at all," I defended. "'I got a scholarship for the trip and I been workin' extra to save up."

"Hmmm," Keisha said blandly, "I wish they had scholarships for people who ain't in school 'cause Section 8 waitlists are bullcrap."

Keisha glanced at her cell phone again, then stuffed it into her jeans pocket.

"Well I gotta get back to my uncle's crib with these groceries. Gimme your number and we can chill before I go back to G.A.?"

"Okay sure, it's 254…"

"Oh, there the chicken flour is," Keisha interrupted,

"finish right quick."

Keisha typed my number into her phone and promised she'd get in touch with me before she left town. I wouldn't take offense if she never called because I knew we'd both probably be busy, and deep down, I knew we wouldn't have much to relate on. She was a mom and had been for quite some time, and I wouldn't be able to talk to her about anything to do with parenting. In a sense, I was still a 'kid' myself, going out to parties as often as I could and not thinking about nobody or nothing else when I went about my daily routine.

Seeing Keisha that day made me feel empathetic for Delilah. Delilah was no longer just my little sister; she was a mother-to-be. I highly doubt Keisha nor Delilah planned on getting pregnant when they did, but sometimes things happened that way and at least they had the courage to accept the responsibility at their ages. Thinking about having kids made my head hurt—I got exhausted just babysitting a few hours a week! Of course I'd want kids in the future, but definitely not now. It'd feel like my youth was over the moment the pregnancy test came up positive, but then again, I wouldn't let a pregnancy happen. I refused to let it happen, and no matter how many times Darrien would try to have me, I will not let him get it easily or unsafely. I wanted to stay young as long as I could and keep partying until I was in my thirties at least, just like my parents did.

On my way out of the market, I called Tamina and told her I had just run into Jakeisha. Tamina was just as shocked as I was—neither one of us had heard from or about her in forever! Even more so, Tamina seemed to be just as excited as I was about my trip.

"It's official, really official now! My plane ticket has my name on it and urr'thing!" I cried to Tamina, "and I'll be picking up my passport any day now!"

"I'm so happy for you Bre," she said cheerfully. The amount of excitement transmitting from my end of the telephone could have been enough to short circuit my phone's wiring. I was glad to have Tamina as my friend. I had thought this before, but it occurred to me again. She always listened to me when I needed to vent and never seemed to have drama around her. At times I wished she wasn't so quiet, but I never picked at her for just being herself. She was timid as a kid and hadn't changed much over the years, so I surely wasn't expecting her to transform anytime soon, and I'm sure she would in her own time.

"We gotta hang out for real as soon as you come back, okay? I decided on the school in Tennessee so I'll be moving a week after you come back."

"You goin' all the way to Tennessee?" I interrupted, taken aback by her official announcement to move and go to school out of Texas.

"All the way? My school's around the corner compared to your school in France. I got cousins out there and I'm wantin' to get to know my family better. I'm just... done living with my mom and I need to move away. I love her of course, but we're just very different people and I don't wanna live lazy, stressed out, poppin' medicines I don't need all day like her. She keeps askin' me for money I don't have and screamin' at me when I don't give it to her. You know how she be, so you understand, right?"

"I guess," I said, frowning as I tightened my grip on my cell phone.

"Just don't forget about us country folk while you're out in Europe enjoyin' yourself, speaking French with your Texas accent," Tamina said.

"I'm not gonna be doin' too much out there," I replied, "you know I ain't got funds like that."

Tamina was silent for a moment, then said "You'll be alright Bre, just thank God for the chance."

I sighed. Tamina, Aunt Trecee, Antoinette, and everyone I knew seemed to be oblivious to the fact that I'd be taking this trip with so few resources. They weren't understanding the worries I had about doing this trip on my own and they seemed to ignore the fact that I would be 'scraping by' for six weeks with the smallest budget known to Beauconte. But the more they started to push aside my financial worries, the more I started to believe in the possibility of a successful 'budget trip.' I had already saved up as much as I could in the last few weeks and was planning to save up even more in the little bit of time that remained.

As difficult as it was, I avoided going to the mall and taking unnecessary shopping trips the weeks before the trip. I added a few more odd jobs to my already busy schedule and constantly reminded Zeke that I was available to work extra shifts. My car repairs would have to wait, and thankfully, Tamina has agreed to braid my hair before I left so I wouldn't have to mess with it while I was there. I vowed to sacrifice all 'costly' activities until the day I left, including my trips to the salons, the movies, and the clubs. No bars, no dancing, no nothing if it wasn't free or extremely cheap. I was okay with being bored in Texas for a few weeks if it meant not being flat broke in Europe. My savings plan required extreme will-power, patience, and strength, and even though I had never saved up for anything this big before, I was determined to make it happen and hopeful that my will-power would pay off.

By the time the third week of June came, I was exhausted from all the hours I had put in at all my jobs and all the nights I stayed out late with the girls. What kept me going was the fact that I had amassed a decent sum of money for Paris, and I would be able to access my paycheck overseas thanks to the direct deposit service I set up with my job. It would only cost me a few dollars to withdraw my own bank account money from any ATM machine overseas, and I would only get charged a small percentage to buy things with my bank card while I was there. According to the information packets, the ATM's would only distribute European money when I put in my American bank card, so banking seemed like it was going to be easy. What a trip it'd be to see cute purple and pink European money spit out the machine after I put my card in (the money looked so snazzy in the brochures!).

My last days in Texas mushed together like a clump of Play-Dough, and the day of my departure came swiftly. I remember avoiding Delilah most of my last week there because I didn't want to deal with her moods or hear about her stupid belly. I remember my boss Zeke being surprisingly supportive of my journey and agreeing to take me off the work schedule temporarily and put me back on the schedule the week I came home, thus helping me avoid any official paperwork or re-hire processing like some people had to do when they left work for an extended time.

My very last night in Texas was the second day of summer, and I stayed out until four in the morning hopping around town with the girls. Tamina agreed to be the designated driver, so Laydee, Nette, and I all got hella twisted! We went to two clubs *and* a house party in between, without slowing down for a second. We ended the night at Club Escapade, our favorite hip-hop lounge in the next town over. We hid miniature shot bottles in our bras and snuck them into the club, then mixed them into the dollar sodas we ordered from the bar. I was a little upset because Darrien couldn't make it out or meet us at any of the parties, but I was okay with it since I knew he'd be dropping me off at the airport the next day.

By the end of the night, I had forgotten all about the disappointment anyway, especially when I heard the DJ say my name in one of his announcements.

"Dresses, Gents and G's, Club Escapade wants to send a very special shout out to Bre-Bre Davis, she's going to France tomorrow y'all, doin' it big and representin' for the dirty dirty the whole way! Bring back some champagne and fine wine for the homies! This next jam is for you. One."

"Oh my gawd, y'all told the DJ!" I screamed, as one of my favorite rap songs, 'Short Dress Shorty,' came blaring out of the nightclub speakers. I slammed the palm of my hand over my open mouth and my eyes started steaming up, thanks to the drinks, but then stopped myself before I got too emotionally carried away. I dramatically hugged all my friends before we hit the dance floor one last time. We were grooving, moving, and shaking until our booties could shake no more! I don't remember much about the rest of the night, the ride home, or how I managed to get in my bed with my proper pajamas and headwrap on, but I do remember waking up late the next morning with my head spinning, thankful to God my flight wasn't until the late afternoon.

When I finally rolled myself out of bed my last day in Texas, I awakened to a text message from Darrien that said: *Sorry boo, I can't drop you at the airport like you want. Something hella important popped up and I gotta handle business. I'll see you when you get back though. Be safe out there.'*

I was despondent, especially because I wasn't able to see him at all during the week leading up to the trip and I was supposed to introduce him to Maurice that day. I wanted to cry, but there was no time to, so instead I just stood up and started rearranging my suitcases again while I thought of who might be able to give me a ride and who'd be able to sacrifice three to four hours of driving to see me off.

It took all of two minutes for me to find a replacement driver; I approached Maurice while he was watching TV in his favorite living room recliner and asked him for the favor.

"Of course Bre Bre," he said without hesitation. "I got the afternoon off, just let me know when you ready to load your stuff."

I was astounded about how laid-back he seemed in agreeing to take me to the airport—I rarely could get him to agree to take me to the corner market! So a couple hours later, he loaded up all my luggage for me in the back of his truck, (thankfully too because I would've broken a nail with how heavy they were!), and we started the extensive drive.

We didn't speak much during the hour-and-a-half journey to the airport, in part because I kept dozing off, but when we finally got there, I felt a small surge of panic flash through my body and an unusual tightness in my chest.

My hands were trembling as Maurice handed me my suitcases. I looked in both directions of the airport drop-off area, which was packed with hundreds of people rolling hundreds of suitcases just like mine, then back at him. I jumped a little when a plane took off right above us and filled the air with that overpowering engine noise. Even though I was trying to play it cool like I wasn't nervous as all heck, I'm sure Maurice could tell how I was feeling and could see a hint of gloom in my eyes.

"Thank you Da... Maurice," I hesitated to say. Father's Day had just passed and I had been wanting to tell him 'Happy Belated' or something like that, but every year the holiday came around, it got harder and harder to say. He nodded his head and looked at me with wide eyes, seeming to be caught off guard by my inclination to almost call him Dad. Neither Delilah nor I had ever told him Happy Father's Day before, nor never called him Dad to his face (just to other people to help make the long story short), so we couldn't blame him for acting all oddly when those 'fatherly moments' popped up.

"Just remember your manners, and keep your brass knucks close," he said with a reassuring grin. I reached up and gave him a quick hug, even though he was never the hugging type. He patted me on my back, then took a step away from me.

"Go on, get to your gate," he concluded, jerking his neck toward the direction of the giant automatic glass sliding doors where I was supposed to enter the airport. I threw my carry-on bag over my shoulder and gripped one of each of my suitcase handles in each of my hands, then shuffled through the glass doors solemnly as the clunking sound of Maurice's old truck dwindled away in the distance. I quietly passed through each of the check-in procedures and security checkpoints, making note to follow the maneuvers of all the people waiting in the lines in front of me so I wouldn't stand out as the obvious first-time flyer.

One of the last things I remember was sitting at the airport bar and being extremely surprised that they didn't ask me for my I.D. (real or fake!) when I ordered and indulged in a few strong cocktails while waiting for my flight. I only vaguely remember boarding my flight, and can only recall a few details of the safety instructions that Donna, the bubbly flight attendant, gave. Donna shot me a dirty look while she was doing her safety presentation because I laughed when she instructed us how to use the plane's seat cushion as a floatation device if the plane landed on water—there was no way in heck that plane was going to float if it crashed into the ocean! But Donna showed us how to use the seat cushions anyway, and pointed out the emergency exits in case we needed them.

I fell asleep right after Donna's presentation, and boy did I sleep good. I wish I could tell you something interesting about that ten hour flight, but all I can accurately tell you is that the airplane blankets were extremely cozy and the earplugs worked amazingly when I asked Donna for a pair when someone's baby started crying shortly after takeoff. I think I got out of my seat once to use the bathroom, and was peeved by how tiny it was. I glimpsed at twenty minutes of the latest Fast & Furious film on the TV in the headrest in front of me while I was eating the complimentary meal, and remember thinking that the meal was surprisingly delicious before I fell back asleep to the sound of race cars. In summary, if anyone were to ask me how my flight went, I'd have to say it was pretty darn peaceful! Every mile the plane moved forward felt like a move toward freedom, and I looked forward to waking up and being as far way I could from the stress in Texas.

PART TWO : THE WORLD

"Life begins at the end of your comfort zone."
-Neale Walsch

Chapitre 18: English Breakfast

"Lay-ees and Gen-ole-men, we ask that you please remain seated with your safety belts fastened until the red light indicates that is safe to exit. Please remember to remove your carry-on luggage from the overhead receptacles and exercise caution when leaving the aircraft. Thank you for flying with UK Airways. We hope you enjoyed your flight and we wish you an extraordinary stay in the United Kingdom."

The pilot's accented announcement was indistinct when Dabresha slowly shook her head and blinked her eyes open to regain consciousness. She surveyed her surroundings and looked up to find a man with a pointy nose peering over her from his window seat and gently nudging her arm.

"Miss, do you mind?" the man said from his window seat. He was trying to step into the exit aisle of the plane and Dabresha's cramped, stiff legs were blocking his exit. She adjusted her position in her seat and allowed him to pass. *Was the flight over already?*

Dabresha couldn't believe that it had gone by so fast and contemplated the possibility of the plane having made an unexpected landing somewhere else. Or worse, maybe the plane hadn't taken off at all and she had fallen into a drunken nap before it had even lifted off the ground. But she prayed that wasn't the case as her mind stopped wandering a million different directions and she slowly came to. She remembered getting out of her seat to stumble to the bathroom, so the plane had to have flown somewhere. She hoped any possibility of being anywhere but London wasn't real as she scooted over to the window seat and gazed out of the tiny window. She surveyed the area outside and stared at a plain view of the tarmac and a terminal building which were without a doubt, unfamiliar to her. The airport she left in Texas was simple looking and the weather was clear when she boarded the plane. The place she now saw out of the window looked like something out of a science book. Not only did the futuristic structure of the building and the airport's ambiance were different, but the sky above the airport was gray and gloomy and looked as if it was preparing to rain. It was like she was in a whole different country, and Dabresha groaned once she realized that was the exact situation.

Her head pounded as she drowsily grasped the armrests around her seat, straightened her knees, and forced herself to stand up. When she raised her arms and attempted to pull her carry-on luggage out from the overhead compartment, her fatigue overpowered her and she lost her grip on her bag as she tried to take it down from the overhead bin. Thankfully, the people seated around her had already filed off the plane, so the suitcase didn't strike anyone when it bounced on the aisle seat across from her and proceeded to landed on the floor.

"Damn those margaritas!" Dabresha grunted as she tried her hardest to walk steadily through the airport passageways, trudging around and around the aisles with her aunt's floral carry-on suitcase in tow. The hallways leading off the plane seemed to continue forever, winding, twisting, and turning at different angles in a maze-like manner. The labyrinth ended at an immigrations inspection area just before the baggage claim turnstile for her flight. Dabresha spotted her suitcases on the turnstile behind the immigrations area right away and was happy that the awful floral print on the suitcase had actually come in handy for something.

Dabresha appeared irritable when a serious-looking older male customs agent with a thick mustache asked her for her passport and questioned her about her trip. *Why are you here? For how many days? Are you travelling alone? Where will you be lodged during your stay?* Dabresha tiredly gave the agent a series of taciturn responses, using as few words as possible with monotone answers before he stamped her passport with a loud slam and allowed her to pass by him. Dabresha heaved her luggage off of the turnstile soon after, then began to follow the numerous signs that indicated where arrivals of the London Heathrow Airport should go. Her legs and back were sore from sleeping in awkward positions all throughout the flight, and her head was swirling from her small hangover and from the massive amount of noise and voices surrounding her. The black girl from Texas was now just a small speck in middle of the hustle and bustle of one of the world's busiest airports.

As she wandered the airport, she looked over her shoulder and scanned her surroundings for some sign of familiarity as she tried to replay the words from her welcome letter in her head; she had read the letter a dozen times before she boarded her plane and tried to memorize the few instructions that were given. *Please remain patient upon arrival and gather near the east satellite souvenir stand. A counselor in an orange AIS logo shirt will collect you at approximately 10:30 a.m. You are encouraged to convene with other program students whose bright orange luggage tags should be identical and easily identifiable to your luggage tags.*

Dabresha looked up at a giant digital clock that peered over the airport's main corridor. It was a little after nine, and she had no idea what she should or could do until 10:30 came. She followed the signs that directed her towards the east satellite and, while making her way through the commotion, scanned the crowd to search for other young faces that were just as reticent and confused as hers. Her head was fixed towards the ground as she walked so she could glimpse at the luggage tags of everyone that passed by her. No one walking near her had orange tags, and unlike her, everyone seemed certain of where they were heading.

Twenty minutes passed before Dabresha realized she had unintentionally walked in a huge circle. She passed the same giant clock twice, clenched her teeth, then decided to take refuge at an empty café she saw on the outskirts of the arrivals area. She lugged all of her bags into a corner that masked a small dining table and plucked the skinny laminate menu card out of its place inside the table's center napkin holder. Palm on cheek, she slowly scanned the menu, stopping herself from lowering her eyelids and dozing off again. She wasn't very hungry, but she would have liked a little something to fill her stomach until the welcome luncheon started later that afternoon at the hotel, so when Tim, a sharply dressed waiter with perfectly placed sandy blond hair, approached her table and asked what she would like to order, Dabresha chose the 'English Breakfast' option that was listed at the top center of the foldout menu.

The provision offered toast, tea, and a tall glass of orange juice for a total of six British pounds. Dabresha wasn't certain of how six pounds would convert to American dollars and didn't have the energy to calculate it, so she ordered it anyway since it happened to be the least expensive option on the menu. She was satisfied that the quaint little café provided her with temporary, still seclusion from the bustling airport activity, and she was happy to temporarily let go of the luggage that seemed so much heavier than it felt back in Texas, as if some sneaky airline worker had strategically placed a few bricks in her baggage while she was sleeping in the air. Dabresha opened her bags to ensure that the items inside were appropriately hers, and when her meal arrived, she zipped them all back up before proceeding to gobble down the toast and drink the orange juice from her English Breakfast without a pause.

Dabresha lingered at the café a while longer to fix her hair and makeup, re-organize her bags, and retrieve her cell phone from the bottom of her suitcase. She powered on her cell phone and adjusted its time to match the clock in the airport; her cell phone would have no other use in Europe but to be a timekeeper and currency converter since her cell phone company did not provide service outside the United States, however she could still access her address book, applications, and old messages from outside of the country.

When Dabresha summoned Tim to provide her tab, he politely asked how she preferred to pay for her bill.

"We accept Visa, MasterCard, and most other currencies, and we can convert your total into the currency you prefer," Tim said politely. His British accent was amusing to Dabresha and made her want to giggle.

"U.S. dollas please?" Dabresha replied with a bemused expression, "and I'll pay with credit card," she concluded. Dabresha felt an air of sophistication ordering her tab in the currency of her choice and proudly whipped out Aunt Trecee's credit card, elegantly placing it on the table for Tim to collect. She wondered if flexible payment options would always be available wherever she went in England, or if it was only an option inside of the airport. She still had no idea what to expect after leaving the airport, and smiled at the cafe's stucco ceilings as she thought of the possibilities.

Dabresha's mouth dropped open when Tim returned to her table with the modified bill and asked her to sign it. The one item on the bill, English Breakfast, totaled $11.60 U.S. dollars, and Dabresha was adamant that there had to be a mistake.

"Eleven dollars, y'all serious?" she asked loudly. Tim assured her that the conversion was correct and showed Dabresha a printed page of currency exchange amounts with the day's date at the top. Tim grew impatient as Dabresha hesitated to sign the bill. Dabresha neglected the idea of providing any form of a tip, and gave Tim an offended look before handing the bill back to him.

"I can't believe you chargin' eleven dollas for lukewarm bread and a glass of juice," Dabresha retorted, "*and* that tea was nasty."

"Yes miss. Six British bounds is precisely equivalent to eleven and a half American Dollars. If you'd like me to verify the conversion once more on our device, I'd be happy to show you," Tim replied unenthusiastically. Dabresha popped her gums and muttered, "no thanks," before abruptly tearing away her copy of the receipt. She couldn't fathom how she had just spent close to twelve bucks on a tiny, bland 'breakfast'. She rarely spent that much on any meal, and the few times she had, she could at least remember feeling full and satisfied at the end. After all, her favorite banana pancake plate at the Waff Spot back in Texas was just under eight dollars and came with a lot more than two thin slices of bread.

Dabresha pouted as she briskly collected her bags and prepared them for another stroll. She had already spent more in her first hour in Europe than she was supposed to spend that entire day. She hoped whatever future purchases were to come in Europe would not be as expensive as an 'English breakfast'. She noted to herself to do all currency conversions in advance before she bought anything so there wouldn't be any future unpleasant spending surprises.

The credit card Aunt Trecee lent her allotted her five euros, or about seven dollars of spending money per day. That, combined with the ten dollars daily stipend that the study program would provide for lunches and snacks would be just enough for Dabresha to eat every day and at least attempt a tiny bit of shopping. Dabresha knew she would have to make a few purchases when she got to Paris, the fashion capital of the world, and she wouldn't have it any other way. She had to bring some fresh new gear back to Texas to show off to her friends—walking around town knowing that no one else could possibly be wearing the same outfit would be an ultimate high! And she was determined to try and locate a bottle of her mom's favorite perfume, no matter the cost, so she could bring it back home.

Dabresha didn't worry about those things just yet; she had to focus on the most important things she needed first, like groceries and school supplies. After all that was established, she would do a huge shopping trip when it came closer time for her to leave. For the next six weeks, the currency converter tool in her cell phone would become her sidekick, and she would have to remind herself that she was in 'survival mode' and would need to pay careful attention to every dollar, euro, or pound that left her wallet. Her manicures and pedicures would have to be placed on hold, and they wouldn't matter as much anyway if Darrien wasn't around. She wouldn't spend money on anything that wasn't completely necessary, like an 'English Breakfast' that could have technically waited since she could have survived a few hours without food and saved herself eleven dollars!

Dabresha fumed as she meandered around the airport with slightly more momentum than she had when she first got off the plane, giving ear to the multitude of conversations around her and to the various languages that filled the air. She felt an aura of excitement surround her. She soon realized that not everyone at the airport was speaking English; she could hear versions of Arabic, Asian, and Latin languages all around her. The airport was full of people just as foreign as her, and people just as anxious to get to wherever they needed to go in London. For Dabresha, that destination was the Hilshire Bay Inn near a famous bridge, and she speculated as to whether or not it was the same bridge she sang about as a kid that fell down on the fair lady.

Dabresha waddled her way to the east terminal, balancing her luggage and heading towards a magazine stand. As she started to pick up a British fashion magazine, she noticed a large brown suitcase next to her sheltering the jeans of a taller girl with wavy hair facing the opposite direction. Dabresha instantly perked up when she noticed the girl's suitcase displayed a large, bright orange AIS tag, and Dabresha inched towards the girl with caution, pondering whether to introduce herself as Bre or Dabresha, and whether or not to offer a handshake. Approaching strangers had never been an easy task for Dabresha, so she politely tapped the girl on the shoulder. "Hi, are you with the..." she started to say.

"Dabresha! So happy to see you!!" the girl interrupted as she threw her arms around Dabresha's neck. The girl's face lit up and though it took Dabresha a moment to realize who was hugging her, she gave a teeth-showing smile at the surprise encounter. Miryam's dad had decided to let her come after all.

Chapitre 19: The Overseas B.F.F.

"Aaah you came through!" Dabresha exclaimed, though her voice sounded at regular volume in the midst of all the commotion around them. Dabresha and Miryam hugged like they were long lost relatives. Although they admittedly didn't know much about each other aside from a few short conversations in the school hallways, the sight of a familiar face in that gigantic airport comforted them both and made them mutually feel more at ease.

"Papa changed his mind at the *very* last minute. The school let me join the trip even though I missed the paperwork deadlines. I had to go all the way to Houston to get a emergency passport."

"Proper!" Dabresha replied, elongating the word and bouncing her shoulders as she took a step back from Miryam. She realized she was standing a little too close to her and smiling a little too hard; she didn't want to give Miryam the impression that they were friends nor did she want Miryam to *think* that she was as happy to see her as she was. Dabresha didn't want Miryam to assume they were buddies just because they came from the same town in Texas, besides, Miryam wasn't black, thus according to Dabresha's Uncle Otey, she couldn't be trusted.

Dabresha quickly found out that she had flown on the same flight as Miryam. *"Crazy!"* Dabresha thought out loud. Dabresha assumed she must have missed Miryam during boarding time and at the gate because had spent all of her 'pre-flight' time at the airport bar and was one of the last people to board the plane, so it wasn't too much of a surprise that they didn't see each other. Miryam had gotten to the airport early and had a seat near the back of the plane, far from where Dabresha was seated, so though they didn't see each other in Texas, on the plane, or in that long maze of the immigration inspection line, they eventually found each other in London. Since it was the first time on the plane for both of them, they chatted about their experiences on the airline. They both shared a common anxiety about flying, and both agreed they were just extremely happy that the plane had landed in one piece.

Miryam told Dabresha there was some heavy turbulence halfway through the plane ride, somewhere south of Greenland, so Dabresha was especially thankful she could not remember the flight and told Miryam that she slept through most of the ride. Dabresha deliberately left out the details of her insomnia the night before and the abundance of cocktails she drank before she boarded the plane; she didn't want Miryam to think she was an alcoholic or some kind of crazy person, so she simply told her she was tired from staying up all night packing and had slept peacefully through the flight as a result.

One by one, other 'orange tag' students started to join the small circle Dabresha and Miryam had started by the magazine stand. By the time Aurelie, the cheerleader-esque ginger-haired program coordinator arrived wearing her bright orange t-shirt, there were almost a dozen students standing in their little group, and almost every one of them could tell that Dabresha and Miryam had some familiarity with each other.

"How do you know each other?"

"Did you guys take the same flight?"

"Are you friends?"

The others asked the Texans the same variety of question, and Miryam and Dabresha simply responded "yes" to every inquiry with a quick flash of a smile to avoid the full explanation of, 'well… we go to the same school and barely knew each other until we both got invited to this program while riding in an elevator and we just found out that we were on the same plane.' Dabresha did try to explain the situation to the first few inquirers, but quickly gave up. Their friendship wasn't that big of a deal as far as Dabresha was concerned, and the only real thing they had in common *was* Texas.

Every student they met introduced themselves by stating their hometown and the program they signed up for. Somewhere in the mix, Dabresha met a Joe from Washington who was doing the London program, a Kate from Illinois who was also studying in London, and a Donald from Ohio who was going to Paris. Unfortunately, Dabresha was horrible with names, especially common names, so she feared she would forget them all by the end of the hour.

Dabresha was better apt to remember names that were more unique, names like her own. She vividly remembered a girl she knew in grade school named January, and a girl in her kindergarten class named Sparkle. Names like those were easy to remember, and if January or Sparkle were to ever reappear, Dabresha was sure she could recognize them in an instant. Dabresha was not very keen on 'average names', and in that regard she was a little thankful to have a name that wasn't very popular. There were already an abundance of Ericas, Christinas, and Jennifers in the world causing confusion to the masses, and Dabresha vowed that her future kids would have original names, nothing too extreme like hers, but at least names that weren't already oversaturated in every school's yearbook and every person's phonebook.

While Dabresha was introducing herself to a school of fish in a sea of common names, she was pretty certain she had forgotten most of them within seconds of learning them. Dabresha did remember the names of the boys in the group because there were only a few there. All but one of the boys was Caucasian, and one was Hispanic. Dabresha denied the possibility of checking any of them out, after all she had a nice chocolate man back in Texas! Furthermore, she never regarded boys that weren't black and never thought twice about looking at a boy outside her race, not even mixed boys, as she was set on only dating the type of dark, rugged men she grew up adoring. She was sure it'd be easy to keep her eyes from wandering around at the abundance of European boys she was sure to encounter in the following weeks.

Every student Dabresha met in the airport that first morning came from various parts of the country; the majority of them came somewhere from the east coast and a few flew in from the Midwest. Dabresha remembered meeting one girl from California who was skinnier than a stitch of grass, confirming the rumor she'd heard about all California girls being built like twigs. Dabresha kept her introductions with every new face short and sweet; she didn't want to say too much or scare anyone off with her country accent since that's usually what happened when she conversed with people from outside the South. They always commented on her accent and asked her to repeat herself on things they couldn't understand, and Dabresha definitely did not want to be singled out in this group. She simply introduced herself as 'Bre from Texas' and told them about her school and her flight.

Dabresha wondered why no one else felt as bewildered as her about being in a new country. She was envious to learn that the east coast students had flights that only took half the amount of time as hers, and considered the east coasters lucky for not having to be on their planes so long. She supposed that's why not one of them seemed to be as apprehensive about their flights as she and Miryam were, and she assumed a lot of them had flown on planes before since many of them mentioned having traveled to Europe in the past. Only Miryam knew that Dabresha had never flown before, so Dabresha felt singled out even though there was no need to. At least now Dabresha could claim she's flown somewhere if anyone were to ask her; the trip had given her that experience before it had officially begun, so she could at least check that accomplishment off her list.

Dabresha's eyes lit up when Aurelie, the program counselor, finally escorted the group outside of the airport after she conducted a roll call. There were several black vans waiting by a curb outside the exit with orange placards on the side doors so the students could easily identify the cars designated for their group. Every student climbed into their car of choice after Aurelie checked their names off a list. Dabresha's driver, a portly man with balding hair, helped Dabresha and her fellow group of students load their luggages into the trunk before everyone took their seats. Dabresha stared at the driver inquisitively when he took his own seat on the right side of the car. How strange it was to see a car with the steering wheel on the opposite side! Dabresha remembered seeing cars like that in movies, but never actually saw one in person nor had the chance to ride in one. When the driver drove, he drove on the left side of the road, and he maneuvered the van's stickshift with his left hand. It made her a bit uneasy since she couldn't imagine controlling her stickshift with that way if she wasn't left-handed, but she assured herself she'd get over it.

Dabresha stared at the cityscape around her with quiet amazement, save for a few "oohs!" and "aahs!" she exchanged with the others in the car. There were so many sights amongst the buildings she passed and all the different types of people on the street, and to her surprise, even black people! She was comforted in knowing that she wouldn't be the 'only one' in London like she feared in the beginning. Even though Ms. Cole mentioned there were plenty of black people in Europe, she still feared she could be an obvious minority until she saw the truth for herself. Then again, she would have to hold her breath until she got to Paris as London would only be included in the first four days of her itinerary. Hopefully, just hopefully, Paris would have black people too.

Something about London felt magical to Dabresha, but she couldn't quite pinpoint where the feeling came from. Maybe because it was an entirely new place to her and the excitement intensified with every unfamiliar thing she saw. No matter what it was, there was something in the air that gave Dabresha a bit of amazement and made her hesitant to blink—she didn't want to miss a thing!

When the procession of black vans finally pulled up to the Hilshire Bay Inn, Dabresha couldn't wait to throw her suitcases in the room and leave to start exploring the streets. She and Miryam agreed to share rooms since the program counselors had given everyone the option of choosing a roommate or accepting an assigned roommate for the first part of the trip in London.

Dabresha and Miryam couldn't stop giggling as they slowly pushed open the door to their room and began to permeate their London suite. The room was narrow and simple, much smaller than Dabresha had imagined and much smaller than the room she shared back home with Delilah. Dabresha didn't care much about the room space since she wasn't planning on spending too much time inside of it anyway; she was preparing to hit the town and scope out as many bars and parties as she could while discovering all she could about London's nightlife in the few days she'd be there!

"Well ain't this cute!" Dabresha exclaimed as she claimed the bed closest to the restroom and hallway mirrors, planking herself across the bed with her arms out to the sides. She flapped her arms as if she were a snow angel and patted the bed's smooth blankets.

"Right?" Miryam responded, planking across her own bed. "The pillows are so mushy and… silky. I feel like a princess!"

The girls savored their few minutes of unwinding time before they both bounced right back up and quickly unpacked some of their toiletries. They left the rest of their luggage standing upright against the wall nearest their beds; they knew it would be senseless to unpack completely since they'd both be relocating to new residences near their respective schools in a few days. Miryam and all the other students enrolled in the London program would move to a dormitory at their university, while Dabresha and all the other Paris program students would relocate to an apartment-style hotel in the center of Paris. Both girls would call these cities 'home' for the next month and a half, and both girls would have to adjust to living away from the only place they had called home their entire lives.

After redressing themselves and fixing up their hair and make-up, Dabresha and Miryam scurried down the huge, winding, soft navy blue stairs that separated the giant hotel lobby from the first floor. An hour remained before the welcome luncheon would officially start, so they decided to meander around the outskirts of the hotel to take pictures. They noticed other students from the program had formulated the same idea and were also outside trying to snap their own pictures in the immediate area around the hotel. Dabresha loved the fact that the program allowed her and all the other students to do pretty much whatever they wanted as long as they attended the mandatory group meetings and went to class every day.

The welcome luncheon would be the first of the many obligatory meetings, and a 'Parisian Culture & Safety Seminar' would follow on the day the group arrived in France. The first twenty minutes of the luncheon would be dedicated to socializing with the other program students and utilizing a 'labeling station' that was set up for students to inscribe their names and email addresses on their most personal belongings in case they got lost. Then, the students would eat and listen to a presentation that the three coordinators prepared. There would be another meeting two weeks into the program in which all the students could discuss concerns, complaints, or grievances they may have encountered; an open discussion of sorts for the students to ask Aurelie and the two other coordinators any pertinent questions about their stay.

Dabresha didn't look forward to the school schedule, which was projected to consume her agenda five days a week for four hours a day, but she looked forward to all the free time she would have after classes were out and looked forward to using the metro to get around town. According to the pamphlets she read, the metro system was much quicker and more convenient than the public transport system back in Texas, and could take her wherever she wanted to go in Paris from early morning to late at night for about the same price. Finally, Dabresha was pleased about being able to attend a real university, though temporary and foreign, and being able to earn class credits that would transfer over to whichever university she would choose back home. It made her feel proud and smart—proud to have won the trip and smart because she would be attending one of the top colleges in Paris. It made her feel like she had accomplished something before the experience had begun.

Dabresha and Miryam spent well over an hour snapping pictures of everything they saw around them. Even the bushes outside of their hotel weren't spared from their vibrant photo spree.

"Get me in front of the hotel!"

"Get me by this fountain!"

"Get me standing on this wall thing by the river!"

The girls couldn't stop giggling as they called out snapshot orders to each other and exchanged ideas for poses. They made sure to smile big and bright, and though they hadn't seen nearly anything particularly noteworthy yet—well at least not any of the famous buildings, monuments or bridges that they'd heard about, they kept on taking pictures.

Dabresha slowed down her excessive photo snapping when she remembered Aunt Trecee's precise instructions about the camera. *The camera shouldn't be turned on for more than a few minutes at a time. The flash has a mind of its own, so don't bother adjusting it. Also, there's a 300 picture limit on the camera so choose your pictures wisely or be prepared to buy a new data card.*

Three hundred pictures sounded like more than enough for Dabresha's trip, but when she looked down at the camera, she realized she had already taken thirty pictures in just the first morning. She figured it'd be okay since she wasn't one of those girls who liked taking hundreds of pictures a night at a club and showing them to all her friends. Up until that week, she had never owned a real camera before, just 'got by' with using disposable cameras during those few times she felt it was necessary to have them. It often took her weeks, sometimes months, to develop pictures from her cameras. Her lack of speedy picture sharing annoyed her friends at times, especially when they were included in some of the photos on the camera and were anxious to see the pictures, but Dabresha didn't care because pictures were never a big deal to her.

Dabresha went through moments of avoiding cameras whenever she felt like she didn't look pretty enough, or felt her hair wasn't right, or thought her stomach was bulging too much. It was a secret, nagging insecurity that subconsciously controlled her thoughts and affected the way she interacted with people. Ever since she began to 'develop' as a teenager, she always thought she looked fat in her pictures. She hated close-ups because tiny pimples occasionally clustered around her forehead and though they were barely visible, Dabresha believed them to be hugely distracting. The rest of her complexion was practically baby-smooth, but all she saw when she looked in the mirror were her blemishes.

Then there was her nose, the wide mountainous thing that kids in her elementary school used to make fun of when she was little. She had grown nicely into her features by the time she was a young adult, but the casual taunts of the mean elementary age kids still swam around fresh in her head. *"Ash-y Bre-ee, nose like a sideways E,"* they used to sing to her, and the taunts a dozen years old reminded her of how unpretty she was and kept her insecurities high. Dabresha was often told she was a beautiful girl, but she was unaware of this herself. She had smooth brown skin, desirable height, favorably shaped plump lips, and curves in the right places. Her natural hair was full and luminous whenever she freed it from braids and extensions, but without confidence, none of that mattered, and to this day she suffered from her view of her own self-image.

Chapitre 20: Free-mails

To: LatreceeSoFly64@gomail.com
From: Da_Breezy254@wahoo.com
Subject: I made it!

Aunt Treceeeee !!! I'm so sorry for not calling you when I landed like you asked. The phone card I got at the airport already ran out and making calls out here cost a lotta dough! People told me it's less money to make calls in France, so I'm hopin' that's truth. Would you believe me if I told you I was on a boat today? Not no little sailboat neither, a real big ship like one of them cruise ships you see in magazines! We left London on a bus, and next thing I knew, the bus drove up this big ramp onto this gigantic ship. We got off the bus and climbed up some stairs, then BAM! I looked around and all I could see was HUGE wood floors surrounded by glass walls. The ship had a bunch of levels and a restaurant and lots of little rooms and an arcade even. It had to be the bigger than the titanic! There was even a whole big space for kids on the boat to play at and it had an arcade. Some of the kids got motion sick though and they had to sit down by the bathrooms in case they upchucked (they call it the 'loo'). Have you ever got motion sick? People kept telling me to expect some on the boat ride but I really ain't felt anything funny in my stomach.

So my first few days in London were THE BOMB!! Me and Miryam, she's this Mexican chick that goes to my school, we spent the whole time there hoppin' around town and chattin' it up with British folk. We went to a few clubs and a house party--it was really different then the college parties I'm used to but it was fun! People out here don't really dance or battle, they kinda just stand around facing the DJ and talk. My first 'international' party, I ain't never gonna forget it! London was coo and I hope the vibe (& the shopping) in Paris is the same. (so speaking of shopping, I kinda went over my daily spending limit... Spent more in 3 days than I should have in a week! But I'ma make sure to watch my spending when I get to France.) and London was tidy! I've never seen a city so clean.

I'm still crackin' up thinking about how these folk talk though. You would laugh your daylights out if you heard 'em! They speak all proper like they in one of them Shakespeare plays we had to read in high school. I didn't understand some of the folks there and some of them didn't understand me when I spoke, it's crazy! I tried to speak slow and tried not to use no slang, but I still confused a couple people. Crazy how we both speaking English and not really understanding each other! Please tell Maurice and his daughter I say howdy. I'll send you another message once I settle into my place in Paris. I'm typin' this to you from a computer station at a rest stop a few hours aways from Paris.. it cost me five euros just to use the internet for fifteen minutes, can you believe it?! But we bout to start drivin' there now. (My place in Paris!? I never imagined those words leaving my big mouth LOL). We'll be 7 hours ahead of time from you, so I'll probably be calling you when it's your morning time, but please keep checking your e-mails 'cuz emails will be way less expensive than talking on the phone no matter where I go (I should call them free-mails lol!).

Much Luv,
Bre Bre

* * *

Dabresha *finally* reached Paris, uncertain if everything she was seeing was real. It was only a week ago when she was in little Beauconte, so sure that she knew plenty enough about the world, and working her butt off to save up money for the trip. Then she got on a plane and landed in a place so odd to her that she could have mistook it for another planet. This place was more than foreign to her; had she gotten on a space shuttle instead of a plane? Certainly she hadn't, but it would take more time for her to believe that she, the poor little Texan girl who was accustomed to a lifestyle of scraping by, was thousands of miles away from home and now whose only concern was not getting lost while she walked the city. Everything about Paris was strangely hypnotic; even the air seemed unusual, but any new place can seem strange to someone who has never left their own neighborhood before.

Dabresha noticed right away how the Parisians walked around with elegant posture and wore trendy, classy clothes. It was fascinating to her, and it was as if all the same people she saw in her mother's old fashion magazines had hopped off the pages and come to life. The younger people in Paris had a style all of their own, a perfect fusion of different cultures and classic influences. Even the girls who appeared to be 'dressed down' looked flawless in style. Dabresha was mesmerized by the endless variety of shoes, leggings, and handbags she saw; not one looked the same and she could not spot one ugly accessory in all of Paris!

The foods she tried tasted different; they were not what she was accustomed to, but definitely not different in a bad way. The French foods contained a lot of rich flavors, savory creams, and thick tangy sauces, so though it was a far reach from the ultra-sweet or spicy barbecue flavors Dabresha had grown up eating, the food was still tasty in its own right. Dabresha *loved* the smells that trailed out of the bakeries every morning when she walked by them to go to school. The aroma from the 'patisseries' overpowered the sidewalks and tempted her to want to go inside and personally sample every single pastry on display. She had tasted all kinds of tarts, macaroons, sweet croissants, and eclairs, and had come to favor a particular treat called 'sacristain aux amandes'. She didn't know exactly what it was made of; it looked like a long, twisted white pretzel stick covered with white sugar and almond slices. It was filled with just the right amount of a sweet cream and it was delightful!

"My God!" Dabresha exclaimed when she took her first bite into the sacristain while walking to class on her third day of school, "this bread is on point!"

Dabresha was so entranced by the treat that she was incognizant to how many crumbs and specks of powdered sugar were tumbling onto her blouse that day. She savored every bite of every new pastry she tried since she knew it'd probably be near impossible to find them in Texas and also knew that the pastries would deter her from trying to lose weight. A lot of the foods were new to her and she was certain she had never seen them before, however she was also content on knowing that there were an abundance of McDonald's, Subway, and KFC restaurants in Paris in case she needed a break from French cuisine and a taste of something familiar.

Dabresha noticed that none of the cars that whizzed by on the street had bumping sound systems or custom paint jobs like the cars in Texas. Dabresha could only imagine how many heads would turn if Darrien's car cruised down the streets of Europe, London in particular. A car like Darrien's would undoubtedly raise eyebrows and stand out amongst the horde of small, simple, uniform cars with steering wheels on the right side. The cars in France had steering wheels back in their normal positions, but she felt the cars still lacked 'personality.'

The Parisian street dancers also caught Dabresha's eye; she would pass by a group of young performers blasting presumptuous hip-hop songs on an almost daily basis; it was quite the contrast to the groups of young trouble-makers she would see gathered on the street corners in Texas. The street dancers in Paris would do breakdancing routines and synchronized dances for the small crowds that gathered around them, then collect donations from their spectators when they finished. If there were ever crowds of spectators being entertained back on the streets of Texas, it was usually because of some form of conflict or nonsensical violence that caught the eye of those passing by or may have been partially involved.

The only place Dabresha felt safe back in Texas was on her college campus, because senseless incidents rarely seemed to happen there. She rarely saw the police or heard people fighting over money or 'baby daddy' drama. Dabresha had gotten used to seeing dope boys and ghetto girl fights around her neighborhood, the kind of girl fights where faces got scratched up and weaves got snatched out. They were all a part of the daily nonsense where she grew up, and though she tried to stir herself away from drama and the petty stuff, somehow drama would find a way to her in one way or another. Drama would throw her off track and demand her full attention, making her occasionally wish she grew up somewhere less dramatic.

Seeing young people gathered in the streets of Paris for dancing and entertaining purposes provided Dabresha a bit of soothing relief. She relished in watching the charismatic performers, and even donated to a few euros to the groups that she personally thought were dope. During her walk home from school on the same day she discovered sacristains, one of the street dancers tugged her arm and asked her to jump in and join them!

"Non, merci," Dabresha resisted at first, shaking her head furiously while smiling at the doe-eyed teenager who was wearing a red tracksuit and kept tugging at her arm. The street dancer would not let Dabresha get away, and pulled her into the center of their 'sidewalk stage'. Despite her reluctance, mainly because she still had traces of powdered sugar on the front of the dark blouse she was wearing, Dabresha let the dancer guide her, twirl her, and lead her and a handful of other audience participants through a synchronal hand-clapping to a fast-paced Reggaeton beat. Dabresha walked away smiling on a liberating high, remembering how much fun she used to have when she danced as a kid. These dancers were much older, but they always looked like they were enjoying themselves even though they probably weren't making much money.

The last thing Dabresha adored was the fact that she could buy anything and everything she wanted without having to show her I.D. The drinking age in France was lower than in Texas, and all kind of places seemed to sell wine and beer; even the Subway Sandwich shops! And though Dabresha claimed not to be a heavy drinker, she simply liked having the freedom to purchase whatever she wanted, whenever she wanted without having a cashier demand to see her I.D. The feeling of freedom was exhilarating and the vanishing of rules and regulations made her feel like she could fly. If there was anything to look forward to, it was enjoying those weeks of freedom and having her classes as her only real responsibility. She didn't have to work, babysit, or keep tabs on Delilah; all she had to do was come to class five days a week and pretend to be interested in the subject matter.

Dabresha perceived the nightlife to be vibrant and accommodating, even though she hadn't personally experienced too much of it in her first week there. She hadn't found a niche of friends to wander the city with yet, so though she hadn't explored the bars as much as she would have liked, she observed that there were plenty of lounges all over the city with friendly-looking bouncers guarding the entrances in style. All the buildings in Paris, including the apartment buildings and nightclub venues, looked like ancient luxury, built hundreds of years ago but renovated to include a modern flare. Dabresha could not imagine what a 'bad' neighborhood would look like in Paris, if one could even exist. Did gang members and drug dealers make their rounds in the medieval looking buildings she saw, in a country where guns weren't legal? No one she came across even slightly resembled a thug, and though she did perceive a few sketchy looking people on occasion, they definitely weren't the same variety of sketchy she was familiar with back home.

Dabresha was not aware of it, but her stress and general 'heaviness' were lighter than ever before. She was mostly carefree, and only occasional worries about money shortages crossed her mind. It pained her to think of Delilah going through her stuff back home or borrowing her clothes and jewelry without asking, but she figured borrowing clothes was probably the least of her pregnant sister's worries at that point. Besides, Dabresha strategically hid her most valued items in a box that Antoinette was holding at her dorm for her, so it put her mind at ease knowing that her most valued items were safe. Even though she was among strangers and didn't feel like she could talk to anyone who would really understand her point of view, she was less tense than she had ever been and less apt to show her 'ghetto' side because she feared no one around would comprehend her anyway.

Chapitre 21: Paris Euphoria

Unfortunately for Dabresha, her 'Paris Euphoria' didn't last very long. Not only was she struggling to make friends with the other students in her residence, but her assigned roommate in Paris was quite complex and far from Miryam's level of relatability. Emily was from Utah, and told Dabresha that her family forced her to do the study abroad program. Dabresha couldn't find any common ground with Emily and rolled her eyes at her everytime she walked by with a frown on her face. Emily was a quiet, sensitive, withdrawn Caucasian girl with no fashion sense, so Dabresha was annoyed around Emily because she looked like she was about to cry most times she saw her. Even when Emily talked, her voice was fragile and wavering. Whenever Emily asked Dabresha questions, her soft squeaky voice sounded like whining to her.

Dabresha liked listening to music on her headphones as she went to bed; it bugged Emily and her bionic sensitive hearing since Emily preferred to go to sleep in complete silence.

"Can you turn down... your headphones please?" Emily would ask, and Dabresha would throw her blanket over her head and pretend not to hear her whining.

Dabresha liked finding European TV stations that played music videos, but Emily preferred to watch the BBC World News if the TV was on and would say,

"Can I... change the channel?"

Living with Emily made Dabresha appreciate having Delilah as a roommate. At least they could agree on most things and had the same taste in music! Dabresha vowed to carefully select her future roommates whenever the time came for her to move out; living with anyone like Emily long-term and having to answer her every night when she asked, "Is it okay if.. I.. take my shower first?" would probably render her miserable.

Then there were her 'program-mates', the other American Students participating in the program who lived in the same residence and attended the same university, though not necessarily in the same classes as Dabresha. There were several girls that came from California and New York that clung together like magnets and seemed to be well off. They openly gossiped about other students on the trip, and not even the program coordinators were spared from their bundles of endless and pointless gibberish. These girls got under Dabresha's skin, but she faked nice in front of them in hopes they would exclude her from their gossip. The leaders of the Spoiled Brat Pack, as Dabresha secretly called them, were Ashley from Los Angeles and Chelsea from Manhattan. Both girls had artificial hair colors, wore extravagant make-up and an abundance of expensive accessories on a daily basis. They carried their school books around in designer purses and talked on their cell phones without regard to the potential cost of their phone calls.

Dabresha was in no way jealous of the girls, just annoyed by their personas as they were a direct contrast to Dabresha's simple lifestyle. These girls would complain about things that Dabresha didn't find problematic. Every time they conversed, they compared something they were doing to the 'last time' they were in Europe. Nothing Dabresha had done in her modest life could ever compare to the seemingly thousands of travels these girls had already done, or to the millions of miles of road trips they had taken in their Beamers and Audis. Dabresha was especially livid when she learned that they had been referring to her as the 'ghetto fabulous one' behind her back, but decided not to confront them in the way she wanted. The girls were nothing short of mean and snooty and Dabresha preferred not to deal with them at all, but depending on the day's excursion, the class, or the meal, she bit her tongue and socialized with them just so she wouldn't have to feel the agonizing sentiment of solitude while she was in a foreign place.

Dabresha began to lose sight about her mission and began to wonder what the big deal about Paris was. She started to perceive the town as overcrowded, muggy, and grimy. The 'city of lights' was littered with transients and trash, and she despised walking around by herself because gross old men often tried to talk to her. Then there was the rain... Dabresha wasn't fond of the fact that Paris seemed to have unpredictable rain showers. The days would start out sunny, then a rain cloud would appear out of nowhere, making it rain heavily for a short moment before the rain cloud would disappear like something out of a cartoon.

She tried to follow the weather forecasts on TV but they never seemed to be accurate. She would glare at the news forecast in the mornings, if Emily permitted her to watch the local news of course, and tried her hardest to understand the French weatherman. It frustrated Dabresha that the weather forecasts were given in Celsius degrees, and since she couldn't remember learning how to measure things in Celsius, she had to guess the temperature based on how warm she felt and based on the cloud symbols next to the temperature readings on the forecast. Any temperature above seventeen degrees Celsius was perfect, and anything under twelve degrees meant she needed to carry a light jacket. Thankfully, the weather stayed moderate and never got too cold or too rainy, which were the two types of weather Dabresha despised.

Dabresha constantly thought about Darrien and tried to

guess what he was doing at any given time of day, especially when she passed by the phone in the lobby of her residence. She would consider the time difference and call him if she sensed the time was right. It thrilled her if she could accurately guess what he was doing before, and if, he answered the phone.

"8pm here means it's 1pm there. It's Wednesday, so he's probably working at the radio station."

"It's 11pm in Texas on a Friday. He's probably at a party with his boys."

It was a little game that preoccupied her and gave her a small hint of satisfaction. Darrien rarely answered his phone, but she smiled anyway when she hung up and assumed she was right. Dabresha missed him and missed being able to reach him easier without having to count minutes to save money. She missed sending him texts and waiting for him to respond, and since internet was the only communication Dabresha had in France, she grew impatient with her limited communication.

* * *

To: D_Dare_Cares@gomail.com
From: Da_Breezy254@wahoo.com
Subject: Answer ya phone!

What it do boo?! I been trying to call you, hope you realize it's me hittin' you up. I'ma try again tomorrow at 10pm your time so please pick up your phone even if you don't recognize the number.

Europe's starting to get wack. First off, it rains hella randomly and I don't like having to carry an umbrella around all the time cuz it weighs down my bag and makes my back hurt. Next off, my roommate be working my last nerve. She's hella weird and pathetic, always whining about something, and on top of that needs lessons in hygiene. Not only does she seem to wear the same outfit every other day, but she forgets to flush the toilet and I keep finding long strands of her stringy hair all around the room. Then, there's these girls in my hotel that I can't stand and I'm two seconds away from going off on them. I call 'em the Spoiled Brat Pack 'cuz they look like those Beverly Hills-type girls that you see in the movies, plasticky and all. I walked in on them talking mess at our residence breakfast lounge. I'm not sure what they were saying but I just know they were talking about me... you know how you can just tell sometimes when people are talking mess, and you can feel it? anyways, when they saw me approaching them, they all got silent. One of them giggled, and one of them told me 'howdy doody ma'am'. That don't even mean nothing! But I just looked at her like she was crazy and chunked deuces at her. Oooh I want to slap the bright lipstick colors off their faces so they can't giggle anymore! These girls complain about everything: the food at the breakfast lounge is never the right taste or the right temperature, the hotel's not nice enough, and there aren't enough outlets in the rooms for them to charge all their gadgets. I don't see nothing wrong with the hotel or the food... why can't they just chill out?

The only somewhat cool chicks in the whole group, we're like 80 deep, are these two filipina girls from Georgia. They're both laid-back and don't brag about what they have back home or how much stuff they bought in France like the Spoiled Brat Pack, and they understand me when I talk! They got southern accents too, though not as strong as mine, and they don't look like obvious fakes like the other girls either. They don't really like going out though and I'm itching to hit up some clubs and wishing the girls were here. Me, Laydee, Nette and Mina would have tore up half the town by now!

So speaking of this town, everyone out here seems to

smoke cigarettes like crazy! You know I'm okay with a little
green smoke, but cigarette smoke gets on my damn nerve.
They smoke everywhere out here: in restaurants and
buildings and hotels even... I'm surprised they don't let
people smoke in the classrooms! I'm tired of having to
breathe it in, my nose ain't havin' it! I keep waking up with
a stuffy nose and I know it's because of all the cigarettes and
I'm tired of it.

Anyway, I gotta get off the computer cuz there's a 15
minute limit on it, which sucks because it takes longer to
type on these keyboards since the letter keys are all out of
order! and I'm also craving some sweet tea, so I'm gonna try
to find some at a café or something down the street
(hopefully at a cafe that's not filled with cigarette smoke). I
looked up the translation so I know exactly how to order it.

xoxo
Bre

* * *

"Bonsoir," the waitress at the café said to greet Dabresha
as she entered.

"Bawn-swar" Dabresha replied as she got comfortable in
her seat.

"S'il vous plait, un tay pe-shay?" Dabresha told the
waitress proudly, ordering what she believed to be a peach iced
tea.

"Quoi?" the waitress asked, squinting her eyes.

"Un tay pe-shay?" Dabresha added, "Cold. Sweet tea.
Peach," she over enunciated in English.

The waitress cocked her head to the side.

"Aaaah okay! Un moment," the waitress replied
enthusiastically, disappearing behind the cafés tiny counter. She

returned a moment later with a boiling hot cup of chai tea and placed it in front of Dabresha with a smile.

Dabresha thanked the waitress with a dismal "merci," then released a heavy sigh as soon as she walked away. Dabresha placed the palm of her hand on her forehead and watched the steam rise out of the searing hot chai tea. She burnt her tongue while trying to sample the drink before it had cooled, then ripped open several sugar packets and dumped them into the cup. The drink still tasted bland even with all the added sugar, and definitely didn't satisfy the taste of sweet tea she was craving as she slowly sipped it down.

Dabresha thought about all the parties and cookouts she was missing back home. She longed for a proper BBQ plate and some real sweet tea, not the savorless bottled liquid she found at the French convenience stores or the lackluster hot tea she had accidentally just ordered. She felt jilted and uncomfortable, and no one seemed to understand her in any language. Most of the other American students would squint an eye at her Southern accent, and the French people did the same when she tried to speak French. By the end of her first week in Paris, Dabresha was not content and sincerely believed she was ready to return to Texas.

"I wanted this trip, right?," she asked herself as she stirred more sugar packets into her chai tea. "I won this trip for free and I wanted this."

Dabresha glumly paid the waitress before she headed out of the café and started walking back to her residence. Thoughts of disappointment and dissatisfaction danced around her as feelings of nostalgia weighed heavy on her mind. She was homesick and longed to be back in Texas where she felt like she belonged—a place where she knew exactly where to find real sweet tea, what to expect from the day's events, and a place she felt connected to.

She entered her residence and went right back to the

computer station, anxious to see if Darrien responded to her email. When she confirmed he hadn't replied yet, she began to write a new email to her Aunt Trecee. After a week of discovering all of what she believed Paris had to offer, she slowly typed the words to the title of her email so they said: *'Ready to Come Home.'*

Chapitre 22: Paris; City of Frights

TO: Da_Breezy254@wahoo.com
From: MiryMexicaniMami@gomail.com
Subject: hey!

Hola chica, how r u? How's the weather in Franceland?? You see any cute guys yet?

I need details like a.s.a.p!! I'm lovin' London, but I think I'd be loving it more if you were still here. These other kids don't know anything about Texas and how bomb it is. I mainly hang out with these two girls from Virginia. They don't really like going out or shopping, and as you know those are my two favorite things haha. They're cool, but they're not as fun as you!

The club scene is crazy out here, and the boys are sexxay! That club we went to on our second night was just a sampler of this place... every club I've seen has gotten bigger and better!

People always ask me where I'm from cuz they can tell I'm not from England, and on top of that most of them think I'm from Spain or 'Maghreb', that's what they call North Africa, but I let 'em all know what's up! Texas by way of the Yucatan and Honduras. I represent all three places!

I still find these people's accents so funny. They're supposedly speaking English but they're really not! British English is hella weird... I don't even understand them when they talk sometimes :-o It's like I wanna shake 'em by their shoulders and scream "stop talking like that!" lol.

How is your room and your roommate? Our new place isn't too far from the hotel we stayed at in the beginning and it's super cute. The building is kind of medieval looking but the decoration inside is so modern and chic! Some of this stuff would look cute in my room back home. I wonder if they'd notice any of it missing...

I attached pix I took of my room. The picture of us in front of that giant ferris wheel is on the wall behind my little desk with a bunch of other pictures I brought of my family and friends back home. I found a place that prints pictures for only fifty pence— it's probably the least expensive thing I've seen in all of London LoL. I'd die of shock if I found a dollar store or a '1 Pound' store in this pricy town.

My eye candy at the moment is this cutie who works at the reception desk. I never thought any kind of arabic boy would ever be on my radar, but he is fiiiiine! and he's tall! We always flirt with each other at the front desk, but then there's Flavio... the hotel's restaurant greeter. I think he has the same kind of job like you have back in Texas. We smile at each other every time we walk past one another, and I think one time he tried to talk to me but his co-worker interrupted us. I hope he gets the cojones to say something to me soon. He's tall and muscular too girl and he's Portuguese supposedly. It's hilariously sexy hearing him speak with a British/Portuguese accent!

My roommate's alright. She's from Michigan and she's my same age. Me and her talked about moving back here one day after we finish school. It sounds crazy right, but this place is friggin' brill! (that's the british word for awesome). The only thing that sucks is how much it costs to do stuff here. Everything is almost double of what it costs in Texas, so if I ever live here I'd have to make sure to have a job that can pay for all of the things I'll need. So update me when you can mija! I know you're probably having too much fun to even check your e-mails, but reply to me when you can, k?

I can't wait for us to reunite in dos semanas! We gotta do it big when I come out there with the group for the weekend excursion so be ready for me!! Being in Europe is like a dream I wish I never had to wake up from, it sucks that it's already almost half over. G2G for now chica: Flavio's working so I'm gonna dress super cute and try to get his attention on my way to class (yea I said that!)

Cheerio mate! (that's bye in British haha)

besitos from Miry

p.s. I just found out I'm going to be an auntie again, so me and you are both going to be aunts at the end of this year! trippy! How is your sis doing by the way?

* * *

"Demoiselle, attention!"

A vendor with prominent cheek bones shouted as he ran to help Dabresha pick up the contents of her purse off of the pavement. An adolescent thief had just attempted to pickpocket Dabresha, but she noticed right at that critical moment and was able to snatch her purse away from him. Everything inside of her purse came tumbling to the ground when Dabresha tried to reposition it and zip it closed. By then, the thief was out of sight and had already scurried off to find new prey.

"What?!" Dabresha shrieked. She flashed a panicked,

suspecting look at the young man who had shouted at her.

"I don't need no help! No thank you! Non merci!" she exclaimed as she tried to shoo him away. She started to collect herself and her things off the concrete. The young vendor smiled at Dabresha and offered her a hand, despite her hostile glances.

"It's broke!" She mumbled as she tried to hold back tears, "the camera," she continued. She looked up at the young vendor then back down at her things on the sidewalk, shaking her head furiously.

"Aah ze cam-ee-rah, yes, it has a scar."

It took Dabresha a moment to realize that she had been speaking English to the vendor and that he had been replying to her in English too. Dabresha stood up and stared into his light eyes with curiosity. He had a darker skin tone than the average person she saw in Paris, but he was definitely French.

"You are British?" the vendor asked politely as he handed Dabresha her passport booklet and lip gloss.

"I'm from Texas," she snapped. She flashed the front of her passport booklet toward him before quickly burying it in the depths of her purse where it was housed just moments before the pickpocket came along. She was mildly annoyed by the young man's inquiries while she tried to gather her things and suddenly regretted choosing to do solo sightseeing after her classes let out. The vendor stared at Dabresha, in awe of the curvy brown 'mademoiselle' who almost got mugged in front of his souvenir booth.

"Ze camera, it is just a zthing. A zthing can be replaced, no?" the young vendor politely asked Dabresha.

"It's not *mine*," Dabresha retorted. She rolled her eyes at the young vendor and continued to abruptly gather the rest of her things from the ground.

"T'en fais pas, don't werr-hee," the vendor assured her

with a friendly wink. He handed her the last of her possessions.

"I'm Gabriel, and you?" he asked.

Dabresha was silent, wary of giving her name to the wavy-haired light-skinned boy with almond eyes. Flustered, she turned to walk away.

"So you don't have name?" he persisted. Dabresha gave him an irritated stare as she rushed toward the metro station. "I gotta go," she called, "but thanks. Merci."

"It's okay, I'll know your name soon or late," he replied with a sly grin. Dabresha gave him a sideways look, clutching her purse closer than ever to the side of her chest and under her arm as she fled. She was already having a bad morning, and the unsuccessful mugging incident surely didn't make things better. She sighed heavily and plopped down on the worn, graffiti-ridden metro seat, scanning the immediate area of empty chairs around her to ensure that there were no other child thieves lurking around in the metro station's shadows. Gabriel's parting comment replayed in her mind like a broken record. *Why did he say he will know my name?*, she thought. *Why was he so damn helpful?*

As Dabresha situated herself aboard the metro train, she started to rummage through her purse with the intent of trying to assess the damage of Aunt Trecee's poor little old camera. The camera was already difficult to operate, and Dabresha had counted three or four pieces, probably all unfixable, when she and the vendor started to pick the parts up off the ground. For some reason, she could not find any of the pieces anywhere in her purse when she began looking for them on the metro. Her wallet, her passport, and make-up supplies were all there, but not one piece of the camera was anywhere to be found.

She searched every corner, crevice, and side pocket of her purse, then continued to search as she approached her student residence. She didn't want to search through her open purse too long while she was standing in the streets as the program counselors had strictly warned every female to keep their purses zipped closed and to not 'look lost', even if they were, in order to increase their safety.

Dabresha tried to walk with certainty as she hesitantly wandered the streets of Paris with caution, positive that she hadn't left the camera on the subway since she hadn't even taken it out of her purse since the incident. Apprehension began to tear at the core of her chest as she climbed the stairs of her student residence and rushed to empty all the contents of her purse onto her bed.

"Ah HELL naw!" she squealed when she realized the inevitable and confirmed her worst fears in the safety of her dorm space. "That *fool* stole my camera!!"

Chapitre 23: The Nerve

Dabresha flew out of her Parisian residence the next morning fully intent on cussing out the sly young vendor that 'assisted' her the evening before. *The nerve of that fool!* she scoffed while bolting down the sidewalk, her head visibly shaking as she boarded the metro. She was prepared to give Gabriel the cussing out of a lifetime if he didn't give her back her camera. She purposely wore small earrings and packed her brass knuckles in case things would have to get physical. She envisioned herself knocking over everything on his cart and running away as fast as she could *if* he didn't give her back the camera. Dabresha was infuriated and ready to fight!

She decided not to tell the program counselors about the incident. Gabriel had stolen her personal property, but the value of the camera was probably not worth involving the program coordinators nor the police in her opinion. She rarely even saw the police when she was out and about in the city and figured they probably wouldn't be of much help anyway. What good could the police do if the vendor just denied everything and pretended he had no knowledge of her or the camera? Dabresha knew how to 'play' things pretty well with the police back in Texas, and doubted there would be much difference in France. No evidence meant no action, plus she'd look ridiculous getting everybody involved for Aunt Trecee's little old camera.

Dabresha paced back and forth down the aisles of the metro with her fists clenched. She was too worked up to sit still in one of the few empty seats and felt she would snap if anyone even slightly bumped into her. She needed to have her space while her furious thoughts were flying rampant. *I'ma cuss him out in English and he better understand me! Shoot I might throw in some French cuss words too just to get my point across. I'ma ask him nicely first to gimme back my camera, and if he don't, I'ma let loose all over his busted souvenir stand.*

Dabresha darted off the train and skipped up the dozens of metro steps with ease. Those same stairs that normally made her short of breath when she climbed them were invisible that day. All the frustration, homesickness, and heavy emotions she'd been concealing since the beginning of her trip were minutes away from being lashed out on that poor, yet cunning, young vendor.

She decided she would wait for the vendor to show up at his stand if he wasn't already working when she got there. She wasn't going to resort to violence unless it was absolutely necessary as the program counselors had forewarned every student that criminal punishments were much harsher for foreigners in Europe. She briskly rounded the street corner where her favorite bakery stood; the smell of fresh pastries nearly distracted her from her goal, but once she eyeballed Gabriel's cart in the distance, she continued on her mission. She saw him and his thick wavy hair shoved under a navy blue baseball cap. He stood with fervent composure in front of his vendor booth. She approached him from behind with incredible energy, aggressively tapping him on the shoulder and ignoring the fact that he was conversing with an elderly madame.

"Hey fool, I *know* you got my camera," she exclaimed as she grabbed his left shoulder and forced him to turn around to face her.

"One moment, mademoiselle," he replied calmly, causing Dabresha to widen her eyes and become even more furious. Her mouth dropped open as she whispered the words "oh hell no," and lifted her index finger.

"How *dare* you act all nonchalant and ask me to wait right

now?"

Dabresha yanked at his left arm, just as he handed change to the petite madame in front of him who was evidently oblivious to the amount of tension in the air. Dabresha's patience had long dissolved, and she began to tap the ball of her foot on the pavement as Gabriel gave the older woman one of the famed double cheeked kisses that she had seen so many times in France. Her nose scrunched up in disgust; Dabresha was having trouble getting used to the fact that everyone in France seemed to greet each other with 'bisous'; friends, families, and strangers of both genders were all subject to the unique French amicable salutation—she even saw police officers exchanging bisous with one another!

Gabriel took a key out of his pocket and slowly started to open a cabinet that was mounted on the side of his booth.

"Did you hear me *fool*? I said give. me. back. my. camera!" Dabresha shrieked with sharp pronunciation, clapping her palms together between each word. Gabriel ignored her insults and reached into the cabinet.

"I knew you'd come back," he said nervously. He handed her a small black velvet case with a wristband attached to it. Dabresha held out the case and stared at it with repugnance. She set it down on the vendor's souvenir stand and started to remove one of her earrings.

"What the hell is this?" Dabresha yelped. "Where are the pieces to my camera? Où mec? Where?" Dabresha shouted with fiery eyes while snapping her fingers.

"It iz there in your hand," Gabriel replied gently. He backed away from the mad mademoiselle and greeted a new customer who approached his stand to ask the price of an item. Dabresha slowly zipped open the smooth black pouch and removed her camera. It was back in one piece, polished, and had new life when she turned it on. There were no more strange whirring noises or clicks, the data card was undamaged and the screen was intact. What caught her eye the most was that the letters BRE were embroidered on the front of the velvety black pouch.

All the anger she prepared to serve Gabriel vanished within seconds, and she could feel her cheeks infusing themselves red as she gaped at him with a puzzled expression on her face and he wrapped up his chat with his customer.

"So, I suppose you name is Bre, because it's written on bottom of ze camera," he said.

Dabresha was flustered beyond recognition and she could feel her face burning red under her brown skin. Her tornado of emotions had swiftly transformed from red-hot rage to stone-cold embarrassment.

"Yes," she said abruptly. "I... have to go." Stupefied, she started to turn towards the direction of the metro station and prepared to take off just as quickly as she had arrived.

"It iz Saturday, and you must leave quickly once more?" Gabriel asked before she could take a step.

Dabresha flung the camera in her purse and started to walk away.

"I hope to seeing you again, Bray," Gabriel concluded. Dabresha didn't know how to respond to the innocent young vendor whom she had nearly thought about attacking just moments before. She was embarrassed for having grabbed his arm and shoulders so violently, and for ruthlessly interrupting his conversations with his customers when she approached him. Not only had Gabriel fixed Aunt Trecee's aged and battered digital camera, but he had made it look practically new. The camera, which was fractured and tarnished the day before, now shined with youthful life and no longer had cracks in its view screen.

It was Gabriel's plan all along, to help the peculiar stranger that had caught his eye. Gabriel was very skilled with electronics and technical equipment thanks to the fact that he also worked at his uncle's electronics shop, so he knew how to repair all sorts of devices. In France, it was typical for children to learn and take over their family's trades, so as an adolescent, Gabriel started learning the ins and outs of the electronics sales business. His Dad and uncle taught him how to build rapport with people, and told him that talking was the most successful aspect in running a business. 'Talk to and listen to the customers, and they will keep coming back' they taught him, thus even as a young man, he had been doing a decent job of helping run the family business.

When Gabriel saw the opportunity to get to know the cute 'rondelette' girl he had been eyeing every time she passed by his stand on her way to school, he did not hesitate to intervene and try to help her during her unfortunate robbery attempt. He saw it as what may be his only possible chance to talk to her.

On the way back to her residence, Dabresha succumbed to a mix of emotions; relief that her camera had been returned to her, stupidity about all the preparation she invested into diminishing Gabriel, and the subtle stress she felt in her struggle to adjust to the odd place everyone called France. The country where everyone drove tiny cars and dressed and walked around like they were on a runway, and where one too many people smoked cigarettes and carried long loaves of French bread around like they were purses. It all seemed odd to her, and though she was living in the center of the capital city of supposedly one of the most beautiful places in the world, she could not ignore the fair amount of litter, dog droppings, and graffiti she saw on the streets and in the metro stations. She was in the middle of a place that many people considered to be a dream vacation, but the 'dream' aspect was constantly overshadowed by the fact that she was in the city with no friends, no family around, and no money.

She had talked to the counselors earlier that week about the possibility of returning to Texas early due to her money shortage. All the money she saved up for the trip was close to being well spent. She tried her hardest to budget herself, but couldn't deny the frequent shopping trips and cafe gatherings with her classmates—she refused to come home empty handed! She thought she may be able to get some of the trip's deposit back if she left the program early and put the money towards her car repairs. Much to her dismay, the counselors informed her that deposit reimbursements of any kind were not possible because she earned a scholarship spot in the program.

She asked the counselors if it would be possible for her to find some kind of work on the weekends, just so she could live a little more comfortably. They told her it wasn't possible for her to work in France without a special type of international work permit, a visa, which she wouldn't be able to obtain within the weeks that remained. They explained to her that work visas were a lengthy ordeal that involved getting a series of documentations authorized in Texas, and that most people aren't able to get an authorization without a job contract in place first.

Aurelie and the other two counselors were as helpful as they could be nevertheless. They recommended supermarkets and shopping centers for Dabresha that had reasonably priced items and also gave her tips on how to save money. In the end, it still did not seem like enough, and Dabresha stayed intent on going home early and abandoning all the hard work and preparation she had already invested in preparing for the trip. She really felt she was ready to abandon every European possibility she had imagined before to return to her safe, comfortable, Texas haven.

"France just isn't for me," she thought, "it's just not *meant* for people like me to travel around the world. Mrs. Vanderkamp had a point. Laydee was right when she said I needed to keep my big, broke behind in Texas. Luxury things and luxury trips just aren't meant for people like me, like *us*. Luxury vacations and luxury cars are supposed to be for the people that are born well-off. Maybe they've all been laughing at me this whole time and just waiting for me to quit."

That night, Dabresha sent her Aunt Trecee another email about her grievances and emphasized the point that she was beginning to feel sick. She had vomited earlier that week after trying fried frogs and her stomach had been acting sensitive ever since. Twelve days away from Texas had been sufficient enough, and she was certain nothing better would come of her trip. That day, Dabresha was absolutely certain she was ready to come home.

Chapitre 24: Ready to Come Home

To: Da_Breezy254@wahoo.com
From: LatreceeSofly64@gomail.com
Subject: RE: READY TO COME HOME

Hey niecy! I'm happy to hear from you even if it's just a e-mail. Sorry I missed ya call- I was at the market picking up cake mix and done left my phone behind.

I understand things ain't been so peachy since you made it out there, but I'm gonna advice you to tuffen up now, ya hear? So you saw someone's shopping bags get stolen in the train staytion, be thankful it werent yours! I know you've seen plenty of wild things in Texas already, you didn't grow up in the Hamptons! Your in a beautiful city seeing things most people only dream about seeing, doing things most people wish of. Stop thinking about whats gone wrong and focus on the good stuff. You have no idea how prouda ya I am right now, and it's not just me, your dad and sister is too. They don't say much bout ya leavin but I know they feel the same. I be tellin' all my neighbors and all the people at the office, "my niece is schoolin' in Paris" and they all got so many questions that I can't answer. They wanna see pictures! Even lil Nattie was askin' about you, you know Ms. Charles' granddaughter. She wants you to take her there with you next time you go.

So your roommate's a little..unique. You know rich folks be sad for no reason sometime. Those pills you saw on her dresser are just gon' help her be a little less sad. You shouldn't be buttin' heads with her much 'cause you should be out doin' things! Remember not to judge nobody honey, you never know what people might be goin' through or what they mighta survived.

If you think I didn't notice you casually mentioning a boy fixing my camera, you aint gettin' off the hook that easy. What's his name and what he look like? I just wanna know a little bit more about anyone who does my niece a favor, he sounds like a very nice fella even if he made you upset at first.

Your trip just started so I know it'll get better. Everyone gets a little homesickn that's all. You a strong young lady, just focus on your schoolin'. There's no point of coming back now anyway! Trust me when I say there ain't much going on at home, and when you do come home in a month, things will be exactly the same as you left 'em. Just keep pushin'! And by pushin' I don't mean squeezing frogs out of your stomach :-p

Even though your new spanish friend stayed in London, I know there's got to be plenty of other nice young people you can find to get along with. It ain't fun spending the hole time with the same person anyway, you gotta have variety.

YOU'RE IN PARIS BRE-BRE! Dont forget all that work you put into your application and think about how many other folks would want to be in your shoes right now. I know it'll get better for ya, I just do, so keep ya chin up baby gal. I'm gonna think of these last e-mails as silly little outbursts and put a little extra something on my credit card for ya. It's not much, but it'll help ya out a bit (The Lucky 7 Scratcher finally brought this old lady a little bit of luck). I'm glad you dont mind your classes and that theres plenty of other black folk out there with ya. You teachin' me things already! I thought everyone from that part of the world were blue-eyed blonds. I love ya niecy, don't give up and remember God's watching ova ya no matter where you are.

Talk to ya soon, Aunt Trecee

* * *

To: Da_Breezy254@wahoo.com
From: Chauvalier_Gabriel@wahoo.fr
Subject: (no subject)

_____

Salut Bré, ça va? Is Gabriel, the man who réparéd your
camera. I write you this message grace to your e-mail on the
camera. I would like knowing if you are in anger at me? I
don't see you walk past my stand anymore even though it's
just near from your school. Before, I often have seen you
walk by. Sorry I didn't say you I took it but I wanted to be a
surprise. Alors, I hope you are ok and your camera works ok
too? Maybe we can see each other soon. You can write me
response in anglais or français, you choose. à bientôt,

Gabriel

P.S. you very pretty

* * *

To: DatDiva888@wahoo.com
From: SunnyDelilahful17@gomail.com
Subject: just read

_____

Hey bff!

Your phone is cut off again so I'd figure I just write u here.
THIS FOOL IS ON A GOOD ONE GIRL!! Puttin' me thru
all kinds of emotions. He had the nerve to ask me if I was

sure it was his, like I been messin' with a whole bunch of boys or some $#!t. I called him back and he said his phone lost service or whateva but I know he clicked on me. He's the only boy I ever been with and he should kn0w that! but he still has nerve to ask. I wanted him to c0me to the doctor wit me but he didn't say nothin when I asked him, then he tole me he ain't want nothin' to do with the baby! I asked him "watchu mean??!" and he told me to figure it out. The NERVE of dat boy! & to think I was starting to fall in luv wit his dumb behind before all dis happened. No wonder why his other baby momma don't give him the timeaday. I ain't trippin, who needs 'daddy' anyway? I'm just fine witout mine, who knows where that fool, and my daughter (I hope it's a girl!) will be just fine without hers. No sense in cryin any more over this fool. I don't need him n0 way. I'ma do me and be a good mom by myself, watch! U gotta help me plan the baby shower in a few months, it's gotta be huge since I never got my graduation party. After my sister's home from her trip I'll ask her to help if she still ain't mad w/ me & I'll invite her friends too even though they ain't fun like we fun. I'll get @ u layta girl.

luv. Lilah

* * *

To: MiryMexicaniMami@gomail.com
From: Da_Breezy254@wahoo.com
Subject: Re: hey!

Miryyyy, what it do in England boo? Thanks for showing your pictures. I haven't had time to figure out how to download mine on the computer yet, but I'll send some ova as soon as I do. Have you met any more cool folks in your group? Of all the Beckies and Ambers I've grown to dislike, there is one girl I'm jellin' with pretty well. She stays on the same floor as me and her name is Angelica and she got huge dimples. She ain't bony like the other girls here, and that's kinda how we connected. There was a night the counselors took us to a buffet in the Chinatown, and none of the other girls were eating much from their plates. Angelica was sitting next to me enjoying her food and she could tell that I enjoyed mine too (I ate quick!). Angelica asked me if I wanted to go back to the buffet line for more food, but I told her no even though I was craving more of the noodles and potstickers.. I just didn't want to look like a pig & no one else was going back to the buffet line so I would've stood out. Angelica grabbed my wrist and insisted I go back to the buffet line with her. She said "us eatin' girls gotta stick together!" and she helped liven that boring @$$ dinner we were at with the whole group especially since I had been eating in quiet for most of the time that everyone else was talkin'. Angelica's coo with a lot of the different clicks here and it seem so easy for her. I wish I had her assurance and.. what they call it.. charisma? She knows how to mix with all kind of folk yet It's hard for me to even introduce myself to folk! (btw, I ate too much and ended up throwin' up some of that nice dinner. I think it was the frogs or the seafood I tried.)

The other night a bunch of us '4th floor' girls went out. Not Emily of course, she's too scared to leave the damn room! but the rest of us normal folk stepped out. It took us a good hour to take the metro across town to some place we heard was gonna be free for ladies, but when we got there they said it would cost us 18 euro to get in (that's like 25-30 bucks Miry!) I didn't have the money, especially not in cash, but Angelica insisted on paying for me when she saw me walking away trying to leave the group behind. She dropped the money in my purse all smooth so no one else would notice. I told her I'd pay her back as soon as I could, but she told me not to worry. I guess not everybody from California is superficial sticks and bones cuz Angelica's from southern Cali and she's sweet as pie! I guess we really can't go off believin' everything anyone says unless we see it for ourself. From here on out I'm gonna make my own opinions on things only after I see with my own eyes. I was kind of in a funk last week thinking I was ready to come home, but I'm okay now. Get back at me, peace!

Bre Davis

p.s. did you ever talk to the cute guy at the reception?

Chapitre 25: Work

"Do you sell the Tweety bird knick-knack? The one with him holding the Eiffel tower?" a frazzled looking blonde woman shouted. She had been pacing the center aisles of a quaint souvenir shop before she rudely shouted her question to the shop owner across the store. She advanced toward the cashier with wide eyes that demanded a prompt response.

"Yes, sell every. Look here," the portly cashier said with a smile. The woman became noticeably frustrated as she tried to explain what she was looking for a second time, causing the little Arabic man's smile to slowly diminish.

"I see these Eiffel Towers, merci. Do you sell the one with Tweety? You know, the yellow bird?" The woman's voice was unpleasantly militant as she stressed her syllables to help the cashier understand. She whistled a chirping noise with her pursed thin lips and made bird-like motions in the air with her hands.

"Bird yes, this way." The balding Arabic man politely escorted the blond woman to an adjacent corner of the souvenir shop. The woman followed closely behind him. The cashier could feel the woman's hazel eyes glaring into the back of his neck.

"Bird here," he said with a smile. He pointed to a shelf with a row of glass statuette models of white and blue birds in front of Paris scenery. The woman squinted her eyes and made a sucking noise with her teeth as she backed away.

"Merci," she over annunciated with a fake smile. She let out a loud sigh as the vendor reassumed his post behind the tiny counter in the corner of the shop.

Dabresha stared at the blond from the opposite corner of

the store; she had meandered into that same shop on her way home from class to take a peek at things she might buy for her folks back in Texas and to see if the shop happened to sell the bottle of perfume her mom loved. She casually glanced over at the blond woman as she scanned the shop's inventory for items priced less than a few euros. She found pencils, magnets, and lighters with Eiffel Tower pictures on them, but the better souvenirs, the more personable and fashionable ones she knew her folks would love, were triple the amount she budgeted for and there were no perfumes anywhere.

Dabresha listened in as the impatient blond woman started up a conversation on her cell phone. The lady emulated the rich folks that Dabresha had heard about back home, the ones who easily took vacations or honeymoon in France. The woman was assuredly American, and likely one of the snobbish types that would probably dine at Zoe's Roasthouse back home and would insist on having a particular table. Something about this lady's demeanor and accent had Eastcoast hints, so Dabresha could tell right away that she wasn't from the South.

The blond woman proceeded to tell the person on the other end of her cell phone line that she had seen a little Tweety bird statue a few days prior, but could not remember what street she was on the day she first spotted it. She wanted to buy the statue as a birthday gift for her boyfriend, a cartoon enthusiast with a large collection of animated figurines, then said she was starting to lose hope after visiting five different souvenir shops.

"The people in this country are freaking useless! I'm like sooo over it. You'd think they'd talk better English when they live in a place full of tourists," the woman grumbled into her phone. The woman shot a look at Dabresha when she heard Dabresha giggle. Dabresha was amused by the lady's blatant disregard and loud insults toward the shop owner inside the store. The woman probably assumed that she was the only English speaking person in the vicinity at the time, and jumped on the opportunity to express her frustrations in loud and bold English.

Dabresha erased her chummy facial expression and continued to circle the souvenir shop. She was humored by the scene, but felt a bit of sympathy for the heavyset Arabic man who was seemingly unaware that he was at the core of the blond woman's verbal attacks. The cashier was used to dealing with rude, non-French speaking tourists and probably didn't realize that some, like the blond lady, could be insulting him right in front of his face. When the blond woman snapped her cell phone closed, Dabresha politely grabbed her attention by tapping her on the arm. The woman scanned Dabresha from head to toe like she was her worst enemy.

"Hi. I think the souvenir shop on Rue Victor Hugo has those Tweety Bird knick-knacks you're looking for. That shop's right next to that science museum right off the metro five station. I see 'em every day in the window when I pass by."

The vendor stared at Mademoiselle Dabresha and Madame Blondie with intrigue as they chatted.

"Finally, someone in this freaking town knows English and knows how to give accurate directions! Thanks sweetie," the blonde woman replied.

"It's nothing," Bre assured her with a prideful smile, feeling happy and accomplished to be able to give someone useful information about her new city.

"Well, thanks a bunch. I'm Kristin, from Mass, here celebrating my birthday with my lovely boyfriend who prefers to sleep half the day at our lovely hotel room," she joked.

"I'm Bre, Texas. I'll be here for another month taking classes."

"Well that's wicked! Classes in Europe. Maybe we'll see

you around the city then? We're leaving for Rome in a few days then heading back to our regular, busy lives. Kudos to you for being able to vacay so long, I wish I could!"

The woman pulled a metro map out of her large, beige, designer purse and started to head toward the exit.

"Thanks again," she called. "Sometimes I wish I could hire a personal full-time translator like you to guide us around on this trip. Ciao!"

The woman rejoined the bustling city streets as Dabresha returned to her quest to find affordable souvenirs for her folks back in Texas.

"You," the vendor called out, pointing at Dabresha. "Here."

Dabresha was startled as she slowly approached the counter after assuring the cashier man wasn't motioning to anyone else. She was the only person in the store at that moment, so it didn't take long for her to confirm.

"Tu parles français?" the vendor asked.

"Un peu," Dabresha replied in a high pitched voice and with a curious stare.

"Why are you here?" he asked in French, "en France?"

"Ooniversi-tay," she replied in perfect French.

The vendor slowly explained that he was looking for an assistant at his shop and that he preferred to have someone who could speak English. Dabresha was surprised that she could follow most of what he was saying, especially since he was only speaking in French. Dabresha raised her eyebrows to show her interest, then replied,

"No visa," with a look of disappointment.

"No problem!" the vendor replied. "You help only weekends when I having very tourists afternoon, I give you little money. My son, he do shit things. He no help. But if you help, I pay." It was now obvious to Dabresha in the vendor's English explanation why the man needed an English speaking assistant.

Dabresha's eyes widened at the man's spontaneous offer, and after introducing herself as best she could in French, she was able to negotiate a small under-the-table salary with the man. She made sure he was okay with the fact that she would only be in France for another month, and he insisted it was 'no problem.' Dabresha's pay would be miniscule, but Dabresha figured that any amount of extra cash would be better than none. She was also able to negotiate the fortuity to take home one medium-priced souvenir at the end of each weekend as part of her salary.

Her job was to assist with keeping the store organized, but more importantly, intervene and assist with any English-speaking customers, most of which were difficult for Monsieur Benziouche to deal with on his own. Mr. Benziouche's final requirement was that Dabresha teach him basic English vocabulary throughout the weeks and write down the words the customers used most often. He asserted he would listen to all her transactions when she helped English speaking customers, and that he would not say much when they arrived. He would only help out with the native speaking customers and invited Dabresha to listen in on his conversations to help improve her French. They were to be a bilingual team in charge of accomplishing the basic goal of selling as many souvenirs as possible.

Mr. Benziouche went on to tell Dabresha about his family in French and broken English. From what Dabresha understood, Monsieur Benziouche opened the souvenir shop with his brother, an English-speaking business-savvy entrepreneur, a few years before, shortly after moving his family to France from Morocco. His brother, however, ultimately decided to move back to North Africa after having a difficult adjustment in Europe. His brother was victim to a hate crime and had a hard time handling the discrimination he felt as an Arabic-speaking immigrant, so he left Mr. Benziouche with full ownership of the store earlier that year.

Sadly, Monsieur Benziouche struggled to run the store on his own. Neither he nor his wife had experience running a business. His wife was a homemaker and made a tiny living from sewing and selling fabrics at markets every week. Mrs. Benziouche also spoke limited English, and her priority was taking care of their two younger children. Their oldest son Kharim used to help at the store, but had recently resorted to abandoning all his school and work responsibilities and opting to party with troublemaking friends instead. The sixteen-year-old bandit had even run into some recent trouble with police, but was legally pardoned for his crimes because of his age. His son was his English speaking shop assistant up until the week before, when his Dad realized he had been stealing from the shop and tried to confront him.

"Much years I care him," Mr Benziouche concluded with a saddened expression on his face. Dabresha didn't understand Mr. Benziouche one-hundred percent, but she could tell that the subject of his son's behavior was extremely sore for him when it made his eyes steam up.

"So, Saturday you here on fourteen hours?" he asked.

"Oui, I'll come," Dabresha replied slowly in French. She counted the conversion of military time on her two fingers. Twelve hours meant noon, so that meant thirteen o'clock was 1pm and fourteen o'clock was 2pm. She would really need to brush up on her French (and military time conversions) before the weekend came, particularly numbers, shopping phrases and business vocabulary. She was excited to take on the challenge and very pleased to find some sort of income, big or small, even though it had ironically found her.

That week, she decided to concentrate harder and harder on her classes and spent several extra hours studying in her room and listening to pronunciation tapes she borrowed from the Paris school's library. If she was going to follow through on this crazy thing, she wanted to be ready and have a least a little bit of confidence talking in French whenever she needed.

When Dabresha's first day of work came, she was a bundle of nerves and qualms. Could she hold her own working in a place with a language she only knew partially? She showed up to her shift ten minutes early, presentably dressed in black as Mr. Benziouche had instructed her to, and ready for what her first day of work would bring.

*   *   *

Back in Texas, Delilah was becoming obsessed with her baby as she continued running over the idea of motherhood. It consumed her every thought and motion, so much so that when she ate, she wondered if the baby liked what she was eating. When she slept, she wondered if the baby was sleeping too. She never inquired on getting an abortion because she just couldn't bring herself to end the life that was growing inside of her, and she knew she was past the legal deadline to terminate a pregnancy anyway. Every time Delilah passed by the mirrored closet door in her room, she lifted her shirt and stared at her stomach to verify that the tiny life was growing large in her once petite abdomen.

Every thought and every action was no longer just about her, but became about her *and* her baby. Everything she ate, drank, and thought of was now done with the baby constantly in mind. Delilah wondered if she'd be able to stand on her own two feet when the baby came into the world and worried if she could she handle the pressures of motherhood while continuing her mandatory high school summer courses. Would she have to give up everything she ever thought about doing to postpone her life to take care of her child? She knew Maurice wouldn't stand for that, and the thoughts concerning her future circulated in her head in a disorienting vortex, every minute of every day, even in her dreams. Elated feelings of joy were bound by feelings of pain, disappointment with herself and her child's father, then doubt. She wondered if she could truly survive as a single mother and if the child's father was adamant about staying out of the picture. She wondered if Maurice or Dabresha would help babysit from time to time or if she would be completely on her own, watching the child 24 hours a day, without a break for herself to breathe through. She hoped her big sister would help out at least a little so she could hang out with her friends just once in a while. She hoped Dabresha would forgive her for being a bratty nuisance to her over the course of the last few months.

Delilah's reflections were taking a huge toll on her, her skinny body, and her limited way of thinking. Before she knew of her pregnancy, Delilah had a narrow-minded way of thinking and behaving, and now she was suddenly forced to consider another person; a tiny fetus that would grow and take form in the next months before finally developing into a living, breathing, crying baby. Delilah had already chosen names—the baby would be named Jomari if he was a boy and Janetta if she was a girl. Whenever the doctor could confirm the baby's gender, Delilah was ready to start introducing her stomach by name and inviting people to the extravagant baby shower she was going to throw in the baby's honor. She knew her child's father wasn't likely to present at the celebration, but she would savor the festivities and celebrate the beginning of the life she committed to starting with her child, with or without him.

Chapitre 26: Might as Well Finish

Dabresha exerted a little extra effort in her classes the following week once she came to terms with the fact that there would be absolutely no benefit to an early return home. She didn't want to look like a big baby to her friends and family; an early return would mean that she was too weak to handle the challenge of being away from home for a month and a half. An early return would make her appear 'soft', like she couldn't manage her own independence. Six weeks was a short period of time, but it seemed like an eternity to her at times when she considered that she still had more than three weeks to go. She vowed to try to make the best of it and take her aunt's advice on appreciating her time there.

Dabresha socialized more and more with the other girls in the program and began joining them on their spur-of-the-moment city excursions and lunch invites. She became meticulous in the way she ordered food when she ate out with her program mates and limited herself to either one dessert or a beer when she dined in the city. Part of her newfound independence involved keeping track of every penny and every euro coin that left her wallet so she wouldn't spend beyond her means. She got in the habit of packing her own snacks every morning so she wouldn't overspend at the corner markets and bakeries, and though she wished she could have gone to a new club every night of the week, she only went to nightclubs occasionally and only if they were free to enter.

Dabresha was ecstatic when she ran into Angelica on campus in Paris and Angelica invited her out to a club with a small group of other girls who stayed on the same floor of the residence. There was a ladies night taking place at a venue called 'Red Circle,' one of the few hip hop clubs in the city. Paris had an abundance of house music and techno clubs, neither genre of music which was Dabresha's cup of tea, so Dabresha was happy that she could finally spiffy up and wear one of the night dresses that she had strategically squeezed in her suitcase with its matching high heels and accessories.

"I'll be there!" Dabresha assured Angelica, with a glowing expression that confirmed she was ready to hit the town!

"Feel free to invite your roommate or whoever else you'd like," Angelica offered, causing Dabresha to scrunch up her nose and shake her head.

"Aaaw she can't be all that bad," Angelica said with a giggle. "Who is your bunkmate by the way?"

"Some chick named Emily from Utah. You've prolly seen her moping around the hallways with a flushed red sad face on."

"Oh yeah, I heard about her," Angelica replied, "but be easy on her will ya? Her mom passed away a couple of months ago."

"Oh, I didn't know." Dabresha replied. "She don't really talk and I doubt she'd come if I invited her anyway. I'll definitely be there though!"

"Yaay, awesome! We're meeting at my room at nine and we'll get the partying started with music and drinks. We'll head out around ten to take the metro to the discotheque, and we'll split the cab fare to get back to the dorms since the metros will be stopped by the time we leave."

"For sure, I'll see you then!" Dabresha exclaimed with lit up eyes.Dabresha hadn't gone out much since her arrival in France, so it was hard for her to hide the fact that she was thrilled to be going to this particular nightclub as she chatted with Angelica about the details. She was looking forward to downing a few cocktails and grooving to a familiar jam or two.

Dabresha couldn't hold her excitement when she returned to the residence after class and walked through the lobby. She whipped her international calling card out of her purse the moment she got there skipped up the steps to the payphone area to try to get ahold of her friends in Texas.

"It's going dooowwn!" Dabresha hollered into the residence hall phone. Antoinette was on the receiving end of the conversation and Dabresha tried her hardest not to talk too loud while she chatted and caught up with her good friend. The residence's general phone booth had three glass walls and offered very limited privacy, but it was on the second floor near a media center and far from any guest rooms.

Dabresha told Antoinette she was having the time of her life and completely enjoying her time in France thus far, verbally contradicting the email she had sent to Aunt Trecee literally just days before. She didn't tell Antoinette about her initial feelings of disappointment, but focused instead on her good news, particularly her new post at Mr. Benziouche's souvenir shop that helped remove some of the financial pressures off of her.

"That's good girl!" Antoinette congratulated. "Now you got some extra funds to help you with your little shopping habit."

"I don't got no habit, I just like keeping fresh clothes and things around. Plus shopping make me feel good, you know how it is!"

"Yeah, shopping every other day! Girl you're a trip but I love ya anyway," Antoinette laughed.

Dabresha asked Antoinette to dial Laydee's number on a three way connection so she could spare her minutes and get two conversations done at the same time. Antoinette knew Tamina was in summer classes, so she didn't bother trying to bring her into the conversation. Dabresha told her girls about all the cute black boys she had seen around town and how surprised she was seeing multitudes of black folks in Paris. She bragged about how easy it was for her to buy and drink alcohol without ever having to show her I.D., and how awesome it was that the sun didn't set until almost ten o'clock every night, which meant the malls and boutiques stayed open later. She glistened when she talked about how the bars and clubs operated all night, and how some of the clubs gave free drinks to ladies only. She summarized as much as she could in the minutes she decided was sufficient to converse with them and basically told them that everything was dandy. Her classes were easy, the boutiques were amazing, and she was still in awe from seeing the real Eiffel Tower and a golden castle her program leaders took everyone to earlier that week. The girls were excited for her and were thrilled to hear about her adventures so far, and as far as they could tell, Dabresha was having the time of her life!

"Don't be having too much fun without me out there," Laydee joked. "You ain't allowed to have no more fun unless I give you permission."

Dabresha wished them well before she ended the conversation by telling them she would try to call them in the next few days and would definitely send them all emails regardless.

After Dabresha caught up with her friends, she left a message for her stepdad and sister on the house phone answering machine letting them know that she was doing okay. Then she left another voicemail for Darrien on his cell since he didn't answer, and she let him know she'd try and call again the next day from the same number at around the same time, instructing him once again to 'just pick up' his incoming calls even if the number on the caller ID looked funny.

"It ain't so bad I guess. I might as well finish this thing," she thought out loud as she walked up the stairs to her residence room. Her friends back home seemed to be in awe of her trip thus far even though she still hadn't seen or done too much. She used her friends' amazement as stimulation to keep moving forward with the study program and to keep her head up in whatever further mishaps might occur.

$$* * *$$

To: LatreceeSoFly64@gomail.com
From: Da_Breezy254@wahoo.com
Subject: 247 stairs

247 Stairs! Would you believe me if I told you I climbed up 247 steps today?? It could've been more stairs 'cause I honestly lost count trying to count 'em, but I think my fitness game has stepped up doin' all this walkin' out here, I might even be losing weight! We went to this place today called Sacred Heart Cathedral. It's a church at the top of this biiiiigg hill and the only way to reach it is by climbing a bunch of stairs (or waiting in an exhaustingly long line for a tram to bring you up the hill). It was SO pretty auntie, the inside too! There was a big picture of Jesus with doves and angels painted on the roof. I took a picture of it for you cuz I know you like that kinda stuff. There were so many nuns inside too that I felt like I was in a Sister Act movie! Some sort of service was going and I couldn't understand the most of it, but I could feel the.. how you call it.. the warmth in there. I heard Europeans weren't really into church like we are in the south, but all the French folk I saw shoutin' and praisin' inside that church coulda had me fooled! On the flipside, at the very back corner of the church, I saw this lady on her knees crying with her face down on one of the benches. Something was wrong with her, I don't know what, but she was crying so loud it made me want to cry. Her tears just kept fallin and fallin.. one of the nuns walked over to

her and placed some tissue in her hand, but she didn't even look up, she just kept goin'. Crazy thing is the other folks in there just let her cry. They prolly thought it best not to bother her, but she looked like she needed a hug. I wonder what happened to her. Maybe she lost somebody special? or maybe she havin' a whole mess of bad luck. I ain't never seen a grown person cry like that before, but I hope she felt better after church. You say church make people feel better, right? Maybe I'll start goin' when I get back home.

And don't worry bout me no more auntie. You was right, I was just havin' a silly little outburst when I sent you those emails. I'm gonna stay and work things out over here-- I found some friends and some work, and things ain't so bad afterall, I was just havin' a bad week.

Talk to ya soon Auntie,

Bre

* * *

To: Da_Breezy254@wahoo.com
From: LatreceeSoFly64@gomail.com
Subject: Re: 247 stairs

Howdy niecy,

I'm glad you gotten round to enjoyin' yaself out there. I figured you was gettin' on well since I ain't hear from you in a while. I can't wait to see the pictures you took of the Sacred Heart and hear about all the other things you done seen out there! Didn't I tell you things was gonna get better? You done got yaself a lil' job and a little boyfriend.. (I'm just foolin' but I really think you should give that nice young man who ficksed my camera a chance). Please call me as soon as you can. I ain't been leavin' the house much so just keep tryin' me till I pick up. Your sister ain't doin' so grate. Please call.

Aunt Trecee

* * *

To: Da_Breezy254@wahoo.com
From: LushissLibraLaydee@gomail.com
Subject: giirrrllllll

GIRL, you need to bring yo black behind back to Texas! so much has happened since you hopped on that plane and I don't got the time or the energy to type all of it! first off, me and Dominican Chris are officially steady. Took him long enough to recognize my flyness, ya know! we been chillin, talkin on the phone and textin' urrday. that boy is too damn fine! He got a NICE whip too, a draped up Mustang, and he likes kissing me now that I got my cheeks pierced-- I finally did it! It hurt like a mofo and I could barely eat the first few days after, but now they feel alright.

so what's up with you and D Dare, is you still talkin to him? cuz he be actin' like he don't know nobody when you ain't around especially when he's conversating with other chicks. I see him and his boys toyin' wit thirsty-lookin red-bone freshmen but idk, it could be casual.. just talk to your man! I heard the police came lookin for him at school too. I aint tryna werk u up or nothin while you over there, but I'm just passin' info along for your own good.

By the way, you missed the crunkest party ever last week! EV-ER-Y-ONE was there, I mean the block was shut down and there had to be at least 300 folks chillin' by the amphitheatre right after the Kingston Midas concert. it went on till sunrise, cuties and beer was on the loose! but I guess I gotta stop noticin' boys now since I ain't completely single no more. you woulda enjoyed it though. I saw Shareena there but she didn't try to start nothing so it was all good. you need ta get back here ASAP, there's sposed to be another party at the same place next week, and hopefully without no drama. That boy Rodrick from school got jumped by some messicans at the party, and bad too. He got took away in a ambulance! I guess he owed somebody money. That's exactly why I don't mingle wit messicans or anyone that ain't black. they all got tricks up they sleeves and knives in they pockets waitin' to stab you in the back, so you best watch your back running around with that Meery chick.

Also, where are you stayin' at while you out there by the way? I hope not a hostel. I saw a movie ad about these college kids who get kidnapped from a hostel in Europe, then they get chopped up in pieces by some murderers in a warehouse, so I hope that's not where you at and I hope you're being careful out there BreBre. The news be talkin' about how tourists be targets for crimes out there and terrorists be messing wit europe too since it's probably easier for them a-rabz to mess w/ those countries closer to arabia. anyway, help me pick out my next tattoo, I put up 2 photos on my web page so lemme know which one you think'll look better on my ankle. ok bye girl! stay fly!

Laydee T

Chapitre 27: Le Réunion

The day Miryam and Dabresha reunited was undoubtedly one of the best days Dabresha had in Europe. Every college student in the London program was offered the opportunity to do a forty-eight hour excursion to Paris and stay at the same residence with their program-mates whom they met during week one. Miry signed up for the excursion without hesitation; she couldn't wait to see her buddy from Texas again. The two hugged like sisters who hadn't seen each other in years when they reunited at the base of the Eiffel Tower.

"Only two days!" Miryam exclaimed when their respective groups found each other on the Trocadero. Miryam asked a classmate to take a picture of them together on the plaza, then she began to snap a few scenic photos for herself.

"You don't want pictures?" Miryam asked Dabresha. Dabresha shook her head.

"Girl I already came 'round here fifteen-thirty times, took pictures on that plaza with my shades on throwin' up deuces and everything! Trust me, I got more than enough pics of that gorgeous thang."

"Oh yeah, that's right. You a Paris expert now! Girl show me all you can while I'm here—take me to the best spots and the best clubs! I'm not gonna stick to the group's schedule so you gotta show me a better time than whatever they planned for us."

"I got you," Dabresha answered. "I'll make sure you have a proper time this weekend and a better time than what the group is supposed to be doin', and trust, we goin' clubbin' tonight!" she said proudly, over enunciating her syllables in a proper voice so that her voice mimicked that of a British pilot. "I just gotta help stock a shipment at my job then we can roll out."

Dabresha accompanied Miryam during her entire time in Paris, adding her two cents of newly acquired knowledge to every attraction they passed by.

"You know there's a restaurant on the top floor?" Dabresha stated when they first walked around the Eiffel Tower, "and they do free concerts at this park every summer for French Independence Day?"

Miryam didn't seem to be 'wowed' by Paris in the same way Dabresha was on her first day there, but she took advantage of the opportunity to discover as much as she could of one of the world's most popular cities in the two days that she was allotted.

"Did y'all come here on a boat too?" Dabresha asked Miryam as she continued to snap pictures of the Eiffel Tower.

"No, we took a train underwater. I was trippin' out girl!" Myriam admitted.

"For reaaaal? Could you see fishes and things through the window?"

"There were windows, but we couldn't see anything underwater. It was just black."

Dabresha contemplated if she would ever be able to ride the 'chunnel' without sweating bullets. She had heard people talk about it in Europe, but couldn't be certain that she could stay collected if she ever had to ride it. Planes and boats didn't seem like such a scary idea after hearing about an underwater train.

After separating themselves from the rest of the group, the girls settled in at a charming cafe with a clear view of the Eiffel Tower and caught each other up on everything they had seen and done in the last month. They showed each other their digital camera pictures while they chatted about their experiences.

"Is this your same camera? You fixed it?" Miryam asked curiously while she scrolled through the pictures on Dabresha's camera.

"Someone fixed it for me," Dabresha stated as she casually took a bite of her food.

"Who?" Miryam pressed, "My camera keeps freezin' and I want it looked at."

"Just some boy who work at this souvenir stand by da school," Dabresha replied as she took another bite of her food.

Miryam smiled, showing her teeth, and cocked her neck at Dabresha while giving her one of those accusatory smirks that friends usually gave each other when they sensed an undercover situation. It was the same kind of look that Dabresha gave Laydee every time Laydee told her she was going to 'study' with a boy she was crushing on, however Dabresha was caught off guard by Miryam's visual allegations.

"What?" Dabresha asked innocently, giving her friend a blank stare. She squinted her eyes at Miryam and added, "It ain't what you think *chica*, I gotta boo back home."

Miryam smirked at Dabresha again and squinted her big brown eyes right back at her. "Yeah, back *home*," Miryam added as her smile widened. Dabresha grimaced at Miryam, then looked back down at her food.

"Okay, he's *kinda* cute for bein' so light," Dabresha admitted. She threw a french fry at Miryam.

Miryam slammed her fist on the table as a huge grin flashed across her face.

"I knew it!" she shouted. "I knew you had to have someone's attention. You are too cute to not be turnin' fellas necks out here, you just don't know it!"

"He's a friend Miry, if that," Dabresha defended. "I ain't said much to him since the day I got my camera back, just replied to one email and said hi to him one time I passed him on the street. It ain't nothin' like what you and *Flavio* got going on back in

British land so don't get it twisted!"

Miryam laughed and threw a french fry from her plate right back at Dabresha.

"Don't hate because I'm on my A-game, completely single and sure ready to mingle. I don't gotta man back in Texas so I'm free to do whateva and whoever I please!"

The girls shared a laugh as they finished their chosen meal of a large 'poulet crudites' sandwich that they had split in half, fresh crispy french fries, and sodas. "I've never been to Vegas, so I'll just say what happens in Europe, stays in Europe."

Miryam's big teeth shined in the Parisian sunset as she formed another grin. Dabresha noticed herself smiling more in the time since Miryam arrived than she had smiled during the rest of the trip. Maybe all she needed was a little something or someone familiar around to comfort her as she endured her journey.

"You miss ya family?" Dabresha asked Miryam softly. Though she didn't want to admit it to them, Dabresha truly missed her friends and family. She was surprised that she didn't feel as huge of a yearning for Darrien, but since he never seemed to pick up his phone and there were too many other things on her mind, Dabresha adjusted to not having him a phone call or text message away.

"Of course I miss them, all six brothers and sisters and all eight nieces and nephews! But at times I wish I could just stay out here a little longer. They've gotten used to me not being there. I think my Dad just wants me around because I'm the more 'responsible' one... what about you? I know you got a small family but it's going to be bigger soon, right? You must be super excited to be a first time aunt, I know I was!"

Dabresha looked down at her plate and moved the remnants of her sandwich around with a fork.

"I'm not going to be an auntie no more," she replied

somberly. She gulped down a huge sip of her cola. Miryam's smile disappeared as she studied Dabresha's face with calm astonishment. "Miscarriage," Dabresha concluded, before Miryam had a chance to formulate the unfortunate question with her own mouth.

"Awww I'm sorry Bre," Miryam replied. She stared at Dabresha, surprised at how casually she talked about the subject.

"It's alright. Lord *knows* I know we can't control everything in this life," Dabresha said as she stood up to throw out her plate of uneaten food. Miryam stared at Dabresha with squinted eyes, wondering how Dabresha could appear so expressionless in a serious conversation.

"Don't be looking at me all sorry woman, can't stand when people do that. Trust me, it's all good, now let's shake this spot and get ready for tonight," Dabresha added. "We gotta show these Frenchies how we get down in the South!"

Miryam solemnly followed Dabresha out of the café, saddened by the news but more concerned by Dabresha's reaction or lack thereof. Miryam wondered how people could deal with bad news so calmly, especially since she was openly used to expressing her motions to her friends and family. She shrugged it off and followed Dabresha's lead out of the café and prepared herself to hit up the discotheque that night.

Dabresha hurried out of her shift at Monsieur Benziouche's shop with intense excitement. She rushed to her residence with remarkable speed and plucked Miryam, who was wearing a golden halter dress with black pointed-toe heels, from the lobby. Dabresha changed into a ruched dark purple strapless dress within minutes, squeezed on a pair of velvet black and purple stilettos, and once she was sure her hair and makeup were on point, she and Miryam 'click-clacked' their way down the street to catch one of the last metros for the night. They were an interesting looking duo and turned heads and caused whistles from all kinds of characters. Their American southern-influenced fashion stood out among all the other Parisian ensembles that the French girls were wearing while they were walking out and about that night. The Texans were an undeniably exotic looking pair and unaware of exactly all the attention they were drawing in their outfits.

"Ça va femmes des rêves."

"Hey baby, where you fron?"

"Où allez-vous sexy mademoiselles?"

The plentiful approaches and various bad pick-up lines caused the duo to giggle every time they passed by a suitor.

"Do you know what they're saying?" Miryam asked Dabresha as she linked their inner elbows together.

"Nothing important," she replied with a chuckle.

The stunning Texan divas sashayed their way into the nightclub feeling like superstars when one of the bouncers insisted on letting Dabresha and Miryam advance to the front of the line. Not only were they fabulously dressed to impress, but the bouncer remembered Dabresha putting on a well-received dance display the weekend before when she came with Angelica and her residence mates. The bouncer tried to persuade Dabresha to dance her routine again.

"L'americaine, you will dance ce soir again for we?" the bouncer asked with a smile.

"Peut-être," Dabresha replied with confidence. Dabresha's pronunciation of the french word for 'maybe' elicited just enough boldness for her to own the V.I.P. entrance. Miryam was especially proud to call Dabresha her friend that night and was awed by the poise and assertiveness she exhibited when she spoke her French phrases.

"O-M-G. You really speak French now!" Miryam exclaimed as she grabbed Dabresha's hand while they walked by the crowd. "This place has done you a lot of good Miss Bre!"

Dabresha gushed as Miryam went on.

"You seem all confident and... relaxed. You ain't the same girl I hung out with in London last month. You glamorous now!" Miryam threw her chin up at Dabresha and playfully nudged her shoulder before the girls pushed their way through the small crowds once they got inside the nightclub. They set themselves up at a quieter end of the long, stylish bar counter. Dabresha smiled as she ordered a drink from the bartender.

"You think so?" Dabresha asked, surprised. "Is it good change?" she asked Miryam as Miryam ordered her own drink.

"Haters will tell you that you changed for the worst whenever something good happens to you. I'll be the first to say that you're changing for the better and you're wearing it well chica."

Dabresha nodded her head to admire the compliment as she helped herself to a second drink and an eventual third.

"I think workin' here is makin' me better in French. Just talkin' every day to people and listening to my boss, it's helpin' more than sitting in class. I haven't told no one else about my job though cuz I don't want word getting back to the program heads just in case they got a problem with me workin' without a visa. Let's keep my international hustle hush-hush, ok? What happens in Europe!"

"Yaaas, to Texas!" Miryam exclaimed with a smile, lifting her glass in the air. The girls energetically toasted their glasses before sipping on their drinks. Both Miryam and Dabresha flirted casually with the bartenders and the 'mecs' that offered to buy them drinks as they sipped their cocktails and waited for the techno music in the club to come to an end. They planned to storm the dance floor once one of their familiar hip-hop jams started blasting through the speakers so they could show the people in the club what Texas was all about.

"If there's one thing I'm not feeling about Europe, it's this damn techno music!" Miryam said with a laugh. Both she and Dabresha had an affinity for any music other than techo or country, the latter of which one could often hear played in Texas.

"They sure do play a little too much electro or whatever they call techno here," Dabresha added, "but thankfully this club got a hip-hop DJ."

A short, pudgy, balding man holding a batch of flowers approached the girls from the back of their barstools in the midst of their conversation.

"Non merci," Dabresha told the little man with a half-smile as she politely waved her open palm and outstretched fingers at him, "Non, no thank you."

Miryam and Dabresha mutually found it amusing that the clubs in France also had their share of pesky flower people; short silent entities who circulated nightclub dance floors looking to sell expiring roses and lily florets to inebriated club-goers at very low prices. This particular flower man refused to leave when Dabresha repeatedly told him that she wasn't interested in his product.

"Yes, for you" the flower man replied with a small look of annoyance on his face, "man buy for you already!" The flower man shoved a handle of pretty pink roses in Dabresha's arm then pointed at another part of the room before briskly walking away. Perplexed, Dabresha looked over towards the area where the flower man had pointed at the other end of the bar. An attractive young man was standing there with a small group of presentably dressed gentleman on the other side of the room. He smiled and waved at Dabresha.

"Oh shoot!" Dabresha whispered loudly. She clutched

Miryam's arm and stared at her with wide eyes. "That's him!"

"Who.. huh?" Miryam replied as she visually scanned the bar area with a puzzled look on her face, just as Dabresha swallowed down the rest of her drink in one giant gulp.

"Gabriel."

Chapitre 28: Gabriel

"Hi, I'm Miry, and Bre thinks you're kinda cute," Miryam blurted with a sly grin as she hopped off her barstool. She swiftly shook Gabriel's hand while tugging at the base of her halter dress with the other to straighten its creases out. Dabresha didn't say anything to Miryam, but gave her a look that implied *I'ma hurt you woman!*

"Restroom, excusez-moi," Miryam said. She playfully blew Dabresha a kiss in the air as Dabresha shook her head and subtly glared at her with puckered lips.

Gabriel chuckled as Miryam walked off. Dabresha squinted at Gabriel as she tossed her flower bouquet on Miryam's vacant barstool and Gabriel positioned himself on an empty seat on Dabresha's opposite side. Dabresha became tongue-tied and unsure of how to respond.

"You don't like the fleurs?" Gabriel asked with a smile.

"They're fine, merci, but you smell like smoke," Dabresha blurted, scrunching her nose. "Tu fumes?"

"Just sometimes when I'm out with my friends, but I won't if it bothers you," Gabriel replied.

Dabresha crossed her legs and swiveled her barstool toward him. She flashed a look at her purse, which was idling inches away from Gabriel's knee on a handbag hook under the bar's counter. She folded her arms and looked back up at Gabriel.

"I won't take your things today, okay?" Gabriel laughed. "I don't wanting you so angry again."

Dabresha observed Gabriel with peculiar skepticism as he ordered a beer from the bartender and offered her a drink of her own.

"The wine is the best drink in all France, are you certain you don't want trying?"

"I'm good," Dabresha politely declined, bouncing her shoulders to the beat of the music in the background. She suddenly craned her neck around the club then looked back at Gabriel with a face that showed pure joy before her mouth dropped open. The DJ had just started playing her favorite Kingston Midas record and she couldn't hold her excitement.

"Oh snap! Okay! This my *song* right here!" Dabresha yelled with a wide-eyed burst of enthusiasm.

Gabriel observed her with subtle amazement as Dabresha rapped along to all the lyrics in the song, waving her palm in the air to the beat:

'♫ *I make paper in the evening, Paper in the day*
Paper on the Southside, Paper in the Bay
Twenty four seven, I burn through trees and paperrr
With my short dress shorty, and her phat money-maker ♫ '

Dabresha stopped her solo performance when she realized that Gabriel was beaming at her and that her rum-influenced concert may have carried on too long.

"Sorry, that's my jam," she said meekly, "I can't believe they're playing Texas rap out here!"

"Yes, France radios play much music American, but so many rappers American talk of paper, why is this?" Gabriel asked, scrunching his eyebrows with a puzzled expression.

"Paper means money," Dabresha clarified with a huge grin, "and there's lots of other words for it: dough, bread, cheese, dead presidents, they all mean the same."

Dabresha finally broke a genuine smile. She couldn't help but empathize for the boy with the flawed English. She remembered how difficult it was for her when she was a beginning

French speaker trying to communicate with fluent Francophones. Gabriel must have been experiencing the same nerve-wracking feelings she underwent, and she respected Gabriel's courage to make effort to speak a language that wasn't his own.

"Oh I underztand now, it's like here when we say 'fric' or 'blé', ze words mean money only sometimes and mostly young people use ze words."

"Y'all say 'freak' for money?" Dabresha chuckled. "I'ma remember that fo sho!"

Dabresha found it amusing that Gabriel and possible swarms of other French people may have been under the impression that rappers were singing about actual paper, cooking ingredients or deceased presidents. She chuckled to herself while she sat with Gabriel.

"I know my English isn't good, so I'll like you to help," Gabriel voiced. "I want to see you next week when you have a time, and assist me to practice. I'm certain my level can advance if I meet avec true speaker of English."

Dabresha tilted her head as she considered the proposition. "I don't know how to teach Gabriel, je sais pas," she replied.

"You won't teach, just talking, and I'll take ze notes and promise not to smoke before I see you. You've taught me 'paper' déjà so I'm already learning from you," Gabriel said with a friendly wink.

Dabresha nodded her head in partial agreement since her rounds of drinks had made her words a bit garbled and she did not possess Gabriel's confidence to make her own language mistakes. He stood up from his seat, right as Miryam conveniently reappeared from her lengthy restroom stop.

"Alors, it's too loud ici for us to talk really, so let me know?" Gabriel said with a charming smile, squeezing Dabresha's shoulder as he bid the girls farewell. He walked to rejoin his group of friends and Miryam gaped at him the whole time he was walking away, her face twinkling while she tried to conceal her excitement for Dabresha.

"So when are y'all meeting?" Miryam asked as she plopped back down in her seat, making sure to pass the flower bouquet under her nose before placing them on the bar.

"I don't know about him, but I *do* know that I'ma hurt you if you disappear that long at the bathroom on me again," Dabresha joked, causing Miryam to giggle.

"I'm sorry chica, but you're a fool if you turn that away," Miryam said loudly as she gawked in the direction of Gabriel and his friends. "You may have a man back home, but that one over there just wants to sit and talk," Miryam insisted. "Plus you haven't said more than two words about your boyfriend since you got here!"

Dabresha sighed as Miryam gave her a funny look.

"Talk huh? I'll think about it. He's just so... *skinny*... and *light!*" Dabresha said with a squinted face. She cocked her neck to the side and looked up at the ceiling, trying hard to imagine herself associating with someone like Gabriel who was so far from her type.

"Psssh if you won't talk to him, you can pass his skinny light info my way. Him *and* his friends were all that. You're loca!" Miryam emphasized by winding her index finger in a circular motion around her ear.

Dabresha could feel herself blushing as Miryam pressed her to consider the 'mec', insisting that no harm would come from one little meeting with the vendor and told Dabresha to stop overthinking.

"No one back home has to know a thing," she concluded. "What happens in Europe!"

"Stays in Europe!" Dabresha finished, "Mayne, we're in Europe yo!"

Miryam started chuckling and she used the back of her hand to wipe some moisture out of her eye, then she flagged down the bartender and ordered another drink before she started chuckling again.

"What you laughin' for?" Dabresha asked.

"It's that we're in Europe! Like, we're really *here,* out of the South and it's crazy! I still laugh thinking how that little elevator flyer became our ticket out of Texas. I'm just... I dunno... amazed by it all," Miryam said as she released a heartfelt sigh. "We both out here enjoying ourselves? This whole trip has been a blessing and I'm just glad I got to share some of it with someone who understands it wasn't easy to get here."

Miryam raised her glass to her mouth to try and conceal a tear rolling down her cheek.

"Aaaw girl, don't get me cryin' up in this damn club," Dabresha replied. She gave Miryam a side hug and grabbed her by the forearm. "Come on, wipe them tears and get up, let's dance these drinks off!"

The girls linked arms and hit the dance floor side by side, swaying and bouncing and grooving to the every song that blasted out of the speakers. They danced in tandem and danced with a few of the guys that approached them on the floor. They danced until their feet were battered and swollen from all the twirling they did in their high heels.

Gabriel approached Dabresha a final time before he left the club, not to ask her to dance, but simply to ask her to reply to an email he would send the next day. Then he respectfully left her with her friend and wished her a safe evening.

Neither Dabresha nor Miryam remembered exactly how

they got home that night, they just know that they were both a little tipsy, so much so that they both fell asleep with their club outfits and high heels on in their respective rooms.

Miryam was the first to wake up, so she knocked incessantly on Dabresha's residence door to wake her out of her deep slumber. Dabresha opened the door for Miryam looking like a verified zombie, then threw herself back on her bed and began to drift back off to sleep.

"Wake up woman!" Miryam exclaimed while pulling at Dabresha's arm from under her blankets. "I only got half a day left in this place and it's already noon, so let's check your email and find something to do," she said loudly.

"Check *my* email?" Dabresha asked with a bemused expression.

"Skinny Light told you he'd be sending you a message, remember?" Miryam said with a smile.

"Oh shoot. Alright," Dabresha grumbled as she slowly forced herself to sit up from under her blanket, "since you all in my business!" Dabresha threw one of her pillows at Miryam, then shuffled toward the end of her bed to rummage through her suitcase for some shoes. She slid on a pair of flip flops and a sweatshirt, and motioned for Miryam to follow her. They dragged themselves to the residence media center computer and Dabresha quickly entered the details to login to her email account. Sure enough, there was a brand new message awaiting her from 'CHAUVALIER Gabriel' when she logged in.

Miryam stood behind Dabresha and they read the email together. It was brief, written in flawless English, and simply asked Dabresha to meet him the next afternoon at his favorite Parisian crêperie. He offered to direct her there from the metro station, and would bring a notebook to write down new words and phrases he would learn during his 'English practice'. He insisted he would pay for anything that Dabresha ordered from the cafe during their lesson.

Dabresha replied to his email with Miryam by her side critiquing her on what to write to officially accept Gabriel's invitation, then the girls got dressed and roamed around Paris for the rest of that day. They walked the entire length of the Champs-Elysées, shopped in the Marais district, ate crêpes at a park bench in the Luxembourg Gardens, had lunch at the top of the Montparnasse tower, and ended their escapade at an Italian bistro in the Latin Quarter. They had a fantastic time their weekend together, and Dabresha was nothing short of dispirited when she had to leave Miryam at the Gare Du Nord to catch the underwater train back to London that evening. They promised to hang out when they got back to Texas, and to keep each other updated on everything that would happen their last few weeks in their respective European countries.

"Thank you for showing me around chica, I had a good time! And don't forget to update me after your meeting with Monsieur Skinny Light," Miryam said as she hugged Dabresha goodbye.

"Of course, you'll be the first to know just in case I get kidnapped," Dabresha joked, smiling warmly at her new friend as she boarded the train. "See you in Texas!"

"Hasta Texas amiga!" Miryam called out as she mounted the final steps. The doors to the train clamped close and Dabresha watched as the train bolted down its tracks and slowly disappeared out of sight.

Though Miryam was persistent in convincing Dabresha to meet with Gabriel, Dabresha mainly agreed to the meeting because she figured she was bound to run into him again before she left the country anyway. Their paths seemed to cross at the oddest places, and unusually so in a city with millions of people in it. Not only had Dabresha bumped into him at the club, but she had spotted him around town in the prior weeks, once at a metro station and once at a market. Both times she saw him, she changed directions to avoid getting noticed because she still felt silly for acting so aggressively toward him the day she confronted him about her camera.

Gabriel had long forgotten the incident however, and was delighted to run into Dabresha at the discotheque that night so he could try to court her once again. Gabriel knew email was the only method for them to communicate since she didn't have a working cell phone overseas, but Gabriel was not going to let that hold him back from talking to her. He was enamored by and had to know more about this unusual girl that captured his eye weeks before, so if he had to fabricate the excuse of wanting to practice English just to persuade her to meet with him, he would do just that.

'Hi Gabriel. I'll meet you at the cafe tomorrow at 18:00. À demain. Bre'

Chapitre 29: American Dream

Dabresha spent some extra time in the mirror getting ready to see Gabriel that evening. She wanted to look decent for her first casual meeting with her new French acquaintance, but her desire to perfect her make-up caused her to be unfortunately late to their meeting.

"Jolie!" Gabriel exclaimed when Dabresha entered through the cafés arched doors. Dabresha could feel her cheeks tingling at Gabriel's forward compliment.

"Merci," Dabresha replied softly and with slight embarrassment. Gabriel was the first boy to tell her she was pretty to her face, so she took the compliments with reluctance, all while remembering that Darrien was still back in Texas. Dabresha tried to conceal her smile when she thought back to that night and how much she initially wanted to kill Miryam for her twenty-minute restroom break.

"I must tell you, your French was a little bad zhat night," Gabriel chuckled as he pulled out a chair for Dabresha to sit down, "and your English," he added, causing Dabresha to burst into laughter. Dabresha cheeks tingled as she continued to think about that night. Trying to speak French with a clear mind was one thing and trying to follow her French class lectures were another, but attempting to formulate the most basic French phrases after she had already threw back a few drinks turned out to be a disaster.

"Sorry if I wasn't making sense that night, and sorry I'm a little late," she said shyly, hoping her intoxication hadn't caused her to say anything dumb during their short talk at the nightclub. She didn't remember every detail of their conversation, just the bits and pieces that Miryam told her they discussed.

"It's okay, you were having fun," he assured her with a smile. He flagged down a server to take their coffee order and pulled a small red notebook out of his pocket and placed it on the table. The cozy crêperie Gabriel chose for their meeting in the west side of town was perfectly tranquil for their lesson. It was chicly decorated with black-and-white artworks of famous Paris attractions nestled in vintage wood frames. There were metallic barstools with teal cushions surrounding all the cafe's high tables, and antique bronze napkin holders on the center of each table.

To break the ice, the two talked about a variety of cultural subjects and everything else from school, to art, to traveling in their conversation exchange. Gabriel asked Dabresha questions about American culture (does everyone own guns?), slang (what's a 'boo'?), and idioms (the term 'hang out' confused him in particular), and asked her to clarify more of the lyrics he'd heard in American hip-hong songs on the radio.

"Drop it like hot, what does zis mean?"

Dabresha couldn't help but smile as the two conversed and discovered more about each other's cultures— she realized it was actually kind of fun for her!

"Drop it like it's hot? It's a... kind of dance that girls do," Dabresha replied with a wide grin. Dabresha found the innocence of Gabriel's questions delightful and continued to smile throughout their conversation.

"The way you speak slowly, your accent Texas, J'adore. It makes easier for me understanding ze English," Gabriel added. It was one of the few times anyone complimented Dabresha on the way she talked and it astonished her!

"Your accent too, it's different," Dabresha noted, "and easier for me to understand your French."

They shared a smile. Dabresha appreciated that Gabriel

spoke in a drawl that was slightly easier to understand than the other French accents she had gotten accustomed to hearing in France, and as they chatted, Dabresha learned that Gabriel was originally from the South of France where people tended to speak with a moderately different accent than the people in Paris. It was a concept Dabresha completely understood since people in her Southern town definitely spoke differently than the people in the rest of America. Dabresha found it amusing that the same held true for the people in France and grew to appreciate Gabriel's accent even more. It intrigued her and made her want to see Southern France for herself, especially since Gabriel insisted that the South was the best part of his country.

Dabresha learned that Gabriel was twenty-four and had stopped going to business school, where he first started studying professional English, to help run his uncle's business. His mother, a Senegalese immigrant, and his father, a French native, produced two children in their marriage with Gabriel being the oldest. His little sister Anaïs was a teenager who wanted to become a beauty professional after finishing high school, thus his family was quite small, just like Dabresha's, and his small handful of cousins were spread out around the country of France.

"Et toi, how is your family?" Gabriel asked Dabresha.

Dabresha shared the basics about her family but didn't go into too much detail, only sharing that she lived with her dad and little sister in a mid-sized Texas town.

"And your mother?" Gabriel asked.

"Elle est mort," Dabresha said bluntly, causing an awkward silence. She sighed as she looked down at the floor, then back up at Gabriel when he spoke.

"My father, also. Desolée," Gabriel replied, quickly changing the subject to a less personal one. Dabresha began to sense a bit of empathy for Gabriel after learning that he too, had lost a parent unexpectedly just two years prior.

Gabriel posed the majority of questions to Dabresha and simply asked her to correct him if his grammar was wrong and clarify any responses he didn't understand. Gabriel pretended to scribble notes in his little red notebook, scribbling scattered phrases of nonsense in child-like handwriting across random lines. Dabresha tried her hardest to converse without giving Gabriel too much of her Southern twang, even though he said he liked it, but it wasn't easy. She also tried to make sure her phrases flowed like an organized speech so Gabriel could understand her better. She felt like a tutor, and essentially she was, so she didn't want to confuse the curious French boy who seemed so enthusiastic about improving his English. She didn't mind helping him, especially since he had agreed to pay for whatever she helped herself to, and Dabresha was not one to pass up on anything that came for free.

In all their talking, Dabresha hadn't realized that several hours had passed in what was supposed to be a short meet-up at a cafe. When Gabriel insisted that they take a walk afterwards around the 'quartier' along the banks of the Seine River, Dabresha hesitantly accepted.

"Mon Dieu! It's already nine? I was supposed to call my aunt half an hour ago," she exclaimed when she took notice to the clock near the cafe's exit as they got up to walk out.

"Do you need to go?" Gabriel asked.

"No, it's okay," Dabresha sighed, forming a small look of disappointment on her face. She had promised Aunt Trecee she would call and hoped she wasn't milling around her house waiting for her phone to ring.

"You are certain?" Gabriel asked.

"Oui," Dabresha assured him. "I'll just call her tomorrow, or if we see a public phone I'll call her up right quick. T'en fais pas," Dabresha said with a strained smile.

Gabriel guided Dabresha out of the cafe and onto the quay of the Seine River. They walked side by side, conversing in both English and French, openly changing between the two languages when the other saw fit. Dabresha was pleased to have a real French person to practice with who wasn't a professor or a program counselor. She was still in awe of the whole situation; she was in France speaking French to French people! And walking around Paris with a charming 'metisse' (mixed) boy who was easy on the eyes made it even more exciting. She had noticed a huge improvement in her own French skills in such a short period of time that sometimes she even surprised herself with how much she could understand, and at times would lose track of which language she was speaking in!

It stunned her that she felt more comfortable walking around France than she felt in her own neighborhood in Texas. The streets of Paris were busy and bustling, but the people walking the streets seemed to keep to themselves. People weren't yelling, arguing or fighting like they sometimes did in Texas, and she didn't see anyone sprinting down the streets like they had just stolen something. When Dabresha heard a loud noise, she didn't jump at it in fear it was a gunshot like she usually did back home. Guns were illegal in France, and the few crimes she would see pop up on their news broadcasts were petty crimes in her eyes. Dabresha felt safe, accepted, and at ease, and those were three feelings that she seldom felt while walking the streets back home.

The English lesson had turned into a full-blown impromptu excursion through the center of the city of lights, with Gabriel acting as the tour guide and explaining some of the points of interest they passed as they continued to walk and talk. At one point, he led Dabresha to a bridge that had a thousands of padlocks attached to its railings. He pulled a tiny gold padlock out of his own pocket and handed it to Dabresha as she gave him a puzzling look.

"What are these locks for?" Dabresha asked him, scrunching her eyebrows.

"They are for good luck," Gabriel replied with a cunning smile. "I have only one, so we'll lock it together?"

"Sure," she replied, fascinated by the immense number of locks attached to the railing. She smirked when she thought of all the superstitious French people that appeared to believe that clamping a lock on a fence would bring them luck, but she allowed Gabriel's hand to guide hers to an empty section of the fence, and together, they clamped the padlock closed.

* * *

Gabriel pointed out various bridges, museums, and famous buildings as they continued to walk along the Seine, including bits of his playful personality in his descriptions of what they saw. He tried to dig into Dabresha's life as much as he could so he could get a better sense of her, but didn't want to make her uncomfortable. Who was this fascinating smooth-faced American with impeccable urban fashion sense and gorgeous hair?

"At ze café, you said you have someone at home. Is he your boyfriend?" Gabriel asked, looking at Dabresha curiously. He patiently waited for an explanation as they continued to walk along the river.

"He's... important. But we don't call ourselves boyfriend and girlfriend often," Dabresha replied with uncertainty. She felt her jaw tighten as they continued to stroll.

"So he is your boyfriend or no? I'm not sure I understand," Gabriel asked calmly. He was puzzled by the concept of anyone having someone in consideration who wasn't their boyfriend or girlfriend.

"Yes," Dabresha snapped, a little nerved. Gabriel sensed the question was making her a little uneasy.

"I'm sorry to bother, it's just you... hesitate your response. In France we don't say we *maybe* have a boyfriend or girlfriend," he concluded.

"It's not easy to explain, and you wouldn't understand anyway," she said in a low voice, abruptly dismissing Gabriel's inquiry.

"When you talk of your life in Texas, you don't seeming cheerful," Gabriel noted. After politely correcting Gabriel's grammar, Dabresha explained the context of her various personal and financial problems, adding that she had earned her trip to Paris for practically free because of a scholarship. Her school debt, her car, her annoying little sister, and her lackluster job that had its good days and bad days, were not a very cheerful situation. Life in Texas was just that: life. Life wasn't thrilling or exciting to her in any sense, and she just pushed through it week after week and partied as much as she could to make up for the dull reality of it all.

"Life in America isn't easy like you think and I know you probably think what everyone else in France seems to think, that everybody in America is living rich dreams?"

"No, I don't think like that. Every place has good and bad," Gabriel interrupted.

"No, listen Gabriel. Écoutes. Every day in America is a challenge. The so-called American Dream is a big fat lie for everyone I know. We all struggle to pay bills month after month and try to save up to move out of our single-parent homes. Every one of my closest friends has been through... merde! My best friend has been getting beat on by her moms' different boyfriends since she was a kid. I have another friend who got touched on by her real Dad and had to go to foster care! And a friend with a mom who's been telling her to give up on everything good since day damn one. Don't let me start on me..."

Dabresha's voice began to crack as she shook her head and scrunched her nose.

"My mom died when I was thirteen and I was raised by a man that's not even my real family 'cause my *real* father couldn't stay clean long enough to take care of me or his damn self. He went to jail twice when I was little, but he's been out of jail for ten years now and still hasn't picked up a phone to call us once. I needed my Mom. I need her every day! This whole France thing? It's just a stroke of luck. People don't travel to places like this where I come from, we just get by."

"Get by?" Gabriel asked innocently.

"We survive. We don't got, I mean... we don't *have* money like that. All we got is survival tactics," Dabresha concluded.

Gabriel slowly nodded his head in agreement though he wasn't fully following. He was an ambitious young man who refused to believe that money could hold him back from anything he wanted to accomplish, nor would he accept any tragedy as a permanent blemish in his life. Dabresha began to feel chafed by Gabriel's abundance of questions. It was getting dark and fatigue from all their walking was starting to kick in too. She halted their stroll and turned to face him.

"Look," she said abruptly, "just realize things ain't the same where I come from. It ain't, it's *not* like you see on TV. We don't have big white chapels around our neighborhood with lines of tourists waitin' to come in, or fancy bridges for people to visit to get good luck. We got police looking to stir us up and crackheads actin' stupid in the streets. People laughed at me when I told them I was coming here 'cause they thought I was crazy! Our parents don't hand us jobs or money; we gotta figure our own way in everything. And it's expensive as all hell for us to go to college. You say school is free in France, so why don't you go back, huh? You know how much easier it would be for us if we had free schoolin'?"

Dabresha was winded when her eyes met Gabriel's. She had forgotten to use her proper English and was speaking extremely fast, and the concerned expression on Gabriel's face showed that he seemed to understand her words.

"No Dabreja, I don't know, and this is why I ask. I'm sorry if I ask too much things," Gabriel replied, looking at the ground. An uncomfortable silence filled the crisp, evening air as an accordion player on the other side of the river helped fill the silence with a classic andante tune. Dabresha turned away from Gabriel and leaned against the stone wall that ran along the border of the river, just as an ambulance whizzed by on the street in the distance with its sirens echoing off of the buildings on full blast.

"May I ask one question more?" Gabriel said softly. Dabresha sighed before she looked back at Gabriel, unaware that they were standing only mere inches apart from each other. Her mind was a little weary from the evening's bilingual conversations and she was in a daze from the emotions that arose when she thought about home in the midst of the passing sirens. She stared into Gabriel's eyes and wondered what else he could possibly want to know about the strange, angry black girl from Texas who didn't know if she had a boyfriend or not.

"Your name is Dabresha, so why do they call you Bre?"

Dabresha was taken aback by Gabriel's final question and unsure of how to answer it. There was a slight delay in the time she parted her lips to form a response and the time that words were actually spoken.

"It's... easier for people to say," she answered quietly, deciding she didn't want to bother to explain more. In her mind, Gabriel could never understand the slack she got from strangers for using the 'ghetto' name that was given to her at birth. She had heard plenty of times that her name and her race would always be a disadvantage to her in her big, beautiful, liberated country. Did Gabriel think it silly for people not to be called by their real names?

"I like Dabresha better," Gabriel replied. Dabresha was so inundated by the conversation that she hadn't noticed that Gabriel had started holding her hand, nor that a tear had formed in her eye and begun to roll down her smooth cheek. Gabriel wiped it away with the thumb of his free hand, and for the next minute, the two of them were silent. Gabriel continued to gaze into Dabresha's eyes, unshaken by the sudden silence. He stared at her in a way that intimidated her and soothed her at the same time. Dabresha exhaled loudly as she dropped her head to face the river over her left shoulder. Gabriel moved in to stand closer to her and raised Dabresha's chin with his other hand to recapture her gaze.

"Tu es belle Dabreja, sympa, and strong. All you survive is good for you."

Dabresha remained silent, a whirlwind of sentiments revolved around her like a tornado. Her thoughts and her stomach were in a knot. It was one of the first times in her life where she did not know what to say, and the ambulance sirens whirring in the background didn't help. To say she was speechless would be an understatement, yet she couldn't label exactly what she was feeling; it was a bewildering mixture of anger, frustration, and relief. Her frustration was at Gabriel's seemingly lax demeanor when she told him about her past and uncertain future. She felt anger towards her friends and family for letting her down so many times in her life without really ever apologizing for their mistakes. She was relieved that she finally had the opportunity to release her thoughts to someone who gave her full attention and seemed to care, even if just for the moment. Finally, she was content with the feeling of pacification that consumed her while she continued to stare into Gabriel's eyes. The air between them was magnetically intense, and Dabresha silently stood there waiting for something, someone, or some incident to break the silence between them.

Gabriel leaned toward Dabresha and pressed his lips against hers, using his free hand to squeeze her chin and tilt her jaw upwards to guide her kiss. Dabresha gripped Gabriel's firm bicep with the intent of pushing him and his arm away, but instead she kissed him back, eyes closed, with sensuality. She jumped and snatched her hand away from his arm as fear began to flash through the core of her upper body. She silently gasped while she swiveled around and started backing away from him.

"I, I can't... I'm sorry," she whispered feebly to Gabriel. The kiss had literally taken her breath away.

"Wait me, Dabreja," Gabriel pleaded as he walked a few steps in her direction.

Dabresha shook her head, crossed her arms, and scurried off down the cobble road that ran along the side of the river, disappearing into the midst of a crowd of people lining the sidewalks on the streets.

"Do you know how to go home Dabreja?" Gabriel called from a distance as he tried to catch up with her. "Let me take you."

Another tear fell from Dabresha's eye and splattered to the pavement as she scampered away without looking back. She felt an unusual burning sensation through the core of her chest as she fled from Gabriel, a physical manifestation of anxiety she had never felt before.

Dabresha thought hard about the whole evening as she rode the metro home. The ride went by faster than usual and all the people and foreign conversations around her were more distorted than ever. She could only hear small murmurs of conversations on the crowded metro as she sat down on the hard plastic seat and contemplated what had just happened. *What did I do? What was I thinking?* Confusion overwhelmed her blurred mind and vexed her with fatigue. She couldn't sit still as she rested her head on the metro window and struggled to get comfortable in her seat.

The kiss was nice, really nice, but Dabresha felt guilty for allowing it happen. *It was just a kiss.* No one would ever have to know about it, and she wouldn't have to worry about seeing Gabriel again once summer was over. She could go back to Texas, back to reality, and everything that did or didn't happen in France would stay there. She wouldn't have to tell anyone about anything that transpired during her trip, especially Darrien, who would probably want to know. She planned to erase the sweet embrace from her memory and bury every emotion that Gabriel managed to pull out of her that evening.

Dabresha was more than relieved when she returned to her residence that night and Emily was nowhere in sight. She took advantage of her temporary, much-needed private solace and allowed several more tears to fall before quickly preparing for bed with the TV blasting as loud as she wanted it to. Dabresha stared hard at herself in the mirror as she brushed her teeth. For the first time in a long time, and with blurry reddish eyes, she saw herself clearly different than the broken, survivor she once was. For the first time ever, she *saw* herself.

She eventually fell asleep that night, her mind on Gabriel and how silly she felt for running away from him once more. The other part of her mind was on Darrien and what he might be doing at that moment on the other side of the world... and if Darrien would care that she had just shared the most passionate kiss she had ever known with a light-skinned French boy named Gabriel.

Chapitre 30: One Day

To: SunnyDelilahful17@gomail.com
From: Da_Breezy254@wahoo.com
Subject: (no subject)

Hi Lilah. I'm so sorry for not reachin' out to you sooner. Aunt Trecee told me everything and I really hope you're feeling okay. I'm sorry I couldn't be there for you and didn't take more time to get ahold of you while you were healing up at the hospital and planning Janetta's burial. I ain't been the greatest sister and I apologize. I'ma work on me and promise to get better at it though... we just gotta be tighter Lilah, we got to. Mom would want us to be closer than we are right now. we can't be fightin' over silly stuff no more. We're sisters and we been through enough already, we gotta find a way to do better than we're doin' and make somethin' of ourselves, work harder and take more classes so we can live better in Beauconte, or wherever! This trip has taught me that there's so much more outside of our town than we could ever know, we just gotta find it! I don't wanna be grown and still strugglin' like we are, do you? Let's get through this thing called life together and get some plans in motion sis! I don't wanna waste any more time than I already have foolin' around in school and making pennies at my job, so I'm gonna get my transfer and my degree done asap, and I want you to visit that cooking school in Austin you was looking into and find out more about it. You cook so good and you should do something with it Lilah! I never wanted to tell u cuz I didn't want your head to get big, but u honestly the best cook I know. Let's make Momma proud and keep Maurice from losing anymore of his hair lol. E-mail me if you need anything before I get back okay? I check my e-mail least twice a day and I'll respond as soon as I can. When I do get home, talk to me about whatever you need and I promise I'll listen. You're my sister and I love you no matter what, and Maurice does too even though he never says it. I'll see you soon sis,

Bre

P.S.: You're gonna LOVE the souvenirs I picked up for you just wait!

* * *

"Mommy, what's that on your keys?" Dabresha asked with a bright-eyed expression. Dabresha was fascinated by the oblong goldish object with steep sides and interesting features.

"It's a Eiffel Tower, it's in Paris baby."

"Where's Parish at?"

"Oh child, it's far far away."

"Can we go far far away and see it? I like big towers."

"One day baby. It's my dream to go there too, and your uncle knew that when he gave me this keychain and the blue perfume bottle when he went there for his military work."

"Can we go?"

"Not now baby, Momma don't have money for us to go anywhere right now, but one day we'll get to see it. I heard it's real different...in a good way. They got the best shoppin' in the world and people don't follow you around the stores there thinkin' you gonna steal something. I heard they treat all ladies like royalty out there and they don't pick on black folk like here in America. As long as you carry yourself right, they treat you proper, the way it ought to should be here."

"When can we go there momma?"

"One day."

"Promise me you'll take me to Parish? and we can see the real fievel tower."

"Yes baby I promise. Me, you and Lilah will have a grand ole time over there. Now wake up, you gon' be late for school."

* * *

Dabresha snapped awake from her dream with a tear rolling down her cheek. She had slept through her alarm, but ended up waking up, or being woken up, just in time so as not to be tardy to class. A smile slowly formed on her face and she felt a warmth that she hadn't felt in a long time—the warmth that accompanied the sound of her mother's voice. Dabresha smiled as she fondly thought back to one of those many conversations she had with her mom about the Eiffel Tower keychain, which happened on a day she couldn't exactly remember, but she knew it was a special day. It was the only promise Dabresha's mom had made to her that never got the chance to come to fruition before her untimely passing.

Dabresha was overwhelmed by her epiphany; her trip to the other side of the world, a shared dream with her mother, was spoken of well over a decade ago and had actually come true. Dabresha never conceived it possible to be able to come true before, but now she was in Paris, free from the hardships that restrained her in Texas, with that cherished memory resurfacing in her dream. In a matter of weeks, Dabresha had traveled to two countries and opened herself up to confiding in the most diverse group of friends she'd ever had in her life. She took chances to try things she never imagined trying before, all while catching the eye of a French boy who treated her like a princess. She stopped thinking about what others thought of her and truly started to get comfortable in her own skin. She felt more content than she had ever been since her childhood, and that moment, that epiphany of freedom, made her tearful with tears of joy instead of pain for an entire day.

Dabresha smiled as she rode the metro to her school in Paris, peering out of the window and truly absorbing the sights she passed. She kept to herself for most of that day and avoided interacting with too many people apart from her classmates that morning. After class, she wandered the Vincennes Gardens in solitude and spent the whole afternoon reflecting on all the trials and tribulations of her past, gradually trying to release her painful memories into the mellow clouds that slowly moved over the waters of the garden's still lakes. She smiled reverently as she sprawled herself across one of the garden's elegant benches and envisioned her future and all the opportunities that seemed more possible with her newfound language skills, interpersonal skills, and travel experiences. What if she could move back to France one day? Maybe for a summer or half a year, and find work that would sustain her throughout her time there? Mr. Benziouche already told her she was welcome to come back and help out at the shop anytime she was in France, so if she were to move back one day, she would at least have a place to start.

That week marked the germination of a new Dabresha, a more collected and open-minded individual whom had been roaming Dabresha's arid soul all along and just needed a little bit of rainfall. When it began to drizzle that day in the park, Dabresha didn't even flinch. She just let the moisture fall on her and watched the tiny raindrops gently dance on the lakes in the gardens.

Dabresha's eyes got misty every time she thought of her mom that day, but then a smile reappeared when she imagined her mother sitting on the bench with her, or walking along the streets of Paris at her side, strutting with her shoulders back and her chin up high, wearing a fabulous sundress and brand new bonnet that she would have likely purchased from one of the French markets. She imagined her mom stopping to peek inside of every boutique they passed and leaving behind a subtle aromatic trail of hibiscus flower in every shop she visited. Without a doubt, Dabresha's affinity for impulsive shopping was inherited from her mother's side, and Dabresha was okay with that.

Some could call Dabresha's trip a stroke of luck or a series of coincidences that led to her journey. Others could start to view it from a supernatural perspective; it was a necessary journey that was placed in Dabresha's path at a very fitting moment in her life, a moment when she was in need of healing and self-analysis. That half-minute encounter in the elevator set these imperative events in motion that blossomed into an opportunity of a lifetime.

What if Dabresha would have taken the stairs that day or decided to skip her counseling appointment all together? What if

Dabresha let her fear of flying ultimately inhibit her plans? Even with all things in her destiny considered, Dabresha's willingness to take the chance to try something different was a primary reason why the trip transpired at all. She suppressed her fears, kept faith that things could be okay, and when things got rough, she still rode the waves (and boy there were some mighty waves!) Drama back in Texas threatened to ruin her purpose, but she fought off every temptation to abandon her journey early. She ultimately succeeded in accomplishing her goal to polish her school records while taking a break from her hometown. The feeling of success was as immense as the blue color of the waters of the lake she laid next to, and that feeling made her blissful.

Dabresha called Darrien several times in the days that followed Gabriel's magical kiss because she felt a hint of shame from what had transpired. The one time Darrien answered the phone, he said he couldn't talk very long and asked her to call back on the weekend. Dabresha ultimately abandoned the idea of telling Darrien about her secret, passionate kiss; she began to wonder if Darrien would even care about the incident if he knew about it, then subsequently began to wonder if Darrien even cared for her at all. He certainly hadn't made a good effort to stay in touch with her while she was overseas; he had only replied to one of her emails and never attempted to call her residence phone even though Dabresha explained to him that it was extremely easy to buy an international phone card at the grocery store. All of Dabresha's friends and even Maurice had committed to picking up the phone and responding to emails, yet Darrien had failed to initiate any line of communication since the day Dabresha left Texas.

Two days after the passionate kiss by the river, Dabresha wrote Gabriel an email in English so she could express how she felt with as much accuracy as possible.

'Hi Gabriel. First, I just want to tell you that you really need to work on how you use words that end with -ing and -ly. You mix them up and you use them a lot of times they're not needed! Just try not using them at all until you get more English practice in and your sentences will sound a lot better I think.

I'm sorry for criticizing you when you were trying to be nice and I'm sorry for showing a mess of emotions. It's difficult when I talk about my past but I'm glad you listened the way you did, it made me feel better. I don't mind meeting you again and helping you learn more English, so let me know if you'd like to try again. à bientôt? Dabresha.'

Gabriel responded to Dabresha's email within hours of her sending it off. He apologized for asking too many personal questions and assured Dabresha that she was not out-of-line for showing her emotions. Gabriel also apologized for the kiss, but Dabresha, in her next response, reassured him he didn't need to.

And so they met again.

They had lunch at a different bistro this time and took walks around the city together. Every afternoon for the last weeks Dabresha was in France, Gabriel improved his English while helping Dabresha master her basic French. They spent every day learning a great deal from each other and discovering they had much more in common than just moderate knowledge of a second language. Dabresha appreciated having a gentlemen like Gabriel squiring her around all ends of the city; he treated her with such respect and 'politesse' that she nearly forgot about Darrien, and was beginning to become okay with that.

Gabriel was an invaluable companion who listened to Dabresha, comforted her, looked out for her, and made her feel secure; he was exactly what Dabresha needed in her time of growth and development: a listener and a friend. No matter what would become of their companionship, Dabresha was thankful for their time together. Every time Dabresha tried referencing the negative events of her past, Gabriel would look her in the eyes and squeeze her shoulder, leading her to change the subject. Through his attentiveness and affection, Gabriel taught her one of the most invaluable lessons of all: to focus on the present and have optimism about the future.

* * *

To: Da_Breezy254@wahoo.com
From: MauriceLFranklin@wahoo.com
Subject: (no subject)

Ms. Pat from the church came by with her nephew- he know how to fix cars. They heard you havin trouble with the buick so I let em pop the hood. Her nephew came back that week with some parts and fixed up whatever were wrong. He was there outside the whole day workin on it. Next day I drove it round the expressway couple times and i didn't hear no funny noises or see no smoke. I cleaned it up for you got it detailed and the tires polished so when you get home you don't gotta worry bout takin' the bus no more. I also fixed up y'alls closet door. It just needed some sandin' a few bolts and a frame. Hope you don't mind I went in there Lilah said it was okay. Delilah better she talked to Miss Pat that day about cooking school and

Miss Pat gonna drive her there to fill out some papers tomorrow. She say she wants to open up her own diner when she finish learning how to run restaurants. Speakin of, I saw your boss from the Roasthouse at the corner store the other day, he asked about you and I told him you was doin' mighty well. Your Uncle Otey also called from the pen, surprised us all since he ain't called in over a year. he says you crossed his mind and that glad you enjoying yourself. We all proud of you Bre. From Maurice.

* * *

To: LovelyNette@gomail.com
From: Da_breezy254@wahoo.com
Subject: update

What it do Nette Nette! What's new in TX?
Sorry I missed your call on my room phone but I did get your voicemail. I've been away from my room more often than usual. Things is really good out here and I'm a lil sad that this ride is comin' to an end! Some days I wake up still wonderin' how I got here in FRANCE! Speakin' French!! Hoppin' around Paris like it's my own town. I'm gonna miss it here when I bounce but I'm sure I'll be back one day cuz I still haven't found that perfume bottle I've been looking for!
I sure gotta to tell you about last weekend. I still can't believe seein' what I seen. This boy I been kickin' it with, that boy Gabriel I told you fixed my camera? he invited me to the south of France and we chilled there all weekend. I know I said I'd never date a lightbright, but I have to take that back because this boy is lighter

than ever, lighter than you and damn near white! But people don't stare at us like they stare at mixed couples out in Texas. Matter of fact I've seen quite a few black ladies walking around here with white men and they don't get stared at neither, it's kinda nice. Anyway, Gabriel convinced me to go with him to a city bout 4 hours away on the train, and I know I know.. you said I need to be careful mingling with folk out here and all, but I trust him and he treat me good and I've met a lot of his friends and his uncle. I've spent more time with him over the weeks than I've spent with Darrien this whole year so that has to count for something, right? And it takes him less time to respond to an e-mail than it takes Darrien to respond to a text message. We got much more in common than I first thought too.

What I like most is that he e-mails all the time cuz he know it's hard (and expensive) for me to get to a phone, and he shows up on time every time we agree to meet somewhere. We started meeting at cafés so I could help him with his English, then things just kind of... blossomed? and we started seeing each other every single day, sometimes twice a day. I can't think of a day where we didn't see each other even if it were just a few minutes. He always pays for whatever we do, he's a real gentleman and a good listener Nette. He keeps me mellow when I feel like getting worked up and he can sense when something's on my mind. We just connect that way, him and me (so I guess D-squared just became D&G lol). And you know what? I think he stopped smoking, well at least around me, because he knows cigarettes bother me. I haven't seen him pick up a cigarette since the day I told him I didn't like it, and I never smell it on his breath.

So anyway, we got on the train last weekend and a couple hours later we got off in this city that was so gorgeous I can't even describe it right girl- you'd have to see it! When we were approaching the city from the train, it looked like something from a storybook! It was the most beautiful city I ever saw, no lie! It had beige and maroon houses muddled together on a bunch of little hills, and there was bright turquoise water all around it. Gabriel grew up there, but he moved to Paris with his uncle to help run his uncle's shop after his Dad passed a few years back. If I lived in that place with the turquoise water, I don't think I'd ever leave and I think I like it more than Paris! Gabriel goes there every other month to get merchandise for his uncle's shop and visit his Mom and sis. I met them after his cousin picked us up from the train station and dropped us by their house to say hi real quick. His mom was so nice and welcoming, his sister too; she did my nails while I was there and they came out so cute! They wanted us to stay for lunch but Gabriel told them he wanted to take me around the city since I wouldn't have a lot of time there.

His cousin brought us to his house, I guess they call it a 'flat', and gave us some instructions about staying at his place (he has a few pets so Gabriel took care of them while he was away on a business trip). His cousin let Gabriel hold the keys to his place and the keys to his car.. that's a nice cousin! And I guess Gabriel and him are real close. Before we dropped his cousin off at the train station, he walked us to a café 'bout ten minutes from his place. It was right next to the turquoise water, the Mediterranean Sea. It was soooo pretty and I couldn't take my eyes off of it, and since the guys were catching up and speaking fast a lot in French, I asked them if they didn't mind if I walked by the water while they chatted. I kicked off my sandals, walked through the sand, and put my feet in the warm water. The water was so clear I could see little fish swimming through it! I went back to the sand and sat down on it. I didn't care that my skirt may have been getting dirty or that my lotion may have been wearing off. I could hear birds yappin' and children playin' a ways off down the shore. I could smell fresh seawater and fresh bread from the seaside bakeries too. I just sat and stared at the water; I closed my eyes for a few minutes and no one probably noticed since I had my sunglasses on, but it was so peaceful, just sitting there and chillin' and... breathing. I don't know how much time I zoned out, but it must have been a while cuz Gabriel came over and said that it was time for us to drive his cousin to the train station.

Gabriel gave me his hand and helped me walk off the sand, and we held hands until we got back to the café and met back up with his cousin. We walked back to his cousin's place to get his car and drop him off, then Gabriel took me right back to the beach. We walked around the beach pathways holdin' hands the whole day and stoppin' by the little market booths on the sidewalk, then we got dinner at a really nice restaurant, probably the nicest I've ever been to. Gabriel convinced me to try some pink wine and a delicious lemon pastry dessert. You know I hate wine but the ones I tried that night were alright! Sitting there sipping wine with him next to the shore made me feel so classy and so... *exquisite* lol. After dinner we walked and watched some street drummers and some brazilian dancers. We even danced a little ourselves with some of the other folks in the crowd! I had so much fun that time flew by QUICK and before we knew it, the 'midnight marketplace' shut down, and we went back to his cousin's place. We watched movies and played some card games and... it was the most special night of my life.

The next day, we went back to the beach in our swimming clothes. I know you probably ain't gonna believe me, but I snorkeled! Yes, me the girl that don't like water or swimming, I went SNOR-KEL-ING. Gabriel's cousin had diving gear at his place and he said it was okay for us to use it. I wore a vest that kept me floatin' so I didn't have to swim really, but girl, it was so crazy! there was red and blue and silver fish swimming all around me and they didn't seem to mind that I was in their 'house'. They didn't bite or nip or nothin! I could see the bottom of the sea and so far out I kept lookin' for sharks even though Gabriel said there weren't any. I got a little mad at Gabriel cuz I told him not to swim too far away from me and he kept diving down to the bottom to play with the fish under the rocks, but he assured me we were safe and kept telling me not to worry. He was the perfect guide and I'm so glad I met him. He says he wants to visit me in Texas someday, but please don't tell the girls or nobody else yet. I know it sounds funny and all with me technically havin' a boo back home, but I'll handle that part when I come back. Anyway girl, I love ya and I hope you're good! Don't forget my flight lands at four o'clock next Sunday, can't wait to see you and thanks for agreeing to drive out and get me from the airport. Tell everyone to roll with you in the van! Dabresha

Chapitre 31: Au Revoir

On Dabresha's final morning in Paris, she was awakened by Aurelie and another one of the program counselors banging at her door asking if she was okay. Dabresha and her program-mates had definitely celebrated quite hard their last night in Paris, and bar-hopping until three in the morning caused her to oversleep her alarm and almost miss the towncar shuttle.

"I'm okay!" Dabresha moaned as she rolled out of her bed and opened the door for them.

"You gotta scoot or you'll have to pay a taxi! We'll help you," Aurelie said as she craned her neck around the suite to verify there were no items left behind. The counselors helped Dabresha quickly zip up and carry her luggage to the lobby before rushing her out of the residence and into the last seat of the town car. A lean, dark-haired driver dressed in black guided Dabresha to her seat in the front of the car, holding the door open for her and waiting for her to get in.

"There you are," the driver said enthusiastically, courteously extending his right hand to guide Dabresha to her seat. His name tag read Benoît and he had twinkling eyes that directly contrasted Dabresha's tired eyes.

Dabresha gave Benoît a faint smile as she plopped down inside the car, where Emily and two other students who had departing flights in the same hour as her were quietly waiting, and prepared for her last ride through Paris. Benoît cheerfully attempted to strike up small talk with the girls as they made their way to the Charles de Gaulle Airport, but the four of them kept quiet for most of the ride. Though Dabresha did not know the other girls, she could tell that they were all feeling the same way as her; a bittersweet fusion of happiness and sadness from leaving their temporary homes to return to their permanent ones. Emily looked more contented than the other two, but Dabresha could tell that there was still a hint of sorrow in her that had nothing to do with the fact that she was leaving France.

Dabresha fell asleep during the ride and awoke when the town car slowed to a halt in front of the airport to let the first two students out. The two girls flying home to the Midwest bid farewell to Dabresha and Emily, then began hauling their suitcases into the airport entrance. A few minutes later, the town car slowed to a halt once again.

"Utah, your turn," Benoît announced from the driver's seat as he energetically bounced out of the car and walked to open the trunk. Emily slowly began to unbuckle her seatbelt and scooted towards the passenger-side car door.

"Hey," Dabresha said as she tapped Emily on the shoulder. Emily was startled and slightly jumped as her right leg dropped onto the sidewalk before she turned to face Dabresha with wide eyes.

"I know we ain't exactly seen eye-to-eye as roommates, but I hope things get better for ya back home. I heard you lost your mom and I know it hurts; I lost mine too and I understand what you feeling like. E-mail me if you ever want to talk, okay? Take care."

There was a moment of silence before Emily sighed and nodded her head.

"Thanks," Emily replied softly as she stepped outside of the car. She lent Dabresha a half-smile, the most of a smile Dabresha had ever seen her make, as she exited the car and met Benoît at the trunk to claim her luggage. She waved Dabresha goodbye as she walked toward the airport entrance doors with slightly more bounce in her stride than usual. Dabresha nodded and waved at Emily as Benoît hopped back in the car.

Dabresha felt a tightness in her chest when it was finally her turn to leave. She reluctantly stepped outside of the car and breathed a deep sigh as Benoît carefully handed all of her luggage to her and assisted her to place them in line on the sidewalk.

"Merci," Dabresha told the driver as he tipped his hat to her.

"Je vous en prie, bon voyage!" Benoît replied with a friendly smile before he quickly resettled in the driver seat. Dabresha watched the shuttle car intensely as it pulled away from the curb and zoomed out of sight; her time in Europe was officially up.

Gabriel was waiting for Dabresha inside the airport when she finally got to her check-in terminal. He was holding an adorable plush beret-wearing beige poodle, and the poodle was hugging a small handle of baby roses between its fluffy paws. The two of them sat down at a bench adjacent to the airport's crêpe cafe, and Dabresha held on to the stuffed animal firmly as they waited for her flight. Gabriel tried to chat with her, but she wasn't in the mood for talking. Not only was she exceptionally tired from the previous night's events, which included a date with Gabriel at the restaurant at the top of the Eiffel Tower before the endless bar-hopping with her classmates, but she was melancholy thinking about what would or couldn't become of her relationship with Gabriel, the boy that had treated her better than any other boy had treated her before. They had spent so much time together in their few weeks together that Dabresha was genuinely dejected that their companionship had to end in the physical sense. They could always keep in touch by phone and email, but Dabresha knew that electronic communication could never amount to being with him in person.

Gabriel sat with his arm around Dabresha's shoulder and

tried to get her to talk. She almost fell asleep in his arms and though hundreds of people were passing by, Dabresha only saw him.

"You will return when?" Gabriel asked her solemnly.

"Je sais pas, Gabriel. I can't tell you that right now."

"But soon?" he asked.

"I hope," Dabresha answered with a smile.

They sat together quietly, and Gabriel's arm stayed around Dabresha's shoulder the whole time they waited for her flight to begin boarding.

"I hope too," Gabriel replied. He gently squeezed his grip on Dabresha's shoulder and leaned his head on hers, making Dabresha feel even more comforted in his arms.

"Maybe one day I come to Tex-oss, and you show me your town, and the cowboys," he joked.

"Maybe," Dabresha said affectionately. "You've been a good friend Gabriel."

"A good boyfriend?" Gabriel replied.

"Oui," Dabresha said with a smile as she kissed him on the cheek.

Dabresha imagined walking around her little Texas neighborhood with Gabriel by her side; people would definitely be able to tell he wasn't Texan, but she would feel so special strolling around with him and wouldn't care what anyone might have to say about his European style of clothes, his light skin color or his foreign accent. Dabresha would make them accept him as he was, and defend him against anyone who tried to swindle or bully him on the streets. She would guide him the same attentive, thoughtful way he guided her. Dabresha couldn't help but smile at the thought of her walking around Texas with a real boyfriend like Gabriel—a boy that wasn't afraid to show a little affection in front of other people and a boy that wouldn't hesitate to take her out to places and buy her an occasional gift—a real boyfriend with a genuine heart! Her friends and frenemies would surely be envious of how he treated her, but she'd make the haters and naysayers respect him as she wished.

Dabresha vowed that things would change when she landed back home. She vowed to take control of her life and speak up when people disappointed her. She had let a lot of people take advantage of her in the past, and she was not going to let it happen anymore. She vowed to put her best effort into her future classes; she recognized the tremendous improvement in her grades when she sincerely started trying, and that effort would surely pay off when she got to a university. She studied her French almost every day while in France, and as a result, she got honorable marks in both of her overseas classes.

Most importantly, she vowed to let go of her past—or at least try her hardest. Her time in France had provided her with ample opportunity to reflect on the things that stirred her the most, and trap those thoughts as they occurred in English while being surrounded by French conversation. France helped her to mentally and physically 'zone out' of her surroundings, and realize the power of her thoughts, and because she was constantly in her thoughts, without interruptions from her cell phone or familiar encounters, she was afforded quality reflection time on her past decisions and relationships. Being in Europe made her pause to think about things before she said them, and separated her from the hustle and bustle of her regular life. She appreciated the beauty in the slow pace, and the low stress living that proved to be crucial to her journey.

Even though Dabresha sat there silent with Gabriel, eyes closed and halfway asleep, she felt like they were speaking a million words. This boy had showed her how to feel loved and appreciated and conversely, how to love and appreciate. Even when Gabriel was busy with his work, he still found a way to call, email, or just show up at her residence to get ahold of her. There were no guesses or games; Gabriel was genuinely a man of his word and a true partner in Dabresha's adventure. She would surely miss him when she got home; Darrien was never as affectionate as Gabriel had been, but she knew it would be a challenge to see him again in the near future, a challenge that would require significant planning, saving and more arrangements to leave her job temporarily. She sensed Gabriel knew that too, but they didn't let that stop them from enjoying their final moments together.

"Flight two hundred thirty-three passenger Dah-breh-jah Dav-ees, please make your way to boarding gate J forty-seven immediately, thank you. S'il vous plait mademoiselle Dabresha Davees aller vers ton gate de depart immediatement. C'est J quarante-sept, merci."

Dabresha stood up and sighed, realizing she had lost track of time when she nodded off in Gabriel's arms. Now it was time to board her plane and bid her monsieur goodbye.

"So…" Dabresha started to say.
Gabriel interrupted Dabresha with a kiss and hugged her long and tight.

"Bon Voyage, Dabresha," he said, embracing her with both of his arms around her shoulders.

"Email me when you arriving, I mean arrive home okay?"
"Oui," Dabresha replied. "Merci pour tout."

Dabresha's name was called a final time and Dabresha rushed to pick her carry-on luggage off the floor. She quickly wiped the tears that were forming in her eyes before Gabriel or anyone could notice.

"À bientôt, no au revoir," Gabriel called.

"Right, see you," Dabresha said quietly as she walked briskly toward her check-in gate. She smiled at Gabriel and waved at him lovingly as she staggered through her gate. *If only he could come to Texas.*

When Dabresha boarded the plane, she was sober, at peace, and unafraid of what the flight would have in store. She smiled as she looked out the small oval window of her plane and got comfortable in her seat. As the plane ascended, she saw the Eiffel Tower protruding high above the rest of the city in the distance. She pulled her Eiffel Tower keychain out of her purse and pressed it against the window, holding it side by side with the real tower.

"There is sparkle. Thank you," she murmured as she nodded off into a deep slumber. The smile rested on her face while the airplane darted across the globe high above the Atlantic Ocean and landed smoothly in Texas.

Chapitre 32: Just Press Delete

"Girl, start talkin' now!" said Antoinette. "I don't care if you tired, we need details!"

Antoinette and Dabresha hugged buoyantly just off the curb of the airport arrivals area while Tamina helped load Dabresha's suitcases into the back of Antoinette's family van.

"Y'all have to go to France! I can't tell everything," Dabresha chuckled as they all settled into the car.

"We're so happy for you Bre," Tamina chimed in from the back seat. "We was thinkin' about you the whole time you was gone."

"And look at you! You look *different!* Did they feed you out there?" Antoinette chimed in.

"Aaaw, y'all sweet," Dabresha said. "And Antoinette you funny. I ain't been gone *that* long."

Dabresha settled into the middle seat of Antoinette's van and laid her whole body across the middle row.

"I missed y'all too, but I liked it out there. Well at first I didn't, but it got better. It's a cool little place, especially the South of France! Maybe the four of us can plan a trip there next spring break or something? We won't need no fake I.D.'s that's for sure," Dabresha chuckled. "They don't even I.D. you when you go to the clubs out there!"

"I'm down!" Antoinette said.

"Me too!" Tamina added, "I can save up seven hundred."

"Laydee says she's gonna meet us at your house by the way, and Darrien couldn't make it cuz he had to work, but he's gonna try and stop by after," Antoinette said.

"It's alright," Dabresha replied. The girls stared at her with curiosity. "Would y'all mind droppin' me by his job on the way home? Just for a few minutes since it's on the way."

"Sure," Antoinette hesitantly agreed. "Delilah's barbecuing for you at the house though so it's gotta be quick. We were trying to surprise you, it ain't huge or nothin', just a few folks and some good food waitin' for you."

"Yes!" Dabresha smiled. "I've been deprived of Southern cooking for six whole weeks! I'll gladly wait out the next hour or so it'll take us to get back to Beauconte."

"So what went on over there? Was it cool? Were there functions? Did you make friends? Did you lose anything?" Antoinette asked in rapid succession.

"I lost somethin', I ain't gonna tell you what it was though," Dabresha said with a sneaky smile.

The girls laughed and playfully shoved her as they buckled their seatbelts and navigated their way out of the airport. During the lengthy ride back to Beauconte, Dabresha talked and talked about everything she could remember, answering every question the girls threw at her way with vivid detail. She told them about the cathedrals, the shopping, and the bakeries that kept the streets of Paris smelling like fresh bread, and the amazing time she had eating dinner at the top of the Eiffel Tower on her last night there. She began to shuffle through her bag as she talked so she could distribute the souvenirs she hand-picked for each of them.

The girls "oohed" and "aahed" as they thanked her for the fabulous gifts: a French bible, pair of earrings and a scarf for Antoinette and two mini statuettes of the Eiffel Tower and Sacred Heart Cathedral for Tamina. She gave them both a handful of nougat pieces and insisted that they try the 'bombest candy' she'd ever tasted.

"Wow that is good," said Tamina. "Is this taffy?"

"It's nougat," Dabresha answered.

"New what?" Antoinette interrupted.

"Noo-gaw. I never heard of it either and I'm not sure what's in it, but I'll hunt these down and find a place that makes it here if I have to, they are too gosh-darn delicious!"

Dabresha accidentally dozed off as the girls continued to ask her about her trip and catch her up on everything (or the very little) that happened in Texas while she was away, according to them. When Dabresha woke up, they were parked outside of Darrien's workplace and Tamina was tapping her on the shoulder. Dabresha sluggishly rolled herself to the side of the van and out of the van's sliding door.

"I'll be right back y'all, I won't keep you waiting long," Dabresha promised. Her eyes were visibly tired and her face had sleep imprints from the way her head was tilted on the seat belt.

"Please don't, it is too hot to be waitin' anywhere in this car," Antoinette urged.

Dabresha strolled into Darrien's work place and, as promised, she re-emerged a few minutes later. She had a smile on her face and her eyes no longer looked sleepy.

"What happened?" asked Tamina, "you look uppity!"

Dabresha smiled as she leaned back into her seat and fastened her seatbelt again.

"I just broke up with him. Done with him and his constant excuses, and I'm not stayin' with anyone just to say I have someone."

Antoinette and Tamina both gaped at Dabresha with wide eyes and open mouths, gave each other a look, then looked back at Dabresha.

"Girl are you sure you're thinking straight after all that time on the plane?" Antoinette asked. "Flying makes everybody a little jittery."

"How much did you drink at the airport?" Tamina added.

Dabresha began to laugh.

"Believe it or not, I haven't really drank at all the past few weeks 'cept for a few glasses of wine, and I promise y'all I'm thinkin' straight."

Dabresha released a sigh of relief as she gazed out of the car window and a smile formed across her face.

"Listen y'all, I spent my last few weeks in Europe being treated like a real lady by a real man. He didn't have a nice car and he didn't live in mansion—matter fact he didn't have a car at all! But he looked out for me and showed me how I should be treated, took me a bunch of places and never asked for nothin' in return. I know I ain't the perfect girlfriend, but I definitely deserve better than 'D. Dare', so Darrien is officially in my rearview and the new Bre is done playin' little games with little boys."

Dabresha made a shooing motion in the air with her hand, then propped her legs up across the middle row of the van.

"Awww, good for you. I always thought you deserved better than him," Antoinette added.

Tamina threw her arms around Dabresha and hugged her warmly.

"I'm alright y'all, trust," Dabresha insisted as she dug her cell phone out of her purse and turned it on. It began to send alerts non-stop; every voicemail and text message that was sent to her while she was away started to alert as her phone reception slowly came back. Dabresha imagined her six weeks' worth of messages hanging in a cloud above Texas waiting for her to signal them out so they could fall down like raindrops. She turned the phone to silent and handed it to Tamina.

"Mina, can you do me a favor while I rest up before the house? Delete every text message you see from Darrien, no matter what it says or when it came, just press delete."

ANASTASCIA DUCHESSE

Dabresha dropped her phone into Tamina's lap as it continued to light up. Tamina's eyes bulged as she slowly picked up the phone and stared at it.

"I think he's trying to message you right now Bre. Are you sure?" Tamina asked.

"Just erase everything from him, okay? That way I can get to the messages that matter when we get home. Now let's bounce so I can get some proper barbecue!"

Antoinette continued to drive down the highways in her usual, over cautious manner as Dabresha dozed off again. She awakened to the sound and motion of Antoinette's van coming to a squeaky halt outside of her house. Dabresha noticed right away that there were more cars than usual parked outside, then she noticed her own car sitting in the driveway. Dabresha hopped out of the van and walked toward her car, gasping when she saw it up close for the first time since she left it. The old Buick looked practically brand new! Maurice had surely done a number on it after Ms. Pat's nephew worked on it because the paint, wheels, and interior were shining like they had never shined before. It sparkled.

"Hope you don't mind we invited a few people. Your Dad said it was okay as long as we keep on the patio. He's working late so we told him we'd clean up," Antoinette said with a smile.

The girls each grabbed one of Dabresha's suitcases from the back of the van and lugged them up the pathway to the front porch for her. Dabresha could hear music playing and several voices chatting by the side of her house. She also heard Delilah's distinct voice say, "here they come!"

Antoinette and Tamina dropped Dabresha's suitcases inside her house by the front door and escorted her to the patio. Delilah, Antoinette's sister Jayna, Aunt Trecee, Ms. Pat, and a dozen of Dabresha's other friends were there standing by a long table that had a small cake on it.

"She look different!" Dabresha heard someone say as she walked closer to the patio's wooden table to look at the cake that was sitting on the center of it. The cake was rectangular and tri-colored blue, white, and red, just like the French flag, and the words 'Welcome Home' adorned the cake in fancy, black cursive letters. Dabresha clapped her hands together and raised them to her nose.

"Y'all serious?" she exclaimed. She walked around and greeted each of her guests with bisous, trying her hardest not to cry. It was the first time her friends and family had surprised her with anything and it meant the world to her even if it was just barbecue and a small cake. Dabresha's eyes welled up the most when she approached and hugged her Aunt Trecee.

"My niece, you are glowing!" Aunt Trecee exclaimed.

"I can't believe you came all the way out here for this," Dabresha cried.

"I came to get my suitcases back!" Aunt Trecee joked, "You best not have messed 'em up! Now halt them tears, we got food to eat made by 'Chef Davis' herself."

Delilah, who was wearing an apron and gloves, began uncovering the bowls and platters of food that were neatly arranged across the patio table. Every single item looked delectable! There were several well-glazed and succulently marinated pieces of meat, greens, gumbo, potato salad, mac & cheese, cornbread, and hot pecan pie all neatly arranged next to a giant pitcher of sweet tea. The smell of the food excited Dabresha's senses as she prepared her plate and everyone else there followed suit, piling up their own plates with as much good food that could fit on it. Everyone stood around the patio and chatted with each other. The surprise gathering was more than

Dabresha could have ever hoped for and filled her heart (and stomach!) with joy. She couldn't stop smiling the entire time.

There were a myriad of questions for Dabresha and she tried answering everyone's inquiries, but eventually just ended up passing Aunt Trecee's camera around while telling stories about her time out there. She relished in talking about how the school she attended in Paris looked like a castle and how she received high marks in her French classes. She talked about the variety of fine wines she had tasted and told a select few about her snorkeling trip in the Mediterranean Sea. And, when anyone asked her about Darrien, she informed them that they were no longer together.

Dabresha tried her hardest not to distract herself looking at her phone nor through any of the older messages that were still coming in, but it was difficult. She sent a message to Laydee, who had yet to make an appearance at the barbecue, and asked where she was at. Laydee never responded and Dabresha ultimately decided to turn her phone back to silent mode and leave it charging inside her house so she could focus on interacting with the people who were there to support her in person.

The gathering lasted until the sun went down, then everyone started to part ways when Dabresha constant yawns hinted that she was greatly fatigued.

"I think baby girl needs some sleep," Aunt Trecee told some of the guests, helping the party to wrap up quicker. Dabresha thanked every person individually for coming by and insisted they take home some of the leftover food. Delilah and Jayna cleaned up the patio while Dabresha hugged and said her goodbyes to Antoinette and Tamina and prepared to unload her suitcases for Aunt Trecee.

"Did Laydee get lost?" Dabresha asked Antoinette before she took off.

"That girl barely talks to us ever since she got with that boy. Maybe you'll have better luck getting hold of her," she replied with a look of disappointment.

"You know what? It's all good. I'm glad y'all are here and I'll talk at Laydee another time about how to keep a friendship," Dabresha replied, causing Antoinette's frown to disappear. The girls lent Dabresha a subtle look of surprise; the new Dabresha was so much more forthright than pre-France Dabresha!

"I'ma introduce y'all to my friend Miry before y'all move away. She's a feisty Latina with a good heart and I think y'all will like her. We hung out in Europe and she goes to our school, so I'll bring her out with us one of these days before y'all move off."

The girls nodded their approval as they said their goodbyes, making sure to each give Dabresha a lengthy hug.

"We're glad you're back Bre," Tamina said.

"Don't be taking off like that in the future without our permission," Antoinette joked, "You still gotta call us at our new schools and ask us."

"I love y'all, thanks for puttin' this together for me," Dabresha said as she waved them off. Antoinette plucked her sister from the patio where she was finishing the clean-up with Delilah and the three of them scooted out the house. Aunt Trecee appeared from the patio as well and helped Dabresha lay out all her suitcases on the living room couches. Dabresha ravaged through them to show Aunt Trecee all of the new French fashions she managed to purchase. Aunt Trecee listened attentively as Dabresha told her all the stories she could think of about France, and gave her aunt several knick-knack souvenirs and an entire bag of individually-wrapped nougats.

"They don't got Mexican food, microwave popcorn, or sweet tea out there, but everything else they had was alright, especially the desserts. I wish I could have brung some for you, but they probably wouldn't have stayed fresh."

"I'm fine with this nougaw stuff," Aunt Trecee said as she stuffed a second one in her mouth. "It's tasty! But we all so proud of you Bre Bre. You really packed up and flew up out of Texas and did something with yourself," Aunt Trecee started.

"It was just two classes auntie, I didn't really..." Dabresha started.

"Don't downplay it gal," Aunt Trecee interrupted. "You did something a lot of us have never even had the courage to try! And you got a passport now and can go plenty more places as you please. Most of us don't even got *that* Bre Bre. You did it. You stuck it out and you made it. Things is only gonna get better here on out as long as you keep on tryin', you'll see. Keep it up niecy."

Dabresha silently nodded in agreement as Aunt Trecee handed her a small yellow envelope.

"From your dad," she said. "And I'm callin' him your dad from here on out expectin' y'all do the same and stop calling that man Maurice. He's done more for y'all than anyone else I know, definitely more than your real father. Looked after y'all when your momma passed and got the courts to keep y'all out the system. He cares more for both y'all then he lets out and you don't need the same blood to be someone's family. If they look out for you this long, they family."

Dabresha nodded as she clutched the envelope and examined it closely. She carefully tore it open with her index finger and removed its contents. There was a plain greeting card inside and a one-hundred dollar bill nestled in the crevice of the card. Dabresha squinted her eyes to read the short scribbled message to herself:

'Glad you home safe. Dawnisse asked me to make sure y'all go to school and do better than us, so that's why I nag sometimes. don't leave the patio messy. keep us proud - Maurice.'

Dabresha's eyes welled up as she tucked the card away into her purse. It was the biggest gift Maurice had ever given her and the first time he had given her a card. Maurice was not the card-giving type—when birthdays and holidays came around, it was rare to get more than a verbal two-word greeting from him. To Dabresha, the paper card was much more special than the money inside of it.

"You right Auntie. I'ma call him dad from here on out and I'll tell Lilah to do the same."

"Yes ma'am! And find some time to come visit me, ya hear? I can't stay long this time, doctors keep nagging me to run some tests so I made the 'pointment day after tomorrow. You and Lilah should take the bus out, maybe for Thanksgiving? Y'all should both have school off 'round that time."

"Both?" Dabresha asked her aunt inquisitively, raising her neck and squinting her eyes.

"Oh you ain't heard? Lilah got a intra-view at that culinary school in Austin next week. She's been practicing for the questions and she gon' come with us to get our nails done tomorrow morning, my treat. She say you inspired her."

Dabresha's lips parted and formed a beautifully humbling smile. She couldn't believe that she would have ever inspired anyone to do anything, and that Delilah had actually taken action to further herself from her influence so quickly. The smile remained on Dabresha's face as she finished unpacking and got ready for bed. She felt an unusual peace that night, one that she hadn't felt in her home before, and an even greater optimism about her future. She imagined she may have brought the peace with her from Paris, packed it with her and unleashed it into the house, and she hoped the peace was here to stay. The peace was rooted in the support from her friends and family that day, and from the release of all the negative things that were hindering her before she released them in the European clouds.

As Dabresha began habituating herself to the art of 'letting go', she began to feel the burdens of her tumultuous past lift away from her and her previous limited way of thinking. Her trip to France had done more than just take her to another part of the world; it had elevated her to a new sense of maturity and planted the seeds for her to evolve into the sophisticated, cultured, virtuous woman that she was destined to become. That she *deserved* to become.

Dabresha hugged her Aunt Trecee long and tight before she went to her room and climbed into her bed. Just before Dabresha dozed off that night, her phone vibrated one last time. She flipped it open and tried to distinguish the odd-looking phone number that had sent the new message. The phone number had a plus sign in front of it and more digits than she could count on her phone's tiny screen. She focused her eyes to read it:

'I hope you are home safely boo. E-mail me to confirming soon. Je t'embrasse (I hug you), -Gabriel'

Dabresha smiled at the message and dozed off peacefully in Beauconte, Texas, snuggled under her zebra comforter.

Chapitre 33: Thankful

To: Myrna.Cole@SRJC.edu
From: DabreshaDavis@wahoo.com
Subject: Thank you

___

Dear Ms. Cole,

I'm writing you from my new email address to let you know that I got home from France two weeks ago and it was *a-ma-zing*! The trip turned out much better than I thought it would. I tried so many new things while I was out there, saw so many beautiful places and met so many people in those six weeks that I'm just so.. thankful! Things at home feel different now, but not in bad way, in a nice way. My time there got me to reflect on a lot of things and now that I'm back in Texas, I feel at ease and I appreciate things more than before. Little things like microwave popcorn (it's impossible to find out in France!), and bigger things like the people in my life that I used to took for granted. I came home with class credits and a whole new outlook on my situation.

My life has been far from a bed of roses, but everything that's gone wrong in my life has taught me something, made me stronger and given me more assurance in myself. France helped me to see and hear things more clearly because I wasn't constantly running my mouth to gossip with folks; instead I was listening and trying to understand people around me. I used to be more of a talker than a listener, but being in France made become better at listening and communicating; France has changed me. I'm smiling as I write this because it's hard for me not to when I think about my time there, and before I went to France, it took a whole lot for me to smile.

So I know America ain't perfect, but we do have a lot of conveniences and opportunities here that a lot of us don't realize (well at least I never realized before until the conveniences disappeared). Being inconvenienced got me thinking of ideas for businesses I could open overseas and stores I saw out there that I would love to see in Texas. Now I want to travel to more places, come up with more business ideas, and do something with them one day. I think it'd be so awesome to have a job where I could travel new places ever so often and make decent money. I'd have to get more comfortable flying on planes, but I could figure that part out!

It was crazy hearing so many French people tell me how 'lucky' I was to live in America and that it was their dream to visit here. I haven't looked at any part of my life as 'lucky' before, but I guess people look at things differently from over there. One of the things I'm most thankful for is that Europe helped me realize that I deserve better in my relationships. The day I got back, I ended a relationship with a boy that I should've never been with from the start, a boy who, by the way, got arrested last week for a DUI and is still in county right not because none of his friends can bail him out. This boy was inconsistent; he treated me wonderfully some days then ignored me on others. Don't get me wrong, it hurt like heck to drop him, but he wasn't fully committed and I let things drag on hoping he would grow up and grow to love me more. I was afraid of being single and afraid to hear what people might say if we split up, but now I don't really care what people think about my decisions, heck, several people told me I was crazy for wanting to go to Europe! If I would've listened to them, I would have missed out on everything. I'll never forget this journey.

I met someone while I was out there, a guy named

Gabriel who treated me so well. We're trying to keep in touch but it's difficult being thousands of miles and seven hours apart. It takes us a while to get back to each other on the internet and we keep missing each other's calls, not to mention the cost for each minute we try to reach each other. I'm not sure how long we'll be able to keep things up, but we're trying, and who knows, maybe I'll end up back there one day or maybe he'll come visit Texas like he says he wants to. Either way, he was a true southern (French) gentleman and I'm not going to settle for anyone less anymore.

Thanks to my journey, I don't worry about the same things I worried about before. My mind was always running, even while I was asleep! I used to be thinking and worrying about things 24/7, but now I just keep calm. Before I went overseas, I was so self-conscious about my body because my hips weren't shaped like the girls in the music videos and car magazines. I kept telling myself I needed to lose weight to make my waist smaller. I weighed myself last week and those stubborn pounds I used to wish would fall off had naturally disappeared somewhere overseas when I wasn't even trying to lose it! I didn't go to a gym once or even *try* to diet! I wasn't thinking about the weight and now it's gone. It's funny how problems go away when you stop giving attention to them.

Another odd thing happened happened when I went to my favorite nail salon with my aunt and sister the day after I came home. Now, the same stylist who has done my nails plenty other times and repeatedly told me to relax my hands, that day she said, "you look relaxed today." I used to get peeved every time she told me to relax before because I didn't understand why she'd tell me it so often when I thought I was relaxing! I didn't realize how tense I was before, but the nail stylist noticed without even knowing me personally. I hope to keep my newfound 'relaxedness' going while I'm settling back into my Texas routine. If it weren't for you, none of this would've happened. I know you had a big part in getting my application accepted and my plane ticket funded, so thank you for helping me find a way to study abroad and taking a chance on me. Now I understand why you want 'us' to travel; I didn't at first but now it all makes sense.

I'm putting together a scrapbook of my time in Paris and adding all the 'flat' souvenirs I kept, the ticket stubs, maps, menus, coins and things. I put a few pictures of my mom in there too so it looks like she's standing next to me at some of the attractions. Now I know why she loved Paris so much, or at least the idea of it, and it's always gonna be special to me. I'll stop by your office when school starts back up and show you my scrapbook. It'll be my last semester at SRJC and I'll be transferring to Jedston A&M in the spring to study International Business with a minor in French. I already met with a few advisors and am on track to transfer there come January as long as I finish my last few classes at SRJC with solid grades. My sister just got accepted to a culinary school nearby Jedston so we'll eventually find a place to stay and move out there so we don't have to drive all the way from Beauconte. Thank you so much Ms. Cole.

Dabresha L. Davis

* * *

To: DabreshaDavis@wahoo.com
From: Myrna.Cole@srjc.edu
Subject: RE: Thank you

Dear Mademoiselle Davis,

It truly warms my soul to hear you had such a fabulous time in Europe! Look at you go—from the 'Dirty South' to the South of France, you did it Miss Davis! Travel surely has that effect on people--with the good and bad it helps us to appreciate 'home' more and place things into a bigger picture. They say true destinations aren't cities, but are new perspectives on things. When I was about your age, I was blessed to take a trip out of the country and it changed me forever. It gave me hope that things could and would get better, and helped me to be comfortable in my own skin. My time there ultimately helped me develop into the person I have become, and I could not imagine having missed that opportunity.

I haven't mentioned to you beforehand, but the two of us have quite a few things in common. My only parent was uneducated, and though my siblings and I never missed a meal, we grew up knowing not to ask for anything more than food and clothes, and to accept that we'd always be short on cash. I was almost one of the 'lost ones' doomed by societal systems that steer 'us' to live in mediocrity, and I sensed you've been through similar things when I read your application essays. My 3 siblings and I 'entered the real world' lacking necessary knowledge: knowledge about how to carry ourselves, budget ourselves, and further ourselves. We were set up to fail, in a nation that already bestows several disadvantages on minorities and impoverished people. By the grace of God, I made it 'out', and I'm constantly encouraging my siblings to break away from the chains that hold us back and not settle for lives of unfulfillment. All of my siblings are capable, competent people with more than enough intelligence to progress, but unfortunately, many people just like my siblings don't want to change and get comfortable living on government assistance. We can, we MUST rise above the statistics and separate ourselves from the negative stereotypes that encompass us. Society will continue to write us off as thugs, hood rats, ingrates, *animals*; you've heard the abundance of terms they've used to belittle and dehumanize us. *We are humans* with more power than we realize, and often times subjected to prejudiced treatment because of our backgrounds and our 'ethnic' names. We have the potential and power to achieve great things regardless of what environments we're produced from or what we've been through. All the "isha's" and "ika's" in the world can overcome.

The power begins with knowledge; the knowledge we acquire when we become educated, open our minds, and travel to new places. Knowledge is acquired through experiences, through making mistakes, and through listening and observing more than speaking. Anyone can get educated. Anyone can travel. The choice to do so is *solely* up to that person.

I don't know where I'd be today had it not been for Chardaine, a loyal customer of the first place I worked at as a teenager and the first job I found right after I had my son. I was a single nineteen-year-old mother elated to have income at a retail boutique because it paid slightly more than minimum wage, so I worked there diligently for 8 whole years without any intention of leaving. Chardaine got to know me throughout the years during her store visits. She, too, was a single mother, but also a successful accountant with her own office in a sky rise building. Every time she shopped at our store, she would chit chat with me about my goals. Unlike the other customers who only wanted to talk about new fashions and sales prices, Chardaine spoke to me about improving myself. She'd constantly encourage me to further myself and seek better employment. She saw something in me that no one else did, spoke visions into my life, and helped me realize that my dreams extended far beyond the retail racks. Because of her, I decided to go back to school and make something of myself so I could provide a better future for my son Gerald. I learned new skills, learned how to interrelate with people from all kinds of backgrounds, and eventually established myself as a true working professional. I have the stability and the income I never thought possible before and will never work for 'a little more than minimum wage' again.

Unfortunately, Gerald hasn't been much appreciative of my efforts. I too, made some mistakes as a parent, but I did my best to show him I loved him even if I wasn't around to spend as much time with him as I wanted to. Gerald's a little older than you and had limitless potential—he was on honor roll several times back in grade school! But as a teenager, he limited himself to whom he associated with. I tried my hardest to keep him away from the 'hood'; I put him in a performing arts middle school and found us a house in the suburbs, but somehow, he managed to befriend acquaintances that led him right back to the hood and all it entails. He didn't finish high school and he did not make the best choices. I pray for his safety and well-being every morning because that's all I can do. He's currently finishing a 6 month prison term as a result of his indirect involvement in a serious crime. Gerald hasn't let go of the negative influences of his past and has fallen into the common societal trap that many of our black men fall into: the world of violence, fast money, and limited thinking. I'm hoping he will be a changed young man when he is released, or will come back to around to being the ambitious little boy he once was, but only time will tell. He has two young sons, my precious precious grandbabies, and the mother of the youngest one doesn't want anything more to do with him (or me unfortunately). She packed up and moved to the East coast, so Gerald's youngest may very well grow up without a father or a relationship with our side of the family. The mom is fed up and she has every right to be, but I'll be crushed if Gerald allows this cycle to continue. I don't want my grandkids to become statistics, fighting their whole lives to try to recover from their childhood setbacks. It will be solely up to my son to mend the broken relationships with the mothers of his children, carry out what he's started in creating those young lives, and step up to be a father to his children. It's never too late for someone to make a change, and if he steps up now, his kids may never even remember his absences or his shortcomings and all could be forgiven in their eyes.

I'm sorry to go so far off topic, but I hope you understand that your future is truly in your hands; even with the odds that have been flung against you, your success is up to you! You don't have to follow the crowd to stay 'cool', because coolness becomes less and less important as time goes by, while character and stability become golden.

I hope you remember this as you further yourself in your life's journey and make progress in your personal goals. Share your successes with others in your community and try to set a good example to those around you. Even with just six weeks of travel under your belt, *you* can be an influence to other young people, older people as well, who'll benefit from opening their minds and getting outside of their comfort zones. All it takes is courage, faith and endurance. Money helps, but it's not truly a necessity to start the journey that begins within. You have to keep pushing even when the roads get a little rough. Like our good Reverend Dr. MLK said, you have to keep moving forward.

You probably won't find me if you try to visit my office this semester; I'm ending my tenure at SRJC to pursue a promotional position at Central A&M University.

Nevertheless, don't hesitate to reach out to me if you need something. I love hearing from my study abroad alumni; you are the eighth student my department has sponsored and we love to get updates from time to time. Let us know when you finish college, start your career, or make any big moves! Stop by the office sometime and talk to 'Senyoreta' Harmonie. She's been through some things like us, and really saw herself grow when she studied for a semester in Spain a few years ago. She'll be relocating to Dallas when she graduates from her master's program next year and already has strong career prospects lined up. We are all so proud of her and will wish her nothing but the best when she moves on from her position at SRJC.

Nevertheless, I wish the same to you and pray for your utmost success. Wherever you go in school and in life, whatever you do, you must keep moving forward.

Take care Dabresha, au revoir (is that right?)

Myrna Sharmika Cole